Let the
story begin...

Published under licence by Brown Dog Books and
The Self-Publishing Partnership, 7 Green Park Station, Bath BA1 1JB

www.selfpublishingpartnership.co.uk

ISBN printed book: 978-1-83952-184-3
ISBN e-book: 978-1-83952-185-0

Cover design by Kevin Rylands
Internal design by Andrew Easton

Printed and bound in the UK

This book is printed on FSC certified paper

MIX
Paper from
responsible sources
FSC® C013604

Let the story begin...

R DONALDSON

BROWN
DOG
BOOKS

This book is dedicated to my BFF
'Potty Potter'!
I hope that you have experienced some of the pleasures!

Let the story begin…

Chapter 1

Lottie closed the door and put on the light in the entrance hall to the empty house.

Today had been long and she was glad that it was all over. Her mother's funeral had been well attended by friends and the few distant family members that she had left. People that Lottie had not seen for years had been there and it made her realise that she had been away from her family home for longer that she could remember. People that she had only known as a young girl were now mothers, fathers and grandparents: time had moved on.

After leaving university she had spent just over three years working in Manchester as an assistant pathologist for the police, earning her doctorate. She had only managed to get home for the last few Christmases, a few weekends here and there and birthdays. It had only been in the recent six months that her visits had been more frequent to the quaint, little village Tudeley in Kent where she had grown up as her mother became ill. She had moved a few things into the house as her stays became longer. The decision to move back had been a hard one, as she had worked hard to get the job that she loved so much after leaving university. But the last few weeks of her mother's care had been demanding, and with no siblings to help manage her mother's business and finances, she had to go it alone.

She walked over to the old piano in the sitting room and lifted the lid. The shining black and white keys spoke out to her, and she was drawn to press one. The sound reverberated in the silent room, so she placed her finger on another white key and the note sprang out. The piano had been a gift to her when she was eight years old from her father. One of the last things he had given her before he died in a road traffic accident. It was that which had started her fascination with finding out how accidents happened and what had caused her father's death that had led her to want to be in pathology. Her mother had always said that she would be better off being a doctor. Well, she was a doctor, just not one that worked with people who were alive!

Another note rang out as she moved across the keys and she pulled the red velvet stool out and sat down. Her fingers quickly moved along the keys to create a tune. Nothing of note, but it was then she felt the warm, salty tears on her cheeks that she realised she was crying.

For a few moments she was lost in the tune, remembering her father and how he had paid for her lessons twice a week to start off with and then almost every day. She had taken to playing the piano quite quickly. Sitting exam after exam to become the best in her class, year and in the local area after entering competitions and winning them. Playing in the youth orchestra at the Royal Albert Hall had been what her father called 'Your crowing moment, my poppet.'

'You could be onstage, poppet, full-time pianist,' her father would say to her as he listened to her play in the evenings after they had eaten the evening meal. Her mother would be washing up, or tidying around.

'Don't listen to him, you would never make a living at that!' her mother would shout through. 'A doctor, that's what you should be!' So, she hoped that they were both together somewhere now looking down at her, she had achieved both, only in different ways. To make some cash through uni she had played the piano at a local wine bar several nights a week. Although she never went short, her mother paid regularly into her bank account and the rent on her one-bed flat was paid for; in fact, her mother had bought the house after a few months of her living there. When her father had died her mother had bought a small house and let it out; over the years she had developed a portfolio of properties and found renting a good source of income. By the time she had died Lottie had been left in sole ownership of 36 properties dotted around the country and local area. It was this little empire that she was now in control of, as well as three shops, two small guest houses, a farm and grassing land, and the local village pub. Her mum had purchased this last: it was going through hard times and she could not bear to see it close, so invested. The same landlord ran the pub on her behalf, and a letting agent looked after everything else. Lottie only had to turn up to meetings, sign cheques for work that needed taking care of, or just pay her tax bills! But sitting at the piano she wondered if that was really what she would do now.

In the light of day, the house was a fantastic Victorian converted farmhouse, and had a great garden, views over the open countryside, an outside pool and stables. It was imposing and she felt lonely the last few nights that she had been alone. She remembered the sound of the laughter the three of them had shared when she was young, even the very rare parties that her mother had held a few years after her father had died, but it would now never feel the same.

She stopped playing and pulled the lid down on the piano. She walked through the open-plan kitchen, turning on all the lights and aimed for the fridge. She had tried not to drink all day, keeping a clear head, but now only a few glasses of wine would help her to sleep. The cold, liquid had no taste, but she found the second glass easier to swallow. Refilling her glass for the last time she turned out the lights, and made her way to the old staircase. The wood creaked as she took the steps and she could hear her mother's voice as she made her way to her bedroom: 'One step jump, two steps jump, three steps aaannnnd … Race you to bed!' It had been the game they had played even when Lottie was thirteen, something her father would do when she was really small in the effort to get her to sleep. The last try to expel some energy and to tire her out.

The wine tonight would have to do that. After undressing and washing the make-up off her face she turned out the light and awaited the sleep she needed to close the day. Silently it came.

Chapter 2

Three weeks had passed slowly and the sound of the letter box clanging made Lottie realise it must be after 8am. The postman – well, postwoman – in the village was always on time. She had been in the kitchen making another coffee when she heard the usual rustle of gravel on the drive, the van door open and the rattle of the metal knocker. 'Morning!' would come the cry as the woman left whatever post needed Lottie's attention that day.

The post had been mainly bills, final details from her mother's solicitors and business correspondence.

She bent to pick up the three items, noticing one with a London postmark. Handwritten. 'No one does that these days,' she thought in the world of social media, emails and the internet. Old-fashioned handwriting was a rare thing. Addressed to her, she sat at the breakfast bar in her nightshirt and shorts and started to open it. Her bare feet resting on the stool bar, she sipped her coffee and began to read.

'Lottie,' the letter began, 'I am so sorry to hear the news about your mother passing away and I hope that you don't mind me writing to you so soon after this sad event. It has been a while since we had any contact but I wanted to write to you in person and I have lost your email address. I rang the village pub to ask after you and I was told your news and your home address.' The letter was from Todd Carter, a friend who she had been at uni with but had lost touch with when he moved to London to start his own job as a forensic scientist's assistant. He started talking about what he was doing and continued, 'I have been working for a new lab here in London and we have received funding and sponsorships that will last for at least the next three years. We are looking for someone to come and work here alongside the police and, well, I thought of you straight away.' She took another sip of coffee and continued to read. Todd explained the work and the job; he had put an application form in the letter but had said, 'I have been given the task of finding someone who would fit the bill, but when I heard of your situation I did not think that you would want to take in on-board, but to be honest the few people I have seen really don't come up to scratch with the way we want to work at the DuPont Centre of Research so, if you are interested, give me a call and we can talk it through. If you want it, I can pull the strings I need to make it happen.' She continued to read his contact details and the rest of the letter.

She put the paper down and stood up. She needed to get a shift on, as she had arranged to meet Agnes and still needed to wash and change.

The letter played on her mind and after an hour of looking through the mountain of paperwork she was looking at, Agnes broke into her train of thought.

'Come on then, it has to be a man making you look lost in dreams, because I have never found VAT bills to be so distracting!' Agnes Deakin had been her mother's best friend. She was an accountant and had started work again after her own children had fled the nest. It was a natural thing that she had looked after Lottie's mother's accounts and they had remained close friends ever since.

'Sorry, well no, but yes sort of!' Lottie managed to get the words out. She explained about the letter, and who Todd was. She missed the bit out about the fact that they had been dating each other for nearly nine months and he was one of the best lovers she had had, not that she had had many to compare him to. Since there had only been Gav, a guy whom she was infatuated with aged seventeen: after he got what he wanted a few times she found out he had a girlfriend and was five years older than her so he was dumped. A one-night stand (or four, actually) through the barren uni years when studying was more important that being weighed down by a man, and Lottie was still very unsure about sleeping with just anyone. Lastly there was Phil, whom she had seen about five times before she moved back to be with her mother. He had visited but after a few failed attempts at a long-distance relationship it had faded away until she got a text to say it was over. By which time she really did have more important things to think about. Her first time, she never spoke about. Not even Aggie was aware of the first time. Her mother had known some of the details, but it was never spoken of, and thanks to good counselling, Lottie never really thought of it either.

'Well. You must have impressed him for him to think of you for the post after such a long time.' Agnes laughed, looking at Lottie over her half-rimmed schoolteacher glasses and the papers she was reading. 'Sounds like you should go for it. You really are not set for the country life, even though you don't have to work to support yourself, I know you and you need to do more than sit at the bar of an evening playing tunes on that old piano, entertaining the village punters like you have been of late. You are young, only 28, in your prime. Grab the opportunity, and Todd, by the horns and go for it!' She smiled, guessing by the fond look on Lottie's face that Todd was more of a friend than she was letting on by the passionate explanation she had given of him.

'Really, do you think?' Lottie picked up her coffee and pulled a face as it had gone cold when she took a sip. 'London's a big, old place for little old me!'

'Tosh!' Agnes exclaimed. 'You survived the city before without a care for us back here. The proper career gal, helping to solve all those crimes, getting your name in the local papers. Your mother used to show us all the clippings, you know. How proud of you she was. We followed your career, and to be honest it would pain me to think that your talents have gone to waste.' Agnes got up from her chair and moved round and hugged Lottie. She could see that mentioning her mother had touched her and she wanted her to know that everyone missed her mum. 'She would want you to. I can look after everything here, just like before. We can find you a nice flat and nice boyfriend and you can come home at weekends to show him off to us all!'

Lottie hugged her back. Agnes had been like the auntie she had never had. Although she was only two years younger than her mother at 53, Agnes showed little signs of being a day over 40. She kept her figure, loved her hair blonde and short in the latest style. She always dressed to impress, and looked stunning in whatever style of clothes she wore, suit or jeans alike, and, although happily married to the same wonderful husband for over 30 years, she did like to, and could still, turn a few heads both in business and amongst friends.

'Don't cast it off until you have seen the offer,' Agnes continued in her businesswoman tone. 'Ring him, meet him, have a drink and flirt with him if that's all you want.' Lottie rolled her eyes as Agnes brought her a fresh, hot cup of coffee from the pot that was on the stand on the office sideboard. 'But don't give it up and regret it. That's all I have to say.' With that, she sat back down and put her head back in the papers she had been working on.

After concluding the rest of their business, Lottie asked that the seven of the furthest-away properties were put on the market. It was not for the money, it was more to bring the properties closer to home and easier to manage with just using two letting agents. She left the office and made her way to the gym. She had packed her kit in the hope that she would be able to get a run in, but it had started to rain so instead she headed into town to work up a sweat. The music in the car, and then on her headphones as she pounded the treadmill, took away the thought in her mind, but on returning to the house and standing in the shower, her mind turned over all the possibilities that this could bring. She even thought about Todd and the possibility that, although it could prove dangerous, flirting may just be what the doctor ordered to bring a real smile back on her face, if nothing else.

Her mobile phone held to her ear, she listened as the ringtone dialled for the third time. 'One more ring and I will put it down,' she thought. Just as she pulled the gadget from her ear she heard a voice.

'Todd Carter's office, how may I help you?'

Lottie shot the phone back to her ear.

'Oh hi.' She paused. 'Um, can I speak to Todd, sorry, I mean, Mr Carter please?' she said, trying to pull herself together.

'Of course, Miss, I will put you through. Mr Carter is in his office. Can I tell him who is calling?' the girl enquired.

'Yes, sorry, Leticia Jenkins,' she replied.

'One moment.' With that the girl had gone and the holding music buzzed a happy tune in her ear and she felt her stomach turn as if she was a child again playing a new piece of music she had learned by heart without the sheet music for the first time to her father in anticipation that she would be note-perfect.

'Lottie!' the strong masculine voice said at the end of the line. 'How splendid you have called, I really did not think that you would.' The sound of his voice made her feel surprisingly childlike as if it was a first date or something.

'Hi, Todd,' was all she could muster in reply. 'Grow up, you are a professional!' she thought to herself as he continued. 'But it is great that you have. So sorry to hear about your mum, but I had to contact you, how are you doing?'

Pleasantries over Todd went onto detail and the DuPont Centre and the job. He was doing a good sales pitch to her, and she found herself jotting down a time to meet him the next day within no time. She had not given a thought of travelling to the city and how she would get there.

'Fantastic! Email me with the train times and I will have a cab waiting to pick you up from the station.' Todd closed the conversation with a final statement. 'It really is great to hear your voice again, Lotts!'

As the phone went dead, the affectionate parting word, 'Lotts', played over in her mind. He had always called her Lotts followed by a whisper in her ear and lick on the inside bit, just where it seemed to do things in the spot between her legs. That usually led to the best orgasm ever to be encountered, until he did it again, and again. Which he often would, and on frequent occasions in one night!

Lottie quickly phoned Agnes with the news, a little shocked at her for saying yes. Agnes's words soon put her mind at ease. Lottie invited her over for supper and the dutiful husband brought her to the door at 7pm as planned.

'I will give you a ring later, love, when I am ready to be picked up!' Agnes shouted as she got out of the car. 'It will not be late, promise!'

'No worries, love, I'm just going over to see Lynne and the kids, I will stop there till you call,' Dick, her husband, called back.

'Kiss them all from me,' Agnes said, standing by the driver's window as he pushed the electronic button to allow the cool spring air in. Agnes bent and kissed him on the lips. 'Dear heart!' she whispered to him as she stood back up.

He smiled and winked at her. 'Behave, you two!'

'Always!' She replied, walking towards the door that had been opened by Lottie as she had heard the car pull up.

'Hi, Dick!' Lottie shouted to the back of the car as it slowly and carefully pulled away. The toot of the horn acknowledged that he had heard her through the still-open window. Lottie smiled to herself when she thought about Agnes and Dick. He was a year-older than her, had been her first lover. They had seen some hard times, but they had travelled through some good ones, too, in their 30-year marriage. They had two children: Lynne, who was the reason that they got married, had turned 30 a few days after her mother's funeral; and Mark, the fun-loving rogue of a son, had followed to complete the family four years later.

Chit-chat over a glass of wine made Lottie relax. They had eaten a light salad and had sat outside in the late-April night air until it had turned too cold when the sun had set. Agnes had dragged her upstairs and laid out an outfit for her to wear. Short, black shirt, red top, black stockings and high heels. A red and pink silk scarf and a light black jacket.

'It's not a night on the pull!' Lottie exclaimed as she saw the arrangement of red and black. 'Who is going to take me seriously wearing that? They will think I am on the game!'

'Here, then.' Agnes changed the top for a white blouse, with a white silk camisole to go under it. 'Skirt and stockings stay! Dress to impress, if that does not work, blow their mind with those long, sexy legs of yours. If they don't want that fantastic brain, men will not turn down the fact that they can look at you all day to take their minds of their frumpy, fat wives!'

Lottie laughed out loud. The wine had taken hold of Agnes, in the way it always seemed to. It brought out a young, flirty woman, and Lottie often thought why had she and her mother been such friends as there were never two people so different? In their looks, lifestyle and attitude to life.

Lying in bed, feeling the effects of draining that last drop from the second bottle of wine when Agnes had gone, Lottie went over the plan for the next day again in her head. Good old Dick had been volunteered (without him knowing) to take her to the station to catch the train into London. Tube and then the taxi to the centre. She had texted Todd the timings earlier, having to take the phone back from Agnes who had put a 'lol' at the end of the text. Lottie deleted it and sent the message. It came back a few moments later with the words: 'Taxi in place and will be waiting for you with a board for the DuPont Centre in the front window. C U Soon Tx.'

'See, he put a kiss!' Agnes had exclaimed. Lottie fell asleep.

Chapter 3

'I'm not budging, deal or not, that is all I need to know. I can take my offer elsewhere, but to be honest, he will not get a better one. Make it happen today, or I am out!' The phone was placed back down in the cradle and the caller turned his chair round to look out of the large window that looked out over the city.

'Mr Dean.' A voice came over the intercom breaking into his train of thought. 'Alex is here to see you.' He did not reply, just turned back around and waited for the door to open. On cue the door opened and the tall, slightly overweight guy bounded into his office.

'Someone looks pissed!' he said, slumping in one of the cream leather sofas that faced the desk and reclining chair housing the occupant.

'Not pissed, just working with incompetent prats,' he replied.

'Well, then, mate.' Alex stood up and moved to the large office desk, putting both hands down looking his friend in the eye. 'Lunch, drinks and we can find you a good woman, or pay for one, that usually works. That's what you need to bring you out of yourself. How long are you going to be like this?' He paused, thinking carefully about how he worded the next sentence. 'Look, losing Mitch must have gutted you. The loss of a brother, well, I can't imagine how that feels, but you really should let it rest. It is driving you to distraction. The police have given you their findings and the verdict was accidental.' He paused again, waiting for the reply. The silence was either good, which meant he was thinking about it. Or bad, he would explode at his friend, as he had in the past and they would come to blows. 'Ed?' his friend enquired.

The chair turned away again to the guy dressed in jeans and designer tee shirt who had been looking him in the eye when he had made the statement. Once more looking into the spring morning sunshine, Edward Dean watched the bustle of the city below him at his feet from the top floor of the office block he owned.

His mind had not been far away from his brother Mitch for the past ten months after his death. Edward had been in New York for the four months before Mitch's death. He had lived over there on and off for the past three years, rarely making contact back with home. The phone call from his PA had rocked his world, and within the hour he was on a chartered jet coming back to the UK.

He should have been there for his little brother. Since he had left the Army he had lived a privileged life, if quiet, which Ed had helped to fund. Partly because he felt guilty that he was not around, but partly to try to make a better life for him after the accident. The Army was all he wanted to do all through their young life. Their father had died when Ed was nine. He was a businessman, although as it turns out, many of his businesses were not so straight and upfront as they seemed. Although it left the family with money and wealth, their powerful friends were not always as friendly as their mother had hoped. And it proved to be their father's downfall. He had had a heart attack, or so they said, whilst fleeing the scene of a crime. Their mother had protected them from much of the truth, but it was the driver that Edward needed to know that he would make a better life for himself, be nothing like his father had been.

Mitch had been involved with an explosion in Iraq, where several of his regiment had been severely injured and two killed. Luckily, he had not been physically hurt, but psychologically it had changed him. Ed had seen this in the few months that he spent out in America with him soon after the event. He had become quiet, withdrawn, losing his outgoing nature. He had become realistic on life and left the Army because he wanted a proper job to make some money and settle down before, he felt, it was all too late. It had made Ed smile because he was only 26, but the loss of friends and the real death experience had levelled him to the ground.

Their mother wanted him back home, and so Ed had found him work and unknowingly to Mitch supported him with his businesslike persuasion in the right circles. He was doing well. Good flat in the city, nice, steady girlfriend who worked in a city centre school. He did charity work, half and full marathons, anything sponsored (which Ed usually gave heavily to); all the other hours he was working for 'Help for Heroes'. He really was making the best of it, with a little help here and there until that day!

The thought brought him back to the guy standing in the room behind him. He turned the chair back round.

'Thanks for the offer but I have an appointment this afternoon.' He fell short of giving the details of where and with whom to spare the lecture he knew he would get. 'Tomorrow I am free: let's make a day of it, book something, anything and let me know.'

'Your loss, pal!' Alex waved his hand in the air. 'I'm off to "The Club" later with that hot chick you turned down last week. Mistake! Big! Huge!' he emphasised with his arms out wide. 'Like a train, mate, goes like a train!' The smirk on his face as he opened the door and turned around to walk out did have to make Ed smile. 'Well, if you won't, then I will. Catch you later. I'll let you know about tomorrow if I have the energy left!' The door closed, but not before Ed had launched a nearby pen from his desk at it.

'Wanker!' he shouted, lightening the mood.

'ARSE!' came Ed's reply.

Ed was glad that he had remained calm. He never meant to offend his friend but as of late he seemed to lose it with anyone and everyone. Alex was right about the girl: she was hot, had the most fantastic tits if he remembers rightly (although not all her own) he had noted, but he just was not in the right headspace at the moment, and very few women had turned his head lately. He had buried himself in his work, and the battle he was having trying to find the answers he needed.

Alex and Ed had been friends since they met at school. After their father's death, his mother had wanted him to come back home, but Ed loved being his own 'little man', as his mother had called him in private. It would have never done for the other boys to know she called him that. It was bad enough that he took a regular beating and continued bullying for years. It was how Alex and he had met: Alex had found Ed in a mess after an incident, and promptly took him under his wing. Although not a sportsman (unless you class bedding every girl above, and mostly below, the age of sixteen) the fact that he was to inherit his father's title and would be a Peer of the Realm one day seemed to have a higher social standing. Although Ed did not much agree with Alex's philosophy in life of taking everyone and everything for granted, they had sort of gelled. Alex had become more distant in the latter years after uni, but he would still come a-calling for a good night out, and had stayed in America with Ed for what had seemed years.

He had even helped Ed win over some of the bullies, taking great pride in the fact that Ed had brought down one of the major Eastern European banks that one of his nemeses had run, giving him no option but to sell to Ed for a steal. That had been the breakthrough less than three years ago that had made him a millionaire. Things had just snowballed from there, now being CEO of two banks, three oil companies, and the silent owner of nine other commodities, including the communications business that his brother had been employed at.

'Zoe.' He pressed the intercom on his desk. 'Call down to the gym and get it cleared. I want a workout, alone, before Pete picks me up in a few hours.' Without a thank-you or other word he stood up and made his way to the sliding door, which revealed a secret room. It was a high-end bedroom/ shower and dressing area. Nothing like what should be in an office, more like a scene from a glossy edition of *Men's Life* or something. Black silk sheets over a gold-framed bed. Black and white tiles that were polished until you could see every detail. And just if you had missed anything that was black, white or gold, the mirror over the bed reflected the light from the surrounding windows! They did not have blinds - after all, who would see you that high up! He started to change into the workout gear and made his way out of the door.

Zoe gave his broad shoulders and muscular legs a quick glance as he passed her by. She had seen it all before, but it was always worth a look. It would look even better when he returned all hot and sweaty! 'Oh God,' she thought. 'Down, girl!' the little devil on her shoulder shouted out. 'You're married and have been for six years. That's the reason you work here. Not only your fantastic skills as PA to the CEO, but the fact that you don't threaten anything about him. It is a work, work and more work relationship,' the angel on the other shoulder reminded her. 'Yes, girlfriend, but there is no harm in window-shopping, is there?!' She looked down again with a smile on her face. Life is sweet! she thought, tapping away at the letters to go out before lunch.

Ed reached the gym and, as requested, the large, open room full of workout equipment was empty. As he passed the desk a few unhappy women were walking out, but hey, he owned the building. After all they worked for him, or at least their husbands did as the gym was open to staff and family only associated with Dean Enterprises UK; they looked like the 'ladies who lunched' set anyway. So they would not dare to complain that their morning plans had been spoilt. In fact, looking at their workout kit, it did not look as if they turned up for more than a chat and a bitch about someone anyway.

'Mr Dean.' A male voice averted his attention in a strong American accent. 'Programme or just killer?' Jamie, the gym instructor, stood as tall as Ed. Blond, as fit as a flea, very tanned and pumped up with his tattoos showing on his well-worked biceps. He had been a top trainer to the rich and famous in New York and Ed had asked him to come to the UK and work the gym for him, at a good price of course. Over the past year Dean Enterprises had purchased several gym chains and Jamie was now well established as the lead UK trainer. Based out of this, the flagship (and only one not open to the public) gym.

'Killer,' Ed replied, reaching for the boxing gloves Jamie had in his hands, 'and you are the prey. This is going to hurt you more than it is me!' Ed pulled on one glove and took a sideswipe at Jamie. His quick reaction allowed him to duck and Ed missed. After several years of practice, he had archived the highest qualification as a Dan in various martial art sports and now this served him well.

'Really, that's it?' Jamie replied with a smirk that hit every piece of male pride Ed had. With a flick of the other ungloved hand Ed planted Jamie in the left rib. There was a loud grunt as Jamie felt the unguarded blow hit his bones.

'Really!' Ed replied. 'You may be three years younger than me, but fitter, really? Ed replied, already raining down blows on the punchbag that sat to the side of the open sparing matted area as a warm-up.

'Put this in, precious. Don't want to spoil those good looks and work up your dentist's bill.' Jamie handed him a gumshield. 'How long we got?'

'Hour, hour ten max,' he said, muffling his voice as he placed the guard in his mouth. And so the beating began. Only stopping to take on water, or as Ed said, 'You only want a drink because I am kicking your ass!' They beat each other, and defended themselves as if it were a street fight, not a workout session.

As the elevator door opened Ed stepped out into the entrance of his office.

'Good?' Zoe tried not to stare, but could not help but notice the red marks on his face and the blood on his vest top. He still had a slight tan from the time he had been in America, although it was fading and really could only be seen when he was sweaty as he was now (or in the shower, wet, Zoe's shoulder devil thought!). She felt a small twinge between her legs and her nostrils flared. She looked fully at him in the face. 'You need any ice?' She looked at his top, circling her finger on her own shoulder to show where the blood marks were on Ed's arm.

'Not mine, but you may want to ask downstairs if Jamie is OK!' he triumphantly announced as he closed the door with a smile that did remind him he had taken a few knocks on his face after all.

Chapter 4

Well, as days went, this one had best get better! Lottie thought as she tried to get the coffee stain out of the white blouse she had on. She rubbed at it with some toilet paper from the train toilets in between stations. It was getting worse!

The Starbucks she had purchased at the station in a bid to remove the pounding band playing in her head had been fine. Along with the painkillers it was working a treat. Until the fat, sweaty commuter had joined them at the last station and knocked into her mid-sip. The brown liquor had gone down the blouse and she thought to herself, OK, Agnes, the red top-pink scarf combo would have hidden this, but the white blouse!? The only thing for it was to take it off. She slipped it over her head and forced it into the bottom of her bag, making everything else in there fight for space. The thin camisole underneath was low, and as she bent down she was aware that her old-fashioned lace white bra could be seen, giving the rest of the commuters at the station an eyeful if she was not careful. She had already felt naked sitting next to the young man eating a pasty for his lunch, who did nothing but look at her legs and give her a wink from time to time, with a flake of pastry and some of the contents of the pie on his chin. Welcome to the city! She was glad she had asked for an appointment after lunch: not only did it give enough time to get there, but if she had to be on the train when it really was busy, she may not have made it out alive at this rate and it would be Todd doing her post-mortem!

Now there is a thought! She smiled to herself whilst still on the train. Todd seeing me naked: Umm, she inwardly sighed, him running his hands over every inch of her body. Some people may think that is sick, thinking of when you are dead, but she cast her mind back to the time they had been in bed and he had drawn on her body all the outlines of her vital organs with red lipstick. He had traced the outline first with tender kisses, and then followed with the bright red cosmetic. He had then walked his fingers over the same spots, tracing the lines to divide the body up into neat sections, before he nibbled and blew cold air across her skin.

She shivered, and the fat man sitting next to her shifted in his seat again. This made her come back to reality again. The train was almost at the station. She pulled the lapels on her jacket up and did the front buttons up. Luckily for her, the stress of the last few weeks had kept the weight off, even losing a bit. As Agnes had pointed out, something about her perfect size 10. 'Lose any more weight off your chest, kid, and no man will want to have a look!' She smiled as she hopped onto the platform, walking along listening to her friend in her head with the conversations they had had last night.

On cue there was the black cab amongst the hustle of the station entrance with a large yellow sign in the window displaying DuPont Centre – Miss Jenkins.

Lottie went to the window and said he was for her; she opened the door and hopped in. The driver made some small talk on the twenty-minute journey. She had made good time from home. It had only taken two and half hours, not a daily commute, she thought, so moving closer had to be an option if this was what she wanted to do. Maybe Agnes was right again: rent a room, home at weekends. Although she had learned that this type of work very often was not Monday to Friday 9 to 5, people really did not have a specific time frame to be found dead in her experience. She had often been woken in the early hours, driven to some remote area to look at a poor soul who had been injured or killed in some way. That was her job, after all, to find out how.

She had been dropped off outside the Centre, smiling sweetly as the cab driver said it had been paid for. She gave him a tip anyway and turned on her heels to face the large mass of glass, windows, steel and a splatter of bricks that the building was built from. Walking to the revolving front doors, she took a breath and said, 'Ready, girl, you go for it, you're a 28-year-old professional,' in a poor mimic of Agnes from last night.

The security guard on the front desk looked up. He gave her a warm smile. 'Afternoon, Miss.' He looked at his book on the desk. 'Miss Jenkins for Mr Carter?' he questioned, although it was more of a statement than a question.

'Yes,' Lottie replied, feeling the heat build up in her cheeks. The guard pressed a button and waved her through the turnstile. 'He will be with you shortly. Do take a seat.'

There was no one else in the small holding area, although through the windows Lottie could see people in lab coats walking around, chatting and using mobile phones. The door to her right opened with a beep and she turned.

'Miss Jenkins.' She recognised the voice as she looked at her old friend, old lover. Todd had not really changed. He had sure been looking after himself as he looked more masculine that she had ever remembered. She held out her hand as the formal greeting had thrown her slightly. He held out his hand in reply. 'Lottie, it is great to see you.' There was no awkward pause as she thought that there may be: he took her hand to shake it, pulling her closer with a firm grip to land a short peck on her cheek. He must have felt the heat from her face on the outside. To her it felt as if she had been face up on the desert floor for a week with no suncream. 'You look awesome!' He stood back slightly to look at her, full length.

You smell awesome! She wanted to say as the deep, musky aftershave he was wearing hit her nostrils. That had not changed over the years and she really could not believe that he still wore the same brand. She quickly replied with, 'Thanks, this place looks amazing,' conscious that her reply had been a long time coming while her mind went back to that distinctive smell of eau de Todd.

'That's a great start. Let's go for a walk round, meet a few faces to see if I can impress you further.' He pointed to the elevator and started talking about the Centre, more details than he had given her before.

After what felt like an hour they had made it back to Todd's office. The smiling lady on the reception must have been the person that spoke to Lottie yesterday. She smiled at her and was not sure that the friendly smile she got back was quite as friendly, as Todd had placed his hand on the lower part of her back to usher into his office.

A coffee pot was on the desk with a small tray of biscuits. Todd poured and Lottie reached forward to take a cup. She took a sip. Watch the top! she thought. Don't spill any. As it reached her mouth she delighted in the hot liquid. She took another sip.

'Well, then, Miss Jenkins, see anything that excites you? Do you think you can handle something so impressive!?' He took a sip of his own drink as the words had come out totally innocently, referring to the work and building she had been shown around. Lottie nearly choked.

'Huph, huph.' She cleared her throat. 'Yes,' she choked out.

'Lotts, you OK?' He quickly moved over to her and put his hand on her shoulder. 'Do you want some water or something?'

Now, depending on what the something was, she was totally in awe that her mind seemed to be on the one track for the last hour. As they had walked around, all she could do was watch his well-formed arms through his shirt as he opened doors. She had, on more than one occasion, looked at his tight ass and the shape of the top of his legs. She had to admit that he had not been in front of her much or she was sure that she would have tried to look to see if the bulge in his trousers was really as big as her imagination was leading her to believe.

Oh God, this is a bad idea, I can't take the job. She thought. What is wrong with me? I know it has been a while, but I am like a bitch on heat.

'Todd, I'm not sure,' she said, pulling herself together. 'It really is impressive but...' She stopped. 'It would mean finding a place to live here, but I still need to be able to look after Mum's business so I need to keep the house at home.' She stopped again and thought to herself. I would have to work close to you each day and resist the current urge to jump on you in your office chair like we used to. That would obviously upset your PA who has a crush on you. She had seen the look she was getting through the glass as Todd was now perched on the desk in front of her, and yes, the bulge was now very obvious in the front of his trousers! She continued out loud.

'I am loving what you offer, I really think I can cope with the workload, it's just other stuff...' She stopped herself from saying the last thoughts out loud.

'I am not sure about the other stuff that you mention: is the money not enough? I can work on the package.' Todd's innocent words made Lottie stand up.

'No!!' she said out loud. She felt as though she was having an out-of-body experience and that this lust was some demon that was taking her over. Never had she felt like this or reacted in this way; even when they were together she had never felt so drawn, so goddamn rude. It ashamed her, and she turned as he caught her hand. She froze.

'Sorry,' he said as he let it go. He was standing now, directly in front of her. 'Listen, I am so excited about this new venture. I think that we really will make a great team. You have so much of what this place needs.' He continued to talk but she seemed to have turned off from his voice and focused. After a deep sigh she said, 'Can I...' She was going to say 'sleep on it', but wanted all terms of sexual reference to be pushed from her head. '... Take a day or so to think about it?' She continued. 'I need to look at places to stay, sort out how to run things my end, you know?' She stopped and looked at him.

'Yer, yer, of course. Come back and talk to the Professor. He is with some very important donor at the moment but he was the one who mentioned your name when we first started out looking for someone new. He had seen recent work you had done on the police cold cases, something of a special area when all leads to the crimes have gone, well, cold! And commented about it. As soon as I heard the name I just knew it was you. I was privileged to say that I knew you. He asked if I could get in touch and ask you to join the specialist team here.' He paused. 'I told him about, well, you know, the past few weeks and that I would speak to you when it was right.' He stopped again.

'Listen, if it helps, my sister, you remember, Jess, has a granny flat attached to the house in Camden; it was built for her father-in-law before he died. It is totally separate from the house. You would have space, be able to do your own thing, give you time to look around for your own place. Listen, you can even bring your man back to stay over it's that private. You would not be imposing on anyone.' What had Todd just said? 'Your man' back. What man? Thank God, she did not have a man to go back to, because if the last hour's worth of thoughts were anything to go back to tonight, she swore that the sexual tension would kill them both!

'Sorry, I don't have a...' She stopped. 'Boyfriend,' she continued. Why had he said that, was he fishing?

'Oh sorry, I thought when you said other stuff you may need to talk things through with someone.' He walked over to the coffee and refreshed his mug. 'Listen, no promises, but I really think we can do this. I am not sure how you felt about today, I was nervous about seeing you, you know after we had been so close.' Lottie had been trying to forget just how close for the last hour. Thanks, mate, for reminding me, she thought. 'Well,' he started again, 'I know that when we split it was for the right reasons: we both wanted to have a career and it took different paths. Remained good colleagues for those few months before I moved, great friends even.' He paused again and turned his back as he walked to the window.

Lottie was not sure what to say. He was right. Their split had been a decision by them both, and they had worked side by side without any issues from that time onwards. They never found themselves jumping into bed at every opportunity, although they had come close after a few nights at the uni bar. They still played in a band together: Todd had the most fantastic voice and knew how to play a guitar: his hands were so seductive! But although her hormones were shouting at her, he was right. They had something special and it needed to remain that way. He turned around and again sat on the edge of the table.

'I'm not saying it's going to be easy, especially if you turn up to work in stockings and a top that low-cut every day!' Lottie could feel the colour in her cheeks rise again. See, he had noticed! she thought. 'But we are professionals, I would love for you to meet the family and become a great friend with us all, and…' He stopped short. 'Well, you know, just make a really great team here.'

Lottie had closed their meeting saying that she would give it some thought and get back to him tomorrow. They parted the same way as they had met, a short kiss on the cheek, but somehow to Lottie it felt different to what it had those few hours before.

Agnes's wise idea of staying the night had been again a good one. Lottie got into the taxi and told him where to drop her off. She had been persuaded to book a high-end hotel, with a spa, so at City prices it would be expensive, but maybe the opportunity she needed to have a really good think about her life. There was a really great restaurant in the hotel and she had booked for an evening meal, too, as a treat.

Before she had left Todd had invited her back on Friday night to meet his sister and her husband. As she remembered she had only met the older sister twice before, but could not remember seeing a husband, although she knew they had young children. They had arranged to meet at Jess's house so that Lottie could see the flat and then go into town. Her husband Bobby was attending a charity works do and they were going to go for a drink in a wine bar that Todd's younger brother managed when he had finished. The bar had not been doing so well and they tried to give as much custom as they could. According to Todd, they often closed with their party staying behind and having drinks as a private group of friends. It all sounded great, and might allow her to relax about moving to London and starting out afresh. Getting back into the city would mean another train journey, but she was sure that it would not be as disastrous as the last had been, and she was sure that Dick would have no issues in being a local taxi for her again if she asked.

As high-end hotels went, she had chosen well. She closed her eyes at the room prices as she checked in at the reception so it did not feel too extravagant. The porter showed her to the room four floors up, and her overnight bag was left in her room. A quick look around the mini-suite revealed the large bath and walk-in shower, and little dressing room with a window seat that showed a great view of the back of the next building. Although she had to admire the Georgian/Victorian architecture, with the details she could see carved into the stone work.

A drink, she thought. Grabbing her phone and the note she had made of the wine bar they would be in on the Friday, she jumped into the lift. She admired herself in the glass mirrors that were on the walls in the lift. Um, the top is a bit low, but no one knows me! She smiled as she walked out the door and looked around for the bar. It was on the first floor so she had not gone all the way back down to the reception. She could see a spare seat at the bar and thought it was a better option to sit at than one at a lower table, so that if anyone did walk past her, she at least limited the view of the pretty white bra she had on.

One drink and then a soak in the tub, she thought. Maybe two and take it back to the room, yes, better idea!

Hopping onto the high stool, she perched at the bar. The bartender looked her way and acknowledged her as he was serving another customer.

'Glass of Merlot please,' she said. Red wine did go to her head, so it would slow her down a bit. She placed the note on the bar and pulled out her phone. Text or call? she thought. Agnes would be on the phone forever, she thought, if we chat, so text was best, although there was so much to say.

Going good, room is lush good choice, hun! Having a drink, I will call you when I am soaking in the bath in an hour or so L x

She pushed herself round a bit on the chair so that she could hold the phone out and tapped in the address of the wine bar. Waiting for a response, she took a sip of wine. Tap and Tune, it was called, sounded intriguing. She had another sip of wine and looked at the website.

She never noticed the guy who had walked to the bar, as he was standing behind her.

The meeting was a success, even if Ed hated going to a hotel to do business. No matter how expensive a hotel was, how nice the meal or the wine, he always thought of them as places to bring a cheap woman, not to make a million, but he wanted to celebrate. The rest of the party were still at the table, but a swift drink would allow him to go back in and make his apologies before heading back to the office.

Walking into the bar, he noticed a slim blonde sitting with her legs crossed. He looked again and tracked the line of what he knew were stockings under the short, black skirt. Nice, he thought. Just another inch and you would see flesh! He moved behind her, and he was aware she had not noticed; even when he asked for a Scotch, she did not move. She was engrossed in the text she was sending.

The way she sat in the chair made him aware that she had a strong posture, and, although he could not see it from the back, his eyes had been drawn to the low-cut top she was wearing. He pulled a pen out of his jacket and wrote a note on the drink serviette that was under his glass and passed it to the bartender. The young man looked at it then over to Lottie and then smiled. 'No problem, sir,' he replied.

In one mouthful the liquor went down, leaving a hot trace in his throat. He nodded to the bartender and walked out the same way he had come in. From the doorway he looked back across to study the blonde from a safe distance. She flicked the strand of hair back that was loose from the rest that had been neatly piled up at the back. Business-like but sweet, he thought. She stroked her leg subconsciously knowing that the shirt was short; she pulled at it to ensure that nothing she had on below was showing: self-conscious, he thought. The little movement allowed the white top to pull across and the top of her chest was revealed for a short moment, but he had seen it. Schoolgirl white, innocent! He thought feeling a stir in his groin. Ed knew a girl like that would never satisfy him and the need he had, but he had ever liked the challenge. But there was something about her, something that would sadden him if he was able to play his games. 'Sometimes there has to be purity in the world to cope with the bad,' one of his therapists had said to him, and God, he could be bad. He smiled to himself as he watched the girl order another drink and the bartender atomically had it ready.

He smiled again as she started to look behind her, uncrossing her legs and swinging the chair around to see who the mystery purchaser was. Her legs parted and a swift glimpse of what he had suspected was confirmed. Innocent but daring! I like that. He was aware that he had been away from the party for a while and so headed back. He sat listening to the conversation, but outlining the white, delicate lace he had just seen in his mind. His train of thought was broken by the bartender standing by his side.

'Sorry, Mr Dean.' The boy paused really sorry that he had interrupted them 'The young lady.' He paused again. 'At the bar, dropped this as she got up.' He was handed a scrap of paper: **Tap and Tune – 8:30 Friday** was all it said.

'Thanks.' Ed pushed his hand in his jacket and pulled out a £20 note and handed it to the young lad. 'Sir!' he replied as he walked off with a grin on his face as if it were Christmas.

Chapter 5

Agnes had the full lowdown that night, starting with the drink at the bar, and concluding with the next invitation to join Todd and his family. After the question, possibly ten times in the course of the call, did Lottie want to go for the job, she finally said it was starting to sound more appealing.

As always, Dick had come to the rescue as the taxi to get her to the train station, and when she arrived on the Friday night in London she really was looking forward to it. She arrived at a semi-detached house, which had a very narrow extension. There was a covered passage along the side of the house that led to the one-bedroom flat that Todd had mentioned. She had knocked on the door, but Todd had heard the taxi and was keen to get her inside and show her around.

He never asked the question once about if Lottie wanted the job, which made the start of the night really relaxed. They were running late going into town. Jess and Lottie had a lot of time to speak, and she felt really at ease with her. Jess was in her middle thirties, and was from Todd's mother's first marriage. He never referred to her as stepsister, though: nice, Lottie thought.

Jess had explained that her husband would join them a lot later, but if it was too much later he would have to go home to look after the kids, as the babysitter could only stay until 11:30. They had a quick drink in the pub at the end of the road and then walked to the Tap and Tune. It was quite busy, but as Todd explained, once people had finished eating, they tended to move on. Even on a Saturday night they often closed at 11:00 just to save on staffing and costs. Todd's brother was serving a table of giggling women. He was a mini-version of Todd, but with slightly longer, messy hair, all the latest fashion. He noticed them and he pointed to a large table in the window. Todd gave the thumbs-up and they all sat down. Menus were passed around for food and drink, and when it was time to order Scotty came bounding over. Todd stood and they had a man hug; he went around to his sister and kissed her on the cheek. He looked at Lottie and said, 'Lottie Jenkins, the legend in the flesh as I live and breathe.' Todd shot him a look that could have killed.

'Sounds like my reputation precedes me!' Lottie said, standing and holding out her hand. Scotty looked at her hand and said, 'Really, a handshake?' He leaned in to kiss her cheek quickly with a squeeze for good measure.

'Right folks,' he continued, 'everything is still on, although I only have one salmon left,' he wrote down everyone's order and then took away Todd's wine glass. He was soon to come back with a bottle of red and a beer for Todd. As he poured the girls a glass, Lottie flicked her mind back to the hotel and wondered if she should comment on the last glass of red she had had in the city! She thought better of it as she sipped the dark red liquid, but then thought that if she had much more of this - 'wow, that is strong,' she said - she felt she would blurt it out anyway.

The meal was great, the company better, the time flew, and after eating Todd sat back in his chair. He had chosen to sit next to Lottie, leaving the chair free opposite for Bobby, who sadly had not yet turned up. Scotty would from time to time give them a few minutes of his time in between the dwindling number of customers. It was when Lottie got up to use the bathroom that she saw it.

A shining baby grand piano, sitting all alone in a raised corner of the room. She had not seen it because of the customers sitting in front, but got a great view when she walked back past it. The stool had a red seat, like hers at home, and she came back to the table and said, 'Scotty, your baby is so beautiful.' Todd looked at her, but it was not quite as funny as Jess and Scotty with questioning looks on their faces.

'You had too much wine and you are seeing things?' Todd laughed.

'No, funny.' She gave Todd a little nudge of the arm. 'The baby over there.' Lottie pointed in the direction of the gleaming piece of furniture.

'Oh right, I think that we all get it, the piano.' Todd looked at her face and was genuinely moved by the look she was giving off, like a child looking into one of those original sweetshop windows at all the candy the world had to offer. He got it, the piano, he remembered she played.

'Glad you are a forensic scientist, bro: see the training worked out well now you got all the clues!' Scotty mocked and laughed from the other side of the table. Todd stuck out his tongue.

'You still play?' Todd asked, looking at her. He remembered how they had spent nights jamming and playing tunes: sometimes she would sing, they would sing together, and he would sit by her side and play a tune of the old uni bar piano, or play the guitar while she played.

'You play?' Scotty said in a loud voice without allowing Lottie to reply. 'Really?'

'It is so surprising?' Lottie asked.

'No, sorry, I did not mean that the way it came out, I mean you play. We had a guy who used to come and play for the punters, but he left. Since then we have not had anyone, and I swear it has had an effect on trade,' Scott finished.

'No,' Todd said out loud quite unexpectedly. 'Lottie, don't let him tempt you to come and play in here every night I asked you first to work with me.' His tone was not a stern one, but she could tell that he felt threatened by the thought of losing her to his little brother.

'Boys!' Jess said. 'Lottie was only making a statement about the piano, not devoting her life to either one of you in any job. The poor girl needs to be able to make up her own mind and tonight was not about putting her on the spot to make that decision. Remember, Todd, you agreed, no pressure.'

Lottie thought of how nice that was, Todd had spoken to them both about why she would be there and he really did want her to make up her own mind about the position at the DuPont Centre.

Lottie looked at them all and took a sip of wine. 'I have to ask,' she said, looking at Scotty. 'Can I?' She wiggled her fingers as if silently playing a tune.

'We are called the Tap and Tune, bro,' he looked at Todd, almost asking permission. Todd rolled his eyes and Lottie leaned over to him, flashing her eyelids. 'Pleeeeaassseee?' they both said together. There was only one other full table of people left. Never one to run down the opportunity to play, she had not played on such a fine piano since her youth. Although her old friend at home was good, and the one in the bar at home was OK, a baby grand gave such a tune, like no upright piano could.

Ed had looked at his watch now several times. Although he would never be so rude to leave, as he was hosting the dinner, he really did want to take some time out. His phone had called three times: it was his driver Pete saying he was outside as arranged, but could not stop as it was red route on the main street, collection only. The dinner had raised good funds tonight, and the champagne was flowing. Ed's mother was deep in conversation with the Lord Mayor's party and he took one last look at his watch.

'Got to be somewhere?' An attractive brunette gently placed her hand over the watch to get his attention. 'Caroline, don't you have someone else you would like to talk to? Why come to me in such a busy room of rich, young and desperate men!?' Ed's mother would have slapped his face for being so rude, but Caroline Pickards was out in life for one thing: to screw you over. In both the financial and the physical sense. While Ed had never failed to impress her on the latter, he really did draw the line at gold-digging slappers.

She liked to play, and play hard in bed. At first Ed had been satisfied for weeks in his habits, but then she turned tricks and spread gossip amongst her friends. One thing that Ed did not want was everyone in his life knowing he liked to play rough, rougher than some in the bedroom.

He thought he had chosen her well, as she responded to all the games. Even the role play in the office bedroom had been fun, but she broke her word on keeping quiet the day after Ed had refused to fund her latest shopping spree, racking up thousands of pounds on shoes and clothes. He paid her off in the end to deny the information publicly, but it was too late as a paper had got hold of the information. Luckily for Ed, he owned a large share in the paper and it went to print on a small column on page 9.

'No one ever gets to page 9 and reads it, they just look at the pictures,' Alex said as he looked at the newspaper. 'Not sure why you could not get it totally taken out?'

'Some legal thing that the lawyers advised: if she claims it again, I can have her for slander or something,' he had replied.

'Move away please.' He sweetly smiled at Caroline taking her hand from his wrist. His phone rang again. He looked at the number: Pete again. 'I'm there,' he said, moving towards the door as quickly as he could.

The destination he had asked to be driven to was only a two-minute drive, but he did not want to walk as it would take longer and he could be back before he was missed. 'Sorry, Pete, I have had a nightmare getting away,' he explained.

'It was just getting so late after the pick-up time you required: what are we going there for?' Pete had been Ed's driver, bodyguard, Head of Security, private investigator and all-round rock for the last five years. Although he was a driver most of the time, he was the highest-paid in Ed's personal staff by a long way. Ed respected the guy who had spent years in the SAS. He could look after himself and when Ed got into trouble the night they met (over a woman in a club who was married to the owner, but naked in Ed's face at the time!) Pete had stepped in and put a guy down. This was the end of his SAS career, getting a police record for GBH. Ed got him off the sentence and paid the large fine to one of his friends in the court. It was not out of guilt he did this: Ed knew that he needed a guy like him around.

'Interested in something?' Ed, replied loosening his bow tie.

'The lease of the place we are going to. Can't you do business in the daytime?' Pete asked almost at the destination. Ed had asked Pete to find out all he could about the wine bar. He had told him the lease was up and it looked like the current owner was not going to renew. Although the manager had tried, business was not good enough as a single property with no other income to support the quieter months. The owner was cutting his losses at the end of the month. The car pulled up outside and Ed opened the door.

The door to the bar was open, to let in some air, and he was stopped in his tracks by the gentle playing of the piano. He looked through to see his red wine girl playing the piano and she took away his breath.

Lottie had chosen Mozart's 'Minuet in G major' as the second piece of music she played. She had only played the first tune for a few moments before returning to her seat, but after some coaxing from the other customers, and Scotty, she had returned to the piano stool to play.

She did not need the sheet music; this upbeat classic piece was something her father loved. She had played it over and over until the notes almost poured from her fingers. She was lost in the moment, helped by the happy memory of her father and also the red wine. But not a note was missed: her slender fingers caressed each note and she never felt the eyes in the room on her. She never did when the passion started to flow. The piano responded to the soft touch of her hands. Her body moved and swayed with the changing phrasing in the piece, she closed her eyes as if the sheet music was embedded on her eyelids.

Ed looked on from the safety of the car. He had closed the door, but had asked for all side windows to be opened. He, like the other guy in the room he had noticed, was transfixed. He watched her whole body as she became consumed in the passion for playing. It was almost as if no one else was in the room with her. He closed his eyes and put the music in his head with the girl sitting at the bar the other day, the back skirt, the white bra. He felt his groin respond to the mounting tension. He imagined her gyrating movements on the piano stool as if she was sitting in front of him, doing this for his own pleasure.

He opened his eyes again, shifting in his seat as his full erection was now painful on his trousers. He had never seen such beauty, such lust for something that totally took over his body. No woman, no matter the height of climax and pleasure he had seen in a woman (and he had seen many from both a distance and at close range!), he had never been so internally affected by, the need to just touch her pale, white skin. To rub a finger down the side of her cheek and softly kiss it. He would have grabbed her there and then, thrust her against the wall and took whatever he wanted. No kiss was ever soft with Ed, he fucked, hard, but he wanted to take her, be soft and breathe in the scent of her, kiss her from top to toe, slowly, sucking, biting and tasting her. He stopped the thoughts before he lost his own control.

The rest of the customers left the bar. 'The manager said he would ask her to play a few nights a week,' one said. 'Doubt it, I heard it was going up for sale next week, so we will all have to find somewhere else to have a drink.'

'Drive!' he said to Pete. 'Go quickly!' He pulled out his phone and made a call. It was 11:30pm but the voice on the other end of the phone was obliging. 'Whatever the cost, I don't care I will have the papers by Monday on my desk to sign?' He listened to the reply. 'Well, pay him to want to leave, then, I don't care about contracts.' He put down the phone in time to return to the location of the dinner. 'Find out what that piece of music was and that girl, I want to know her name.' He wanted to get out when they pulled up on the roadside but was still aware of the reaction his cock had had. He took some deep breaths to control himself and put his jacket over his arm and walked into the venue. He would have to go to The Club tonight to get over this: he was damn sure he was never going to sleep without some form of release.

Chapter 6

Lottie had woken from a good night's sleep in the flat. Todd had said his farewells, but would be round again in the morning. Jess had said to come in whenever she awoke, so after her shower she knocked on the back door. Bobby beckoned her in, they introduced themselves and he apologised for not being able to make it last night. He made a coffee and explained that Jess had taken the kids swimming, but she would be back before 12. Lottie explained that she wanted to head off after lunch and get home.

'I hear you have a talent at the end of your fingers,' he said, 'I mean for the ivory,' he quickly put in, not wanting any wrong meaning to be taken from his words after he said them over in his head. At that very moment Scotty walked in with the largest bunch of red roses, four dozen to be exact.

'Left at the bar while I was cleaning up this morning, some guy in a black car, looked like someone's driver to me.' He placed the flowers on the worktop before he dropped them. 'The cards here.' He had to look hard for it amongst the vivid red petals that gave off the most stunning smell. Lottie looked shocked.

'For me?' she questioned, taking the small envelope being handed to her. 'Yep.' The guys looked at each other. 'As impressions go, you made one on someone!' He knew that they were not from Todd, else he would have been giving them to her himself; it was not Todd's style anyway.

Although he was Todd's little brother, they had had many drunken nights and chats when Lottie had been mentioned, and he knew that, although the boat had sailed, his brother really had loved Lottie, and in the short time of meeting her he could see why. 'She is an infection,' Todd had said. 'Although we split amicably I really missed her and the more I did, the more I knew it was the wrong thing to have done: my one regret is I never told her, always acted so casual. When it was too late to go back we had moved on too far. Scotty had not really understood how you can become that attached to someone, as he had never really had a long-term or short-term girl.' But from his brother's reluctance to become close to anyone again, and become career-driven and minded every hour he could, he knew that she had left her mark, and only hoped that any old wounds would not spoil any hopes Todd had for the future.

'Come on, who is it?' Bobby asked, looking at Lottie's face as she read the card:

Red roses for the red wine girl

'I don't know.' Lottie read the words again and in an instant knew what the connection was, but a streak of fear showed on her face as the realisation that someone was watching her, almost stalking her, made her put the card on the table and look away.

'What's going on?' Todd asked, walking into the room. 'Flipping heck, Bobby, what have you done now to have to give our Jess them?' he innocently asked, gesticulating to the roses. Lottie walked out of the room into the garden as quickly as she could. She was overcome to the point of tears and did not want to let anyone see; to make it worse here was Todd. 'What?' Todd asked the two men. Scotty shrugged his shoulders. 'They were for Lottie,' he said.

'You bloody creep, I told you she was not playing for you at any price; you can't buy her with flowers, you know!' He raised his voice at Scotty.

'They are not from me.' Scotty held up his hands and backed away slightly in submission. Todd picked up the card and read the words. Both of the other men in the room stayed silent. 'I don't follow.' He looked up at Lottie who was now on the phone. 'She said that she was not seeing anyone.'

Scotty shoved his hand in his pocket and felt the paper of the crisp, white envelope. God, he did not dare to get it out and show any of them now. When the roses had arrived, a letter was dropped off with his name on. The guy had simply said, 'From your new boss, best take a look.'

He had opened it immediately. It was from some London solicitors saying that from the 30 April (that was in two days' time) the bar was under a new owner and that he would be paid a full salary to keep it running. They were offering a lot more, almost double what he was on now, under one condition: 'the girl from last night' plays again once a week at least. If not, then the new owner would pull out and the bar would be sold, losing his and the other staff their jobs. Was it a threat to him, or worse, was it a threat to Lottie? Judging by her reaction, the latter was a possibility. He must have gone pale as Todd continued to look at Lottie who was now taking little steps forwards and backwards while talking. Her arms pulled in close to her, her back to them. From her body language something was wrong.

'Spill, brother, you know more that you are letting on.' Todd shot him a look.

'Don't go all detective pathology on me. I know as much as you, as much as we all can see that something is not right. Maybe it's you pushing her for a decision on working down here. You know, thinking about it, she has had some pretty shitty months of late, and none of us really know what crap she is having to deal with.' Scotty grabbed a cup and poured coffee out of the pot into it. He filled Lottie's mug back up. 'Here, take it to her, she looks like she has finished on the phone.'

Todd held out his hand and took the hot mug and slowly opened the door. Lottie turned around after wiping her face and looked at Todd.

'Sorry,' she said, 'a bit of a drama queen.' She took the coffee that he was offering but did not drink it. She looked up at the sky to resist another tear falling down her face. Todd took the cup back off her and put it on the patio table nearby. He held out his arms and she willingly disappeared into them. Her tiny frame rested again his chest. She could feel his heart beating quickly. His arms felt warm, safe and, although she had no siblings, like a brother would protect his sister. He placed a gentle kiss on her head and they stood in silence for what felt like the rest of the day.

'This may not go well,' Bobby said to Scotty as they tried not to look out of the window. 'He needs to back off a bit, I don't do too much male bonding with him. God, we have only known each other for ten years, but I can see her pain is hurting him, whatever the story.' He sipped his now cooling coffee. 'Jess and I saw the last time he became obsessed with her, and despite what he thinks, he is nowhere near over her. Well, after two years there is no way that this is going to be a platonic working relationship. I hate to say this, but I hope that she does not decide to take that job. Whatever life she had before, maybe both of their better options is for her not to stay.'

Scotty looked out; they had not released the hold. Todd was gently brushing her hair with his hand, but no words were spoken between them. No way on this earth was he going to mention the letter. But he had a lot to lose, and his friends who he worked with did, too. He had to find out who had bought the bar. He walked out of the room to ring the boss – well, the boss for the next two days if the letter was to be read as true.

'What do you mean you don't know who made you the offer?' Scotty said as quietly as he dared. He could hear that Todd and Lottie had come back inside and the kettle was starting to boil. 'You must have an idea.' He listened to the reply on the other end. 'Well, thanks, money talks, I can see that.' Scotty turned on his heels and headed back to the kitchen: he put the phone down. 'Money-grabbing twat!' he said under his breath.

'Problems?' Bobby asked.

'Not really. Just something I need to go and do,' he said. 'Anything you need me for, bro?' he asked Todd. Todd shook his head. 'No thanks, kid,' came the reply. Scotty left.

Todd had insisted on taking Lottie to the train station. If he had his own way he would have driven her in his sister's car home. But she was adamant that she wanted to get home on her own.

They had parted, agreeing that she would call him on Monday when he had had the opportunity to talk to the Professor. Although Lottie was sure that she did not want to move to the big city, she wondered if there was any mileage in suggesting she did some distance work for them, almost as a consultancy just for a few months until she got her head in a better place.

While she had been outside she finally said to Todd, 'I just think that the past few months have caught me up, and I need time to readjust to losing mum, before taking such another life-changing task on as this job would be. I want to, Todd, it is no reflection on us, you past or present, but I really think I need some space away, maybe a holiday and then I will see. I understand that if the position has been filled then, well, I have missed the boat and as we have said before, things happen for a reason, but just now, I can't commit to this.'

It had been a poor night's sleep on the Saturday. Although Agnes had been with her, she tried to lose herself in other stuff. Todd had called, and bless so had Jess. She was sure that they would remain good friends, but she was even surer that she needed to get away somewhere. She looked at the piano in the living room and did not want to play. For the first time in her life she did not want to play. That did not feel good. The run she had done would help to keep off the pounds she would no doubt be putting on with the second glass of wine she sipped as she watched the TV. She had looked earlier at a holiday. Agnes had a friend in France with a villa that could be used for a long weekend if she wanted to: they were away for the next three weeks. Sounded good, but would she have time to book fights?

Another glass of wine would help, so she poured the rest of the bottle into her glass. She had found that drink had helped the time she had left Todd, and for a few weeks after, but she knew it was not the answer, but for now it was helping. The house was too big and the silence too loud. She needed to get this out of her system and she promised that Monday would be the start of the beginning.

'Anything Pete? It is Sunday afternoon, how long do you need to find out the information?' Ed said down the phone. He had gone to his mother's, the usual Sunday lunch date. Sometimes it was a pain in the ass, but this week it was a welcome distraction. The Club visit had proved useless. The fact that naked women were draped all over the men in the club, and the occasional woman who paid for that type of thing. Alex had offered several choice ladies, but also Ed really did not have the taste. He went to the dungeon, his favourite room in the venue, to watch a short, thin man whip a young girl, but when they were replaced with a tall, long-legged blonde, all he could see was her face. He went home and for the first time in what had to be three years gave himself a hand job. He could not call it self-gratification, as he was not satisfied, but it removed the primal male urges he had had since he had seen her again.

You're going mad, you idiot, get a grip, he had said to himself as he stood in the shower that morning, allowing the heat of the water to penetrate his skin. He turned up the heat on purpose so that he could feel the pain; sometimes it was the only release, to feel the pain like he had when he was younger. Pete continued the conversation.

'I have made a good start. The hotel was more than willing to give me what I needed to know.' No surprises as you own half of the chain! he thought. 'Can you give me another couple of hours and I will have something I think you would like to go with? I am not sure on what your aims are with her, but...' Pete paused. He never interfered with his employer's professional or private life but he felt that Ed had to know this young girl was in a vulnerable place. 'She has recently, quite recently, lost her mother so...' He stopped himself from saying 'treat her right and don't be the usual bastard you are to women.' But he held his tongue.

'Fine, collect me at 4pm and then we can talk.' Ed put down the phone and went back into the room where his mother was washing up. 'Mum, why do you do that when you have a dishwasher?' The conversation continued. He did a few odd jobs for his mum. Even though he was one of the richest men in the country for his age, she liked to keep him level-headed, although he found it a bit hypocritical as she lived in the three-million-pound house which he had bought for her, with a live-in housekeeper five days a week! His mind did fall on how he would feel if he lost her, too. He could not dwell on that as it was far too painful.

Pete pulled up in the car and Ed kissed his mum on the cheek. 'See you next week, Mum,' he said, waving to her as Pete held the door open.

'It's on the seat,' Pete said as Ed slipped in past him. 'I think you will be pleased with the contents, although it may take a while to read through.'

Pete had not been wrong. Ed had flicked through the folder as he could not wait to find out some information. There were pictures and clippings from newspapers, from when she played piano in her younger years. Although the privacy screen was up in the car, the speakers sprang into life with a haunting tune. It was being played by someone on a piano. That was it, the piece she had played.

'Pete, you are too good,' he said. 'But you know that, don't you?' and that was why Ed paid him well and appreciated him a lot.

He resisted the temptation to look any more at the folder. He wanted to be able to put it down on the desk and sit with a well-earned whiskey in his hand. He got into the penthouse apartment and bid Pete goodnight. The place soon came to life as Ed opened all of the blinds with one push of a button; to complement this, some lights came on in the darker areas of the large room. He put the folder down on the large coffee table in the centre of the open-plan room. The London flat was minimal, plain even, but it was OK for Ed. Between here and the office bedroom it really was all he wanted.

The cut glass crystal shone with the amber liquid as it sat on the table. He sat back on the sofa and picked up the folder. He had turned on the CD that Pete had handed him as he got out of the car. 'Really, bro, classical shit is for old people who have lost the will to live,' Alex had said to him one day. It was not the choice he would make to listen to, but if the radio was on he would not turn it off; if something was playing in the background he would not ask for it to be changed, he would just not listen to it and focus. Music really for him was what played on your iPod when you were running. But he found the piano tunes something that could help him focus, and maybe he should do more of it.

There must have been over 100 pieces of paper: each one was read, reread and notes taken. He had refilled the glass more than once, but then stopped and powered up the coffee-maker to make an espresso. He wanted to keep a clear mind.

Ed had not noticed that the day had given way to the night and he had been looking through the file on Leticia Maria Jenkins for the last four hours. It was going to take some negotiation, but he had a plan to be able to get close to her, and win her over enough so he could taste that pale skin, that innocence, something that you could not find in a woman of her age or professional status. He had to hope that she would see his better side, something that not many of his business acquaintances experienced, but he was sure that from knowledge he had gained in the folder, he would be able to.

He really was not sure what she had done to him that day. Just a glance of her: it was so fickle to him to have noticed, but like a dog with a bone he would not let go until he had what he wanted.

Although it was late on a Sunday, he had made several phone calls to his lawyers. He paid them well to be at his beck and call and he knew that first thing on Monday morning they would start to put his plan into action for him.

He had a list of jobs for Zoe, although he would not call her: he emailed them all over to her. He was still looking over the folder when his phone rang. He looked at the display: it was Alex. One thing Ed was sure of was the fact he was not sharing this one with Alex.

He was a good friend, one that could be the best a guy could ask for, but he had a habit of taking over, and at times wanting the same thing for himself if he knew he could get one up on Ed. Miss Jenkins was something he was not prepared to share. He had shared many women in the past. Lottie, no: for some reason he was adamant about this one.

Monday morning started to bring several areas of the plan together before he got to the office. For the first time in ages he was late. He had been to the gym, having a really good session, and he stayed longer than he had intended.

'Morning, Zoe,' Ed said as he walked past.

'Your meeting with Dr Douglas has been booked, and I have arranged everything apart from the suit. I just need to find somewhere that will take the ones that don't fit back.' She looked up and met his boyish gaze.

'If they won't I will keep them and take them to a charity shop.' He raised his hand. He stopped in the doorway and turned back round to her. 'Nice hairdo, by the way, get it cut at the weekend?'

Zoe could have fallen off her chair. He never made comments to staff, let alone something that meant he was taking notice of anyone. 'Yes,' she simply replied.

'Looks good,' he said, shutting the door. Zoe ran a hand over her hair and straightened her shoulders. Yes, it does, she said to herself. He's up to something, she thought, but as always would never ask.

Lottie came back in from her run. For the start of spring the morning had been cold for the last day in April, but it had stayed dry. She looked at her phone and noted that she had three missed calls from the same number. A number that she did not recognise, although she noted it was a London prefix. Maybe Todd from work, she thought. She grabbed some milk from the fridge and made her way upstairs for a shower. She took the phone with her and as she jumped up the stairs, still pumped up from the run, she stopped when the gadget started to ring in her hand. The same number that she had missed.

'Hello,' she said, almost out of breath. The informal greeting was on the understanding that this was Todd.

'Miss Jenkins,' an unknown voice said.

'Yes,' Lottie replied, stopping in her tracks.

'I am ringing from Flavell and Parsons solicitors.' It was not a company she had heard of, but then she had only dealt with her mother's company. Well, she supposed they were her solicitors now. Lottie continue to listen. There was an introduction to who was calling, and Mr Simkins outlined that his client wanted to make her an offer of the properties that she had recently put up for sale.

She was quite excited at this, and he continued. 'My client also has a proposal for you, Miss Jenkins. He would like to put in an offer for one of your properties that you do not have for sale. With this in mind, he had requested a meeting with you. I am not sure if this is something you would consider, but he would like to make a meeting with you this week, so that we can discuss further.'

'Oh right,' Lottie replied, still taking in the information that she was being told. 'A meeting, in the city?' she asked.

'My client understands that this may be out of your way so would like to offer a driver to collect you. He also asked if you would take the time to visit the area where the property is located to further his proposal, therefore would like to ask if he could accommodate you in a hotel for the evening?'

'Oh,' Lottie said again. It was all a bit sudden and she was taken aback. 'Um, well, I would.' She stopped mid-sentence as Mr Simkins continued. 'It would be the Kensington Green Hotel and Spa. My client will not be able to join you until around 5pm, but you would be able to check in anytime after 11am, so please feel free to use the facilities.' He continued. 'Of course I understand that this is all sudden and maybe not what you expected. My client does not want to put you in a position where you may feel intimidated, and therefore the offer is extended to two persons should you wish it.' He again gave little pause for her to reply. 'He would like to meet at 5pm this Wednesday, and then follow up with a site meeting on the Thursday at 10am. Miss Jenkins, can I ask you to think about this and get back to me as soon as possible so that I can make the required arrangements?'

'Oh, yer, can I call you tomorrow?' Lottie asked, with the running through her mind if Agnes could go with her too.

'Today would be better as the arrangements for the further visit need to be made. There is nothing cloak-and-dagger, but if I explain over the phone, then the proposition that my client wants to make will not be as he wishes. I can personally vouch for this request and if you pass on your details to me, I will confirm in a letter that will be couriered to you this afternoon.' Although Mr Simkins sounded like a nice guy, Lottie could tell that he was under pressure to get a reply from her.

Who was this client he referred to? 'Can you tell me the name of your client so that I can pass the details to my accountant?' Lottie said. 'Dean Charity International Holdings.' Mr Simkins gave the information freely. 'Oh OK,' as if Lottie had ever heard of them, but she could Google search.

'I will have a reply for you by 12 midnight,' Lottie said. 'I have your number on the phone: I will call you back.'

'My thanks for your time, and I look forward to hearing from you.' Simkins put down the phone and Lottie looked at it in her hand. What was that all about? she thought.

'Oh Agnes, that would be great if you could come with me, I would feel so much better,' Lottie said to her friend whom she had called within a second of putting down the phone. While they were talking Agnes was searching for the company that the solicitor had named, but no pictures of anyone came up and she had not heard of them.

'Don't like it, though,' she said to Lottie. 'I have to say the fact that he is going to offer the full asking price for all the properties, fees etc, you will have a tidy sum for sure, and less hassle if they all have to be sold individually. You say that all the tenants will be OK to stay as it is now?' Agnes enquired.

Lottie explained that Mr Simkins had assured her that no one would be asked to leave the properties while the tenant contractors were in place, and that there was no question, all of the fees and costs would be taken care of his end. 'Too good to be true, Lottie: there is motive,' she replied down the phone.

'But if you are there, then I will be OK!' Lottie exclaimed. 'Please.'

'Yes, I can come with you, not turning down a night in a spa.' Agnes laughed. 'What are you doing for dinner tonight anyway?' Agnes continued the conversation.

'Morning, Zoe, Mr Dean please,' the voice requested.

'Yes, Mr Simkins, I will put you through.' Zoe pushed the button that was flashing on the console; she knew that Ed was on a call, but he had asked that he be interrupted as soon as the solicitor phoned, without delay. 'Mr Simkins for you.' She pressed another button that put the original caller on hold.

'Simkins, we good to go?' Ed asked.

'She is calling me back before 12 noon.' He was a bit nervous that he had not got a definite answer for him; he knew his client and he knew that he only liked solutions and final answers, he was not a man to keep waiting.

'Her response was a positive one, I think that she will take up your offer, but I felt that too much pressure would have put her off.' He made the parting statement to try to calm the reply he was about to get.

'You called me without a positive outcome, Simkins, don't waste my time. I have someone waiting on the other line and you tell me this?' Ed was not pissed, he was just disappointed that he had to wait.

'Sorry, I just wanted to keep you in the loop. I did not want you to think I had not made progress,' Simkins said.

'Yes, of course, sorry, thank you for that. Ring me again as soon as you know anything.' Ed switched back to the original conversation he was having and his business day continued like any other.

Lottie did call Mr Simkins back, and explained that she would take up the offer, and to send the details through to her via email. Agnes would be joining her. She asked to be collected, but declined the return home as they thought it would be a good opportunity for the two of them to get some shopping in before they returned to Kent. They had even contemplated staying in the hotel for a second night; they would see how that went on the day. They did talk about the meeting several times before the day itself, but Lottie was no wiser to who this person could be. She had, however, spent a few hours looking at the website for the charity and could see that over the past few years they had done so much towards the injured service personnel. She felt that whatever was to be offered, she really would listen to the reason and if possible help.

It was 9am and the phone rang. Lottie looked at the caller ID.

'Hi, Aggie,' she said, 'all ready to go?' She had been up for a few hours, quite excited about her trip and what it would hold for her.

'Lottie, I am so sorry, I am not going to be able to come with you, I have woken with the most horrid chest and cold, and I really am struggling to breathe. I need to go to the doctor's as I have used up all my inhalers, and I just feel lifeless. I went to bed early last night to try to shake it off, but it seems to have come back worse.' Agnes sniffled and coughed as if to confirm the fact that she really did feel ill. 'You know that I would not let you down, but Dick has said he is not happy for me to go feeling so ill, so for once I think I may have to do as he says.'

'Oh Aggie, you sound awful, I will ring and rearrange,' Lottie said, wondering if that was an option.

'Well, I am happy to go with you when I feel better, but maybe it would be wise to go while it is still a good offer all round.' She sniffled. 'I am only on the end of the phone if you need me, you know that?'

'Yes, but I was looking forward to some girly time away, bit of shopping and lots of wine,' Lottie said.

'Well, get the meeting over with and then stay that extra night, and book a good back massage or something. No need to rush home, is there? In fact you could get in touch with Todd and stay the weekend, I am sure that the cost will not break the bank. If the deal really does play off, you could stay all year!' She tried to laugh, but it made her cough again.

'Not sure I want to stay that long, but meeting up with Todd may be an option. I will see how things go.' Lottie put down the phone, really disappointed. She picked up her large overnight bag and thought about adding a few more bits in case she did stop longer. 'I'll buy something if I need it,' she said to herself 'as a treat'. There were enough clothes already in the bag to last a week, and the dress bag lay over the top so not to crease the suit and dress she had already packed. Two pairs of trainers, shoes and boots were a bit over the top, but she never knew what to wear when standing in front of her wardrobe, let alone when the options had been narrowed somewhat by the restrictions of a bag.

Chapter 7

The car had arrived as planned at 9:30am. Pete had introduced himself to her and assisted in putting her bags in the boot. Lottie looked at him and blushed: although he was older, she found the neat suit and crisp, white shirt very smart and attractive. He was not tall, and she could tell he was fit from the ease with which he opened the door and held her hand to help her get into the car.

When the dark green Bentley had pulled up in the drive, Lottie gave a little gasp as she really could not believe she was going in that. The windows in the back were blacked out, so no one would see her anyway, but as they drove out of the village she was dying for someone to see her to notice her so that she could tell of her adventure when she got back.

No one was around: even as they went past the pub the place was its usual quiet, nothing-ever-happens place. Pete had asked if Lottie had an iPod or if she required any type of music. She had packed her iPod for the expected gym session, or to help her sleep if the place was a little overpowering, and she thought that maybe he was not a classical sort of a person.

'With the screen down, Miss, I am not able to hear it. I will have the radio on for the local traffic and the sat nav to keep me company,' he had said. 'So, I don't mind if you have an eclectic mix.' He smiled and the dimples in his chin squeezed tighter. Lottie noticed that they were not all dimples, though, one was a scar, old, but looked as though it had been painful.

As she sat in the car she wondered if Pete worked for the boss, or the charity, although if a charity could afford a driver and a car of this type, then people paying towards it would get a bit miffed, if that was where the money went. She wondered if he was ex-service. He looked like he could be, made sense with what she had read on the website. The charity was not just for injured servicemen and women, but tried to get them back to normal life: maybe he was one of the successes.

Mozart, Vivaldi and Tchaikovsky had played for the duration of the journey and she had flicked the magazine she had brought lightly; she was becoming nosy as they approached the city. She loved to people-watch, to think about all of these people going about their lives. Where did they go and what were they doing? Maybe that was the reason she loved her job – her old job, she thought.

The traffic got slower and as they pulled up outside the grand building that pronounced itself the Kensington Green Hotel and Spa, Lottie felt like a superstar as the footman opened the door and offered a hand to her so that she could get out.

'Welcome, Miss, to the Kensington Green Hotel and Spa, I hope that you have a good stay,' he said politely. Pete had the bags and was walking her into the reception. They were met by a young boy who took the bags and nodded to Pete.

'Miss Jenkins,' the receptionist said as if she was telepathic. 'We have your reservation for two people.' She looked at Lottie who explained that she would be alone. 'Thanks, that is no trouble at all, I am sorry to hear your friend is not well. Was it just for tonight?'

'Yes,' Lottie said and then caught in the moment she said, 'I had wondered if I could reserve for longer, maybe until Sunday morning. It's not a problem if you can't, with it being last-minute.'

Without even looking at the computer screen in front of her the young girl looked up. 'That is not problem at all. The suite has no other bookings, so until you let me know, the rooms are yours. If you need anything please call down. The bar, restaurant, shops, the gym and spa are open for you at any time day or night as a guest, you will find all the information you need in your room, or again just ring down. The personal trainers will be more than happy to assist if you require.' The young girl pushed a piece of paper forward on the counter. 'Can I just ask for a signature as confirmation of the stay?' Lottie went to take the pen, but the question had been directed at Pete who was silently standing at her shoulder. He obliged and passed the piece of paper back.

'Perfect.' She passed back a small golden key and a golden card. 'When you order food or drink just show them this.' She smiled at her. 'The card gets you access to everything as a gold customer. Enjoy your time with us, Miss Jenkins.'

Lottie turned to Pete and the look on her face must have spoken for her as he said, 'Mr Dean will be with you at 5pm in the top-floor bar.' He smiled and could tell that she was still a little unsure. 'He has asked that you stay in the penthouse suite, so it is only the next floor down to the bar.' He walked her to the lift and pressed the button. 'I need the card.' He pointed to the slot. 'You get exclusive access to the top floor. You will be alone up there but please be assured that no one without permission from yourself or reception will be able to get up there.' He paused, thinking: did that make her safer or more isolated? The doors opened. 'Want me to come up and settle you in?' He smiled at her again as if he, too, now could read her mind.

She smiled back at him. 'Thank you, Pete, I am guessing that you can tell I am not used to any of this glitz and glamour, being a country girl, it's all a bit overwhelming. I am not sure what I am letting myself in for here and I am way out of my comfort zone.' They walked towards the open lift door and Pete pressed the penthouse button after putting the key in again to release the security system that allowed access.

Pete did know that she was not used to this type of lifestyle. After all, he knew everything about her, maybe more than she would want him to know. There was something about her, though. Her perfect skin without a hint of make-up. Her eyes that could draw you in, and held nothing back. When he had first picked her up and seen her in the flesh he had felt the hairs on his arms stand up as the pictures he had seen really had not portrayed the girl standing in front of him.

She was dressed in jeans, boots and a smart but very casual jacket; the white tee shirt had shown the shape of her body, but in no way flaunted what she had in your face. He was amazed she had achieved so much in her life being so quiet and unassuming, and was still so innocent to the world around her. Maybe, he thought, it's the way that she copes with seeing dead bodies and having to cut them up and make sense of their lives, that she sees good in all things, and remains this innocent to protect her from such cruel sights.

They had reached the top in silence and when the door opened Pete held out his hand to show her the way. He used the key one last time and opened the door.

The space opened up into the Royal penthouse suite. From the door Lottie could see the bank of windows one side, with doors leading to the left and right of the large sitting room. It had two TVs on both side walls with large, cream sofas to sit on at one side, and formal Chesterfield seats and sofa for four on the other. There was a bar area, and a large, leather-topped writing desk along this side, too. Pete walked to the windows and undid the latch. The day was really sunny and the view out onto Kensington Park was fantastic; in fact, through the heat haze most of this side of the city could be seen. 'Wow!' Lottie said as he opened the doors and they effortlessly folded open to make the outside space come inside. The noise instantly hit her from the traffic below and she was drawn to walk outside and look closer.

'I will get them to check the heat on the hot tub.' Pete pointed to the large, wooden area to the right. 'It should be on as it activates as you open the front doors. If you need the heaters' - he pointed to a control panel - 'and lights they are all here.' Lottie looked at him: something clicked into place.

'Have you been here before?' she asked. 'Am I being set up here?'

'No, I mean, Mr Dean uses the hotel from time to time. I often check the rooms before he comes up, just to make sure.' He stopped. He had told her how safe the area was and he was just about to say he checked the rooms were clear and secure when he changed his tack. 'I usually just get the place ready, you know. get lights on, pour a drink etc.'

'So, Mr Dean is so important that he has hired help to turn on the lights.' Sceptically she walked back into the room and made her way to the large bathroom. Looking at the double sink and the largest walk-in shower that she thought would house an entire rugby team (nice thought) she smiled to herself. 'And does he have help in the shower!?' she unwittingly shouted, looking at the gold taps and neatly folded white towels.

'On more than one occasion yes,' Pete said under his breath. With more than one at a time, he thought to himself but did not say out loud. He appeared at the door. 'Can I leave you to it?' he asked. 'Please do call if there is anything at all you need. Reception has my number but I have put it by the phone as well. I am sure you will soon fit in. There is champagne and all manner of drinks and snacks in the cupboard and the two fridges, but if there is something they don't have please let reception know: there's a phone in every room and one out on the balcony.'

Yer right, and pay for the privilege of the minibar! Lottie thought, 'I'm fine, going to hit the gym, and then a swim, although could come back up to do that!' She pointed behind her at the door to the bathroom. 'I may need to ring down for a lifeguard if I use that!' She laughed and noted to herself that if the rugby players did not fit in the shower as she had first thought, they could always fit in the bath, it had four seats in it and three sets of taps – really!?

She wandered to the other side of the suite and opened the last two wooden doors. The room was clinically white, contemporary, with one large painting of a person playing a piano. The single white leather chair was positioned as if the occupier was glancing out of the windows, the same sort as in the main room that opened out onto the private balcony area. She walked in and moved towards the centrepiece. A large, white, full grand piano, Steinway: the best, she thought. The lid was up as if tempting her to touch the pure, white ivory keys. She did and the note echoed around the room with a soothing tone.

He had known she was on her way after the first two minutes of the car pulling away from her drive. Pete had phoned through as instructed.

He had not expected the news that she was alone, which may have him changing a few plans, but not for the worse, he thought.

He had another call to say that she had settled in the room, and from the conversation with Pete he could tell that some of the words he spoke were almost of warning. As if he was going to eat her alive up there! He was almost jealous of Pete, that he had just spent the best part of two and a half hours with her, more than Ed could ever want to think about at this point.

The hotel was totally aware that anything would be done for her, at any price. The deal that she could stay had only been for one night, but he would pay for every second she was there, and he hoped to make her stay longer. Pete had mentioned the request if she could stay longer, as if music to his ears. It had been no issue to secure the suite for longer, although the other guests that had booked would have to be disappointed, but he did not care about that.

'It's all included in the room, Miss,' the young valet had said as he stood embarrassed at the door. Lottie had been to the gym, had the best massage ever, and had stood for ages under the teeming hot shower. She had thought about the team of rugby players that could have also been in there with her, and had laughed with Agnes when she phoned her shortly after and relayed everything in fine detail.

There was a knock at the door. Dressed in the hotel robe and slippers, she had answered the door to a young man, dressed in the hotel livery and holding a bottle of Cristal champagne.

'I never ordered that,' Lottie said as she gingerly opened the door, although not naked: she did not want him to see her fully with the towel wrapped around her head.

'It's part of the deal for the room, Miss,' he said again. 'Can I leave it on the table?'

She doubted that the expensive bottle was anything to do with the room, but she could see that he was looking fearful for his life if she did not take it. 'Can I open it for you?' he asked, looking more relaxed that he had got into the room, almost achieving his mission.

'That's fine, I will do it later.' She pointed to her hair. 'I sort of want to finish before I have a drink,' she replied. He nodded at her and quickly left.

It was a small lie, as she had opened the bottle of white wine that had been in the fridge and had a glass while she was on the phone. 'Dutch courage,' she had said to Agnes, after enquiring if she felt better. Lottie guessed, as Agnes had suggested, that the elusive Mr Dean was putting on the show to impress her. While it was nice, Lottie could not help but ask of the ulterior motive that this could have. 'You're ever the detective, aren't you?' Agnes had snivelled. 'Just let him do it, you have the power to say no. After all, you have something he wants!'

Yes, Lottie thought, but what exactly was it to be treated this flash, and they had not even met? 'Rich people are like this all the time. He probably has a deal with the hotel, or it is something he claims back on the taxman!' Agnes had said with a hint of sarcasm in her croaky voice.

20 to 5 and she was ready. Looking finally in the mirror, the black dress looked great as she smoothed it one last time over her hips. Neckline not too

low, but enough to emphasise her bustline. The daytime bustle was growing below her, and with a short time to wait, she thought a glass of bubbly could now do the trick. She opened it and placed it in the ice bucket, pulling ice from the fridge to add to the silver receptacle. She walked outside, leaning against the rail that ran around the edge of the building. She had never been afraid of heights, and in the spring early evening the sun helped the warm glow in her cheeks to build as she sipped at the cool liquid.

She looked at the sky. Well, Mum, she thought, I am sorry if I am doing something that you would not approve of, but here goes nothing. She drained the glass and closed the doors behind her. She locked the door and then smiled: who would break in up here, Spider-Man?!

She took the lift to the next floor and came out into the most lavish of areas. Almost like another building. She scanned the room and looked at the bar area. Tall, mahogany doors led through into what she assumed was the restaurant. She had another five minutes to go, so wandered to the bar. No one else was around. She sat on the stool and was quickly attended to by the bartender.

'Miss? the guy asked.

'I'm just waiting,' Lottie replied. 'Just a soda water, thanks,' she said, thinking that she could not sit with nothing. He placed the glass in front of her and smiled. He continued to clean the glasses from the shelf behind the bar. The phone rang and he picked it up. Without a word he replaced the handset and pulled a bottle out of the fridge. With a controlled pop the champagne was poured into two glasses and set on the bar to her right. It was at that moment that Lottie was suddenly aware that someone was walking into the room. She turned the stool around to see a tall, dark-skinned, blond-haired man walking towards her. He was looking in her direction and her heart suddenly fluttered. Blood rushed straight to her cheeks, even more than the wine and champagne cocktail she had already had, and she knew this was him. She bit at the side of her lip in an unconscious, nervous response. Arrogant, elegant, very sure and commanding, but G. O. D. he was stunning. How ever was she going to sit and have a conversation with him, let alone control herself as she ate dinner? As he got closer she could see his bright blue eyes which hit her, and they with her own. His face turned from this powerhouse to a smile, which she felt was genuine warmth.

'Miss Jenkins, I am so sorry if I am late. The traffic was really bad tonight, and I hope that I have not kept you long.' He held out his hand and accepted hers in a formal greeting. As he put his hand back to his side, he flexed his fingers slightly as if an electric current had run through them. 'Please.' He motioned to the glass of creamy bubbles as he picked it up from the bar and offered it to her. He took a mouthful.

'Edward Dean,' he said. 'Really great to see you at last, I am sorry I have not been in contact, and you had to deal with Simkins and Pete. How was the drive up here? I hope you have been welcomed by everyone, and there has been nothing you have needed?' He knew how she had been treated, and that she had been to the gym and had a massage. In fact, it was that information that had made him stay rooted to his chair for half an hour in his last meeting. As they talked about the contractors for the offshore oil rigs his mind had wandered to her pale skin. Knowing that she was being rubbed over with lightly scented oils until her skin become supple, this had turned him on.

Wishing that he could have been there, not just to watch, but to trace his own hands along her shoulders, down her collarbones, up her thighs and… He had to stop at this point: not only did he not care about 3 million dollars' worth of oil, he also felt that his dick would explode under the table. He was sure that the others in the meeting saw his state of mind. 'OK, Ed?' one had said and dismissed them with a nod and a word to carry on.

'Pleased to meet you,' Lottie had replied. 'Please call me Lottie.' She hoped that the less formal name would lighten the mood. 'You're not late, but I could see that the traffic was starting to get busy. I made use of the balcony and the view, and the champagne, which I guess I have to thank you for? I have to say, Mr Dean, it's all very impressive, but you will have to excuse me, as a simple country girl, and a student for many years, I am not quite so sure about a lavish lifestyle.' She bit down on her lip again, nerves showing again.

Ed noticed this for the second time: he felt the pull in his lower gut. Don't do that! he thought. I would love to bite on that lip and see you react to the intense, erotic pain it would bring, and then let me kiss it until the stinging stopped. He pulled himself back to her statement.

'I am sorry...' He stopped correcting himself as he was about to say 'Miss Jenkins'. '...Lottie. I use the place a lot as I find it really relaxing. I did not want to offer you a meeting at the office: one because I felt that neutral ground would be better; and two, well, I am starving and wondered if the deal, offer, package,' he corrected again, fumbling for the right words to find, 'would sound better if it was over a nice meal. And boy, do they do great food here.' He smiled again and Lottie felt the hair on her arms stand on end.

'Shall we go through to eat?' he asked, gesturing towards the door that led to the dining room. As they walked in Lottie again could not help but notice that there were no more guests. The large, imposing room had windows looking out over the city skyline; they did not open or lead to a balcony, but Lottie could tell that she was directly below her own rooms.

'If the food is so good, how come we are alone?' she innocently asked as she was shown her seat. He pulled it out behind her and she got the hit of his scent. Light, with a clean, fresh smell of man. She could feel his breath on the back of her neck as she sat adjusting herself.

'I hired the lot, I like to relax, but I also like to concentrate on business.' He caught a glance down at her full breasts as he pulled out the chair and then quickly looked away as he walked and took his own seat.

'I really should have guessed that!' She looked at him directly then said, 'I hope that you are not disappointed with the outcome of the meeting, then.'

'I rarely get disappointed.' He stopped and glanced at the menu. 'Red or white?' he asked, changing the subject with ease.

'My preference would be red,' Lottie said. I know! he thought. 'But please, you choose.' She bit on her lip again as she looked at the food. She really did not know what to have: it was hardly her local pub grub she had become used to of late.

Stop that! the voice in his head wanted to shout, but he kept his cool and ordered a bottle of both red and white. Lottie smiled to herself, and then informed the young waiter of her choice of food. Ed did likewise and they had a few moments of conversation about the hotel and the room they were eating in.

The first course arrived and Lottie was amazed at the food.

'Good?' he asked, seeing that she was just as passionate about food as she was playing the piano.

'Um yes, thanks.' She took a glance at him and their eyes met quickly. 'Can we talk about your package!? Sorry, deal, then?' Lottie blurted out. 'Not that I am in any rush but I am intrigued as to your offer. This whole business thing is really new to me since...' She stopped short and looked up. 'Since I took over from my mum,' she finished.

Ed felt his heart pull. He had never felt anyone else's pain, not in this way. Pain, yes, he liked to inflict and also to receive as long as it was the right sort. Business was just that. No hard feelings, no regrets, you get what you want, at any price, at any cost. But her pain felt different to him, and why?

'Well, I often find getting the business out of the way can help the meal go better, so here is my proposal. I will lay my cards on the table to you,' he started after taking a drink of water, as if to clear his palate.

'I was alerted to your properties for one reason to start with. There is a warehouse that I had asked my agent to keep an eye out for any such properties that came on the market. I have a gym business.' He went on to explain about the requirement to expand this. He also said that he would be prepared to take the other properties at the full asking price, and would ensure that all the tenants had the same terms and contracts that were currently in place.

'However, you must know, Miss...' - he corrected himself again - '... Lottie, I had my agent look into your portfolio and there was one property that is not for sale but very much something that I would like to acquire.' He looked at her and she was listening to every word he said. 'Orchard Farm and the land that is tied in with it.' He stopped to take in her reaction, which to his surprise was a warm smile. 'The farm is close to one of my charity projects and I would like to expand it. The land and the buildings would perfectly develop my idea and I would like to make you an offer.' He stopped: it was her turn to speak, but she was still considering the information. 'Want to add anything at this point?'

The next course was put in front of them and the suspense of her reply was killing him. In a normal business meeting, he would have said by now 'take it or leave it' or 'well, make up your mind', but he was in awe of her calm computing brain processing the information.

'Let me get this straight,' she started. 'I am sure that your agent has looked into my business and I can only presume the rest of my life also. I am guessing you had a file produced and you have done your research well, or someone you have paid has done it for you and just picked out the interesting details.' Her voice was not cynical or patronising. 'So you will know that the property was my grandfather's and has a tenant who rents the land and supports his family. Not only is the place very dear to me, but I have no interest in the income, just the fact that my mother was born there, my grandparents both died there, and I have spent many happy years there when I was young on days out, but you want to acquire it. Knowing that I hold the building so dear, which is why it was not up for sale with the rest of the outlying ones in my portfolio, you offer me fine food and wine to appease me and your offer?' She took another mouthful of food and smiled at him. 'Which I do feel is currently working in your grand plan. But I think I need more information and a better understanding before I commit to anything.' She took another sip of wine. 'As for the man who is rarely disappointed, I hope that the information you gained on my personal affairs did not disappoint, but nowhere in there would it have said 'pushover', as I, as you may have gathered, really do not care for the money. Although you have me at a disadvantage, my concern is what does the tenant farmer do if I pull out from under him?' Well, Lottie was not quite sure where that speech came from, but you go, girlfriend! the little voice in her head said. She looked at him: had he been stunned to silence, or was she about to walk out?

He considered her words carefully. He would like to think she was being playful, but he somehow guessed this was her best poker-face. She was right, the businesswomen he was used to were strong-willed, strong-minded and he had slept with most of them before the business meeting was even arranged. It was usually the woman who made the first move in that department as a way of ensuring his deal was achieved. She was different and unaccustomed to it.

'I am sorry if you think it intrusive of me for researching you and your business: it is just what I do.' He pushed back in his chair. 'I assure you that no offence was intended, purely for me to be able to approach you with facts and figures, cutting to the chase really. I do employ many staff, for various jobs, amongst the various organisations I own, but I can assure you when it comes to my chosen charity, I have to make the right choices as people's health and the rest of their lives depend on me getting it right.' He paused briefly. 'At a point of not wanting to sound as if I am coming on to you, the more I read about you, the more I wanted to know. In fact, I wanted to ask if you could come on-board as a partner in all of this. I understood' - although he did not - 'the family connection would be strong for you, so my proposal is this. I fund all of the works, fees, plans etc, but you remain the sole owner of the property. As a charity we can afford some rent, but

I would subsidise this to you myself. Your farmer, when approached, was happy to accept the new farm I am prepared to purchase for him at the same cost and rental agreement that he currently has in place.' He stopped, allowing her to interject.

'Should have known that you had already spoken to him.' Lottie took the last mouthful of the beef and put her knife down. 'I need to know more and get back to you,' she finished.

'I would hope that you do take time to think about it. The first part of the deal will make you a cool million; the rest may not be of financial gain, but it could, if you let it, allow you to become involved as an active partner in a really worthwhile cause, or if you wished to sit back and relax, you could just have a feel-good factor every day knowing that you have helped along the way.'

'And is that why you do it, the feel-good factor, or the taxman?' She knew it had been wrong as soon as the words came out of her mouth. Your mother had not brought you up to be so rude, she thought, scolding herself inside. The look on his face gave an expressed 'I'm pissed at that comment' look.

'I'm sorry you see it as that, although as you have pointed out, you have not researched my background, so how could you know the personal tie I feel to the responsibility and trust the board of governors have in me to ensure that I continue to make these lives better. You visited the website, I presume.'

'Yes, and I'm sorry if that was curt.' She knew that helping injured servicemen and -women was a really good cause, but could not connect him to it. She bit on her lip again and he said, 'Lottie.' He moved closer over the table as if he was going to whisper. 'If you do nothing else for me today, and I do not have the good fortune of winning you over, come into partnership with me.' He paused and sat back a little, almost afraid he would kiss her, but more to stop the restricted material of his fly zip wrecking the rest of his life from damaging the mounting swelling that was taking place between his legs. 'Please, stop biting your lip, you really don't know what effect you are having on me!'

Lottie was taken aback, not knowing whether to smile, or laugh or walk out offended. Was he playing with her? Luckily the waiter came and asked if they wanted coffee. Although the look from Ed could have required Lottie to do her first post-mortem in months on him, she said, 'Yes please,' just to get him away from the table.

'Should I be complimented? By that request?' she asked.

'I have no issue with telling you that before we met (he never said "tonight", as he did not want to slip that he had followed her and watched from a distance) I had never thought to be so attracted to...' He stopped. He was never attracted to women: he lusted after them, shagged them because they offered. Did things that you would not believe because they were willing, and could go further if you paid for it, but he was right: he had never been attracted to anyone so strongly. He had to be in control and one thing he knew from the second he had seen her, the feeling inside him, was way, way out of control to be sane. 'I'm sorry. If I could rewind that statement I would.' Lottie smiled and lowered her brow, the dimples in her cheeks showing. God, the look was even more devastating than the lip-biting. I'm in trouble here, it is all going wrong! The thought of panic went through his mind.

Lottie stood up and his heart sank: she was walking out. She walked round to him and he shot up like a jack-in-the-box. She held out her hand to shake his.

'Mr Dean.' She took his hand and shook it. 'It has been a pleasure.' She turned her back on him.

'Wait!' he shouted but she continued to walk. The few staff that had been in the room seemed to scuttle off as if they were cockroaches when a light was turned on. 'Miss Jenkins,' he said, not knowing if he could halt her by putting his hand on her arm. He resisted.

'I'm going for a drink in the bar, please feel free to join me. There will be other people, unless you can pay them off in about 40 seconds flat. So please curb your lustful thoughts, although I take them as a compliment, and thank you kindly. I can listen to your plans and proposal one more time and then...' She stopped. 'I can have that coffee I just ordered?!' She turned back, walking towards the door. 'And maybe we could start again?'

Sitting in two easy chairs, side by side with a small drinks table in front of them Lottie had asked for the half-consumed bottle of red from the table to be brought over. Ed had asked for another, but she had thought it wasteful as it would not be drunk. They chatted about the proposal, and at times the conversation had wandered from business to general life. There was even a sprinkle of laughter at the odd joke, or something funny. Ed had removed his jacket, a sign he was relaxed, and surprised himself how at ease he was now than earlier at the table.

They found equal ground on subjects such as going to the gym, the solitude of running, skiing holidays and travel (although Lottie had not done half compared to Ed, but Ed had hardly done any travel during his adult years that was not business-related). As he noted this fact he said, 'Apart from the odd weekend when I take to the roads on my motorbike and see a bit of the countryside,' then he laughed. 'Although if you asked my mother she would say I don't see much of it as I go too fast!'

Lottie felt at ease with both his business ideas and the conversation in general. She was drawn to his charm and good looks: any woman with a pulse would have been for sure, but she could tell there was a part of him that she was sure not many people got to see. A darker side of something personal, although as she thought to herself while looking in the mirror in the toilets, don't we all have our secrets?

They had sat for over three hours after their meal. Ed had tried not to look at his phone, but knew that the constant vibrating was the indication of emails, and calls that he would at some stage have to take before the night was out: this he did not want to leave too late, although Lottie he did not want to leave at all. As a parting comment he said:

'Listen, how would you like to go up to the site tomorrow, and drop into the hospital and meet a few people, it may help you visualise my plans. I can ask for the other details to be drawn up on paper from my solicitors, and get them back to you to read over before you make a decision. If we get too late, then you could stay here tomorrow, and I can ask Pete to drop you home Saturday?' He drained the last of his coffee and replaced the cup down on the table. He looked at his phone: it was Pete calling to say he was in the car park waiting for him. 'Oh,' he said, 'Pete has a day off tomorrow, you may have to put up with my driving!'

'I'm sure I can cope,' Lottie replied, watching as his body flexed as he put his jacket on over his strong, broad shoulders. 'How about a spin on the bike up there? We could grab a bite to eat on the way back or something. I will be free from 10, so I could come and get you and then we could be there in an hour, or so, if I slow down.'

'Sounds great. One problem: no kit.' She gestured her hands down her front. 'Skirt not going to hack it on a bike, could be a bit draughty!' They laughed.

'Leave it with me...' he started to say.

'...And you will sort it,' Lottie finished. 'How did I know that was going to be your reply? Why do I think that was the master plan all along?' He stood and held out his hand. 'Miss Jenkins, it has been my pleasure to do business and I can truly say that not many of my business meetings are pleasurable. I am not sure what you mean by the master plan, but there is one thing (well, really there were lots more than one thing he would like to do, but none of them clean enough to verbally report to Lottie) I would like to do, and that is to let you know I will not try to make you, or persuade you to do anything you did not want to do.' She held out her hand and he took it. He held onto it longer than she had expected, but she did not pull away. She could feel the warmth of his skin. She caught him with a glance of his blue eyes and he lifted her hand to his lips and placed a gentle kiss on the back of it.

The vibration was as if the whole building had shaken. It went through Lottie right from the hairs on the back of her neck to the spot between her legs. She held his gaze for a moment and then he released her hand.

'I will get reception to call up when I arrive. I will make sure that you get some "kit".' He gestured back with his hands along his own body as she had done before. He continued. 'Goodnight, Miss Jenkins.'

'Mr Dean.' Lottie smiled and he turned his back on her and walked off.

'Home?' Pete asked as he got in the car. He had to ask as usually after a hard business lunch he would wind up at 'The Club' with friends until the small hours.

'Yes, thanks,' Ed replied. He sat in the back of the car and stretched his feet out. Bumpy, but he had managed to get the plan back on track. The courier was already in possession of the leather motorbike suit; all it needed was the text to say what time to deliver. He had the helmet and he would give it to her when he arrived. They could get to the hospital for about 12 and then go to the site after. He had booked a table in a really nice bar for the way back so he knew that she would be late and would take up the offer to stay in the hotel for one more night. There was no need at ask the solicitors to draw up any documents, they were already in place – forward planning is the key to success, he had once said, although at one point in the evening he was not sure he would make it this far into the plan!

He smirked to himself and could not resist a smile.

He called through to Pete. 'That bar, the one from last week?' It was more of a statement than a question. 'Changed my mind, can you take me?'

Pete looked at him in the rear-view mirror and nodded. It was not far out of the way and, although the time was almost 10pm, he would just have time to have a look around his new business venture and maybe add some thoughts to his plan while he was there.

Chapter 8

Lottie phoned Agnes in the morning after she had been to the gym in the hotel. The conversation was long and she was still talking to her when a knock on the door came. She took the phone with her when she received the large box, with a full set of motorbike leathers, boots and Under Armour top.

'How did he know your size?' Agnes asked.

'The guy has no concept of not getting what he wants. I would not put it past him if he had not had a fashion guru watching me or something, guessing my size over dinner.' She laughed but could see it may be the sort of thing he would do.

They chatted for a few minutes longer and then Lottie jumped into the shower. She laid out the clothes and then, when she had dried her hair, up or down, she thought, putting a hair bobble on her wrist so she could make that decision thinking that she still needed a helmet on.

She had only ever been on the back of Gav's bike in her youth, and her father had let her sit on the back of his scooter, but they had never gone far.

She pulled the trousers on. Lucky, she had only toast for breakfast and had worked it off in the early gym session. They were so new that the leather needed time to warm up and adjust to her curves. Finally getting the zipper to hold up she bent, and sat back on the bed. They were tight, maybe too tight in some places, and sitting on a bike for an hour may prove a test in itself. She put on a red vest top, then the white thermal Under Armour. Guess it gets cold as the wind rushes past you, she thought, as it was a warm, dry day and maybe no need for all the protection. She struggled with the jacket that did up, pulling her chest in tight. Looking in the mirror she could see how some people found it kinky to wear leather. It hugged and moulded you. Made you feel safe, but she took another look at her chest: really does nothing for my boobs! Her mind wandered to wearing leather for another reason. Not that she ever had, but she could see why the women in some of her books liked wearing leather: maybe less than a full suit, something with the boob holes cut out!

The shin boots were matching the suit, all black! Odd colour really for bikers: she would have wanted to be bright yellow with flashing lights so the other road users could see her and limit the chances of knocking them off! 'I have faith, although I am out of my head to do this with a guy I have only just met,' she had said to Agnes.

'You don't have to, but you know me, live a little. If I had been well enough there would be no stopping me. If I had been there, you would have to get a taxi to go see his plans, I would be the one holding tight to someone who sounds like the better older brother of Adonis!' Agnes had a way of relaxing her, making her laugh, and when she had quoted it in her call Lottie had an image in her mind that was wicked, but exciting.

Her phone rang on the dot of 10. They let her know that Mr Dean was awaiting her in the reception. She grabbed her purse, but then could not find the space to put it, so just put a debit card in the chest pocket. The key she would have to leave at reception, as there was no way that she was sitting on that as well as the thick leather seam that was already running and separating the cheeks of her ass.

She got out of the lift, handed over the key and went to the main doors. She could see him chatting to the porter: boys and their toys, she thought, but the red, shiny metal beast did look impressive. Polished within an inch of its life not by you, Mr Dean! she thought and smiled. Dressed in a full leather suit himself, holding two black helmets. She admired the view. 'Hell, yes!' She was not sure if the rubbing of the leather, or the thought of him tightly bound like a swaddled child made her feel sexy, almost turned on. Every curve of his body could be made out without too much imagination. His hair was, as normal, a natural style: one hand rubbed through it, no product, 'that would do' type of style, just touching the collar of his jacket and looked still freshly wet from being washed and showered. Lottie shuddered at the image of that and had to focus.

So, engrossed in conversation, he did not see her admiring the back view until she stepped out of the door and the porter turned and held it open for her. Edward instantly smiled.

'Morning,' she said, not sure how to greet him. Were they formally over the handshake stage yet, although this was still business?

'It arrived on time, then?' he asked. 'Fit OK?' Stupid question, he thought: of course it fitted just fine, in all the right places. She was divine and he hoped that the next leather suit he bought for her, she would be equally obliging to put on and ride with him!

'Snug, I would say.' A bit like yours, she wanted to finish. He handed her the helmet and a pair of leather gloves were folded inside.

'Few ground rules,' he started to explain. 'If you want me to slow down it is two taps, if you want to stop it is three taps, if you are OK when I ask it is one tap.' He continued. 'If I squeeze in my elbows on your arms it means hold on tighter. You are OK with holding on round my waist? Or you can hold with one arm around me and one hand on the back.' He pointed to the hand strap across the back seat, that only looked big enough for a child to sit on. 'If you like, when we go slow just one hand is OK, but I would prefer that you got a good, secure hold all of the time, especially if we are going faster,' he said. 'You OK with that?' Lottie nodded. 'Right. One tap is?' He repeated the ground rules and Lottie replied correctly to them all.

'Like safe words.' She shut her mouth as quickly as it had opened to let the statement out, her inner brain astonished. What, girlfriend? Where did that come from? You just quoted something that was as inappropriate as Mother Teresa wearing a bikini in a photo shoot! 'I mean safe actions, actions to let you know I'm safe, OK?' She shut up: the hole was growing around her and she hoped the floor would take her soon, but not as fast as the embarrassment on her face that was glowing as red as a poker in a fire. She bit her lip.

He turned away: he knew what she meant but not only did she bite her lip, again! He had every hope that when, if, she felt the need to use her safe words it was for a different reason, in a more private setting than this. He was aware that the custom-made leather suit had not accounted for the growing desire in his groin, and he moved behind the bike to give him some privacy. He would let the comment go as he could see she was struggling, but he could not help but think that this innocent girl had more hidden depths. That he was really interested in exploring.

Lottie flicked her hair up and put the helmet on as fast as she could, although she feared the heat from her face would steam it up. He did the same and through a muffled voice said, 'Ready?' She gave a thumbs-up back. Straddled across the seat he held the bike still; she swung her long leg over and sat on the narrow seat. With a wiggle, she put her arms around him and he squeezed them with his elbows and she gave one tap. The beast had been ticking over, but as soon as the accelerator was opened up, the vibrations of the bike went rumbling through her body and they set off.

Traffic had calmed down as they met the M40: it was a clear road until they needed to turn off towards Towcester. She had relaxed, but did not dare to release her hands. He had felt her start to sway with the movement of the bike and he could feel her body move with his. Perfect he thought, although he had promised himself that whilst riding his mind would stay on the road and not wander. His life was expendable; hers, however, was a totally different thing, another feeling he had never had the concept of grasping before he had met her.

They arrived outside the gated driveway to the farm. Edward slowed right down as the single track became quite bumpy. As they pulled up outside the old Victorian farmhouse, Lottie had several fond memories come flooding back. They had met with Mr Thompson, the farmer currently at the farm, and whatever price Ed had offered he was willing to go along with their plans.

Although she was sure nothing would fit inside his jacket, Ed had managed to pull out some very small plans of the site and the proposed building, and they stood in the kitchen looking through them over a cup of coffee. Going to the loo had been an experience; although the leather had become like a second skin, getting the zipper back up still proved a task in itself.

Their meeting was over and they made their way to the hospital. It was less than ten miles away and no sooner had she got back into the feel of the ride than they came to a stop outside an old Georgian manse that had been modernised and extended to maximise the facility. By the time they had taken off their helmets, they had been greeted by several staff. Dr Douglas wore the stereotypical white lab coat. He held out his hand to make the formal greetings.

'Miss Jenkins, Mr Dean, it's great to have you here, please do come in. Can I offer you any refreshments?' They followed inside and Lottie followed Edward, although he opened every door and found himself ushering her through, placing his hand lightly on her lower back. She did not find it intimidating, it was almost a comfort in a place where she felt so overwhelmed.

They had taken off their jackets for the walk round: it was a warm spring day now. Lottie met some of the men and women who were staying at the facility; she was truly humbled. Edward fitted in with ease, chatting and sharing conversation. She took time to look at him and it felt like she was witnessing a different person to the stern-faced man who had greeted her yesterday at the start of their meal. They chatted about how another place would work to complement the hospital, and possible timescales for the development. There was still much to plan, but the trip had done what Edward had intended and Lottie was sure that this would be the right decision, now she had seen it with her own eyes.

Before they left, Edward noted that he knew a village pub they could stop at to break the journey back, and with the same ease they soon pulled up outside a well-maintained gastropub. The car park was quite full; the bike stopped outside the door and Lottie jumped off. The beer garden had a few families in it and a great view of the countryside. Towards the bottom was a canal, something that she wondered if it helped with trade as the pub was quite remote.

'Shall we sit out here?' she asked, pointing to a picnic table next to a nice couple with a young baby. Edward pulled off his helmet and had to think. No, the plan is inside, table booked so we are not disturbed. 'Yer, sure. Why not?' he replied as if an alien had taken over his mouth. 'I'll get a menu.' He placed his helmet on the wooden bench and went in. He changed his arrangements with the landlord, who seemed OK when Edward said he would pay for the table anyway. He returned and they looked through what was on offer.

'I was hoping for chips in a basket and a pint.' Lottie put down the menu that had some really nice gastro meals outlined on it, all of which she was sure would be delicious.

'Chips and a pint, are you stereotyping a biker chick?' Edward laughed.

'I suppose, but I love finger food, and I have a taste for country pub ale. You will have to come to my local and I will show you.' The offer had come out as if she was inviting a friend she had known for years.

'I will hold you to that, maybe next weekend's trip?' He stood up and walked towards the building. 'Chips and a pint of?' he asked. 'Local bitter please,' came her reply. His mind was now thinking of next week. Oh yer, we are going well, he thought, and had a little smile to himself and he quickly turned around just to check she was real and still there.

Lottie had taken off her coat and was peeling out of the top layer: it was warm. She had her back to the pub: good job because as she pulled the tight garment over her head, the light vest top followed up, showing off her lower back and the black bra she had on. Quickly grabbing the cloth, she pulled it down, only aware of the people in front of her, not giving a thought to how the view from the back had looked. She sat down in the hope that not too many people had seen, and folded the top and placed it with her jacket and gloves next to her.

He closed his eyes: he could smell her he was sure. God, he hoped no one else had seen that. He wanted it all for himself. The pale tone of her skin against that black lace, knowing that what was under the top would totally distract a saint. A hint, just a small hint of a tattoo, which went from her lower back and continued below the line of the high-backed leather trousers. Now that I want to kiss, a bold, bright red rose. He was feeling the heat under his jacket; he paid and went back outside, stripping down to the black tee shirt he had on and sitting opposite her.

He looked across but did not speak. She took a sip of the cool, amber liquid, closing her eyes as it refreshed her.

'Yes please,' Lottie said with no prompting of a question beforehand.

'You may need to expand on the preceding question. Multimillion-pound businessman, check.' He made a tick in the air. 'Mind-reader ... no.' He smirked at her. He had a thought of various questions he would like to have put before her to answer, like, Can I taste your skin? Do you want me to lick you here? Harder, my lovely? He stopped there in his train of thought: he knew the pub did a good B&B but it was not sleep that was springing to mind, and it was not just his mind that was springing into a response.

'I will take your package, the proposal, the offer, all of it under one condition.' She had sat up straight to get a more businesslike approach. She was after all asking this man to part with a lot of cash, and make a commitment to many people to take over as their landlord, and assist in creating a place that would help those in need.

Like a business android he, too, took on a more formal reply. 'Miss Jenkins, I don't want you to make any rushed decision. It's going to be a lot of hard work to start with. I, of course, will do everything for you, unless of course you want to be involved. A prospect I feel can only have benefits all round'.

Please say you want to be involved every step of the way, please, please.' The voice in his head was like a little child asking for ice cream after tea.

'I want to be as involved as I can. You, along with every other businessman out there, will eat me alive so I am going to need a lot of guidance. It's not really my line of work, and so different to what I have been used to. But I think I can trust that you are investing enough, for this not to be some fad.' She stopped. 'Or an open attempt of flamboyance to get me into bed!' She took another sip of her bitter.

'Guilty, Your Honour, you have foiled my plan.' He tried to hide it, but God, she really had foiled his plan. But his plan was changing the more time she spent near him. Lottie laughed.

'How can you joke about parting with well over a million pounds? Does it really come so easily to you? She was not direct with the question, but he felt he had to give her an answer with respect.

'I guess I know I want it at any price, as I know for whatever my reasons, to whoever may be looking, and to be honest, I give very little attention to what others think of me. I know it is the right thing to do, something I am passionate about, and something I will achieve.' He looked up and stood. 'Miss Jenkins, I thank you for accepting my offer. I welcome you into the charity as a partner, and I will make sure that you have as much involvement as you want, and need. If I can offer you a kind word, I will not eat you alive, I cannot say the same for some of the bastards out there in business, but as a part of the charity, I sure will do my utmost best to protect you all the way.' He said the last words with a genuine gut feeling. He would: he would crush the first wanker that even looked at her funny, let alone anyone who upset her.

Lottie stood up and shook his hand; she missed the kiss from last night and hoped he would do it again, but he did not. 'Your one condition is?' He sat back down. They took a moment of silence as the food was served and placed in front of them.

Lottie bit her lip as if she dared to jest with him after the very touching and what she thought was a very sincere reply.

'You eat your chips with your fingers!' She held his stare with the best poker-face she could, as if she had just said, I up my price by another million pounds.

'I'm sorry?' he asked with an astonished reply as if it was not a million but about 10.

'You got me out of my comfort zone today, putting me on the back of your bike, and pushing to see if I would tap to go slower.' She smiled, remembering the safe word slip-up. 'Mr Dean, do not think I was not aware that you were going faster and faster, pushing my limits. Now show me you can, too, do something a little out of the norm, and eat your chips with your fingers. Forget the million-pound price tag for once, and enjoy.'

He placed his hand over his chin and rubbed the smile that was beneath it. I will show you 'limits', lady, and how to push them, of that I am sure. He made a metal note of all of the other innuendos she had made in the last 24 hours.

'Perfect,' he said and dared to dip his fingers in. He took a mouthful and smiled at her. She did the same and he dared to smile at her again. You're perfect and I want you at any cost, he continued to say but without the words flowing into earshot of anyone.

He looked around as a child gave out a playful scream in the garden behind them and they continued a light conversation in the afternoon sun.

The drive back to the hotel soon saw Edward part with Lottie at reception, giving his consent to her staying in the hotel as long as she wanted. Another night would be a break, and she could go home on Sunday. There was no changing his mind: that a driver would deliver her to her door, he had given her his mobile number and said, 'Just call me when you are ready to go home.'

She called him just before lunch on the Sunday: they had a brief conversation but Edward had explained that he was with his mother making lunch so could not come along for the ride, as he would dearly have liked to, but that they would talk soon after she had been through the paperwork and the details of the deal.

He had kept his promise that the paperwork would be with her by noon the following Monday. A courier had delivered it by hand and Lottie signed for the large document holder she was passed. She had spoken to Agnes most of the Sunday afternoon, giving her the low-down on both the business side of the deal and the pleasure. Lottie had heard the objection that Agnes had given to the ease with which she had said yes to his guy no one really knew, without even a night to think about it, though, as Lottie had explained, she did not need time: she was sure this was the right path to take. She had seen for herself how this was going to be good, and could only be a good thing all round.

'I've looked at people that are dead for the first part of my working life, and, although I intend to keep that going in some way, I feel it is time to give the living something back,' Lottie had explained.

Agnes had her business head on and outlined how much they could have made if she had asked for more. Though she was well aware that it was not about the money, even without selling some of the assets, the income alone from the rest of the business would have kept Lottie well for the rest of her life. This was icing on the cake really, and she was made up for her. She thought how proud her mother would be of her now.

Lottie did not ask Agnes to come around straight away as she wanted time to go over the documents herself. She sifted through the sale documents and came to the larger agreement of the sale of the farm. This came with proposed plans etc, copies of what she had seen during the visit. She skimmed them over again and picked them up off the counter, when a small note fell out.

Miss Jenkins, if you are free next weekend I would like to invite you to one of our charity evenings. Although it is not a fundraiser for the farm project, you will get to meet many of the other stakeholders and some influential people with money that could be of help, if you persuade them to part with it.

Lottie carried on reading. The letter was handwritten, the words were well formed, and the handwriting looked familiar.

Of course, I will be your host and at no point leave you to the wolves. I will arrange an overnight stay and collection and return home, all you need is yourself and that smile and charm.

Yours

Mr Edward Dean CEO Dean Charities LTD UK

She had planned a night in because the next day she had foolishly agreed to do a 20k cross-country run for charity. She had agreed to it a few weeks before her mother had died, and then felt it was even more important to do it afterwards as it was for cancer research. They had started out a few in number from the village pub; several had dropped out, and the last one through injury, so it was really important that Lottie showed commitment to the cause, although she had managed to get their sponsor money from them so she would run for the pub. She picked up the phone and dialled his number. It rang only for a short time before his voice came on the line.

Ed had sat in his office all morning, mentally thinking about what she would be doing, at which point she may find it. He had written her a note and had it sent to his solicitors to be put in the package as soon as he had returned home from dropping her off at the hotel.

As his phone rang he halted his meeting.

'Gentlemen, I must take this call, please excuse me.' He had stepped to the window and answered. 'Good morning, Miss Jenkins, I hope I find you well?'

Lottie smiled to herself. 'I am well, Mr Dean. Yourself?' she replied.

'The afternoon just got brighter. Have you been able to work over the offer? I have to say it has not taken you long, I like a business partner that does not dally around.' He turned his back to the room of people to look out of his window.

'I have not been through it all yet, it was just your note, for next Saturday. I would love to come but...' She paused only slightly and if she had been standing next to Edward she would have seen his face drop. 'I can't. Well, I can, but I have a commitment on the Sunday that I really can't get out of and I need to have a clear head. I don't want to be tired, or hung-over for that fact,' she continued.

'Well, Miss Jenkins, whatever it is that is so important we can work around. Do explain, you have me intrigued.' He smiled to himself as he turned around and held his hand up to one of the guys who said so that he could hear, 'You having this conversation, Dean, or what?' He turned his back again and listened to Lottie explain her reasons.

'Miss Jenkins, I have the world's most impudent man sitting at my desk trying to work his way out of a deal that will save his poxy company from going under. Can I have a think about this and call you straight back? I take it I can get you on this number?' Lottie agreed and apologised for interrupting his meeting. 'It's not your fault.' Ed said goodbye and walked back over the desk.

Slamming his hands down so hard that Zoe heard it at her desk and jumped and the other security guard at the lift doors stood up and looked at her.

'I suggest, Mr Hawkins, that you get your sorry ass out of my office and go and explain to your father why this deal has just broken down. My conversation with you is over, and the only way that I am going to save your sorry little ass now is if your father comes over here and plays the deal himself. Me personally, I have another company that can do the job just as well, but for some goddamn reason Alex asked, as a favour for a friend, if I would put it your way due to your situation. Something I guess your father does not know the full story about. So, take your accountant out of my face and leave.' He pointed towards the door that was now being opened by the security guard as if something in the last statement had been a code word to assist them from the building.

'Sorry, Ed, Mr Dean, please, my father knows only a little of why I have come to you, he is not aware that...' He stopped as Edward moved closer to the door and the security guard moved closer to the couple who should have been gone by now in Edward's eyes. 'My father!' Edward cut him short. 'Will have to learn of your addiction to whatever it is that has lost his company thousands over the short few months you have been in charge. Women, or drugs, gambling, you explain that to him if he wants to come and see me this time tomorrow then the deal may still be on the table. Frankly it's not my loss.' He moved back to his desk, sure that they had gone.

'You will regret this, you think you know it all, and have it all, you wait and see, Dean, you're not as squeaky clean as you like to make out...' His words trailed off as he was assisted out of the door towards the lift.

The thought was out of his head as if it had been nothing to dismiss them. He started to tap into his laptop and found what he was looking for. Using his mobile he made a call. Smiling at the outcome, he spoke to Zoe with a few requests, and then pressed the caller log on his phone, hitting the call button when Lottie's mobile showed on the caller ID. She was in his phone book anyway so it was not an issue finding her number. In fact, he put her home number in, as well as the pub number, the gym number and Agnes's contact details, all of which he had gained from the folder Pete supplied him.

They made their introductions again and Ed apologised that it was not as soon as he had wanted to reply.

'Listen, I have a plan,' he started. 'I had a look on your website for the race: how do you fancy another person joining the team?' He was not aware that people had dropped out, although he had been told that entry was closed. The large sum of money that was about to be forwarded into their bank account was the only invitation he needed to change their minds. 'Or I could come and watch after dropping you off. Pete has a day off, but I can drive you back early in the morning?' She had gone quiet. 'I don't mean to muscle in, and turn me down if you must' - no, no, please don't turn me down, his brain screamed - 'but I have to warn you, if you are not up for the stiff opposition to be beaten in the race then you only have to say,' he joked.

'So, you had to say that last bit as you know I can't turn down the challenge!' Lottie sighed. She did rather relish the idea of him in Lycra shorts, running behind all the way just to get a look at that cute ass and his muscle-bound legs. She hoped for hot weather just so that shorts were the order of the day! 'It's a long way to drive and it will mean a really early start. I suppose that I could be changed and we can go straight there. You could come back for shower at mine and then have a bite to eat before you go back?' she asked as if they had known each other forever.

The plan was better than he could have arranged himself. He liked her thinking: of course it was a yes but as he stayed silent Lottie added, 'Or not if you are too busy. I know you said that Sunday lunch for you was a family thing.'

'No worries, Mum will be OK with a bit of notice: she can go out for lunch with friends, I'm sure. Anyway, you will meet her on Saturday night, and once she sees you then I am sure she will forgive you the love of her devoted son for one day.' Edward already knew that she would be OK with it; he often dipped out of Sundays after a charity night out, usually because he had been at the club with Alex for hours after and never got up until it was night again. Seeing her son up and about would please her more than anything, knowing he had not been with the 'boy who leads you astray,' as she called Alex instead of referring to him by name.

'So, we're on, then? Can I arrange to pick you up and book a room for you?' he asked, knowing that was what Zoe was already arranging.

'Yes, but can I get to town early? I would like to meet up with a few friends first. If it's not good, then I can catch the train,' Lottie explained.

'You set the time and place and it will be arranged. We need to be at the Grosvenor by 7pm, though.' He was wondering who she wanted to meet, biting his tongue to the fact he was desperate to ask.

'That's fine, I just need to pop to Camden. I can go on the tube if I drop off my things at the hotel first.' They continued to arrange the night. Lottie asked what she should wear. Why she thought he was the fashion police after she had asked the question she was not sure, but she only had a long dinner dress and did not want to be too overstated; in fact she could pop into the city and get something new while she was there. Her meeting with Todd would only take an hour at tops.

As Edward clicked down the phone he had to fight every bone in his body to ring her again and ask her who she was meeting. He had a long think and knew that Pete would be on to her anyway, so no matter: he would find out.

Lottie continued to work through the paperwork and after her evening meal she rang Agnes to set up a meeting the next day to go through everything. As it turned out, she did go through everything with a fine-tooth comb, including the details of the weekend and the one to come.

Edward had a business trip that took him to Paris for the day, but all week his mind was on the Saturday night. He had double-checked and double-checked again everything for the event. Alex had turned a shade of grey when he turned down the offer of drinks on the Friday. So much so that he said he would come and see what the fuss was about himself. 'Bit of skirt turned your eye, then?' he said. 'I wish I had not said anything to you. You won't get in as you're not on the guest list.' Ed knew this to be true, but Alex was one to make an issue out of everything if he wanted to. Edward was sure that he was not ready for Lottie to meet Alex, for many reasons; most of all, this girl he was not sharing, even with his lifelong friend.

Todd had texted Lottie on the Sunday morning, and, although she had delayed in answering him, she had called him later in the evening. She never said anything about Edward or her deal, but she had said that if they needed her advice then she would be there. His text had said they had a case that she may be interested in and he wanted to give her the information, so she could take a look. She did want to keep her hand in, so when they chatted she said she was happy to pop over. He had offered to take her out on the Saturday evening. Maybe with his sister they could go for a drink, but she had used the excuse that she needed to get back not to stop. Only a white lie, she thought to herself. He bought the idea and when he met her off the tube, they had a short embrace as old friends and went to a nearby café.

They chatted and Lottie was brought up to speed. The folder of information had some graphic photos, and she did not think it was the right place to open them. Todd talked about his brother and how well the Tap and Tune was doing under the new owner, although it was a mystery who he was. Todd had done some digging, but they could not find the owner. Some big organisation, foreign, they thought, and it was left at that.

They arranged to meet again as soon as she had worked on the information, and she would email him in the week if she needed anything else. He said that he could get her clearance for information to be sent via email after talking to the professor, who was OK with the remote working thing, as he still wanted Lottie on-board.

After several coffees and the biggest muffin Lottie had ever seen, they had laughed and said she would run it off the next day. Todd even went online on his phone and pledged some money to her sponsor account. Finally, they said their goodbyes with another hug and they left.

It was a sunny day to shop, and walking down Oxford Street the usual throng of people did not spoil her mood. Lottie hated crowds and hated shopping if she did not know what she wanted. 'It's bound to be black!' Agnes had said. 'You need me there to guide you.' She had been quite serious, but Lottie wanted to do this alone, be more positive about everything and make her own mistakes if this was what it was. 'Well, if you won't let me choose, at least make me gasp at the price tag. No tat, please, lady, designer at best, Harrods if you want the best, no arguments: spend that cash of yours, before I manage to put it all in a Swiss bank account without you knowing!' They had laughed on the Thursday when she went around for a drink. Lottie had every faith that Agnes would never do that, but she would be on her case if she did not heed her advice, so she jumped in a cab and went to Harrods, a place she had only ever been to once before and got totally lost and bemused by the whole experience.

She was dressed in jeans and loose-fitting top, with her big, baggy handbag that was bulging with everything, and the folder Todd had given her. Hardly a WAG, she thought to herself as she looked at the other shoppers. Once she had got past the first floor that only seemed to be full of tourists, she made her way to ladieswear. After just looking at one dress she was jumped on by a young assistant. More than shopping, she hated being pushed and pampered by the person who would get 12% service charge just for saying how absolutely stunning it looked and she had to buy it! She carried on walking until she came to the underwear. They seemed more laid-back and Lottie was able to feel some of the silk and lace items in her hands. It was nice, soft and sexy. An older lady approached her and said, 'Let me know if you need anything. I'm over here just shout up.'

Now that's the kind of assistant I need, Lottie thought.

'Thank you, it's not the underwear, I need a dress, but I have to say I am a fish out of water really, but I guess you can tell.' She pointed to her clothes.

'My dear, after working here for so long, I am no judge of anyone. You have money, you don't have money, you want to buy, you don't want to buy. It's all the same to me. Manners cost nothing, and those who need help will more than often ask, those who don't are welcome to look.' She was well over middle-aged and lacked the make-up her young counterparts wore. Another young assistant looked over to her and gave her a stare as if she had heard what she had said. 'I'm through beating the monthly targets. It was a dress, you said?' She looked at Lottie. 'Size 10, something for evening, party, husband or lover?' she whispered.

Lottie laughed. 'Party tonight, charity bash, large hotel...' she trailed off. 'No husband, sadly no lover.'

'Well, turn heads we can do, then maybe the next time we meet it will be for one of the latter!' She laughed a deep, hearty laugh that made the young assistant turn around and tut out loud. 'Isabel, Bella, pleased to meet you. Shall we have a look around for a while?'

'Lottie.' She introduced herself, holding out her hand. 'Yes please, but I have to say I like these.' She held out a cream silk lace nightgown set. Last time she stayed over she had brought her favourite pyjamas; this time as she knew she was in her 'usual room', as the bellboy had said to her when they checked in at the Kensington (good old Edward, she thought: money talks), she felt like taking Agnes's advice and spending a little more than usual.

Bella picked them up and held them across her arm. 'We can try them: tell me what you want in this dress, then?'

'Bla...' She stopped before the whole word was out. 'Not black,' she finished. 'Not low at the front, has to be long,' she continued. 'I don't like too much frill and fuss, I don't do sparkle.'

'Hair up or down?' Bella asked as they continued to walk to the ladieswear rooms.

'Not sure, had not got that far, and I have not brought any hairbands so maybe down,' Lottie replied as she was offered a seat.

'First things first: red or white, or bubbles?' Bella asked. Lottie looked confused. 'Let me.' Bella picked up the in-store phone and made a call. 'Right, give me a moment, I will get these put in a fitting room.' She held up the nightwear, and pulled open a mirrored door where Lottie could see there was a large seat and table, more like a whole room itself than a fitting room in a shop. Bella spoke to two other girls and gave orders that Lottie did not hear. She looked up as a young man dressed in Harrods livery offered her a glass of champagne. 'Madam.' He held it out and then it clicked with her (red/white or bubbles!) 'Thank you,' Lottie said, taking the glass from the silver tray.

The girls had come to the room with several bags, none of which Lottie could see into. Bella had been in twice and finally said:

'Right, young Lottie, here we go. This way if you please.' The door opened up and several dresses had been arranged on a free-standing hanger. The table had various bags and shoes and she could see some delicate hair accessories; all matched the array of colour. Not one black dress to be seen. 'Now try them all before you decide, keep an open mind to what you asked for, although I have a favourite in mind. Let's see if I really know my stuff and see if it is the same as you choose.' Bella handed her the first dress. A dull gold, not glitter but a simple-fitting, strapped dress. She held out shoes and hair jewels. Lottie put it on. 'Nice, but we can do better.' Bella said, holding out another dress. Grey, fitted bustline. Short puff sleeves. The skirt was more free-flowing than tight. Shoes and hair down had been decided. 'Still going to beat that one.' Lottie quickly unzipped: she had by now lost the embarrassment of Bella seeing her in her undies, it was just the two of them in the room and the older woman found no embarrassment which put Lottie at ease.

A dusky brown dress lower cut at the front with thin, gold-jewelled straps, A-line bust with a fitted skirt that was split to the knee to help you walk. 'I would never have picked this, but it is amazing,' Lottie said, daring to have a little twirl in the mirror. 'Mostly what you said you did not want?' Bella asked as a rhetorical question. 'Yes, but…' Lottie gave another twirl and held up her hair. Bella dazzled her with a fine matching jewel for her hair. 'Um nice,' Lottie said.

'Last one, then.' Bella took out a gown from under a bag as Lottie shed the other like her second skin. 'Come away from the mirror and let's get it all on before you look.' Lottie did as she was told: after a few sips of the drink in between fittings she was now getting into this WAG shopping.

It was a dark blue, almost French navy but it shimmered in the light like a crystal blue sea. It was low-cut at the back, fitted and had a band of blue beads from shoulder to shoulder to stop it falling off, as the back was so low. It slid along her thin legs as if it was being poured over her like bathwater. Bella stood at her back and gently eased the dress together. She adjusted the back strap. She took her long, blonde hair with one swift curl up and let a small piece fall over her face. Placing a silver clip to the rest of the hair, it held it in place. The shoes where a silver velvet, full in the toe with a strap heel; clutch bag to match lay on the table ready for the wearer to pick it up. Bella knelt in front of her and twisted something at her leg: the dress slipped open all the way to the thigh and Lottie could see that shape of her thigh. 'Before you say it's too revealing, bear with me. Those legs could melt the polar ice cap and need to be out there, my dear. Now take a look at this.' Lottie turned to the full-length mirror and had to look again at who was in front of her. 'The best till last, you agree?' Bella's question was said with triumph in her voice as she admired Lottie and her fine handiwork with a sense of pride.

'Bella, is it really what you think I should be wearing. It's… beautiful!' Lottie gave a small twirl, not wanting her leg to show too much. She noticed that the back went all the way to her defined lower spine, but just covered her rose tattoo. The jewels on the shoulder were secure, and where they met one small line of them free-flowed in the middle of her shoulder blades.

'You are beautiful, young Lottie.' She paused. 'The dress has brought it out, that's all: it is nothing on the hanger without the beauty within.'

Lottie twirled again and giggled. **Oh yes Aggie take a look at me girlfriend L xxxx** she put in the text that she had sent. Bella had taken a photo that she had attached to the text and had not even put the phone in her pocket when a reply came back. **O.M.G.! A xxxx** Without even asking for the price she said yes to the whole lot. 'I'm not looking at the price just take the card and do what you have to.' She smiled, handing her the debit card and she got dressed.

Walking back into the main fashion hall other shoppers were not aware of what had happened in the fitting room. But Lottie had to control the shrieks of excitement and the joy on her face as the porter took her bags to the door. A taxi had been ordered and Bella took her down to the main doors.

'Thank you again, Bella, you are the best, and, although I am not going to shop here every day I will be back to see you if I need anything else from this shop, even a cheese sandwich, which I am sure the food hall does, but you will know how to order it just right.'

'My pleasure, young Lottie. My only ask is that you hold your head up high tonight and you enjoy every second. And if any young man refuses you a dance or does not hold a door open for you, you send them my way. I will happily show them our range of glasses!' She gave another hearty laugh and Lottie could not resist her a hug before she got in the cab and closed the door. The taxi driver repeated the name of the hotel and Lottie was on her way back.

'So, she got something, then?' Ed asked.

'Yes, she's heading back,' Pete said.

'And she was only with this guy in the café? He never went shopping with her?' he asked.

'No, and before you say it I did not go into the fitting rooms with her. I can be good at undercover work but even three would be a crowd and my cover would have been blown in there!' Pete said with a hint of sarcasm in his voice.

'Message understood,' Ed said back. 'I will see you in a few hours, then.' He put down the phone. How he hated not knowing. Pete had given him chapter and verse about who she was meeting and where but had not been able to get him any more information, although he was aware she had been given a folder and they had hugged on meeting and leaving each other. Was this Todd bloke any threat to him? No chance, he thought to himself as he put his boxing gloves back on and continued to hit the bag hanging from the wall in front of him in the gym in his apartment block.

Lottie had got back and had a swim, although she knew that a day off should have been in order, she could not help herself. Showering and drying her hair, she had noticed that the hotel had a hairdresser's and she had asked if it was possible for her to use someone to help her dress her hair for tonight. On cue, there they were at the door. She had the nightwear on, pulled tightly around her so not to show off anything, although she knew on introduction that the guy who came to do her hair was not the least interested in anything she had on under there.

She was pushing it fine and she jumped as the phone rang. The reception said that Mr Dean was waiting in the lobby. 'God I'm not dressed, and he is early!' she exclaimed, putting down the phone.

'Send him up. I'll help the creation, in you go in there. I'll get the door.' He pointed to the bedroom door. The hairstylist left the door open and he followed. By the time he got in, Lottie had stepped into the dress, just waiting for the back to be tightened up.

Edward walked in. 'Hello!' he shouted out.

The hairstylist pushed his head around the door 'Hold on, handsome, we are creating a beauty in here, not for your eyes just yet so easy, tiger!' he said.

Edward looked slightly amused. He had been called many things by many people but not handsome and tiger in the same sentence by a gay hairdresser wearing red trousers and a God-awful shirt from the 60s! He wandered to the windows and looked out at the view. The evening was warm, dry, perfect, he thought.

The door opened and the stylist stood hands on hips. 'Tadarrrrr!' He pointed in the direction of Lottie as she walked out the door. 'Chin up, remember tits and teeth love, work it, work it,' he whispered as she walked past him.

Edward turned around and felt the thud hit him like a high-speed train. He opened his mouth to speak but the words stuck in his throat. He instantly felt his hairs stand on end, and in his mind he had rushed over to her and kissed her red-coloured lips hard. He looked at her, still wishing his feet and mouth would work.

'It's too much, I knew it.' Lottie looked at the stylist. 'Oh God, it's too much,' Lottie continued.

'Tosh, baby girl, it's perfection personified, cat just got his tongue.' He had already admired the brut, perfect form for a man: 'or stirring something in those tight trousers,' he said to himself but neither party heard the comment.

'Wow' was all that finally came and the stone legs he had suddenly let him take a pace forwards.

'"Wow". Oh man, that's all you can find to say to this smoking hot creature? You don't deserve her!' He held out his hands and took Lottie's hands in his. 'You go, girl and remember whenever you're here next you owe me a drink.'

'Thanks, Georgie, I'll make sure you are paid for your time,' Lottie said.

'Oh my, no way, all my pleasure, this one was on me, would not have missed handling those locks and that dress for the world, you've made my day. Even if the dumb one over there is not saying much!' He nodded his head in the direction of Edward who had finally been able to walk as his semi-erection in his trousers had finally allowed him room to move, although still aware that he was more than happy to see her.

The door closed and they were alone.

'You like?' she said, giving him a twirl, and if the front did not appeal the back of the dress was too much. He swallowed hard. 'You don't like!' Lottie now started to sound disappointed. 'It is too much, I told Bella it was for this type of event.'

Edward was dressed in black dinner jacket and black bow tie, pure white shirt, gold cufflinks and black, polished shoes.

'It is very much that type of do, but I am not sure I can cope with the smile I will have on my face all night standing next to you!' Or the throbbing in my groin, the pure need to rip off the dress and show you things that a young girl should not see, or even experience! He rubbed his hand through his hair.

'Well, stay behind me, then,' she joked and turned around and he just caught a glimpse of red from the rose petal.

Worse, he thought, definitely worse, for me! He had fully expanded again and he was using his years of skill not to explode inside his boxers there and then. This was a test for you, Mr Dean, a test of your willpower indeed, he said to himself.

'Shall we go? Pete is waiting,' he said. She turned and walked towards the door. He savoured the shimmer of the dress, the way it hung to her curves, leaving nothing to the imagination.

They stood in the lift both smiling but not speaking, as if not to let the bellboy hear a word. As the doors opened Edward left the car first and held out his arm. 'Shall we?' he said. Lottie hooked her arm in his and he leaned into her just for a second. 'You look amazing, Lottie,' he whispered.

She instantly felt the heat in her face as she turned to him as they started walking. His closeness had left his smell in her space and she felt the male spices of his odour and aftershave awaken her every pore. Pete held the door as they approached and he tipped his hat.

'Miss Jenkins.' He gave her a smile. She does scrub up well, he thought, a lot different to the jeans and tee shirt she had worn all day. 'Pete,' she replied, trying to get into the back of the blacked-out limousine the best she could. It was inevitable that she would show her leg at some point so she thought it best to do it now. Edward went around the other side and helped himself into the car. It was not long before they started chatting about what to expect of the evening. But Lottie noticed he had been right: he had not taken that smile off his face, and it made her feel quite flattered.

The glitz and the glimmer of the evening were everything she had expected. She hugged her glass of champagne, aware that if she let go some kind soul would take it and give her a full one. She had already said in the car that she did not want too much to be ready for tomorrow; Edward had said he was going to do the same, but seemed to handle the drinks better.

She had been introduced to some nice people, all of whom Edward had done a formal induction for her, and she had noticed that through it all he had placed his hand slightly on her lower back as if a steadying gesture. The first time he did it she jumped slightly, wondering who was touching her bare skin, but after that she accepted the touch of his warm, soft, masculine hands: they made her feel safe.

His mother was a wonderful woman. Small, immaculately dressed, not a hair out of place, but so down-to-earth. She had asked for Lottie to sit next to her so she could have a gossip. Although Edward had been reluctant to let her go, he knew that arguing with his mother was a waste of time, and besides, he got to sit opposite her, to enjoy the view from a better angle. Several of the conversations could have been in Mandarin for all he knew as he got lost in the thought of what was under the dress.

Lottie took occasional looks at Edward, and at times their eyes met. At one point he held her gaze and smiled. One other time he mouthed, 'Are you alright?' and she had nodded. He had been right: she learned so much about the charities that Edward funded or was involved with, or a silent partner in. How come when she had 'Googled' him she had not found any of this on the internet. She had been aware that he did not have his picture taken when they arrived, and Pete did his best to keep the few photographers away from them as they went from the car, but she was OK with that, too. They had arranged a time to go, and it did seem too soon that that time came for Lottie, but they said their goodbyes and got back in the car.

'How was that, then?' he asked. 'No wolves about tonight?'

'No, I'm sure some of the older ladies did not appreciate Bella's choice of dress,' she said.

'Only because their husbands were talking to you, rather than them,' he relayed.

'You are full of compliments tonight, Mr Dean,' Lottie said. 'You're very kind.'

He took her hand in his and she felt the warmness of his breath. 'And you are very welcome.' He kissed the back of her hand and placed it back down on her knee.

Although it had taken the last effort of a dying man he departed at her door as they had said goodnight. He would see her tomorrow early. Lottie closed the door and leaned against the back of it. She went to the fridge for some water. She seemed to be drawn to the room where the piano was: as she opened the door she noticed this time a single red rose was sitting on the top. She looked at it, picked it up and smelled it. It was fresh and vibrant. The lid had been lifted as if to say, 'Play me, Lottie, please.' She put the water on the floor next to the stool and sat down. It took seconds for her fingers to start to caress the keys and the notes flowed out. The sound was amazing in the room.

'I'll take it back up to her,' Edward said when Pete picked up the red lipstick that had fallen into the car from Lottie's bag. Bonus: not in the plan but I will take it, he said to himself as he impatiently tapped on the lift wall as he went up to the top floor. He had been given a key from reception as he said he did not want to alarm her to a call-up before he arrived. As the lift door opened he could hear the soft playing coming from behind the door of the suite.

He stopped and did not tap; he stood still and leaned against the wall. He closed his eyes: he could see the way she would be sitting, the way she would be swaying. He had never felt like this. As much as he wanted to burst in the door and take her, with or without her consent, he wanted to stop and listen, be restrained. Take it slow and make her want him as much as he wanted her. He had never had to wait for anything in his adult life. He had made that promise to himself years ago. He knew that she had to be won over to get her to play the games he wanted her to, to get the trust he needed to show her the power within herself to do things he knew she had never done before. Good things come to those who wait, his mother would say to him, and maybe he had to take her advice this time, maybe he had to wait and learn this lesson finally in his life.

He put the lipstick back in his pocket and called the lift back, and got into the car.

'We good?' Pete asked as he held the door for Ed. 'Anywhere else?'

'We're good, and no' home please. Tomorrow I need to get my running shoes on: I'm in for a long race,' he said.

'That you are,' Pete said from the driver's seat. 'And I hope that you enjoy it all the way with no casualties.'

Edward knew his driver by now that there was a double meaning in what he had said, not just referring to the next day, but the next few weeks, months - God, who knew? - years to come. Now that thought scared the shit out of him. Edward Dean had never seen a girl longer than three dates, if that. The only exception had been Caroline and look where that got him. But was this girl, this young woman, what he had been looking for and what Mitch had talked about: being settled?

'Nice car,' Lottie said as she slipped into the seat of the private-plated Porsche Boxster Spyder convertible. 'Another little play toy?' she asked.

One of many, he thought, but replied, 'I don't like to drive the bigger cars. Pete does a better job than me, and as I don't often have passengers there is no need for anything with more than two seats!' He smiled as he set the car in motion.

'Nothing to do with the 160 mph top speed, then?' she asked with a smirk.

'If that is a gentle reminder not to go too fast, then your wish is my command. Impressive car knowledge, though,' he added. She had been looking at cars during the week on the internet as she wanted to get a new one herself. She had been driving her mum's car and now, with the added funds, wanted something a bit more fun, although she had not wanted to pay the £90,000 price tag that a top-of-the-range one could cost like this!

It was early as predicted. He was dressed in tracksuit bottoms and a light sweatshirt top. He had packed a light overnight bag that had already been in the boot – well, under the bonnet technically - when Lottie had put her bags in there, too. They made light conversation for a start, but Lottie could not help that her eyes felt heavy, and she was resisting the urge to go to sleep. Edward could tell and he knew that the journey would be a few hours, so he said, 'I won't be offended if you want to catch up on some sleep. I'm sorry we were out so late.' Lottie smiled and said she was Ok, but soon found that she was more than willing to take the offer and lost the next hour in a relaxing slumber.

Edward glanced across at her: she looked so peaceful, relaxed and sexy, and if he had been with any other woman by this point sleeping would not have been an option. The only ride she would be getting was not in his car, but in a lay-by they had passed miles ago. Her tight running leggings showed her legs off, and he had mentally worked his way up and down them several times with his hands and his lips.

'Feel better?' he asked as she opened her eyes and tried to stretch as much as the car footwell would allow her.

'Strangely, yes, where are we?' They had only a few miles to go to the venue. It was not long before they were parked up and removing their outer layers ready to make their way along with the other thousand or so runners to the start line. Lottie felt quite nervous. The fact that his shorts showed off his legs just as she had imagined made her conscious not to keep looking at them.

'I'll meet you here if for any reason we get split up, or you can't keep up!' he said.

'Dream on, I will be here waiting for you at the end.' She gently nudged his shoulder in jest at her comment and she felt the strength in his arms as she did not move his frame at all.

'Game on, keep up if you can!' he said back as he stretched and warmed up. As the starting gun went off it took some time for them to get going, but they soon found each other's pace easy to work with. Lottie had her iPod, but did not put it on, and although they did not talk much they seemed to be equally paced. They had been jostled at the start and she could tell that he was putting himself in the way of others so that she did not get pushed around. As the field spread out it became easier. They stopped once for a bottle of water, but that was it: they had stayed together all the way round. Under an hour and half and they got to within the finishing line. The spectators were cheering and it gave them both a lift to the end. Lottie started to sprint the last 100 yards and Edward kicked in to keep at her side. They came in together and as they stopped she gave a smile to him.

'Did not want to beat you really,' she said, slightly out of breath. 'Well done, feels good?' she asked. Without her noticing he had picked her up and swung her around.

'Well done you,' he said, putting her back down. She looked slightly put out and for a moment he thought he had overstepped the mark. 'Sorry, slightly overwhelmed with the old adrenaline!' he quickly said. She placed her arms around his shoulders and kissed his cheek. 'Feels great,' she said, savouring the moment of being so close.

They remarked on areas of the race, and Lottie gave him directions to her house, only twenty minutes' drive from the finish line. As they pulled up to her house she had a need to shower and eat; she thought he would feel the same.

'This is nice,' he said as they went in through the door. He had all the bags and Lottie's things in his arms.

'Let's take them from you.' She held out her hands. 'I'll take you to your room, I bet you need a shower.' She went back to the front doorstep where a cool box had been left. 'Aggie did a shop for me, and her husband dropped them off, I texted her last night to see if she would.' Lottie carried on explaining as she showed him upstairs. She pointed to the guest room. 'Towels and everything in there, water takes a bit of time to come through but it should be OK. Make yourself at home, I'm here.' She pointed to her room at the other end of the hall. 'I'll get changed and then make us some food.' As she heard the water start to run she imagined him in the shower. As if their minds were on the same page, Edward let the water cascade over him and he was doing the same thing about the person in the room across the hall.

He made his way back to the kitchen. As he walked past the living room door he noticed the piano and smiled to himself. She had not come down yet, but she had heard him on the stairs, so she shouted down, 'Help yourself to anything! Water in the fridge, but the coffee pot is on if you want one!' Before she had showered she had been back downstairs and put it on. He looked around and found a cup, and poured some of the hot, black liquid into it. He noticed a large, brown folder on the other side of the worktop, and recognised it as the folder she had been given the day before. He glanced at the door, to check if she had come down the stairs; knowing it was safe, he looked at the file.

Lottie, can you cast your eyes over this? I will ring you, and arrange to come over on Wednesday. We can go for lunch or something, Todd, the note on the front said. He pushed it back as she came down the last few steps.

'Want one?' He held up the cup.

'Please,' she said, also getting a bottle of water from the fridge to ensure that she was taking on some more fluids. She started to open the box that had been left and there was a note on the top. She laughed and then read it out loud. **Everything you wanted, we will be in the pub about 6pm if you care to join us, enjoy. Aggie.**

'I will text her, not sure I want to, unless you feel up to the Spanish Inquisition at meeting them all?' she asked, continuing to get the supplies from the box.

'Up to you, although the view from your kitchen window does look inviting to sit out there with my feet up!' He went over to the door and looked out at the well-manicured garden. 'Like gardening, do you?' he asked, making small talk.

'I have a gardener. Mum used to like it more than me.' She paused. 'Steak and salad OK?' She changed the subject and Edward did not go back to it. He nodded and Lottie came to open the door for him. 'Have a seat, rest your legs: you must be tired after that long run, impressive as you were able to keep up with me!' She laughed over her shoulder as she walked away. 'I will shout you when it is ready: we can sit out there if you like?'

'Funny!' He took his coffee outside and sat down. The sun was still high in the sky, and it was a real suntrap. You did not find many spaces like this in the city, and it was only at times like this that he thought he should have a country bolt-hole where he could forget the toil of his life and really relax. He found himself listening to the birds, and the quietness of the place; in fact there was nothing else to listen to, no noise pollution. He could hear a low hum of music as Lottie had put on the radio, and he smiled to himself. Never had he thought three weeks ago that this would be something he would do. In a way he had to shake himself as it was quite frightening how he was becoming too relaxed around her. If he dropped his guard, he would lose the game.

She broke his train of thought to bring out some condiments and asked if he wanted another drink, as she had put down a large bottle of water and some glasses. She had also brought out a bottle of red wine and two glasses. 'I know that drinking after exercise is bad for you, but never mind, who wants to live safe all the time?'

The meal was welcome and they chatted about the house and how long she had lived there. Some stories of her childhood came out and Edward reciprocated with a small insight to his life. His phone had been silently vibrating throughout the meal and Lottie had asked if he wanted to get it several times. It was calls and emails coming through and, although he had glanced at them, it was nothing he could not leave for now.

One bottle of red went well with the meal and he offered to get another after he was given the directions to where the cellar was located. Time had flown and the evening sun had turned colder. Lottie had put on a light dress after her shower, and had left her hair wet but tied back. She felt the chill but did not move to get up for a jumper. As Edward came back he placed his sweater over her shoulders. 'Thought you may be feeling the cold,' he said as if he had read her mind again. She could smell his aftershave on the top, the one he had on in the car on the way down here. 'Thank you,' she said as she wrapped herself in it more.

They chatted some more; she talked about Bella and her Harrods experience, and they got onto the subject of Lottie's work before her mum had become ill. Without prompting, she had offered him the information about still working for Todd. He listened intently, although the thought of her spending more time with Todd did piss him off. He could see how important it was to her, and he said to himself he would live with it for now.

Although the wine had warmed her face, the sun had gone and Lottie was cold. She had got up several times to clear the plates, and bring out the summer pudding that Aggie had made them. She could feel the effects of the wine when she stood up to go to the toilet, and asked if they could go inside.

When she got back, Edward was in the sitting room looking at the family photos. He joked at the baby photos of Lottie sitting above the fire and then noticed one where she was playing the piano. He picked it up for a closer look.

'That was just before Dad died,' she said. 'Chubby, wasn't I?'

'Yes,' he said, no expression on his face.

'Oh! You're supposed to say no!' She pulled a face at him and she took the photo out of his hand. They were close and she could feel the body heat from his bare arm as she brushed past him to put it back on the shelf. The hairs on his arm stood on end and he felt the pull of her being so close. He moved away without a thought, but Lottie had moved in the same small direction, and they touched once more and held the other's eye for what seemed like hours, but it was only seconds. Embarrassed, she moved back and placed the picture back where it lived.

'Want a coffee?' she said. 'Or a nightcap?' She gestured where the whiskey decanters were in the corner of the room. She walked over to the bottles.

'I'm fine,' he said, then to himself: Well, I'm not fine, you are driving me to distraction and I have never had such unexplainable bloody feelings. I should get in my car and drive as far away as possible, if only for your safety and my own sanity. 'Maybe in a bit, although I have to say I am beat. Today has been really great, thanks, maybe we could do something like it again?'

Lottie went into the kitchen and placed the rest of the dishes into the dishwasher. She hung around in the kitchen, if only to take some time to think. She was confused because sometimes it felt like he did not want to be near her, yet the gestures he made were totally gentlemanly. Maybe he is just going to be businesslike and keep this platonic. Really, Lottie, that is what this should be if we are going to have to work together for a long time, she thought to herself. That was it, he was remaining the businessman and she had been reading him all wrong.

She made her excuses for going to bed and said she would be up in the morning. Although he needed to get off early, she did not mind as she could get on with her jobs and catch up with Aggie. Closing her bedroom door, she heard him close his, and if she listened enough she could tell he was making a few calls, catching up on his day.

She laid her head down and fell asleep. It had not been the same for Edward: he had made a few calls, but then could not sleep knowing she was just along the hall. He emailed his therapist and asked for an appointment for the next day; he also had something else he wanted to do, but he could not do anything about that now. He tried to sleep, but the whole house made him think of her. Slowly creeping down the stairs, he took her up on the offer of a whiskey. Without putting on the lights, he could see where he was by the moonlight coming into the windows and his eyes had adjusted to the light. He sat on the red piano stool and took a sip of the warm liquid. Brushing his hand over the wooden lid he looked in the direction of the photo again. Chubby! Even as a child she looked like an angel. The game had to stop; he had to stop this before he went too far, or could he?

He showered and could hear the radio again downstairs. He was not sure what time Lottie had got up, but when he went in the kitchen he regretted not slipping out as he first thought he could, without having to see her again. She had slippers on, fluffy, sporting a dog's face on both toe ends. Her short skirt only covered her long legs to the thigh, and her sloppy black top fell off on one shoulder. He had to breathe slowly. He had put on his suit trousers, white shirt but left the tie and jacket for later. He regretted that now as the stiffness in his trousers was, he was sure, more than obvious.

'Morning. I hope that you slept well. I was not sure if you are a toast or porridge sort of person, forgot to ask last night.' Lottie had put on a spread and was munching a bagel while serving the coffee.

'Toast is great.' He wanted to sit at the breakfast bar, but thought that was too close to her. He needed help with this; he needed someone to make sense of it all for him. He had never had breakfast with a woman. He had eaten breakfast off of women! But not in such a domestic setting as this. 2.5 children and a lawnmower, Alex's voice was going through his head over and over. Who the fuck wants to be tied down like that? Not you, man. The voice of his friend continued to play in his head. Lottie noticed.

'You OK? I mean this must feel a bit weird.' She stopped as his phone started to beep. Saved by the bell, he thought to himself, and looked at the screen.

'Sorry, just normality calling.' He was grateful for the excuse because if he had said what he was really thinking he would blow this out of the water. 'Can I call you, maybe catch up in the week? I want to get everything signed off this week so that we can get moving on some of the plans.'

'Yes, of course,' Lottie replied, not taken aback but now seeing it clearly: business. He was not interested in her: why the hell should he be? He was a rich, very rich, have it my way or the highway, businessman. She was a country bumpkin, who just lately had fixated on any man, maybe in desperation as she had not had anyone for so long. So why would he want anything more than the business deal?

He wanted to kiss her: get back out of the car, drag her back into the house, and kiss every pale, unblemished inch of her skin. Unless he had glue on his trousers, if she waved at him from the door for a moment longer he would have to do it. He looked at the drive in front of him and revved the car engine and as fast as he could he pulled away. His therapy session was in four hours, so sod the office, he needed to kick the hell out of something and his personal trainer was always a good bet. He made the call on the hands-free while driving, then called Zoe's desk to leave a message to say he would not be in until way after lunch so to cancel everything. Then he would be going out again, shortly after.

He had six missed calls from Alex, so he knew he would have to catch up with him today, but not this early; he would never be out of bed at this time, he may be up, but he would sure not be out of bed, even if he was in his bed at all!

Chapter 9

Todd had been over to the house on the Wednesday as arranged. They had time to go over more notes that he had brought for her and chatted about the case. Lottie had spent some time looking through it and was sure that he needed to look at more leads. They chatted about how it would work, with her working this remotely for the DuPont Centre, and was reassured that the Professor was happy that this continued. Even though she was worried about data protection, Todd had reassured her that all of the emails and electronic communications had been secured. They had agreed that names of people that she was looking into would not be added so they were less traceable, but it would be easy for her to find out if required as the DNA database was often a good place to start.

Agnes was overjoyed to see them as they walked in the pub for an afternoon drink. She had flirted in her usual manner with Todd, who took the compliments she gave. They chatted about their time at uni, although Agnes knew the details; they never lingered on their relationship. She was also under strict instructions to keep the charity business to herself. Lottie did not want anyone knowing her business yet until it had taken off.

With this on her mind she had communicated several times with 'Simkins'. Edward had emailed but had been called back to France for a few days from the business the week before. As they were going to keep this business relationship, Lottie resisted the urge to call him, although she had to hold herself back at times as she just wanted to hear his voice.

'You had a therapy session, man?' Alex exclaimed as he was speaking to Ed on the phone. 'Save yourself the bother and spend the £400 per hour on a nice French tart. That advice was for free, mate!'

Edward had phoned Alex on the Tuesday as he had landed in Paris. He had spared him the details of why he had booked the session the day before as he did not want his advice on what he was feeling for one woman he had met briefly and not even shagged yet!

The Harley Street doctor had been someone that Edward had visited in his past, finding it a welcome release after Mitch died, in particular.

'Mr Dean' – although they had known each other years the formal greeting was always used until the end of the meeting - 'your feelings are normal. I know from your past that you say you are different but your sexual preference is not as deviant to others as you think. We all have our thing. Although yours is more physical than some may prefer, you never impose this on others, so there is no harm. But I do have to say from what you have told me that these new feelings are not normal to you, but are very normal! Caring for another individual in life is a very special feeling, and, although you loved your sibling, and you do your mother, these new feelings are different. If you let them in, embrace them, let them grow, don't be afraid of them. You rely on control, always having your way: that is part of your problem. Being dominant in every way in business is what has made you who you are, for whatever reasons. Being dominant in a relationship can be overprotective and overbearing.'

'And dominant in the playroom?' Ed interjected.

'Is your way, Mr Dean: not wrong if both parties are willing and consenting adults. As long as you know your limits and never harm another by your play, your private life, is well, that: private.' Dr Morgan had tried to ease his mind. One reason that Ed had started to use him was several years ago they had been introduced at a club in town. He was also a dominant, professional man, although he had been in the club with his wife at the time, and they still had a happy relationship with grown children, so Edward knew that it could work.

As he sat in his hotel room on the Wednesday evening he had the doctor's words in his head as he was resisting the need to phone Lottie. 'Overprotective and overbearing'. But was it? Was it because he wanted to hear her voice because of his 'new feelings', or the fact that he knew she had been in the company of another man all day, someone who he knew had been very close? Damn it, that makes me mad, he thought. He has had her in a way that I can only dream of! He got up and called reception for a cab. Alex was right: he needed to get out.

The strip bar was not full. It was quite dark and music played in the background. Several ladies in various stages of undress were dancing, walking around and serving drinks. He had not been to this one before so he was treated with no more courtesy than the next man in there. It was not long before the young brunette had his attention. He had slipped money in her tiny G-string as she danced and moved around in front of him with nothing else on. She touched him, sat on his lap, rubbed his body, and preened his hair. She sat at his feet and caressed his legs, his thighs, but to no avail. He could not do it. He was slightly aroused but could not remove the feeling in his gut that it was wrong. He swilled down the rest of the liquor he had in the glass in front of him and thrust more money in her hand.

'Merci monsieur,' she said as he got up and walked off. The night was cool, but refreshing to his skin. He had to think about this, it was off-plan. If he made his move would she feel the same? If not, rejection was something he handled badly. If she did reciprocate to him would she accept that he could be a normal lover, but at times he wanted and needed more? Would she then run a mile once he was totally hooked on her? More than he was now, which he found hard to believe. Could he stop the possessive nature he had and the dominance of her being his exclusively, in everything. The one thing he knew for sure was that he could not let her go without trying.

He sat on a seat outside a café and ordered a coffee with a whiskey chaser. He looked at his phone: only a few messages, none from Lottie.

He read a reply from Pete to one that he had sent out earlier. The little annoying git Mr Hawkins had sent him a death threat, something to do with his father disowning him for sending the business down. The deal that had fallen through with Dean Holdings was the direct result of his now misfortune. Oh well, Edward had thought and continued to admire the night and the bustle of the city. His mind as always wandered back to Lottie.

'Miss Jenkins?' the female voice on the end of the phone enquired. 'Zoe March from Dean Incorporated. I have been asked by Mr Dean to invite you to a meeting on Friday this week as a final appraisal for your business deal, and I ask if you are available?' She hoped that she said yes, she had spent all morning carrying out the instruction of her boss, booking rooms and tables for dinner, ensuring that everything would go well for her stay and that nothing was left to chance, apart from she could say, 'No I'm busy,' and she really hoped this would not be the case.

'Oh hi,' Lottie replied. She hoped that Edward would phone himself, but guessed that was not the sort of thing he would do. 'Yes, but I will not be able to make it until after 5pm. I'm sorry, I have a few things I need to do for a friend first.' Todd had asked her to send over the files but she thought it would be a good time for her to go to the centre herself and present the evidence that she had found in person. This way she could make best use of her time.

'No problem, the driver will collect you and drop you off at your required destination. If you are OK for your personal items to be sent to the hotel then you can arrive as you need to. Mr Dean will be in the office until after 5pm, so I will ensure that he is free when you arrive.' Zoe continued to give her a number of a hired private taxi that could be used for the journeys in between; although Lottie had said this was too much, Zoe had been able to persuade her. It was one way that Ed could keep tabs on her whereabouts. There was no surprise that the usual room had been booked for her, and the reception clerk explained that it was free for the Friday, Saturday and Sunday evening if she wished to use it. Another way of him knowing where she would be.

'Just as another request, Mr Dean has arranged a charity event in Harrogate for the following Thursday evening, and has asked if you could attend. It will be an overnight stay, but he would not collect you until an hour or so before. He will be arriving by helicopter and could arrange for you to be picked up on the way. Is this something we could arrange now?' Zoe was so matter-of-fact as if this was normal everyday conversation.

Lottie was taken aback by the statement, and then realised that's what rich people do! So she continued to go through details with Zoe and marked the dates in her diary.

Putting down the phone she then thought about what to wear. 'Another trip to Bella, I think. I wonder if I can arrange to meet her so that she is not busy,' she said out loud to herself although no one else was in the house with her at the time. She called Agnes and explained, and as always Agnes produced a phone number for the store to be put in touch with your personal shopper. 'Check you out, "personal shopper": all I can see is that the money will run out soon enough, young lady. Just to let you know the car place have found you a car and you can collect next week sometime.' Agnes finished her lecture about what if this does not go through and she had spent the money?

'Well, then, you will have kittens if I said I am going to look at a flat while I am down there. The work with Todd and working for the charity, I can see that I will need to be closer, and I am sure I can find something that will not break the bank, another property to rent out if I don't need it,' Lottie said quickly as a saving grace.

They debated this for some time, and she explained that her agent had found a few that could work: nothing plush or in the heart of the city but close enough to commute in.

Life was going well, but she was really not sure how she could continue the façade with Edward: if only he could feel the same for her as she knew she was feeling for him. Maybe it was just not to be. It was the thought that sent her to sleep and woke her up until Friday arrived.

It was not Pete who had collected her, but he was a nice enough guy. Steve looked very similar, same age, same no neck and huge shoulders, and she guessed same ex-profession, Army.

Todd had waited for her and she was soon in the centre going over her findings. She had an appointment booked with Bella for 2:30pm and was really aware that the time in the labs was passing her by, but she was sure that the new information would help them get to the bottom of this cold case.

As arranged, she arrived at Harrods and was greeted by Bella. A gentleman dressed in the store livery winked at Bella as she walked through the door that was being held open for them, and Lottie laughed. 'An admirer?' she asked.

'Oh, I jolly well hope so, he's my wonderful husband. We met here when I first started, oh over a hundred years ago!' They both laughed and she continued to tell the story of how they met and courted before getting married and having three beautiful children. Although sadly as the story continued with the hurried trying on of clothes, Lottie soon found out that she had lost a son in Ireland when he was in the Army. Not during any fighting, but in an accident on the base. She could not help but think of the farm and that how she hoped one day to be able to help families like Bella and her husband.

As the time pressed on, Lottie was sure that she would not make it to the city for her 5pm appointment, but in true Bella style she suggested that she wear one of the new suits and go straight from there. With help in the staff toilets Lottie quickly washed her face and freshened up and put on the new, dark blue, two-piece suit, a pale blue silk blouse underneath, and some low court shoes finished the outfit.

More that she could carry, the dress bags had three dresses for next weekend, and a few other items that made up three more casual but smart outfits. Lottie had gone for one of the dresses she had tried on the week before, and also indulged in some more underwear; these were a bit more daring, black lace and very see-through. She had resisted the glass of bubbles this time, wanting to keep a clear head, and as the car pulled away with her, and another had been ordered to take the items to the hotel, Lottie felt the real rush of meeting Edward again. She had a sick feeling in her stomach, as if butterflies. The city was busy, and the cab made its way through. City folk were rushing about their business and they pulled up outside a large, glass-fronted building. From the ground it was stark, as if everyone had gone home. Only the lone reception guy and the security guard on the front door made it look as if the building was used at all.

She pressed the buzzer and the door opened. She enquired at the desk and was let through the door to the back of the hallway. She could see no other people, but oddly the glass front of what looked like a gym. 'Maybe a shared building,' she thought. She pressed the top-floor button and wished that she had taken that drink now: she was so very nervous coming to see the king in his castle, she thought as the door opened and she was greeted by the beaming face at reception.

'Miss Jenkins, we have been expecting you.' She looked over and Pete was sitting at the table by the large glass window that showed the view of the city streets below.

'Hi, Pete,' Lottie managed to say.

'Afternoon, Miss, everything OK?' he asked, but he knew it was: the driver had been in constant contact since dropping her off at the DuPont and then getting her here now. 'I gather you had a good weekend, very gallant of you to let Mr Dean win the race!' he said, smiling at her.

'Is that his side of the story?' she asked. 'I was ever the lady and we came over the line together, but if it makes him feel better at winning, then I will not take that away from him!' She bit on her lip as she thought how she could scold him for this, or whether the banter would be appropriate.

'You have him weighed up already, then, Miss: he is never happier than when he is winning.' And then to himself he said, Or thinking about being with you.

'He is on the phone, but he has asked that you just go through.' Zoe stood to open the large glass doors for her, and as they opened she said, 'I will get the coffee on and be in shortly.' She walked out and left Lottie standing.

He had his back to her, but she could hear what he was saying; he was looking out of the window and she was not sure if he had heard her come in or not. Should she stand, sit at the desk where there was another leather chair, lie on one of the huge sofas, or cough to let him know she was there?

'Thanks, that is great to hear, I will do it now. See you later.' He put down the phone and spun around in the chair. As if he had a spring or an ejector seat, he was round to her like a flash. He held out his hand. 'Miss Jenkins, welcome to my world.' He gestured with his other hand the large, open-plan office. Lottie could feel his warm hand as he took it and shook it, a little longer than maybe he would any other client. 'Please have a seat.' He pointed to the chair in front of the desk. Formal, thought Lottie.

She looked amazing: he knew where she had been and he made a note to go and see the lady responsible for her look and thank her in person. Her hand had been warm and soft to touch; she was sitting there looking around, taking in all the new surroundings. 'Great view,' he said.

'Sure is,' although she had to say that she had really only looked at his perfectly toned physique, the dark grey trousers and the clean, white shirt and pink tie he had on. The shirt was well fitted and showed every line of his shoulders and arms: she bit her lip unknowingly.

'Now Miss Jenkins, I signed the paperwork today, and the call I just was on was to confirm the payment has been received by your accountants. I just need to sign the receipt and then we are all done.' As if on cue the door opened and Zoe came in with a tray of coffee. She put it down on the desk and spun the paper round so that it was facing him. The Post-it note showed where he needed to sign and, without hesitation, Lottie was 1.25 million pounds better off. 'As easy as that.' He pushed the document over to the desk and said, 'Just one from you and then I think that we need a drink?'

Lottie looked where she needed to sign. 'Oh sorry.' He shot from behind the desk and leaned over her, pointing to the space where her name had already been typed. 'Here, use my pen.'

He could feel the heat from her shoulder, the fresh scent of her. The thin blouse showed a hint of a promise of black lace below, and he had to move away in fear that he would invade her space too much. As Zoe was in the room, this was not the right point at which to take out two weeks of frustration on her.

'Thank you.' She signed her name and continued to bite her lip when doing so as if it aided the concentration 'All very formal,' she said as Zoe took the paperwork and left the room in silence. He looked away from the lip-biting thing: he was going to have to say something again but remembered where that had got him last time. But oh God if there was one thing that turned him on it was the lip-biting thing!

'Yes,' he said, 'do you mind if I lose this, it has been a long day?' He pulled at his tie to release the knot and undid the first button to his shirt. Lottie did not say it out loud but she knew that her inner voice was saying, 'Go for your life, don't just stop at the tie, the shirt, maybe the pants would make you feel more relaxed.' She blushed at the thought and that he did see.

'Miss Jenkins, not undressing me with your eyes, are you?' he asked without a flicker of his face as he took a sip of coffee.

'May have been,' she replied, 'but more wondering why Pete is under the impression that you won the race?' She continued to blush. He laughed. 'I can't let him know that I have met my match now, can I?' he replied. 'Where has all the male pride gone to?' He took another drink of coffee. 'So, can I interest you in a drink and some supper? I wanted to go through the plans for next week. Zoe told me that you are happy to come to Harrogate. Are you happy to fly up? I can't get away from here until late so I thought it best.' He continued to talk to her as an equal, something she liked. As they got in the car he asked, 'Where would you like to go?'

'There is a place called Tap and Tune, not sure if you know it, Pete, I know the address.' She rooted in her bag to find the piece of paper that she thought she had, but could not find anything. 'Well, I thought I had the address!'

'Got it.' Pete held up his handheld device and placed it on the dashboard. Of course he had it, he had been before, but Edward was slightly put back by her choice.

'Have you been before?' Edward asked with his best poker-face, looking at Pete to close the privacy screen as they set off.

'A good friend runs it: it has hit some hard times and I said I would try to pop in if I can, I am sure they have some fine champagne that I can buy you to seal our deal,' Lottie explained, totally unaware of anything that had happened before. Edward was now sweating that she would find out he had followed her, and it really had been all about that first meeting and then the spying that had got them there today.

'Maybe just a drink but I am not sure they serve food.' He looked at her as she settled into the seat and he smiled.

'Sorry, have I spilled coffee or something on me?' she asked, wondering why he was looking at her in such a way.

'No, I am just blown away by you, Lottie. I have never had such a beautiful woman in the car who has offered to buy me a drink, and someone who wants so little, and seems so happy to adapt to anything.' There, he had said it: that was as close as anyone could ever get to laying their heart on their sleeve. 'I don't know how to be around you because you leave me standing. I could see that last week.' He stopped talking as he felt the hole he was getting into was growing deeper by the minute.

She smiled at him: every fibre in her body knew that she wanted him, and statements like that gave her the hope that he wanted her, too. He turned to look at her, concerned that she was not saying anything. The car suddenly jolted and made them both lurch forward in their seats.

'Jesus, Pete!' he shouted through the blacked-out glass. 'You OK?' He looked at Lottie. She was fine: it had brought her back to reality anyway.

'Cyclist, sorry,' Pete replied.

'Fine, although it's good to know my heart is still working.' She put her hand on her chest and he smiled. She was not sure what else to say and they both remained quiet for the rest of the ride. As they arrived he jumped out of the car and Pete had the door open for her. He moved to take her hand and said to Pete, 'Randolph, about 7 please. Table as usual please.' Pete nodded and walked back to the front of the car, reaching for his phone in his hand. As they arrived she could hear the piano playing and Edward opened the door for her. She eagerly looked around to find Scott but could not see him. A young girl asked where they would like to sit and Edward replied, 'At the bar would be good.' As Lottie hopped onto her chair he held the back of it so that it was steady and she thanked him.

Without warning, a pair of arms wrapped around her neck and planted a kiss on the side of her cheek.

'Lotts, how great to see you.' She spun around to see Scott with a beaming smile on his face. 'Does Todd know you are in town? I must phone him: he never said you were coming over.'

'Scotty, I thought we could surprise you.' She looked over at Edward and introduced him. He held out his hand and almost ripped him a new one for being able to get so close to her without warning. 'Mr Dean and I are celebrating a new business deal: a bottle of your best bubbles please.' She smiled and he held onto both of her hands. 'For you, the moon on a stick.' He kissed her again. 'I will be straight back, and I will call Todd to let him know you are here.' He rushed off and Edward was grateful that he was gone.

'I booked a meal: we may not stay too long,' he said, 'but I can change that if you want?' It was a rhetorical question that he did not want her to answer. As he went to carry on speaking her phone rang. 'It's Todd,' she said, answering the call.

By now he would have been on his feet and away. The green monster was well up inside him and he had no idea why. Why should this affect him? Christ, he owned the place after all, but that sort of news would devastate her.

'No, we are not stopping long that's why I did not call,' she explained. 'Yer, that's fine, I will email you, maybe Tuesday. The agent said it will be ready by then.' She ended the call and said, 'Sorry, Scotty had called him quickly but I doubt he would make it over in time, he is still at work.' Ed gave her his best smile, hoping that his blood would calm soon. As the overeager manager came back with a bottle and two glasses, he said:

'He is not as good as you, but it seems to have picked up trade.' He gestured over to the piano that was being played by a young man. 'He is earning a bit of money while in uni, bit like you did, Lotts, with Toddy when you both used to play.'

POP! The bottle went and he poured the glasses out. 'What is it with calling her 'Lotts'? And what makes him the one to know all about her past? Edward thought to himself. The devil in his blood was rising again and how he managed to touch glasses as she said, 'Cheers' to him is something that Dr Douglas would be proud of, although it was not making him feel any better.

They were left alone to continue to talk and Edward felt more at ease, although he caught the young man throwing Lottie a grin or a wink from time to time and he really wanted to get out of the place. I will sell up, that will wipe the smile off his face, Edward had thought, but he had to realise that she had lived before and would continue to do so quite happily without him if he did not tread carefully.

They said their goodbyes and went across town for a meal. Another beautiful place, Lottie thought, although she felt slightly underdressed and had said so to Ed. His usual comment of not worrying what other people thought did ease her mind, but she was aware that they had several stares from other guests. She put it down to this stunning man sitting next to her, who from time to time acknowledged that he knew someone who walked by.

They talked about the next weekend again. The charity had groups all across the country and Edward and his mother, tried to attend as many as possible. Alice, his mother was going to go up there a few days before for a social visit to friends and also to take some time out. Lottie knew the area was a stunning place to visit and commented so.

'If you want to stop over you are welcome. Sadly I need to get back, but I can make the arrangements,' he had said. Lottie had declined. She had a full week planned; she was looking at flats with the agent on Monday, and hoped that when she met up with Todd on Tuesday they would have only two or three on the shortlist to physically visit before making a decision. She was also collecting her car on Thursday. She had recklessly purchased a red sports car, not quite the Porsche she had been in, but a high-end BMW she had seen in a showroom. It had one careful owner and only 4,000 on the clock, and was not yet a year old, so it was a bargain. Something Agnes was pleased with.

When it came to the end of the evening Edward walked her back to the hotel reception. They walked over to the lift and called it down. She stepped in and he hesitated.

'Walk me to the door, it is a bit lonely up there,' Lottie said in all innocence. She really had found staying in the suite a lonely place, although she had been reassured by Pete that it was safe.

'Sure. If you are not happy staying here then I can get one of the porters placed outside in the corridor all night,' he said as he pressed the button and the door closed. Or I could stay with you! he thought to himself.

'That's fine, it's just...' She stopped and placed her hand on his. 'Thank you again for another wonderful night, I really have enjoyed your company. I am not sure I could get used to your lifestyle: I like to be independent so it is taking some getting used to you arranging...' She stopped and waved her hand around to show the plush surroundings of the lobby as they stepped out of the lift. 'But I did want you to know that I appreciate it all.'

He took her hands and kissed them softly. 'You are welcome,' he said, looking at her, still holding her hands close to his chest. Lottie bit down on her lower lip, feeling the closeness between them. The heat and smell of his skin, the slight stubble on his face from a long day, made her tingle between her legs. Her nipples pushed out against the silk blouse, and she knew she was turned on by him, more than maybe she should be. Edward cracked. 'Lottie, I'm sorry, forgive me.' He pulled away and she felt the pain and disappointment of his action like a boulder from a cliff hitting the ground. He took two steps away, not turning his back but putting obvious distance between them.

She sighed and looked at the floor momentarily. So he did not want her that way - well, it was good to know where she stood.

Edward looked at her face: he could not leave her like this. He had to do something. 'Carpe diem', seize the day, he thought to himself.

Within one stride he was in front of her, and with a swift movement he put his hand on the side of her face and placed a kiss onto her lips. He placed his other hand around her waist and gently moved her towards him, drawing her closer.

She closed her eyes as the soft sensation of his mouth met hers, slowly parting her lips as she could feel the kiss deepen to accept the gesture. She relaxed into him and kissed him back, moving her arms to his sides, taking him into her space.

He slowly licked at her lower lip, resisting the urge to bite into it. As if they did not need to breathe, the kiss continued and increased with urgency. Lottie could feel his body next to her; she felt the heat rising in her own loins, taking her to the same urgent place he was, wanting more.

He was hard, pushing against her to let her know how much he wanted this intimate contact. He moved his hand from her face round to the nape of her neck, moving her head so that the kiss could become more controlled. He broke the contact and moved his mouth to the outline of her ear. 'I want you to be mine, Lottie,' he slowly whispered in between the small nips and licks of her earlobe. She gasped as the wind in her lungs was thrust up by the desire in her stomach, and she moved her head further to the side to allow his attention to carry on down her long, slender, exposed neck.

She tasted good, soft, sweet. He could feel the pulse in her neck racing away and she gave a short gasp as he moved his hand below her waist and caressed her backside. She rubbed her hands up and down his lower back and he brought his attention back to her mouth. With short gasps of breath, he licked her lip again. 'This little place here.' He gave it a short nip which sent an electric shock up her spine. 'This bit has been driving me insane since I first saw you.' He nipped it again. 'I have longed to taste it, bite it for myself.'

She was breathing out of control and was worried that at any point her legs would give way. She felt his arms taking the weight of her body, and without noticing he had moved her up against the wall: it gave her more support but also thrust his body closer to hers.

He felt her nipples hard as bullets beneath her top that had slightly parted to allow the soft silk to brush against his shirt. She moved her hand down his waist, towards the top of his thigh and pulled him, rubbing her hip bone into the print of his trousers that were straining under the pressure of his dick. He gasped at the sensation; the restriction his trousers held was unbearable.

As if time stood still, this went on for what may have been seconds, but felt like a lifetime to them both. The sexual energy that was created by this action was so high that it was impossible to see how this could end in any other way.

He stopped kissing her and looked at her. She had her eyes closed with her head against the wall. 'Lottie, tell me what you want me to do, tell me that you want this, too.'

She opened her eyes and he once again placed his hand on her face to hold her gaze. 'I need to possess you; I need to know that I have you. I am going out of my mind. For the first time I have no control and I am out of my depth with the way you make me feel.' He held her gaze and Lottie felt that she could see into his soul, a place that not many people had been, she guessed.

'I...' She faltered still breathless. 'I have been feeling this, too, but I am not sure that you need to possess me, I am here if you want me, although whatever this turns out to be I hope that we can remain in the same relationship with the charity and the deal that we just struck. This all remains the same for me on the business side, personal feelings aside,' she said. 'I am out of practice with sharing my life, and would not give up my independence, but I am willing to try if we take it slow.' He had moved slightly away from her now and his hand had dropped to her waist, but he remained in physical contact with her. Edward took the time to think about his reply, how easy would it be to pick her up and take her now as he wanted. He was an all-or-nothing kind of guy.

'I want to be your equal, not the girl on your arm,' she continued, aware that he was not saying much. 'Please say something.'

'It's hard for me, Lottie, I have fought this for days. Tonight, I was as jealous as hell with your friend touching you, knowing that I had not been able to. I'm not sure how I would cope knowing you are mine, and knowing that he can still...' He stopped.

'I get you are possessive, protective, but that alone will be the fact that this will not work, not the fact that I don't have feelings for you, because I do. If you remember that, then we stand a chance.' He took her hands and kissed them.

'You amaze me, and I am hearing what you are saying. I am not sure that I am the waiting type, but I sure as hell know I want you, and so wait I will try. You may have to remind me of this at times, and I will let you know there are things that you will hate about me.' He stopped, still holding her hands. He kissed her mouth again, quickly. 'Help me become a better person,' he said, looking into her eyes where he could see small tears forming. 'Never knowingly would I hurt you: that is my promise to you, Miss Jenkins, that final part of my business deal.' He smiled that childlike grin that really did something to you, like a naughty boy that you just could not tell off for stealing sweets. 'I need to go. I guess it is Pete texting me because my phone is going nuts.' He tapped his trouser pocket. 'And I am not sure that I will be able to keep the other issue in my trousers away for too much longer if I don't!' She giggled as if it was she that should be embarrassed. 'And you said take it slow so that is my first show of control, however.' He raised his eyebrows in a suggestive way.

Lottie playfully nudged his arm with her elbow. 'Mr Dean, I don't know what you mean!'

'Spend the day with me tomorrow. We can do anything, go anywhere, you choose. Pete can drive, we can take the helicopter somewhere further away, or we can be alone, if you trust me!' he added, again lifting his eyebrows.

'I need to be back for 7pm. Agnes is doing supper for a few friends, but apart from that we could...' She never finished her sentence. He had kissed her, more strongly this time, with more commitment that he now knew she wanted it, too.

'I will come across for 8:30am and we can have breakfast and you can tell me your plans. I will get you home in time wherever we decide to go,' he said, not wanting to let her go, but the lift door opening and Pete arriving around the corner made them both move apart.

Edward closed the car door. 'No worries,' he said in reply to Pete apologising again for interrupting them. 'I should have replied to you. I would worry if you had not have been concerned, given what happened up there last time!' The car pulled away and he headed home.

Chapter 10

Well, Lottie thought, I should have expected that. No need for me to make plans of where I wanted to go: I should have known that they would already be sorted! Control freak!

She was sitting nervously in the helicopter on the private runway at City Airport awaiting Edward to jump in by her side. He was giving final instructions to Pete who was, as always, listening intently to ensure that he carried out his orders. A short trip, he had said: well, it's not every day you go to the champagne vineyard for lunch and home again, she had retorted to herself. The smile on her face must have been huge, as Edward jumped in and tapped the pilot on his shoulder. He put on his earphones and Lottie could hear him breathing, as well as the instruction to the pilot through the set she had already put on herself.

'OK, Miss Jenkins?' Edward turned to her. 'First time?' he asked and she nervously nodded her head. He reached over and found her hand on her lap and held it, squeezing it tight. 'It won't take too long, the weather is good today. You should get some great views, only an hour or so: this baby can move!' he exclaimed as they took off.

Another boy's toy, she thought, but he was right: the city below them faded into green fields, that soon were replaced by the coastline, the pale and dark blue colours of the sea.

The pilot made various comments about their location, but mostly Lottie looked out of the window, or replied to the odd question Edward had asked. Edward took out his phone and sent a text or email. Slightly embarrassed to say, Lottie asked if that was wise. 'Does it not interfere with the controls or the electrics or something?' she asked.

He laughed. 'Would I do it if I knew it would put you in danger?' was his reply, in quite a serious tone. It was the only answer she was getting to explain his actions.

The sun was warm, and the boots and jeans Lottie had chosen for her day would have been OK, if they had gone for a walk somewhere like she had planned! They had been dropped off outside a large French farm building. When they had flown over the rows and rows of vines below they had looked fantastic, all in perfect rows. Edward had explained that he would meet Philippe, the grower and manager of the vinery.

'You own this!?' she had exclaimed before they got out of the helicopter and Edward was explaining the reasons for them being there.

'E.D. Incorporated does, so yes, I would say that I do,' he replied. The story of how he got it would not be information that he passed to her. Master Cherylle had been on his hit list from school: when he heard that the company was in trouble after a few bad years of rain and fruit harvest he took the pleasure in ensuring that the 2,000-acre site and the properties and business came his way. It did not make much profit, if anything really, but it gave him a place to visit, kept local people employed, and it seemed to give him one more enemy in the world who had to live with the fact that for three years in the past he had caused Edward hell, and now it was payback.

After time to go to the loo they had a whistle-stop tour of the site. Impressed by the conversation Edward was having in fluent French, she tried to keep up in her broken understanding of the language but to no avail. Although they had kissed when he first arrived and the occasional hand-holding, the only way that anyone would know that there was sexual chemistry was in the way that he looked her. She was OK with this; public displays of affection could come with time, and after all, she had been the one to say that things need to be taken slow.

They had lunch in a little café not far from the vineyard, and it was a surprise to Lottie that Edward did not own that as well. She had almost taken him seriously when he said, why, did she like it and want him to? Then she realised he was not joking. Was she really going to be able to keep this lifestyle up? Was it really so easy for him to do that? What if all of this started to lose who she was? The question played on her mind over the rest of the day. Not showing it, she continued to enjoy the food accompanied by the great champagne.

Forward planning, Edward had arranged for all Lottie's things from the hotel to be taken to her house by Pete, and the helicopter had arranged to drop them off almost on her doorstep. The pilot had joked about landing in the garden, but they were able to get the permission of the farmer who had a field next door that was clear of stock.

Lottie had battled with her eyes several times on the way back. Edward had moved closer to her and she rested her head on his shoulder. She still had questions, as anyone in a new relationship would, and she was sure that she would find the right occasion to bring them up.

They arrived back in the house and Edward called to see where Pete was. He had been delayed in bad traffic and was trying to get there, but was almost an hour late. Lottie put the kettle on and offered him a coffee; as she arranged the mugs on the worktop he stood behind her and started to kiss her neck. She closed her eyes and put her head onto his shoulder. He enclosed his arms around, pulling her towards him holding her hips, and rubbing his hands along her stomach. The top she had on was not tucked in and he ran his hands up to reach the bare flesh beneath. He moved his hands up and rubbed the lace of her bra, brushing her nipple that responded by becoming erect.

He felt the desire stir in his dick and continued to kiss her, using his strong arms to turn her around to face him. Their lips met with a fury of passion and she pushed her hips into him. She could feel his erection straining to release. He pulled her top over her head to reveal the white lace bra, he admired the plump, firm breasts, both of which were showing her pleasure with hard nipples. He rubbed one again, causing Lottie to moan.

'Tell me, Lottie, that you want me,' he whispered in her ear. 'I need you, tell me you need me, too,' he said, still working the nipple between his thumb and finger.

'Yes,' she said, pushing her head back once more as if to present her body to him in acceptance. She rubbed her hand down the front of his body and allowed her fingers to trail over the large bulge in his trousers. He flared his nostrils as the passion pulsed harder in his thick member.

Not wanting this first time to be anything less than perfect, he picked her up off her feet and walked her to the bottom of the stairs. She placed gentle kisses on his head, pushing the hair away from his face. Their words were silent but the actions were speaking for both of them. As he took the stairs without effort, with her in his arms, she could feel the strength in his body to perform the task. Her bedroom door was open and he pushed them through, standing her by the side of the bed.

He pulled at his jumper: as it went over his head Lottie was faced with his lean torso, defined with every muscle line that lay below. She unbuttoned his trousers and he stopped her by holding her hand. He kissed her, allowing his tongue to slip between her lips. She accepted his tongue and grazed her teeth over it. The electric bolt that went through him sent a shudder through his body that Lottie felt. He increased his kiss, unclipping her bra, and as soon as the prize was revealed he took his head to the pale flesh and slowly blew air across the plump mound.

She again attempted to undo his trousers, and this time he allowed her to. She undid her own jeans and with his help pushed them to the floor.

Gently he lowered them down to the bed. The power in his upper body allowed the movement to be performed only using one arm the other hand never left the attention of her breast.

He ran his hands down her flat stomach and outlined the white lace bikini bottoms. Lottie could feel his hard erection against her leg, and her eyes wandered down as he quickly removed his boxers. She gasped at the sight. She had not had a man for months and she was shatteringly aware that he was big, and this was going to hurt. She could not resist the urge to touch it. She wrapped her hand around the shaft and slowly moved it up and down. The animalistic noise that he made came through his teeth and he bit the nipple that he had in his mouth at the time. It was like a hot rod directly to her sex, and she felt the pit of her stomach turn, with the internal muscles tensing and releasing.

'Tell me, Lottie, tell me you want me,' he said again as he moved on top of her, parting her legs without effort. He leaned on his elbows so he was close to her face. Although she still had her panties on he had pushed them to the side and she could feel the head of his cock rubbing on the outer part of her sex. 'I need to know you want this,' he said again in between the gentle kisses he placed on her neck and face.

'Please,' she said in desperation. She was not sure how long she could go with this before she would climax. She could feel the small discharge of pre-cum from him on her. She moved her hips to allow him to be a little further inside her. Gently, as he was aware that this could be painful, he eased his hips down, holding her arse slightly to allow a better angle to enter her. He started to push, gently. Lottie could feel her body trying to accommodate him. He pushed and breached her inner wall. She gasped. 'Sorry,' he said, slightly withdrawing. 'Please don't stop,' she continued, pulling him closer with her hands on his backside. He readjusted her hips and pushed again. God, she was tight, and warm, and he knew that he would not hold on much longer. Bending his head down, he drew his attention to her nipples again, thrusting slighter deeper with each nip and lick until he was able to withdraw and push due to the wetness of her desire.

His rhythm started to speed up. Lottie lifted her hips to meet his rhythm and soon she was taking him all in, feeling his balls hit her as he thrust in and out. His breathing was quick and a small bead of sweat rolled from his temple to his cheek. Lottie noticed it and used her stomach muscle to reach up and kiss it off. The movement of her body made him push her G-spot and he felt her inner muscles tighten as a response. How he did not explode into her then he was not sure. He looked at her chest and the warm, red glow was starting to rise from her breast to her neckline and he could tell that she was close. 'Do you want me?' he said. 'Do you want this?' and he thrust hard into her. 'Oh God, yes, yes. Ed, please make me come, I need to come, please!' she shouted. He powered into her and felt her body start to shudder. She had her eyes closed, and the sight below him was of pure desire, lust and passion. He felt the first spasm of her tighten around his cock and he knew that, within a second, she would be consumed. 'Aarww!' she shouted out as the second wave hit her. He was done, it was useless, although he had used all his powers to let this be her moment. He bit down on his lip and pushed his head back.

She felt him as he released into her, the first pump, and the second. Her climax continued, but with each thrust of the stem of his dick on her sweet spot, it came back again. This time uncontrollably and she dug her nails into his back. 'Lottie!' he shouted. 'Jesus baby girl, I've got you!' His last few thrusts had been quick, hugging her as close as he could. Then one final stroke had released him into her completely: he was spent. His heart was racing, his breathing laboured; he flicked the loose hair that ran across Lottie's face out of her eyes and she opened them. She smiled and bit down on her lip. He gritted his teeth and, although he did not know how, his dick responded to this small action that from day one had driven him insane.

'I have warned you about that lip-biting thing,' and he thrust into her again. She could feel that he was becoming hard again. He kissed her lip and she released it from her teeth. 'I warned you last time what would happen if you kept doing it!' he said, smiling. 'But I have to go,' he said, rolling to his side but keeping her in his arms. He pulled the sheet over them and embraced her. He could feel her beating heart; she, too, was still out of breath. It was usual at this point for him to get up and leave, but he could not, did not want to. 'You OK?' he asked. She had not spoken a word to him and he was worried that he had hurt her, or she was regretting what had just happened.

'Yes,' she said, smiling back up at him, and he placed a kiss on her nose. 'Well, Mr Dean, I am not sure where that came from but I can safely say that is one hell of a way to end a perfect day!' He rolled onto his back and pulled her onto his chest.

'Miss Jenkins, the pleasure, I would like to say, was all mine, but I am hoping that some of it was yours, too!' She leaned up on her arm so that she could see his face. 'I can confirm, Mr Dean, that satisfaction was reached with our conjoining. I could be tempted again, at a later date, you understand, as you have to go now, to do it again.' They were both aware that Pete had arrived sometime ago, although the car engine was now turned off and the lights did not light up the drive. 'To resume our business another time in the near future,' she continued as she was drawing a line along his chest, following the line of his pectoral muscles, and down to his perfect six-pack, then along the line of muscle stretched over his hips towards his dick. He quickly turned and pinned her arm to the bed above her head, towering over her with all his weight. 'You may get your wish sooner than you think, Miss Jenkins, if you continue to run your nails over my skin like that.' He took her other hand and in a vice-like grip held them above her head. He could see that she was not happy so he let go of her hands, but she kept them there. He stretched back on top of her and she could feel that he was fully erect again. 'But you must learn restraint!' he said, dipping his head to kiss her exposed nipples one at a time. 'You have me at your disposal anytime, but the art of waiting, well...' He again licked down her stomach towards her belly button. He had her pinned down with his legs; she did not try to squirm, nor protest, but seemed to be frozen still for a second. 'Waiting is something that we all have to do from time to time.' She managed to buck him and he moved without effort. This allowed her to push, and he gave way to her letting her lean over him in a similar way. She straddled him, feeling better that she had more freedom and movement; she stopped the panic that she had felt building inside her. She placed her hands each side of his head.

'Mr Dean.' She began trying to position his cock between her legs, happy that she had more control of the situation and so that he was close to entering her. She was wet, not just from his release, but from her own wetness of the sex they had just had. 'I don't think you have ever had to wait for anything in your adult life.'

He shot up, pinning her hands to her side and he held her in place with his cock that he had thrust into her. 'You are right, Miss Jenkins, I can be impulsive.' He thrust and she gasped. 'I do get want I want.' He thrust again. 'But I can hold on for the right deal and strike at the right moment.' He tightened his grip on her hands and pushed into her with all his force. Lottie shot her eyes open, the pain of the size of him and the position they were in first startled her and she wanted to get off: it hurt. But he released his grip and held her backside to take some of the weight. The pain turned to a pleasurable feel in her stomach and her sex was responding to the strokes he was now making into her. 'But I can see with you that I am going to need to use all my powers of negotiation.' He kissed her stomach as she bounced up and down on him with her head back. He drew a hand down her shoulder, along her chest, brushing her nipple as he passed, and she gasped. He stopped her moving and she opened her eyes. 'You said we take it slow: who is breaking the rules now?' he asked.

'If I beg?' she asked as she was unbelievably aware that she had a need for her own climax again. Oh yes, baby I am going to make you beg, but not today, he thought to himself. He smiled.

'I have to go.' He kissed her one last time on her stomach. She put her head on his shoulder and sighed.

'How could you leave me like this?' she said with a sad face and wicked smile.

'I am asking myself that very question, but I have to, to get back to the city. Pete is outside and...' She stopped him with a kiss on the mouth. She placed her finger over his lips.

'I know,' she whispered. They kissed one last time, and it was with real regret that he moved to leave her in bed. He had never had any issue with walking away before, but the act that had just taken place had just sealed it. Any bond he had with her from before was now even stronger. He went into the en suite to freshen up and texted Pete while he was there to say he was on his way. When he went back in the room, Lottie had spread out over the bed on her stomach, the sheets lying to just cover her backside, and he looked at the tattoo. He knelt on the bed after he had put on his boxers and trousers.

'I never got to kiss this,' he said, planting a kiss in the red rose, 'or to know its story of how it managed to grace such a wonderful place.' He kissed it again and Lottie dug her hips into the mattress. 'So, Miss Jenkins, can we do this again sometime?' he asked as she rolled over and sat up, the covers totally revealing her naked breasts. He pulled her close, just so that he did not have to look at them: he was getting hard again.

'I guess so, Mr Dean,' she replied.

Pete dutifully stood by the car as Edward said his goodbyes. They had already arranged to meet for the next weekend, and, although asked if she could be in London anytime during the week, she had declined as she really wanted to do her own thing as she had arranged. She could tell that this did not sit well with him, but as he had, said he would just have to get on with it and wait till the weekend. Lottie had the idea that she would surprise him, though, if it all went well at the flat hunting, something she had not let on either.

Knocking on the door on a Monday morning was not something the post lady did, but due to the largest bouquet of flowers and case of champagne she had to deliver, she thought that she had best not just leave it on the doorstep without alerting the occupant that a parcel had arrived.

Miss Jenkins, Baby girl, my weekend was a dream, enjoy (but not too much without me!)

Mr Dean CEO ED Holdings

Lottie smiled and sent a 'thank you' text back. Only seconds later, as if he had been guarding his phone awaiting the correspondence, he replied with a *'You are welcome'*. She continued with her day.

Todd met her from the train.

'So, you thought better of bringing the new car?' he asked as he kissed her cheek.

'Yer, I need a bit more driving to get used to it.' She had made the trip down as arranged on the Tuesday to look at three flats. They had planned to see four, but were too late as one had been taken off the market, although the agent had said for a higher price they could outbid if they wished. They were all within Camden, and as the weather was good they walked from one to the other.

They had both laughed when the agent met them, and during the introduction had welcomed Mr and Mrs Carter. Lottie had explained that they were not married and he had apologised for being presumptuous. Although Todd had tried to persuade her that his sister's annex was still free, Lottie really did not want to stay there full-time: tonight as arranged would be fine but she wanted her own space. Two of the flats were a 'no' as soon as she saw the area, but she fell in love with an old converted house that was shared by two other tenants, with the top floor made into an apartment. Two bedrooms, nothing on a grand scale, but they had put on a roof deck that gave her some outside space, and there was a garage at the back that you could get to by going under the archway two houses down that made it very private. She loved it and the deal was done there and then. Affordable, she could walk to most places and catch the tube to the centre of the city, or the DuPont Centre, or better still to Edward's office. She would head there in the morning and surprise him.

She had not mentioned a word of Edward or the past two weekends she had had with him to Todd. Somehow, she did not feel the need, although she still could feel the soreness between her legs for the epic session she had had at the weekend. She had not noticed until she woke the next day and, although he had not been rough in any way, her body was telling her it had been a long time since she had experienced anything like that.

'Well, now that's over, can we go for a drink?' Todd asked. 'Scotty is not working, but Suzie and Bob are about. I thought we could go to the Tap and Tune, you know, to show willing.'

'I'm starving: can we get something to eat first?' she asked. 'Suzie's got a curry on, she said we were welcome. I can give her a call?' Lottie nodded and with that they made their way through the streets to her house. They had the meal that they had been promised with a glass of wine, and the day was going really well. Lottie had missed the phone calls displayed on her phone. She had put it onto silent and had forgotten to turn it back on when they were in the first flat, so it continued to ring with the owner unaware.

'Right, take me to her! She is not answering any of her fucking calls.' Edward dialled the number again and it rang out. 'What the hell is she playing at anyway? She said that she was not coming into town, and with him.' Pete had ducked once from the pad of paper that had come across the room when he said that Lottie had come to town over an hour ago. Now he had to tell him that his man had lost her, and it would not go down too well.

'Fuck it, Pete, what do I pay you for?' he had shouted, again pressing the speed-dial on the phone. Pete would give an opinion to his employer if he thought it would help but, on this occasion he was holding his thoughts back. In their time together, even when Mitch had died, he had never seen him react this way. Zoe walked into the room.

'Mr Dean, Dr Morgan on line one.' She held her stare at him. For whatever, fury, temper, poor business deal, he had the respect and the manners and would never shout at her. He looked at her and rubbed his face with his hands. He took a deep sigh and sat in the chair. 'Yes,' Edward said as he picked up the phone. It was all he said, but Pete could see by the conversation that he was slightly relaxing. Zoe had some balls ringing him without asking, but then he thought, like him, she knew her boss inside out, but this time would it work?

It was a one-way conversation, the doctor talking and the patient listening. If it worked or not he put the phone down after just saying, 'Thanks.'

He then picked up his landline and called Alex. After the usual abuse for not returning his calls, Alex agreed to meet for a night out, as long as it was out of the Dean wallet. As he dropped him off at the club, Pete almost thought this was a good idea, but if Edward continued in this mood, it could go wrong for someone. And within three hours it had!

Pete had been sitting in the car, keeping tabs on the text of where Lottie was when the buzzer went on his personal alarm that Edward had on a key chain in his pocket. Without hesitation he was out of the car, round the back of the building and in through the kitchen doors.

Locating the fracas was not hard, as there were raised voices and club staff running around. Edward was mid-punch when Pete caught his hand, immediately ducking, knowing that the assailant would be looking to chastise the person stopping him. Alex was making some attempt to get him off the person on the floor, but looking at his face, he could see the result of Edward's current mood. With another scuffle Pete had him in control. Sirens wailed and the club bouncer had informed them that the police had been called. Pete knew that this could be avoided and went out the same way as he came, dragging the figure behind him. It took all his strength, but the fact that his employer was drunk made it easier to disorientate him. The barrage of abusive language was aimed at Pete and anyone who got in his way. Like a whimpering puppy Alex was following up behind.

Pete flung the car door open and deposited the struggling body in the back, not worried that the blood from his face would go on the seats, just wanting to leave the area as soon as possible.

'Get in, you dick!' he said to Alex. The two men had never seen eye-to-eye in the whole time Pete had worked for Mr Dean, but tolerated him. God knows why, because this was the usual thing Alex got Edward into. He always suspected that Alex was in some way jealous of him. Whatever Edward had he would try to take, or use, or steal, especially when it came to women.

He locked the doors and pulled down the privacy screen.

'What happened?' Edward just sat there not answering. 'I said,' looking in the rear-view mirror, 'what happened?'

'The twat, called me out,' Edward said in a slurred reply. 'Said I was a loser,' he muttered again.

'Alex, plain English please,' Pete asked.

'I never really saw it start,' he replied, in no way as drunk as his friend. 'Ed was on a mission to get pissed.' He paused as Pete said, 'Worked, then!' Alex continued. 'Some loser spoke to Ed about his brother, said how he had been a druggie loser, taking his life by driving off the road or something and he just exploded. He just launched at him over the table.' He paused. 'I tried to stop him,' he said, rubbing the side of his face.

'Yer right!' Edward interjected. 'You pussy, he didn't even punch you hard.'

Pete took Alex home and started to make some calls. Edward was asleep by now in his own drunken world, but Pete knew the knock-on effect. He called the lawyers who were not best pleased at being dragged out of bed, although the call to Mrs Dean was even less appealing to him.

'Peter, thank you,' his mother said as they got back down from leaving him on one of the spare beds in his house. 'You don't have to stop, but the other room is made up if you do.' Pete did not want him to go home, so thought that his mother would be the best person to look after him.

'Mrs Dean, I will stop, thank you, although he will have the blackest face tomorrow, and let's hope a bag of regret. I want to be here for that!' he finished.

'Want to tell me what is going on?' she said, offering a glass of whiskey to the bodyguard, who refused. 'Not sure it's my place.'

'It has to be a woman, it always is with the boys.' She still referred to her 'boys', although it was just Edward now. Pete started to explain about how it had been a reaction to something said about his brother, but he did talk about how close Lottie and he had become, and how it had panned out over the last few weeks and how that had started the drinking as he could not get hold of her. He did omit, however, that Edward had been sent a death threat last week, something that he thought he had been able to solve.

If Edward had been in the land of the living instead of the drunken sleep that he was, he would have seen his phone ringing.

Lottie had not checked it until she left Suzie's house to call Agnes, then realised that all the missed calls (all eleven of them) had been from him and now he was not picking up. She did not know the number for the office, although she was sure that if she just dropped in he would be OK, although she was worried with the number of calls that he wanted her urgently.

She pulled the card from her bag and called Pete's number. 'Hi, Pete, I had some missed calls from Edward last night and I wondered if everything was OK?'

He really was not sure what to say, but as he was standing in front of his boss, he said, 'Hang on, Miss Jenkins, he has had some issues with his phone, I will see if I can shout him.' As soon as Pete had said her name Edward had looked up. He had wished that he had not done it with as much speed due to the thumping head and the stinging pain in his cheek for the reddening bruise that was appearing. 'What do you want to do?' Pete asked him.

He held out his hand to take the phone and take the call. 'Lottie,' he said, trying to sound as happy as possible.

'Hiya, everything OK? You called and it seemed really urgent. I had my phone on silent while I was busy and forgot to turn it back on, sorry,' she explained.

'No issues, it was just a change of plan for the weekend, that was all, I wanted to let you know as soon as I could so that it would not affect you too much.' He was trying to lie the best he could but for the first time ever it felt so wrong. He had been over it with his mother and Pete to make sure that the story was straight. He would say that he had to work away, but Lottie could go up and be with his mother, then he would join them on the Sunday, give the headache time to go away, the bruise to fade and any media issues that may be about, time to be eliminated so she could not find out. He explained this to her.

'Oh, that is really bad news.' She was disappointed but not too much as she was almost on the tube that would take her to the office and she would see him anyway.

'Sorry,' he said, 'bit of urgent business, but you will be OK with Mum, won't you? How about you ask Agnes if she wants to go? I can make all the arrangements,' he offered.

'I am sure that you can, and thinking about it if she is free I bet she would love it.' Lottie got quite excited. 'Should I call you back, are you in the office?' She asked. It was a sneaky way for her to confirm his location but it worked.

'I am but just ring the mobile. I don't have that much on until lunch,' he said.

'Well, I hope you mean you don't have much on in the diary and not referring to your lack of attire?!' She laughed. He smiled down the other end of the phone but winced as his cheek hurt.

'Miss Jenkins, please,' he said. 'Oh yes, Mr Dean, yes please.' He thought, although he felt like he had done ten rounds in a boxing ring, he still felt the desire for her that such thoughts evoked.

She hummed as she sat on the tube; she hoped that he would like his surprise. Although she had a newfound wealth, she was not one to give such gestures of flowers and champagne, so she hoped that a visit in person would do.

She soon found her way back to the huge building, and on letting herself in she was able to stop the reception girl from ringing up to him. She explained it was a surprise. Unknown to Lottie, Edward had already ensured that all of his employees knew who she was and that she had unlimited access to the apartment and the office without question: anything that she wanted they should do. And it worked. She was in the lift and onto his floor. As she opened the door, Zoe looked up. She must have gone pale as she focused on Lottie. She was about to pick up the handset when Lottie pleaded quietly: 'No, please, I wanted to surprise him,' she said, moving closer to the console.

'Oh, he will be surprised,' Zoe replied. 'I will let you in.' She thought to herself that this was cruel: he was looking awful, and that was really hard as he was a god with legs normally. He felt ill, although self-inflicted he would survive, and he would kill her for this, but she could not resist the game. She stood up and opened the door. He had his back to the entrance, sitting in the chair looking out of the window.

'Coffee, Mr Dean?' she said, holding her head up so that Lottie did not just walk in.

'Oh, put it on the desk. Thanks, Zoe. I did not ask for it, but thanks anyway. Any chance of some more painkillers?' he asked. Zoe thrust them into Lottie's hand along with the fresh coffee pot from the stand. Lottie frowned but walked into the office and put them on the desk. He remained facing out of the window and she could see he had his phone in his hand just looking at the screen. She waited to see if he noticed and then coughed.

He spun round and she looked at his face: both together they voiced their surprise. 'Lottie?' 'Edward?' He almost wanted to stand up, but the throbbing in his head was unbearable. She never gave him the chance as she went around the desk and sat on his knee without invitation. She placed her hand on his face and asked, 'What happened?'

'Nothing,' he said, dismissing her. 'Gym, sparing this AM, got a lucky punch in.' She looked at it again. He was living and breathing but her pathology brain kicked in and she knew that it was more than a few hours old.

'I thought that we would not meet up until the weekend?' he asked. 'Why are you here?'

'I wanted to surprise you.' She gave her finger a kiss and placed it on his face, trying not to make him wince. 'I was looking at flats with Todd. I did not say anything because I wanted to come and surprise you here, afterwards, and that would have ruined it. Before you get all 'I could have come with you'. I wanted to do this for me, not be influenced by anyone. I am sure that you will approve of the area, and I would never have accepted that you pay for a place for me, so I came and I went with Todd who is totally aware that anything he said was useless. I had made up my mind!'

He took a moment to compute the information in his brain. 'You were flat hunting?' he asked. 'And you did not say anything because you wanted to surprise me?' he asked again as if he were a parrot.

'Yes, and yes, and yes, I found somewhere, in Camden. It is only to rent for now, just somewhere I can be close to town, the centre and you.' She placed a kiss on the other side of his face, hoping that this side did not hide an injury that she could not see.

Edward Dean, you prick! he thought to himself. You got pissed off because you could not control her, and she was doing something all along for herself, but more importantly she had done it thinking of him, and even before the weekend she had done it thinking that she would be closer to him! You are a cock, getting pissed off, wound up, and it all had a simple explanation. And now, now you are going to lie to her. Get a grip, man.

'That's great.' She shifted back off his knee and stood. She walked to the window and without turning around to ask she said:

'Going to tell me how you got that face really? That has to be maybe sixteen-hour-old post-trauma, increased bruising, so maybe done when the heart was beating fast, maybe due to rage, or alcohol or some other form of stimulant. The area is too round, unless your trainer is a bare-knuckle fighter, and if I am not too mistaken.' She turned back round just to make sure he was still sitting. 'There is more than one mark, so maybe two lucky punches, looking at the angle, from the other person who was below you at the time?'

He was so taken aback that he did not know what to say. He put his head in his hands and knew right there that he was going to confess.

'That's amazing: once more you have done it. Left me speechless, seen through the twat that I am and proved how so very smart you are.' He stood up to walk towards her. 'I was pissed off that you were with him.' He paused, realising that he then had to explain why she was being followed. He sat her down in the chair that he had occupied. 'Listen, Lottie,' he started to explain, 'I wanted to know all about you, so...' He stopped.

'You had me followed, at a guess,' she interjected.

'That sounds so bad, but yes. He lost you, I don't know what I was thinking.' He stopped and bent on his knees to be in front of her. 'You have done something to me from the very first. I have never had something that I have wanted so much. But I realised that it was not just that I wanted you. In my possessive, dominant way, the more I knew, the more I knew I needed you to be the influence of my life that could give me something that I have never had. An equal in all the right ways, not just my personal life but my business and my general life as well. You are so calm, caring and passionate in everything you do. I wanted...' He corrected himself. 'I want to be part of that. But me, I have to have it all, now, no questions, and the more you challenged me, the more I knew that I have to have you.'

He paused and she stood up. Everything in her body said, Walk away now, Lottie, go and chalk it up as an experience in the School of Hard Knocks. Sit as the silent partner in the charity and you really would not have to see him again. He started talking again.

'Everyone sees this ruthless businessman, who has everything done and can do anything, but I lost so very much when Mitch went.' He sat in the seat as if the very mention of his name made him weak. 'You, have lost so much, too, but seem to fight back, undefeated and want for nothing, but give everything. You are by nature my very opposite and you astound me how you do it.' She now had her arms folded across her chest but she could feel his pain. Yes, she was pissed off that he felt he had to have her followed. And this thing about Todd, it was going to be a challenge, and she guessed it would be to any man who he felt would be a threat when they were around her, but something had clicked for her, too. Something that maybe she knew what he was talking about. Not the money, or the wealth, but the something that is missing.

'So, the not going this weekend was what? So that I would not see your face? Would you have just sat in the background spying on me?' she said.

'Yes.' It was honest, it was the truth. She walked over to the chair, and while he still sat she stood in front of him. She took his head and laid it on her stomach. He unfolded his arms and placed them around her waist.

'I am mad at you for the stalking thing for sure, but to see you open up to me is more than I could ask. I believe that your last statement is not a lie and that, that is what means so much to me that you trust me enough to be honest to me. We do need to talk, maybe not today, or even this month, but we can work this through. You, you and your honesty are all I ask for. The other things that money can buy are nice, but for us to work, it has to be that we, together, trust each other, support each other. Not smother and suffocate. I know you need time, we have talked about this already.' She paused. 'Look at me, Edward,' she asked and he did. She could see the tears in his eyes and her heart lurched out from her chest. She knelt now in front of him, taking the position he had done only a few moments ago. 'I said I accept your deal, and I do. I said I wanted you and I do. We can do this. I need you to trust me.' She looked into his eyes. 'Do you?' she asked.

He held her out at arm's length so that he could see her through the water haze that had gathered in his eyes. 'Can we try again? I am not going to say that it is easy for me to make the changes to the control issues I have had for years, but I will try. You will have to pull me up when I get it wrong, tell me that I have gone too far when I do.' He took a natural break in the statement.

'Have no fear of that, I will.' She laughed and it lightened the mood. 'So, you do not have to work this weekend, we could go to Harrogate?'

'I am not sure how much money I can coax out of people looking like this?' he said, pointing to his face.

'We could still go up there, though?' she asked.

'Yes, but I can't leave here till late,' he replied. She was now sitting on the desk at the side of him.

'Well, if Zoe knows the hotel details, she can let me know and I can change things around a bit. How about you come up to me on the bike, stay overnight, and then head up around that area? It is a fantastic part of the world and the weather should still hold. We only need to pack light so I could have a backpack and we can take it from there.'

The arrangements were sealed with a kiss, and as much as he did not want her to go, she left him to continue his day. His headache continued but the weight that had been on his shoulders was slowly starting to feel less of a heavy burden.

He phoned his mother and had a long conversation. Pete had listened in to most of it, so he knew he was getting some time off, but Edward confirmed this when he called him into the office.

Lottie had taken Zoe's direct line number before leaving and she had already made some phone calls on the train on the way back, changing some of the plans for the weekend to come.

The next few days went along. Lottie busied herself with moving some bits to the rented flat after the weekend, and Edward carried on building his many branches of Dean Incorporated.

Chapter 11

The weekend had gone to plan and the next four weeks seemed to go by without a hitch: it was now the first week in July. The hot summer was continuing giving long, hot days and warm, pleasant evenings. Lottie had moved into the flat mid-June. Edward had been round the same day, and in the most incredible sex fest had helped her move in and christened every room over the twelve hours he had stayed. Although he was not sure if he liked the area, he understood why she had turned down his offer for her to move in with him in his apartment, although he was sure that he would be asking her again in the future.

They had many deep and meaningful conversations, spending one night a week at Lottie's flat and then away at the weekend, staying either at Lottie's home, or a venue Lottie had booked if they were going away. Usually when she booked it, the accommodation was a B&B somewhere. These weekends were the ones she loved the most because Edward was starting to take down his guard. They had been mountain biking in Wales, walked up Snowdon, stayed in a youth hostel, and been paintballing in the forest around Derby. No one knew them; no one interrupted them unless they made conversation with other couples in a pub or the place that they had chosen to eat. They could be themselves, just a young couple enjoying time together.

Lottie loved his competitive nature, and she had genuinely beaten him at some of the things they had done. The mix of doing something and being together was strengthening their relationship.

Back to the Monday-to-Friday, Lottie became more involved in the DuPont Centre, and was overjoyed that the first case she had been working on had eventually led to the prosecution of the assailant. With the evidence she had supplied, the once accidental death had been overturned by the court, and the guy's wife was now facing a life sentence after confessing to her part in his murder. It made the papers but Lottie was more than happy that her name was nowhere to be seen from the reports. Todd took the lead and the credit: she could live with that.

Edward and Todd still had not met, and, although she knew that the increased phone calls and text messages she got from Edward whenever he knew she was with Todd were still his way of knowing what they were doing, she could accept it.

She had explained to Todd about Edward. She never went into details of what he did, or that she was seeing one of the richest men in the city, but Todd had a good idea that he had some cash because she had been dropped off at the Centre by Pete or another driver on more than one occasion. Lottie had also not met Alex yet. Although she had heard Edward speak of him, every time she said it would be good to meet him he had avoided the subject or on the one occasion they had booked a lunch with him, he never showed up.

The farm project had moved on and the contractors had already started to clear some of the site ready for the building works. Due to the land contamination from the farm some of the building work had to be put on hold till later in the year, but it would not hold anything up.

'Shall we go up this weekend? Ed had asked. 'Have a look at how they are doing? You can book the accommodation, although I am not sure I like the idea of youth hostels. My back has never been the same since that,' Lottie laughed down the phone to him.

'Mr Dean, my recollection of the night was that there was not much sleeping taking place, and some of those positions you were in - no wonder your back hurt!' she had replied to him. They had continued the conversation, then he asked, 'I know that you don't want lavish gifts but your birthday is the Friday after. I wondered if you could get the following few days off after the weekend? I wanted to do something special.'

She had not got any more plans, no family to see and her work for the Centre was as and when she wanted it to be. Agnes would be put out for sure, as they had spent many birthdays with her mum and Dick and their family, but now that Agnes knew Edward, after their first meeting, she was smitten with him. He had explained to Lottie one night that she had given him a talking-to on the quiet when Lottie had taken him out to the pub for a drink and introductions two weeks before. He had found her quite to the point and could see why Lottie said she was like a mother hen to her. He knew how it felt to only have her best interests at heart. Edward had reassured her that he would take the very best care of her as he could. It had only taken a few hours of Agnes seeing how he doted on her, then she believed him to be true to his word.

The hot summer weather moved the days on. It was a normal thing for Lottie to sit on the back of Edward's bike and they would get out of the city for a few hours. They met over a weekday lunch or an early evening, usually Wednesdays. It was after they had arrived at a country pub out of the blue that Lottie said, 'I want to learn to ride, I want to take my test, it's not that I don't love sitting on the back, holding on tight, but I want to be able to keep up, feel free like you do.' Edward was not sure that he wanted her to be exposed to the risks that this could bring. While she was behind him he knew that he would take care of her, but if she was alone, it could be really dangerous.

There was only one thing that she could have done less to persuade him, but the lip-biting sealed his fate after she had asked. He wanted to ensure that she had lessons from the best, and so as part of her compromise he insisted that she had full lessons and extra practice by one of the best instructors around, and he would pay.

'Well. You have the best time whatever you are doing and be sure to call me,' Agnes had said as Lottie had been to her house the day before her birthday for tea. 'You know I would not put it past him to propose to you, Lottie. Don't do it, it is too soon.' The comment had made Lottie laugh.

'Aggie, I'm almost 29, I need to live some first, although I am not promising that he is not the keeper I have been looking for. Anyway, you are a fine one to talk, you and Dick are joined the hip.'

'It's not always been that way, and no one says that trying before you buy is a bad thing. In my day if you tried it usually went wrong and you had to buy!' She was referring to the fact that she fell pregnant and then had to marry Dick, although it was undisputed that they loved each other over the years in their own special way.

'I'm being careful,' Lottie replied, hoping that would satisfy her.

The car pulled up and Lottie got in at 9am as planned. She had been told not to bring anything. This had confused her as she was going to be away for a few nights, so had packed a small bag of personal bits just in case. She was excited as she was going to be dropped off at the penthouse. It was the first time she had been there and could not wait to see what he had in store for her. She had been asked to bring her passport, so something he was planning was outside the UK.

'**Happy birthday**' the text came through within minutes of the journey: he must have known she was in the car by that time. In fact, it was because Steven had called him to say he had collected her. The young driver was a new face that Lottie had seen only once before. The privacy screen was up, but he dropped it down lightly and said:

'Miss, please look in the compartment to your right.' Lottie pulled the drawer down and a red envelope came out. The front said: *Happy Birthday Lottie.* She could see that it was Edward's writing and so she opened it. The card was simple, a sketch of a person playing the piano. It was really detailed and she looked at the signature at the bottom. Hand-drawn, it was a special touch, although she did not recognise the artist. As she opened it, another envelope fell out. She read the note that was enclosed:

I am sure that you are wondering what is in store for you this weekend! I will explain as we go along. I hope that you enjoy. Please open the glovebox on your left, I hope that you like it. ED

Lottie leaned over again and opened the box on the other side to where the letter had been. The box was red and sealed with a proper wax seal: it was too large for a ring box was her first thought. She looked at it wondering how to open it without damaging it. She tried, but thought that she would just have to break the seal. As she did, the box opened up to reveal a necklace, like nothing she had seen before. A full, encrusted diamond choker. She gave a gasp and Steven asked if she was OK. 'Yes, sorry,' she said, still looking at the piece of jewellery that shone and glistened, even though the blacked-out windows limited the direct sunlight into the car.

She noticed that the box was thicker, and pulling a piece of ribbon out at the bottom revealed another layer. It was a bracelet identical in design to the necklace but in a smaller form, and a pair of drop earrings. Wow, she thought. There was enough glitter to have fed a starving country for the price that this must have cost. She took the bracelet out of the box and felt it. It was quite heavy. She held it against her wrist and admired it. She could not put it on as it needed two hands to do the clasp and safety chain, but she smiled to herself. Then the guilt of the cost set in and she thought of all the good that the money could do if better spent somewhere else.

She smiled at them again as she put them away, back in the drawer for safe keeping. I hope we don't crash, she thought! If this was the start of the few days she had better get used to being spoilt, so she thought better of it than to mention the cost to Edward. She simply texted him back. **They are beautiful, thank you.**

Edward had been in the apartment all morning making sure that everything he had arranged was going to plan. His housekeeper, Mrs B, had been overseeing the cleaning for days, although it did not need it. He had asked that the cleaners were on extra time to make sure. The fresh flowers in the hall allowed the sweet small to linger through the rooms. Some would say that the apartment was too clinical anyway, but he liked the new, modern look of the place. As always it was at the top of the building. It allowed for the best security and privacy money could buy. The hallway went off to one side with the sitting room, which led through to the large, open-plan kitchen. It had a formal dining table by the large patio window and a breakfast bar that came out for the worktops like an extension.

To the other side of the hall was a closed door. This was where the office was, and then two bedroom doors to the side of this. Both rooms could have the inner wall pushed back to make one very large space if required. But today it remained closed. In the first room was his bed, large enough for four people, draped in black silk sheets. It was a mirror image of his room in the office, built in storage space that you could not tell was not the walls, but held wardrobes shelving etc for clothes. True to form, the room included having ceiling mirrors above the bed. His bathroom was again back, white and gold. Dominating the centre was a large, free-standing bath, double-wash handbasins and a large walk-in shower.

The other room was decked out in cream and pastel greys, cool, pale blue, with a hint of gold. The bed was smaller in size, but had scatter cushions to give it a homelier feel. The bathroom was cream, beige and dark brown. A copper bath stood to one side, with a walk-in shower and toilet to the other side. Again, it had two basins, with gold taps and fittings. Edward stood in front of the large wall of wardrobe space and closed the door. He was happy that everything had been delivered: all the outfits he had asked for had been supplied and hung ready for the occupant to come along and put on. He looked at his watch: he still had time to shower and change before she arrived.

'Mrs B, thank you, everything looks great,' he said as he went back in the kitchen. She was a middle-aged lady that he had employed for years. She cooked and took care of the apartment for him, which was really handy when he was away. She lived in a small flat herself in the same block, paid for by Edward as part of her salary. In fact, all of his staff lived in the same apartment block, including Pete. It was not that expensive as 'Dean Holdings' owned the apartment block anyway. It sat on the side of the river on the east side of the city. It meant that they were on call if he needed any of them; also it meant that he could choose his direct neighbours, which could give him increased privacy if required. The rest of the floors were leased by various business people and young couples, although there were no families in the block. The apartments below had small, decked balconies, but the advantage of being on the top was that the roof garden allowed for outdoor space, and on a day like today, it was great to open the doors and invite the heat of the sun into the rooms.

Mrs B had been cooking all morning, and as Edward walked past the fresh pastries he pinched a handful.

'Edward, I have been cooking for us all, not just for you. If you are hungry sit down and eat, don't just pick, and if you get crumbs on my floors, you will be in trouble!' she said, standing with her hands on her hips. He quickly jumped towards the open door leading outside, using his hand as a plate, and as soon as he had cleared his mouth he shouted back, 'Sorry, Mrs B!' He stood on the decking looking at the traffic below. He had been over the plans for the weekend several times now in his mind and hoped that it would all come off without a hitch.

He was waiting by the front doors as the car pulled up. Lottie stepped out of the car as he opened the door that he had beaten Steven to.

'Happy Birthday.' He greeted her and she smiled at him. 'You liked them?' he asked. She shot back in the car while the door was still open, not that she had forgotten about the jewels, she was just eager to get to him for the kiss he planted on her lips as they met. Edward could not help but admire the rear view as Lottie reached the glovebox. Steven also noted the tightness of her jeans and the way they curved around her ass, but was quickly shot a look from his employer that made him look away. 'Thanks, Steven,' she said as he dismissed himself, totally knowing he would get a reminder from Pete later about that as he was bound to find out.

'They are divine, but...' He stopped her.

'You promised that you would not mention the money. I said it is a birthday treat and that is what you are getting. So, baby girl, they are beautiful and when you wear them, they will look even better around this slim, fascinating little neck.' He pulled her hair back and kissed her neck as a reminder of where she had to wear it.

'Mr Dean, in the street, how very shameful!' she said as shocked as she could be without laughing at the comment. He also whispered in her ear at the same time.

As they arrived in the apartment, Lottie could not help but look around her. She had guessed it would look like this: it was all very Edward. Humming from the kitchen reminded him that they were not alone, yet, so he led her into the room by the hand to introduce her to Mrs B.

'Hi,' Lottie said, slightly embarrassed on introduction. The housekeeper looked at her with a warm, cheery smile and wiped her hands on her apron so as not to get flour on the young girl's hands. She leaned into the grinning man standing with his chest proud as if he was showing off a prize he had won at sports day and whispered, 'Well, Edward, you had best treat this fine young lady well, and ensure that she eats something: there's not an ounce of fat on her!'

He smiled and put his hand on her shoulder. 'We will be fine: is the champagne cool?'

'I will bring it out when you are ready,' she said, scurrying off to find the glasses she had washed twice already.

Lottie had walked outside to look at the view. 'Nice place, although I am not sure I expected anything other. Always on top looking down,' she said. He moved in behind her and nuzzled at her neck again.

'Not always on top!' he grinned.

'Mr Dean, have you got any more thoughts in your head today apart from...' He stopped her short with the soft touch of his lips on hers. His tongue gently eased into hers and licked her lower lip. She instantly responded to his touch as he rubbed his hand along the back line of her jeans and under her top.

'Nope!' he replied, carrying on kissing her neckline and nibbling her ear. 'We have to christen the apartment as we did your flat!' he said with a beaming smile. 'And something is missing?' She looked at him not sure of what he meant. He pulled back and reached into his pocket. 'The other one is for special occasions, this one is a more day-to-day type of thing.' He opened the small box and pulled out a solid gold choker chain. The centre diamond was small but perfect and shone with a real red colour, not clear like other diamonds, like no other she had seen before. 'So, you can have me with you wherever you are,' he said as he did it up at the back. He admired his handiwork once the clasp had been done up. 'Perfect,' he said. She was not able to look at it, but felt the smooth cool, precious metal against her skin. 'I was going for a ruby, your birthstone, and then I saw the pink diamond, and it seemed the perfect fit, rare, unique, exquisite, like you.' She looked at him and bit her lip unconsciously.

'I'm not going to say "and expensive",' Lottie replied. 'So thank you, it is beautiful.' He kissed her and whispered in a firm voice, 'Stop the lip-biting thing or Mrs B may get more than she bargained for!' She looked at him under her eyes. Stop that as well, he thought to himself: it has just the same effect and we don't have the time.

'Come and have a look, I will find you a mirror.' He led her back into the flat and showed her around. As they went into the spare bedroom she noticed the flowers by the bed, she went close to the console and looked into the mirror and the bright, shining trinket.

'See, beautiful,' he said, standing behind her. 'Yes,' she replied. He looked at her and could see that something was not right. 'Lottie?' he asked. 'What is it?'

'You are showing me the room as if it is mine: are we not sleeping together?' He held her hand.

'The room is for you to use whenever. I have had some things put in here, and your bathroom has been filled with all manner of your favourite toiletries. I wanted to show you this.' He walked towards the wardrobe. He continued. 'Later, but I will show you now.' He opened the doors and Lottie could see that it had been filled with a number of items. Several dresses, formal and evening gowns, a few skirts, trousers, blouses and tops. The shelves had shoes, boots and trainers, jeans and tee shirts all waiting to be worn. She was taken aback on both counts. Not just because of the cost, but how had he known? It clicked as she recognised one of the dresses she had tried on before.

'Before you blow a fuse...' He could tell by the look on her face that she was having reservations. 'I have not done this to choose your wardrobe for you. I went to see your friend Bella, who was more than willing to help me, and we got a bit carried away!' Edward put on his best puppy face to try to lighten the mood.

'A bit, I would say. Really, do I need all of this?' she asked.

'Well, not all this weekend, but you could keep it here as a backup, if for whatever reason, I don't know, you want to take it home. She was so infectious and lovely, I was only going for a few things and I came out loaded.' He was trying to make light of it. It had been true. He had gone to Harrods requesting time with Bella from ladieswear. He had found her so helpful, remembering Lottie so well. Showing him all the items she had tried, or looked at, that he had lost half a day in her company.

Lottie was not sure if she was angry or quite overjoyed: looking at the expensive clothes hanging up she would never have gone so overboard, although she totally knew what Bella was like. 'I accept this only because it is my birthday, you understand. I am quite capable of shopping for clothes myself, although I am pleased you met Bella,' she continued as they left the room. He never showed her his bedroom; Mrs B had called them through and they walked back to the sitting room.

'I am off now, Edward. You and Miss Jenkins have a great weekend and shout if you need anything.' She put her light jacket on once she had removed her apron. 'The bottle is still in the fridge: I was not sure how long you would be in the bedroom.'

Lottie went red wondering what Mrs B had thought that they were up to in there, then her mind wandered to whether this was something Edward had done before. Welcoming women to his apartment, something Mrs B was laid-back about anyway.

'Thank you, Mrs B, we will.' He gave her a little wave as the door closed. 'Shall we?' He gestured to the table that had been set with strawberries and other fruit. He went to the fridge where he brought out the bottle of champagne and a tray of prepared oysters. 'We have until 4pm then Pete is picking us up: you need to be dressed for dinner at the Mandarin, table for two.' He started popping the cork on the bottle and pouring her a glass. 'To the birthday girl.' She smiled still not totally OK with everything so far. She was about to hear the rest of the plans and wondered just now much this was all costing. A simple meal and night out would have done.

'We are off to the races tomorrow, Ascot, and then we will be back for an evening at the Albert Hall: you will have about an hour to get changed in between. We will be back for the night and then you need to pack a little overnight bag and your passport. Something nice to wear in the day: we will be walking around, it will be warm hopefully, and swimwear is an option as well if you want.' He took a sip of the pale yellow liquid and downed an oyster after putting pickle and lemon on it. 'Formal evening dress as well for the night-time, and your other birthday gift.' He pointed to her neck. 'And something to travel home in, again whatever you are comfortable in. Monday, I planned a gym session: I thought you could meet my trainer. We have a table booked at 5pm and then another show. Tuesday, I wanted to go to the farm: they had made good progress and the last part of your gift is up that way.' He stopped and looked at her: she had been listening to him all the way through, not taking any oysters or drink. 'Then, sadly, Wednesday it is back to reality, although I don't have to be in till late so we can have a lie-in if you want.' He flashed her his eyes and smiled a cheeky grin.

'Do you think we will have time to breathe?' she said. 'And the clothes have all been planned with this in mind?'

'Yes, more than one option for each occasion, and Bella has put in some undies and sleeping attire, but,' he said, getting up from the stool and sliding his hands around her back. 'I was hoping that just this...' He caressed the necklace. '...May be all you have on!' He kissed her neck again. 'Even under your dresses.' He continued to kiss her and she felt the warmth of her arousal deep in her stomach. It had seemed that over the past few weeks they had not been able to get enough of each other. As they had become aware of each other's needs they had started to get more adventurous in the bedroom, or out of it as the case was on Lottie's garden terrace and in the back of the car. She had not been too happy with that as she was aware that Pete was driving, but after she was shown that he could not see or hear anything and that the screen could be locked their side, she had succumbed to his lust.

Lottie had never been too exposed, but she was more and more aware that Edward was well experienced in having fun. She had not felt pushed into anything, in fact he was showing her that she had a need and an animal lust that she never thought existed. They had tried several positions, locations, played with some toys, for her benefit really, she had even dressed in her white lace as he had mentioned how he remembered her in the pure, innocent way, but nothing too heavy.

She put her head back on his shoulder and his hand slipped down the front of her bra. He pulled a nipple: it was erect and already hungry for his attention. She reached behind her, trying to find his groin. 'This is your day, it is all about you,' he said as he pulled away from her, but he kept hold of her arm behind her to restrain her from doing it again. The soft groan in her throat was quickly followed by a gasp as he pulled at the other nipple, kissing and nibbling her neck without stopping. She moved her hand again. 'Keep it there or I will have to restrain you.' She opened her eyes. His voice had changed to the no-nonsense businessman, dominating, controlling. They had not done that before and she had to take a quick think about how she felt about that. 'Would you like that, Lottie? Would you like me to be in control of your pure pleasure?'

She was not sure: if she was going to think about it for much longer it was going to ruin the moment for her, for them both. Was this the time to have an S & M discussion or should she put a little trust in him? 'Would you like to be out of control and in my hands completely? Would you like to see how you can become consumed by pleasure?' he continued. His voice was not as strong, but still had controlling tones.

She was not sure. They had joked about things in the past; God, she even made that comment about safe words the first day on the bike. Maybe he was some sick, sadistic psycho and she had got him all wrong. She suddenly freaked out inside and her heart rate and breathing became noticeably increased. She turned around to try to face him: it was hard sitting on the high-backed stool, but she was able to push his upper body around to her. She pushed back to look him in the face.

His heart froze: what had he done, what had he said? He could tell that she had a troubled face: it was the same one she had shown when she had almost walked out of the restaurant on this first meeting. He had hoped that he would not see that face again, but there it was. He knew that over the past few weeks he was getting her out of her comfort zone sexually. They had not talked about it, but each time they met he tried to inadvertently do something that increased her pleasure, made her feel more liberated, both with her own body and his. He could do vanilla sex, but he so wanted to explore what he knew she had inside. It was just how far he could go to get it to come out. He knew that he did not want to sleep with anyone else; he did not want to take or find pleasure in anyone else. Faced with a life without Lottie and just vanilla sex, he could sacrifice some things but, at this moment in time, he thought that he had gone too far, too fast for her.

'Lottie, you are scaring me, what is it?' he asked, moving away from her space, but still holding onto her hands. God, don't let this go down the pan now, I would not cope if she walked out, he thought as she jumped off the stool. Luckily for him, she picked up the glass of champagne. That's good, she would not walk off with a drink in her hands, and she went outside onto the terrace. That's good again: she had not headed for the door! The voice inside his head was reassuring. He quickly caught up with her and stood by her side where she had come to rest on the balcony looking out over the bustling city. He had also brought his drink out: he had taken a few large mouthfuls just to try to clear his head.

'Sorry,' she said. 'I just needed some air and now I feel stupid.' She looked at him and smiled. 'Sorry,' she repeated and then sipped her drink.

'There's something, something that just happened in there that you are not happy with. I have not hurt you, have I?' He really hoped he had not. He had played with her like that before and she had not done anything like this. It had to be what he had said. 'Was it what I said?' he came straight out and asked.

'No.' She took another sip. Did she really want to have this conversation today? The only other person who she had told this to, with the exception of her mother, was Todd.

'Lottie, please, don't clam up on me, I need you to trust me in everything. If there is something I have done, please let me know.' She could now see the desperation in his face, even though there was a demanding urgency in his voice. She turned towards him.

Here goes: I think that if I just blurt it out the traffic noise may cover some of the details and then we can get back to where we were. If not, I have just ruined the whole birthday thing and maybe more, she said to herself.

'Please don't think that this is you, and this is not the start of an "I'm leaving speech".' He took her glass from her and placed it on the table to the side of them. 'I was almost sixteen, well, the day before my birthday actually.' She took in a deep breath, knowing that the date had also had something to do with her remembering not just the conversation. 'I was with someone whom I had known for a really long time, he was a friend – well, almost the brother that I did not have. His father was the local policeman. My mum got on with the family really well. We had played together since we were in primary school. He was only a few months older than me.' She took another breath. 'We had arranged to go for a walk; Mum put some food in a bag with some fruit and a drink. We had walked for miles, then we got stuck in a storm. We managed to find this really old shed: it did not have a roof really but we huddled together to try to keep dry. At first it was fun.' She stopped again. 'I never stopped him as I thought he would not go...'

She stopped. It must have been the look on Edward's face. He was starting to get where she was going with this. He needed to stop her, knew that she did not have to tell him the rest. She put her hand on his; he had turned away from her. 'It's OK, I want to carry on. I went along with it, the kissing and fondling, I thought that if I carried on he would not do anything more serious, but when I said stop because he was trying to pull down my pants he, he hit me, said I was asking for it, kept saying I was asking for it and that he would tell everyone I had said it was OK. I was quite strong I was able to get out of his grip when he put my hands above my head and held me. I managed to push him off at first, get out of the shed, but I tripped, then he used his belt to tie me up and...'

'Stop, Lottie, I don't want to hear any more.' The rage in his face was echoed by his voice. He paced to the other side of the decking, almost back in the house. He was so angry with himself for making her say this, today of all days. Why the hell had she not said anything before. He had held her hands, he had trapped her under him before now and she had not mentioned a word. She walked over to him.

'It's OK, really, I'm over it. Look, see, not even a tear.' She made him look at her in the face by holding his face in her hands. 'I just wanted you to understand that, even though we have played around, I have always been able to get free; you mentioned being tied up and I just wobbled. I trust you, you have always said that you would not hurt me and I believe you, I just need you to know about this so that if I do have a moment where I panic, you will know that it is not you I am panicking about, and...' She lowered her hands. 'I never said I would not try, pushing limits remember?'

'Yes, but Lottie, how could...' He stopped. 'Fuck it!' He looked away. 'I'm sorry.'

'Why are you sorry? It was not you, was it?' She smiled at him. 'Really, don't apologise for all the men in the world, not that I have known that many of course.' She tried to make light of what had turned into a really dark subject. She then managed to break a smile from him. 'We said no lies – well, no secrets, too.' She bit her lip. 'For me, please, I am over it. I don't hate him, it was a life lesson well learned. I have passed him in the street, seen him in the village pub, and I have no feelings at all. I just needed you to know this bit about me.'

He was furious to the point of wanting to hit someone. Never hit a woman, son: it was the only thing his father had told him that he wanted to remember from his childhood. It is an unwritten law. Although strictly not true; he had hit women, but never to cause them harm. Pain, maybe yes, but never in malice or self-indulgence. It was consensual at all times; no matter what he had done, it was always under total agreement. No meant no, that was it. But in true Lottie style, she really looked like she had bounced back from this. How did she do it? Why did she not resent him? How could she talk to him? God, I hope that our paths never cross; in fact, I want to know who it is, pay him a visit. He changed his mind with that thought.

'How do you do it? How can you say that you have spoken to him since? Who is he?' he asked.

'No one that I even want to dwell on any more. He ruined some part of my life, but he has been a no one for years. I knew that I would kill the mood by telling you, and you would no doubt want to kill him! It's over, life is too short, I'm over it, move on. Now can we finish this bottle or what?' She walked over to the ice bucket and brought it out. Refreshing the glasses, she put it in his hand. His face totally said that this was not over, but she had to salvage the day. At a guess this was a no sex weekend after that bombshell, but she was sure that she could work him round.

He was quiet; although she had made the best to make the effort, she knew that this had an effect on him, more than she could have ever known.

She had changed into one of the dresses after her shower; Edward had gone to his own room. Lottie had tried to peek in but thought that there was enough time to see his room later. Good choice, Bella, she noted as she did the back of the dark blue dress up. It was short, just above the knee, but the skirt flayed out. It was made of really light chiffon, cool and floating. She could not do the back up all the way: she needed a hand. She gently knocked on the adjoining door and waited for an answer.

'Can I ask you to do me up please?' she asked as he put his head through.

'Just a moment,' he said. She pulled her hair up in one of the pretty clasps that had been placed in a box on the console, and when Edward came in he had a real smile on his face.

'I'm here,' he said, gesturing for her to turn around for him to do the zipper up. He pulled it all the way to the top and placed a gentle kiss on the back of her neck. The hairs on her arms and neck stood on end. He had not touched her since the conversation earlier. 'I'm sorry,' he said, 'I just can't begin to think of how, why, that could happen, to you, Lottie. How can you move on like you have?'

'Because I trusted you enough to tell you, because I trust you enough to understand, and not to let it make a difference,' she said, turning around to look at him. 'Promise me this will not affect us, what we have, what we could have?' She smiled and bit at her lip, knowing that always got a reaction.

'Low blow, Miss Jenkins,' he said. 'Every time you do it, every time. That lip and my gut must have been separated at birth because they seem attached every time you do that, gets me here!' He pointed to his stomach.

'Or here?' She placed her hand on his trousers and he took it away swiftly. Yes, right, just there, if you must know, but I was not thinking of that on this occasion, although I have to say he has been affected! he said to himself.

'Here.' He placed her hand over his heart and she smiled. 'And that is why the thought of anything happening to you kills me,' he said. Maybe the shower had given him time to think; maybe the shower had given him time to calm down. Whatever it was, he had to try to put this behind him; she had, and so should he, for today, for the weekend. 'Want to wear this?' He lifted up the red box that held her first birthday gift. Her eyes went wide like a child who had been asked if they wanted more sweets.

'Please,' she said. He swapped the necklace that was currently around her neck, gently putting it in the box, then took out the bracelet and placed it around her wrist. Lottie took the earrings and removed the small gold studs she always wore putting, them in the box to keep them safe.

'Better than perfect.' He kissed her so gently it was as if he thought that she would break. She pulled him to her as if to assure him that she would not. The kiss deepened just as the apartment doorbell rang out.

'Not so perfect.' She referred to Pete's timing: he had arrived to pick them up.

'Later.' He tapped Lottie on the nose, and sealed it with a quick kiss in the same spot. She was now sure that the conversation had not ruined the day completely and that it was done now, and they could get over it.

The meal was lavish and tasted superb; so it should be for a 3-Michelin star restaurant, Lottie thought. As always there was a piano playing in the background. Edward had made it an ambition to ensure that everywhere they went there was one playing. It was the only thing that Lottie had not done: play for him. Yes, he had stolen several moments of her playing, but he wanted her to pay for him, just him, no one else. His terms, his location, his setting and his rules.

He had tried not to let her hand go all night, even lingering around the ladies' toilets when she went. She thought it was sweet, but she knew that he was still feeling unsure about the conversation they had had earlier. Although she knew no one in the place, several men had said hello, each one warned off by a look or a stare: his body language said it all, as if the male lion had the final say in the forest.

As they got back up to the apartment he placed his keys on the side, and quickly grabbed her hand. He looked at both of the closed bedroom doors. 'Your place or mine?' He laughed and for a moment Lottie was not sure what he asked, they were in his apartment. Then she got it.

'Not been to your place yet,' she said.

'Well, come on in, Miss Jenkins, and tell me what you think of the décor.' He opened the door and put the light on, then used the dimmer. She opened her mouth. 'Wow,' she said, 'very manly.' She looked around, noticing the ceiling. 'Very, very male...' She lost the words she was looking for. 'Well, let's just say it's not Laura Ashley!'

He almost rugby-tackled her to the bed, she stared at herself in the smokey grey ceiling mirror. 'Kinky,' she said.

'Good for checking spots on your back,' he joked.

'Disgusting,' she laughed.

'I can be,' he replied. He lay at her side and placed a hand over her waist. 'Had a good day?' he asked, knowing that the blip in the middle would play on his mind for a long time to come, hoping that he would be able to keep that from her.

'Great day,' she said, 'thank you.' She closed her eyes. The wine, cocktails and champagne were a light mix in her head and she knew that it was a good thing they had left or she would have definitely wobbled off the dark blue Jimmy Choo shoes that Bella had chosen to go with the dress.

'Sit back, Miss Jenkins, enjoy the view,' he said, kissing her through the chiffon of the dress, along the line of her waist. He lifted the floating skirt up around her thighs and kissed down to her feet. Carefully taking off the shoes, he kissed the tops of her feet. He found out the hard way that she was ticklish there a week ago, so he held her feet as carefully as he could. He did not need another kick in the teeth from the reflex she had if you touched the wrong place!

He worked his way back up the legs, letting his hands go first to move the skirt up, and then, hooking his fingers in her black lace pants, he gently slid them down. She arched her back as he licked the very top of her leg, just breathing along the line of her outer lips. She had shaved ready for the weekend and her soft skin had her musky scent that he loved to breathe in. He avoided her full sex, but ensured that as he kissed her bikini line his chin pushed into her, massaging her vulva. She moved and swayed her hips in a bid to get him to rub where she needed it, but he did not.

He moved up her body once more and slid his hands around the dress. With the speed of lightning the zip was undone and he pulled her arms free. She had done what he had asked. No bra, he had noticed when he did the dress up, but did not want to say anything. Shame about the pants she had on, but in all fairness the skirt had blown in the wind getting out of the car. Happy for him to see, but no one else at this point, he thought.

He kissed her collarbones, down her sternum, avoiding her breasts that were heaving with her increased breathing. He was starting to get uncomfortable but he would have to hold on, he was not going to take her, he promised that this was her day and it was not over yet. He took a nipple and rolled it in his finger and thumb. She drew in breath through her teeth and sighed. The throbbing in her clit was driving her mad. She had sometimes masturbated, but never in front of a man. If he did not touch her soon, this was going to be the first time. She resisted by rubbing her hands along the sheets at her side.

He went back down her body, kissing all the way, this time taking the dress with him. Tossing it to the floor, he turned her over using his hands on her hips. She moved her arms out and spread them on the pillow. He continued to kiss along the line of her spine. There it is, my red rose girl: he kissed the petals in the spot that he had grown to adore. He straddled her as he kissed up her back again and she rubbed her arse into his trousers. She could feel his dick straining to get out, and she wanted him out, too.

'I'm not here for that,' he said, moving down her body, not just to reach his target area, but to stop her rubbing on him. 'I'm here for this.' He thrust his tongue between her legs and hit the back of her sex: she was wet, really wet and hot. She opened her legs to let him get to her, closer, deeper; she lifted her hips in a bid for him to reach where she wanted. He pushed his thumb down the crack of her arse, letting it rest at her outer lips. She was so wet it took no effort to push his thumb to the top of her sweet spot again; this allowed his fingers to rub outside her, then gently with each rub he pushed a finger in, part of the way, another thrust, all of the way, another rub, and another finger, part of the way, all of the way. The small circles he was performing with his thumbs and the rubbing, gliding, of his fingers in and out of her came without effort. The pace was not altered or affected by the continued kissing of her pale skin. He nipped at her arse cheeks and then licked the red skin, finishing it off with kisses. She was really trying hard not to come, but when the internal muscles started to tighten around his fingers he knew she was almost there. He moved up her body, skilfully not allowing himself to rub up her. His fingers never stopped their pace, their frantic rubbing.

'Feel it, Lottie,' he whispered to her. She had grabbed a handful of the sheets and was squeezing tight in a bid to stop the blast of power that was building up in her clit. 'Feel how strong you are.' He slowed his pace and she tried to reach behind her to hold his arms. 'What do you want, Lottie? Tell me,' he asked.

'You!' she shouted. 'This, please I need to, please faster.' She was just on the edge and he knew just how to keep her there. 'Edward, please?' He quickly moved down the bed spinning her round as if she was a rag doll. She gasped and held onto his shoulders as he placed her down. He put his head between her open legs and placed his tongue where his fingers and thumb had been. 'Look at yourself, Lottie, see how beautiful you are.' He referred to her reflection up in the mirror. She did as he asked; she could see his shoulder supporting his weight and moving in time to the electric flicks he was causing on her outer lips. Easing her apart with his chin, he thrust his tongue into her and licked the warm, sweet secretions she had made with her lusting.

'Please, Edward, please I'm begging you!' She grabbed his hand to make him apply more pressure on her sweet spot and to try to get him deeper into her. He reached one hand up and chose the nearest nipple. As if he had a stun gun he applied pressure between his finger and thumb, and she went. Her hips bucked and she orgasmed from her very core to the last hair on her head. She arched her back and gasped as her pulsating, throbbing sex was being sucked by him, increasing the feeling, almost to the point of pain, but it was not pain it was something that she could not contemplate as she was still shaking in the throes of her pleasure. He had been down on her before, but never like that. He continued to blow on her, and she still had shivers of the orgasm that made her sigh out loud.

He moved back up to kiss her. 'Taste your pure pleasure, baby girl, see what you made me do.' He kissed her and bit playfully on her lip. She could feel him next to her: there was a damp patch on his trousers, where he had pre-ejaculated, she said.

'How can you not want to?' she said, feeling the area with her hand. He took her hand off.

'Don't mistake not wanting to with being able to give pleasure before having your own. I do very much want to, Lottie, but you are my first thought here. I must learn to restrain, but it will never stop me wanting you.'

He pulled the sheets over her and undressed as quickly as he could. Sleeping was going to be hard while he was so worked up, but he knew that he had to show her that he was not just in it for himself; he would get the chance to take her, but he wanted her fully and she was not ready for that yet.

She fell asleep in his arms. He looked up at her through the reflection and her necklace sparkled in the moonlight that came in through his windows. A collar of shining lights that reflected on her pale skin: his statement to the world that she was his, and he, in return, was hers.

The day at the races was fun for them both. Lottie had chosen a cream dress, which was overlaid with lace. It had a matching short jacket, and the hat which was a mass of feathers and bows. She had felt really silly getting in the car dressed like that, but soon mingled with the other ladies at the course, who looked just as flamboyant.

Edward had dressed in grey tails, with a tall black hat; he, too, fitted in at the royal box as they walked around looking at the horses. She had admired how he looked as he came out of the bedroom, although she had preferred how he looked as he had brought her breakfast in bed. His boxers did a poor job of hiding his cock, as he had slipped them on when he got up. She was disappointed they could not continue the activity from the night before, but he made the excuse that Mrs B was about already and that they could not be late to start the day.

He knew various faces, all of whom were introduced to Lottie. He held her lightly by the waist throughout the day, increasing his hold if particular men started a conversation with her. She instantly forgot most of their names, something that became worse the more champagne she drank.

She was overjoyed when one of the horses she placed a bet on came in first, jumping around in a circle like an excited child. She had been to local point-to-point races as a youngster, but never such a grand meeting as this. She insisted on putting her winnings in a charity box for 'Help for Heroes': there was a tent set up and it soon became obvious that Edward had set the place up to raise funds. He greeted everyone and moved around the crowd with ease and confidence. She admired him several times and when he caught her looking, he pulled her close and whispered, 'Happy, Miss Jenkins?'

She had replied with a 'Yes, very.' She understood by now that he was not one for kissing in public, but the occasional smile and show of affection were enough for her. One thing that she did note was that he never posed for any photos. There were many opportunities for him to get in front of a camera, for the glossy magazines no doubt, but he always moved away.

Mrs B had made up the most fantastic hamper, luckily with handmade lemonade, a welcome drink from the alcohol she was consuming. The day was another warm one and as they got in the car to come back she pulled off her cream Jimmy Choo shoes and rubbed her feet. Sitting next to her, he said, 'Here, let me rub them.' He held out his hand.

'It will tickle!' she said, knowing the strange feeling that she could rub them without any problems but anyone else seemed to touch the wrong nerve every time that made her jump and giggle. Even having a pedicure was a modern form of torture for her.

'I won't, I will be gentle, trust me.' He beckoned again with his hand and reluctantly she swung her legs round and handed over her feet. He started to rub and she closed her eyes. The shoes were great, but she was really not used to walking around on heels all day. It felt good: as promised, he was gentle and she soon relaxed for the journey home.

The quick change from one event to the next had given her time to shower and refresh. She stood on his balcony looking out at the early evening sky as he joined her. 'You OK?' he asked.

'Yes, I really enjoyed that, tired but ready to go again.' She looked at him and he said as he fumbled with his cufflinks, 'I remembered you saying how you loved horses and really regretted not having the time or commitment to still have one of your own.' She took hold of the little metal buttons, noting that they had a military crest of some form on them and she pushed them through the cuff of the shirt on both sides. 'They are pretty,' she commented.

'They were Mitch's,' he said, looking at them momentarily. She held his hand, seeing how something of no financial value meant so much to him; she never continued or pushed the conversation.

The Albert Hall was packed. All manner of people had turned up and again it had a military theme to the night. The Duke of Gloucester sat in the box next to them: they had the best seat in the house overlooking the stage. All the young players were fantastic, but when a young boy from China started to play the piano, Lottie gasped at his grace and elegance as his fingers caressed the keys. The notes came out fast and loud, soft and gentle. She felt her breathing slow down and speed up as she could feel the passion as if he was sitting next to her. She found herself slipping towards the edge of her seat, as if she tried to get closer to him. When he finished she clapped so hard her hands stung. She felt the wetness in her eyes and she tried not to look round at Edward, who she knew was looking at her, and had been for most of the session.

During the interval she excused herself to go to the toilet. On the way back, she noticed the young boy standing in a crowd of people. They were all asking him questions and all Lottie could glean from the conversation was that he was a young scholar from the Royal Academy. He had been here a year but this was his final performance because he had to go home: his parents, who were not with him, could not afford to fund him anymore. That was sad, she thought as she went back to her seat. The usual question from Edward asking if she was OK: she nodded and smiled, still concerned as to the young, talented musician's financial issues. It was a shame that such talent had to be missed just because they could not be funded.

More young people performed a range of musical pieces: young singers, injured soldiers, and several military bands all took their turn. At the end they mingled for only a few minutes. Edward placed a cheque that he had prewritten into the charity box of a young girl, who was in a cadet regiment. Her buckles and buttons shone so brightly, Lottie knew that for hours she must have been polishing them to create such detail.

'Thank you, sir,' she said as he placed the donation in the box. 'You are welcome,' he replied with the smile that could melt ice, and, although Lottie gave her about sixteen years old, she knew that from the puppy dog eyes she gave back to him, he could charm them young or old.

Another day was done as she lay in his arms. They had joked as she had asked if he could stay in 'her house' tonight, and so they slept in the pale blue silk sheets, both exhausted to muster more than a goodnight kiss.

The private jet had touched down on the airfield, and it was in no time at all that they arrived in Monaco Bay. Lottie had slept for most of the journey which had allowed Edward to catch up on some work. They were the only two on the back of the plane; it had soft chairs, a couple of tables and a private bathroom that included a shower. Pete and Steven were up the front.

Edward glanced over at her several times to check that she was still asleep. He smiled to himself as he noticed the pink diamond sparkle around her neck.

She had noticed it was hot as they walked towards the awaiting car on the tarmac at the airport; this was confirmed by Pete as they got in the car. She was busy watching the world go by that she had no idea what Edward was saying as he was explaining her day. She got the bit about yacht and lunch, and she paid attention to a few hours' sunbathing as that sounded great. She had packed a bikini - well, if the few bits of material and the string holding it together classed as swimwear, then she was OK!

'I'm sorry that I am going to have to leave you. I have about an hour or so's worth of business, but the resort spa, pool and bar are all yours. Steven will stay around if for any reason you want to go shopping, although I would prefer if you stayed in the complex. We can browse the shops before dinner and I can come with you.' He said as they crossed the harbour towards a yacht, something that only film stars went on in Lottie's eyes. And for more than one reason she started to be filled with dread at where they were heading. To keep a light note she said, 'Another Dean Holdings asset? He helped her walk along the gangplank, getting onto the yacht.

'Dean Corporate international, branch of,' he said. It had been during one of the nights they had lain on Lottie's sofa in the flat just taking about life when this conversation came up.

He had explained to her that his business had many branches, UK-based, international and U.S.-based. Some were holding companies, some were part of the cooperation, and others were individual business in his own name, or other company names where he was a silent controlling partner. He was CEO of most of them, or Chair of the board in others. Others he stayed on the payroll but was independently run, although he had a stay in control. It was all a bit high-powered business to her at that stage. She had asked how many people he employed and he did not know the number pulling them all together. She had laughed that it all sounded a tax nightmare, and he said he had a company accounting firm and a bank of lawyers and solicitors as well, for each branch of the business, so he really left it to them. The only thing he did was to be involved with what he bought and sold in it all.

'So, you are worth a lot, then?' She smiled. 'I ask not for personal gain, you understand, but just to keep my eye on The Sunday Times Rich List!'

'I am in many cases asset-rich, more than numbers in the bank, so I don't appear on those, thank God,' he said to reply to her question.

'So, you don't know is the answer?' she asked, amazed that he was so not in control of his finances, this the control freak that had a take on everything.

'If I had to check my bank statements at the end of each month, I would be there for hours, I have personal allowances from various business as CEO. I don't get a pay packet at the end of the month. I have private personal property, such as accommodation, and as you know I have recently acquired some more to that portfolio, cars, these 'boys' toys' that take my fancy, but most things are in a business name, not me the person,' he joked, 'so there will be occasions when you can buy lunch!' She laughed, still really having no comprehension that with her income she was statistically a millionaire herself.

'So, have you lost a lot?' was her final question.

'Sometimes, I enjoy taking a risk, but I have to think about it when I know lots of people will be affected by my judgment. At times it can't be helped, but I don't go out of my way to destroy lives, unless...' He had stopped short and tried to change the topic of conversation, taking her mind off it by kissing her.

'Unless?' she had asked. 'Am I prying too much?'

'I have upset some people who have not taken it well along the years, let's just say that,' he continued, to distract her. He was not interested in telling her that the Italian mafia had tried to have him killed, and the Russian oil magnate had sent in the heavy mob, showing their annoyance by tampering with his mother's car, and the fact that he had had death threats. It was the main reason that Pete had been employed instead of a normal driver. Keeping this to himself would protect her: ensuring that these people did not know about her would protect her, too, he hoped.

The conversation had moved on and he hoped that she would not think too much of it. He was just Edward, Ed to his selected friends and that was who he wanted to portray, as he lay next to her, making love to her.

The skipper welcomed him aboard; he also tipped his hat at Lottie who was really glad she had chosen flat shoes because she could feel the boat's movement the moment her feet left the wooden deck. Although the weather was nice, sea legs was one thing she did not have a lot of. They were only going a few miles out, just to have lunch; she hoped it would be OK. The yacht was serviced by three crew members as well as the captain; Lottie refused the champagne and took a soft drink when it was offered. Once more with the attention of a ninja Edward asked if she was alright. Lottie had started to feel sick before they had even left the land; the feeling was becoming increasingly worse, but did not want to make a fuss, hoping she could get a grip and get over it! It was only a matter of time when it would all go wrong.

And one way to spoil a perfect setting was to throw up in the on-board loo, but she could not help it. She thought that she had done well but the first smell of the seafood that was prepared and presented to her for lunch finished and sealed the deal. Being on the water was not for her. They were sitting on the deck but spontaneously she dashed past Edward and shut the toilet door with a slam.

She was green as she went past him and the crew looked at him as if they had done something wrong. He got up and followed her; he tried the door but she had locked it. There was no mistaking from the sound of her retching that she was ill.

'Lottie, open up, let me in,' he said.

'Not a chance,' she said as she knelt by the basin retching to remove her breakfast once more.

'Please,' he said.

'There's nothing you can do. I don't have sea legs, that's all,' she said as he put his head on the door. Well, note to self: don't do this again, he thought. 'I'm sorry, I never thought, I should have asked. I will get them to take us back in.'

'How were you to know!?' she shouted back, still responding to her convulsing stomach, although it had been drained of everything now. 'It's me who is sorry, I have ruined your day.'

It was about ten minutes before she emerged out of the cabin. Edward sat in the sun on the deck just outside the door so that he could see when she came out. He had a short-sleeve tee shirt on and three-quarter-length shorts. He took the time to soak up some of the sun. He jumped up and she sat down in the cabin. 'You are better off outside. Get a look at the shoreline: it helps, or so they say.'

'I'm so sorry, I bet I look like death, what a glamorous date I have turned out to be!' She had washed her mouth and face and cleaned her teeth with the mouthwash that was in the cabin toilet. She thought to herself that maybe it was there for this very reason, but it did not make her feel any better, as she gagged it back up seconds after gargling.

'Your perfect baby girl,' he said as he sat her in the shade on deck. They had made it quite a long way back to the mainland, although Lottie doubted that looking at the shoreline helped as she dashed to the toilet one more time before they moored back up on the jetty.

'Land legs only,' he said to Pete as he helped her get in the car. 'Thanks for coming back sooner than planned.' She was feeling a bit better, but he asked him to take it steady driving to the resort. They checked into a room and Lottie stayed in the air-conditioned room while Edward and the guys

179

went for something to eat. They came back through the door laughing, almost as friends not boss and work colleagues.

'Better?' he asked as he noticed she had helped herself to a cup of tea.

'How embarrassing!' she said. 'But better, thanks.' She had also got changed into an overdress that showed her bikini through.

'It's just another part of you that I have learned today.' He placed his hands around her neck and ran his hand along her stomach. 'Do you want to try to eat something?'

'Phew, not yet.' She blew out breath just thinking of food. He kissed her head as she placed it back on the couch pillow.

'Pete's coming with me, but Steven is outside. He will show you to the pool if you want: you can have a snack in a bit if you do get peckish, just order on the room. I am just going to freshen up and change.'

'Need a hand.' She smiled and bit her lip, knowing that would get a response. 'So, we are feeling better?' he smirked. 'Sadly no time, but hold that little lip for me till later and then maybe.' He kissed her lips and sucked the one that she had bitten before leaving her to change.

With the promise of only being an hour, two max, he had gone. He had arranged to meet a business acquaintance: it was cheeky of him to mix the two but it had been some time since he had been over to Monaco, and he wanted to touch base. Last time he was there he had taken a few days out with some local girls they had picked up the night before and he – well, Alex - had caused an issue with some Frenchman's wife and they had to leave after a scuffle had broken out. It turned out she was the hotel owner's young wife. He only went back to the hotel because it was the best in the resort, and it was secure, no one minded who you were or why you were there; no paparazzi or photographers were let in. You had to be on the guest list and, although he had been asked to leave on that occasion, money could talk better to get you on any guest list. So, he was happy to leave her knowing that she would be OK, especially as Alex was not with them!

Lottie was sure that Steven must hate sitting around in a suit on such a hot day. They had gone to the poolside and she found a sunbed, and he sat on a chair in the shade out of the way with a bottle of water. She had found the little toiletry bag that even had sunscreen, and as she sat down to admire the surroundings she applied it to her pale skin. Not that the sun had much chance of turning her anything else but red in an hour, so the warmth in her bones and deep into her muscles was appreciated.

From another part of the pool bar he watched her through his dark glasses as she arrived and sat down. Nice, he thought, as she stripped off to the bikini and applied her suncream. He continued to watch her as she sat in the sun. Sometime later, the waiter had asked her if she wanted another drink and she just ordered water. He intercepted him and took the bottle over to her, and sat on the end of the sunbed. It made Lottie jump as she had her eyes closed.

'Your water, Mademoiselle,' he said in a strong French accent.

'Thank you.' She looked a little startled noticing it was not the waiter that had returned, and glanced towards where Steve had been sitting, but he had gone.

'Orange. Pleased to meet you.' He held out his hand and Lottie held hers out to return the handshake out of politeness. He took it to his lips and kissed it: she was taken aback by the gesture. 'Your little friend has gone to the boys' room if you are worried we are now alone. I am aware that Mr Dean does not like his ladies to be shared.'

'So why have you come to talk to me, then, sir, if you know that he will not be pleased?' She sat up on the bed and covered her legs with the see-through dress, not making much difference.

'Because everyone can share for a price, or I would not tell him if you do not!' His smile was not sincere at all and his tone and manner were lecherous. He ran a finger along her lower leg and she pulled it away. 'I notice that he has claimed you.' Lottie was not sure what he meant by that comment so she looked confused. Little did she know that he was referring to her necklace, which shone in the sun. He gave out a hearty laugh. 'Well done, Dean, an innocent, even better.'

'I am not sure what you are implying, but I was happy minding my business and I do not wish for your company.' She moved her legs to the side of the bed. She wished she had not chosen the one so close to the table as she was restricted to get off his side as he blocked the lower part of the bed. Without moving him down a bit, she had no choice but to be by his side. She was about to get up when he placed his hand on her wrist and gripped with a lot of force; he placed his other hand on her thigh and it pinned her down. She could not see now if Steven had arrived back behind her. She hoped if he had, he would come and help her, but to no avail.

'Headstrong and independent, I can see why he likes the fire in your eyes.'

'Can I ask you to leave?' she asked.

'You can ask, ask away, but I would like to stay and keep you company, get to know you better,' he replied, moving closer into her personal space.

Lottie could not believe that, although there were people around, no one seemed to be taking any notice and she was not sure if she should shout out.

'I will ask again then, excuse me.' She used her other hand to remove his from her thigh and pushed as hard as she could and was able to free her way past him. He had a tight grip on her wrist and it caused her a lot of pain to pull it free. Steven came rushing through the bushes that backed onto the pool.

'Miss Jenkins,' he called out and it was enough to make the Frenchman stand, release her and scurry away. He was out of breath as he reached her side. 'I'll go after him. Are you OK?' he asked.

'Don't worry, take me back upstairs, I'm fine. Are you OK?' He looked pale and washed out.

'Yes,' although clearly he was not: he was sweating and looked like he would pass out.

'You're not OK,' Lottie said, putting her dress back on and picking up her bag as if the situation was now over and she was concerned about him.

'Don't worry about me, too much heat, I have a bad stomach. I'm so sorry I left you but I had to. Mr Dean is going to kill me, if Pete does not!' Maybe the fear of Edward was more of a worry to him than the effects of the heat that he was clearly feeling, but Lottie smiled at him and started to walk away. 'No harm done, let's get back,' although the red throbbing in her wrist showed that the statement was not totally true.

She chose to sit on the balcony of the room where it was safer, but still in the sun. Steven was able to get a cool shower and sit in the air-conditioned room. She had told him to take it easy: looking at the clock she hoped that they would not be long. As she picked up a magazine that was left on the table she was soon able to relax again. She had some ice on her wrist: it had swollen and she guessed that it would bruise from the red patches that were already showing around the protruding bones.

The door opened and she heard Edward and Pete return: he came straight out to her and kissed her head.

'Feeling better?' he asked. She was able to hide her wrist from view.

'Thanks, good meeting?' He made chat as he got a water from the bar. Pete had gone into the other room to Steven, and Lottie wanted to get to him to explain.

'Yes, really good. I'm going to grab a shower and I will come out and join you. We have some time before we need to leave: you OK with that or would you like to go for something to eat?' He playfully flicked water at her. She gave a little squeal as he ran off but it gave her an excuse to get up and go back in. As soon as the water was running in the shower room she went into the other sitting room where she found the guys.

'Miss Jenkins, I am so sorry,' Pete started. 'Steven has explained and I cannot apologise enough.' He looked at her wrist. 'Are you OK?'

'In no way do I want you to blame Steven: the poor guy is ill and it could not be avoided. God knows I felt ill enough earlier. No harm done,' she said.

'Your wrist?' Pete enquired.

'Is fine, really, looks worse, or it will tomorrow anyway.' She finished his sentence.

'But how are you going to...' He did not dare to finish his own question. He knew that once his boss saw it, he would have to be told how it happened and then, well, someone would get his ass kicked. Regardless if Steven was ill or not, he sure as hell would be the first, and then there was no doubt, Pete himself would be in the firing line second.

'Go out and wait in reception, leave us, don't answer his calls or texts. If I need you I will call reception. Look after him.' She pointed to Steven. 'Edward will be fine, trust me.' They all left the room together. Pete gathered a few things, and Lottie wanted to wait until he was out back in the sitting room before she said anything.

Edward walked into her, grabbing a bottle of wine as he came through the kitchen area. He heard the suite door close.

'Pete gone out?' he asked. He had not asked him to.

'Steven has a bad stomach, he has been feeling the effects of the heat: they have gone to find a chemist's.' She was keeping as calm as she could.

'Oh,' he said. It was strange that he had not asked to go but he continued to pour the two glasses and took one over and placed it on the table. 'Coming back in the sun?' He had not put on a tee shirt. His rigid torso was still slightly wet and his hair was brushed back from his face. His shorts came above the knee showing off the outlined muscles in his legs and Lottie had to take a little look, just in case this was the last time ever: this conversation could go either way, good or bad.

She was able to allow the dress to drape over her arm and she sat down. He was lying back with his eyes closed: God, he looked good enough to eat. She felt her lower muscles clench at the thought of him, touching him, rubbing cream into him. She grabbed the sun lotion in her good hand and splattered a dollop onto his chest. He shot up like a spring and as a reaction he grabbed her other wrist. She yelped like an injured dog as the faint sound of a crack and searing pain coursed across her wrist into her forearm: a white heat shot through her, almost making her swoon. He could see in her face that it caused immense pain, and at that point Lottie did think that maybe this added action had caused a deeper injury than the first; now it felt more than just the soft tissues. The crack was definitely bones. She held her wrist out from the elbow, not wanting to touch it.

'Christ, Lottie, I am sorry, I don't know my own strength. Fuck!' He was mortified that he had done this, but he was sure that he had not gripped her that hard. He wanted to cradle her then thought better of it: she had tears streaming down her pale face as the realisation that the pain was not going away hit her. 'Let me look,' he said, gingerly drawing her arm to him. 'What the fuck?' He instantly went red in the face as his voice was raised more than she had ever witnessed, 'Lottie, what the hell happened here? That was not me.'

She did not want to cry, she tried to control herself: the tears were not from the incident, but the increased pain that she was now feeling. She tried to make a fist but could not without instant surges of liquid heat travelling from her hand to her elbow. She had to sit down as she knew she would be sick but her legs failed and she was dizzy: anticipation of the situation or the realisation that she may have fractured the delicate complex bones around the wrist area and she was genuinely going into shock. This mixed with being sick, and not eating anything for all of the day was making her weak. She looked at him.

'Don't go off on one.' She started feeling fainter by the second.

'Well, if you don't explain how that happened how in hell's name can I make that decision not to?!' he replied, shouting at her.

She had to take a breath to compose herself. She explained what happened and within the first line he was on his feet with his phone in his ear. 'Fucking pick it up, you waste of space.' He started to text instead. **Shit, Pete, where the fuck are you?'** He rammed and shouted the voice message down the phone as he rang his number again with no answer and hung up, looking at Lottie. She was still trying to explain as he rushed to the door. 'I will kill the prick. If Pete is not around I will do it myself.' She stood, putting herself in the way to stop him using the door.

'Move please, Lottie.' His voice was deep, commanding and loud. He reached out to the couch for his tee shirt he had left there when he came out of the shower.

'No.' She stood her ground. 'I don't want you to go downstairs, I asked Pete not to reply to you, I don't want to make a scene, please Edward. I am here, I am fine. I promise you, please! I handled it and Steven was there to help.' She held the door for two reasons: first, she did not want him to get out; and second, she was close to blacking out from the pain.

'He was too fucking late to be there to look after you. Move, Lottie, I am not asking you again.' He hated raising his voice to her, but he knew her too well that she was not moving. 'I will move you out of the way if I have to.'

He did not have to; she collapsed to the floor and it all went black in her world. She hit her head as she went down on the corner of the table by the door. Edward was just too blinded by his anger to react any quicker to catch her as her temple made contact with the marble top.

She never heard him scream her name, or see her collapse at her feet as he tried to apply pressure to the area of her head that was leaking her lifeblood. With his other hand he texted Pete's number: **Get here Now! Lottie's collapsed.**

She had been wrapped in a sheet and put in the back of the car. She had never left the confines of Edward's arms until she was placed on a trolley at the hospital. Pete had arrived in the room within seconds of the text to see the scene and, although he had not said anything, he gave Edward a look that suspected he had caused this. As they walked to the room that Lottie was taken into Edward turned to his driver.

'I never touched her, Pete, she collapsed by the door. She was trying to stop me from getting out to you, or that prick that started this, but I was standing nowhere near her. If I had been by her, I would have caught her when she fell.' He took a breath and looked at the doctors working on her. He had relayed the story to them as they arrived, and now he was doing it to his employee in the hope that someone would believe him.

'She will be fine.' Pete tried to reassure him. 'What else do you want me to do?' The flight had to be cancelled and tomorrow's plans were discussed. Edward wanted some clean clothes as he had her blood on them. 'And Orange?' Edward only gave him a look and Pete left the corridor. He turned back round to the window: she had not moved or woken up. He needed someone to tell him what was going on. He hit his head on the glass and left it there. This is my fault, all my fault: once more I have fucked it up for her. He took a deep breath and sighed, and continued to watch them plug in leads and drips to her frail body.

It was well over 40 minutes until the doctor came out to speak to Edward; his English was good. He explained that she needed to go for a scan as they suspected some swelling on the brain. This would also confirm the wrist injury. He could tell that he also was sceptical of how it happened, and Ed tried to defend himself. He needed her to wake up soon and remember what had happened to ensure that people knew the true story, but the doctor had explained that they sedated her until they knew more about the head injury. He was sure that she would be in for over 48 hours, and that if any relations from home needed to be contacted: they were welcome to visit.

Edward had not thought about anything else. He followed her from the scan room back to the trauma room, and then onto the side room once she had her arm in plaster and the bandage changed on her head.

'You may sit with her now,' the doctor explained, 'but we do not expect her to wake as she is still sedated. There is mild swelling to the brain but we are not worried, although she must be very careful for a few months not to have impact there again. The wrist has a hairline fracture in the scaphoid.' The doctor pointed to the top of his wrist showing where the bone was. 'She is also very weak and dehydrated, I guess from lack of food, and you mentioned she had been sick in the morning, so maybe this caused the blackout. All the other tests for her are fine.'

Edward still knew that he doubted him and his story but he did not care: he was able to sit with her, be with her. He sat to the side of the bed and took her good hand in his. He stroked her hand with his thumb and placed his head on her arm. At all costs he would not lose her. He had asked Pete to contact Agnes, and if she wanted he would arrange to get her out there. The flight was only two hours, and now that they knew Lottie would be in the hospital for at least 48 hours, he thought that she should know, if not, be there when she woke up.

As the night came, they arranged to move Lottie to a better room. One that had a bathroom and larger sitting area. Edward had insisted on paying for a doctor and another nurse to be available to her at all times. He continued to sit by her side, only leaving her to use the bathroom; he had even changed his clothes whilst standing next to her bed.

What little he ate he did by her side and he slept in the chair at the side of her bed, pulling it close so that he could hold her hand while he caught a little sleep. He talked to her as much as he could. He had a radio brought in and played music in the background on the hope that Lottie could hear him. She was checked every half an hour and it was early morning, with the sun breaking through the half-drawn curtains that the doctor said they could slowly bring her round from the sedation. They felt that the worst had passed.

Pete opened the door first, followed by Agnes.

'Mr Dean, you promised me that you would take care of her.' She looked at the young man who was showing strain and signs that he had not slept much, or showered or shaved. Although his form was still perfect, the past 24 hours were taking their toll on him. 'How on earth did this happen?' She moved to the other side of Lottie and gently rubbed her arm above the plaster; she gave her a gentle kiss on the cheek. Although Pete had outlined the events when he had collected her from the airport she wanted to hear it from him.

Edward stood and replayed the day verbally out again, listing each detail as it happened. When he had finished, she, too, had the look on her face that said she was not sure that he did not push her. Or his anger had more than anything to do with this.

'I want her back with me,' Agnes said, 'as soon as she is fit to come home. Dick and I will look after her for as long as she needs us.' She took breath. 'I have known Lottie a lot longer than you have, young man, and I am sure from the looks of this I can take better care of her. I know she will want to be at home.'

Edward had presumed that she would stop with him and had already asked Pete to forewarn Mrs B. He did not want to argue here but he could feel his temper rising at the prospect of having to let her go. He was about to say something when he felt her squeeze his hand.

'Lottie,' he said, looking at her face to see if her eyes were opening. 'Baby girl, I am here,' he whispered in her ear, kissing her lightly on the face. She squeezed it again and in a croaky voice said, 'Ed?' He pressed the button to call the nurse, although she would have only been another five minutes for her rounds she would have been in anyway.

'We're here.' Agnes touched her arm, too, so she knew that there was more than one person in the room.

'We are both here,' Edward added.

'What, what happened?' She winced, realising that she had pain in her head.

'You can't remember?' Agnes said. 'Do you know what happened, did you fall?' Her question cut deep into Edward's stomach as if she had a blade and thrust it into him.

'Agnes, why are you here?' Lottie asked. 'How long have I been out? I'm not sure I remember.' Lottie tried to sit up but the nurse entered the room and stopped her.

'Miss Jenkins, the doctor will be in to see you.' She looked at both Edward and Agnes. 'Can I ask you both to leave so we can assess Miss Jenkins?'

Edward kissed her cheek. 'I'm outside the door,' he said, reluctant to leave but he did.

For what seemed like an age the doctor stayed in the room with Lottie doing checks. The blinds had been drawn so they could not see in. The doctor asked her what had happened while he checked his charts and took her blood pressure. At first it had been hazy, but without any prompting, she said, 'I am not sure if it was the pain, or shock or the fact that I had not eaten, but I blacked out. I'm guessing I hit something on the way down.' She looked at her wrist. 'And it was fractured in some way?' She licked her lips that were dry, and the doctor passed her a drink. 'We were playing about. He did grab me, but the injury happened before then. I heard a crack so I gathered I had damaged something.'

'Mr Dean has explained himself, as you have just outlined. I am happy that there was no foul play.'

'No,' Lottie said, making him turn around. 'It was nothing like that, he never...' She stopped before saying 'hit me', thinking how everyone must have thought the same as it looked from the outside world. One very angry man, one woman with a couple of injuries, no one else around in the room, raised voices - hey presto, domestic violence.

'I want you to rest, Miss Jenkins. You will not be flying home today, maybe tomorrow afternoon. Mr Dean has assured us that you are on a private flight and one of the nurses has been assigned to stay with you, so

I will be back in later to see you.' He went to the door to beckon them in. 'Sleep as much as you can, and I suggest that Mr Dean goes back to where you are staying and gets some rest. He has not left your bedside: he looks drained.'

Within a second Edward was back at her side, holding her hand. The doctor repeated himself about her sleeping and when she could go home, and Agnes said, 'Then you will come to stay with me and Dick. We can look after you until you are fighting fit.' Instead of just fighting, she finished under her breath. She patted Lottie on the arm: both Edward and Lottie had heard the last comment.

'Agnes, it was an accident, I explained to the doctor and he confirms what I said, to what Edward had explained happened. I don't want anyone to think it was anything else. He lost his temper, yes, but not with me or at me, so you had better get that straight.' Her blood pressure monitor beeped noticeable faster as she was becoming quite anxious that this was not all Edward's fault.

'Mrs Deakin, if you feel Lottie will be safer with you, then please, let me arrange for the nurse to be at your house. I know how this all looks to you. Lottie is, of course, right: I was very angry at what had occurred by the pool, but I would change it all if I knew that this would be avoided.'

'Please don't fight, I'm too tired. Edward, you look as bad as I feel: please take some time out of here to eat and change.' She looked at him 'Please, I really don't want to upset either of you, and for practical reasons I know I should not be left alone for the first day or so when we get home, but can we think about it when it happens?'

He asked if she was sure; Agnes disagreed and wanted to stop, but finally the door had closed and they both left. Lottie closed her eyes. He looked so dejected from it all. As she sat, various memories came back to her and she was sure that she had heard Edward talking while she was unconscious. She remembered him talking about how sorry he was for booking the trip, and that he would never stop at the hotel again, it only had bad memories, how he should not have gone to do business while she was with him. She held her breath: it was in that conversation she was sure he said, 'Baby girl, I love you, please wake up and let me tell you! She must have dreamt it.

Chapter 12

However the conversation had gone with Edward and Agnes to where Lottie would stay, they had been overruled by her own request to go to stop at her own flat. Neither was happy and as a compromise the nurse whom Edward had hired stayed with her for the first day. This meant that there was not enough bed space for Agnes to stay, and to allow her to rest, by choice (more like at Lottie's request). Edward had also gone home that night. He had asked Pete to stay in the flat, and as a gesture that Lottie really wanted this all putting behind her, she asked for Steven instead. Edward had asked Pete to sack him, so she knew this was a saving grace for him and he would not fail anyone again. She was also not allowed to drive for a week and, although she had not planned any trips, she knew that she was not confined to the flat if need be.

'You give too many people a second chance,' Edward said to her when she requested this from him. He knew deep down at least someone would be there who could keep in touch with him as to her whereabouts.

'We all need a break in life. By the sound of how people thought I got these injuries, you should be grateful for that advice.' He had seen her point.

Rest was something she found hard between the phone calls, text messages, delivery of flowers and more flowers in the days that followed. Pete had dropped off her bags, making a point to hand her the gold and pink diamond necklace that Edward had taken off in hospital and kept with him. The stuff they had taken away on the trip was sent back to Edward's apartment. They had joked when Lottie said it could hang in the wardrobe at her house there. The comment made them laugh for the first time during the whole event, and she thought that maybe they could move on. He still seemed to be walking on eggshells around her, and she was worried that this had affected him more than she thought.

He had not told her that he had been to see Dr Morgan on their return, but it had cleared his mind on how he could avoid such a rage of feelings raising their heads again, although that was to be proved with time!

Lottie had spoken to Todd on the first day she was back, while Edward was out of the room. He was devastated that no one had called him; although he was not able to do anything at the time, he had wanted to at least know.

'Edward would not have thought to call you,' Lottie explained.

'Well, at least I know that the guy exists, if only in name: when am I ever going to meet him?' he asked.

Lottie was not sure that she should explain about how very possessive he was, but wondered if he could come over on Friday lunchtime: they could chat about work and he could bring the new case that she was supposed to get on her return on the Tuesday. Maybe if Edward came, too, they could meet on common ground. He would no doubt be over after work to see her and to give Steven a few hours' break as he was still posted in her flat, much to her annoyance now. It seemed a simple thing to do.

Lottie dropped it into conversation with Edward the night before, just as he was leaving her flat.

'You should not be working, Lottie.' He looked at her, wanting to be forceful, but one look into her eyes and he knew that he was on a losing foot from the off.

'It's not working, though, is it? I will be sitting here at home, with Steven or you, or Todd just reading or using the internet. Granted, I still have a headache and yes, the stitches and the yellow eyes and forehead from the bruise are most unattractive, but a folder of paper is not going to mind that, is it?' She almost pleaded, wondering why she had to reason with him.

'Why do you have to be so stubborn? Will you ever listen to people who love you.' It came out without even a hesitation from his lips. He had only used the love word once before as she lay next to him in the hospital bed. He was not really sure himself if he understood the meaning of the word. If it meant that being insanely jealous, more than ever before of anyone else around her, was it love? If it meant that not being next to her felt like he was incomplete, is that love? If it hurt like hell to know that she was in pain, how can that be love? If he wanted her body and mind, but respected them also, is that love? And if it meant that she was the only person he had ever told his true feelings to, then he was in love. And did he regret saying it? No, he did not.

At the point of not wanting to prompt him to say it again, she kissed him and replied, 'I always listen to the ones I love, I just may not do what they want me to!'

He smiled at her, knowing what she meant, if that was her reply to say she loved him, he could live with that for now.

'One last thing,' he said. 'Pete did bring back your necklace, didn't he?' He softly kissed her neck in the area that he wished it to be adorning.

'Yes, sorry, I have just not put it back on, my neck is still a bit stiff. I will go and fetch it.' She wandered off to her bedroom where the item had been put safely away from sight.

As he helped her do up the clasp at the back, his placed a kiss in the crook of her neck.

'There, where it belongs: beauty with beauty', he said more at ease now that he knew she was connected in this way again to him.

Todd arrived early, and kissed her on both cheeks as she opened the door. She asked Steven to run to the shop for some milk and it was a nightmare now that he had to ring Pete, or Ed himself before he left her side. It was getting a bit too much for her to cope with, but she was sure that when she returned to normal after the weekend and she could drive herself it would be better. 'Can you get another bottle of red? No make that two, and some chocolate biscuits for coffee later,' she asked after he confirmed he could go. Todd looked on, amazed.

'Really, is he that controlling?' he asked when the door had closed.

'Protective after what happened,' she replied, 'although I have to say wearing a bit thin now.' The next comment from Todd was so flippant that he never thought about it, but something, something seemed to click with Lottie. It brought several other comments together, too.

'Surprised the collar does not have a chain so he can have you totally housebound,' and pointing to the necklace. 'I presume it was another lavish gift?'

'Not jealous of him, are you? I am not going to have two testosterone-fuelled brutes on my hands tonight, am I?' She tried to make light of the comment but it sat at the back of her mind.

'Been there, done that, over it now!' he mocked her. She punched his shoulder as a playful gesture. 'I was about to say and what a pleasurable time it was, so yes, maybe I am.'

'Well saved, then, I take it back,' she said, rubbing the place she had playfully hit.

'We never had money, Lotts, did we? But we had fun,' he asked.

'We did. And I am so glad that I have you as a work colleague, and a friend now,' she replied.

'So, is he Mr Right?' he asked as she passed him the glass of wine she had opened and had been pouring while they talked.

'I am not sure I can totally answer that; he is not Mr Wrong, though,' she said. 'Cheers,' as they clinked glasses.

'Explain that comment, and is it not too early to be drinking?'

'It's twenty past three and I have been stuck in here all day, so no!' she replied. 'I thought that I was getting to know all of him, breakthrough what everyone else can only see, but then what happened here?' She pointed to her face.

'Are you saying he hit you?' he retorted with his nostrils flared. 'Or he was rough with you?'

'No, why is everyone saying that straight away, jumping to the wrong conclusions? I fell, get it? I mean there is something.' She took a moment to almost think of the right words. 'Something dark. I guess, that I have not seen and it worried me that if, or when, I do I won't like it.'

'Like it less than the fact that he is a dominating control freak, that has too much cash and had more women than hot dinners and probably has never had anyone say no to him in his life. Butter would not melt to look at him.' He sat on the stool by the small breakfast bar.

'How do you know what he looks like?' she asked.

'Google is a wonderful tool.' He laughed.

'I did that and did not get too much,' she replied, sipping again at her wine.

'Google and some of the most impressive electronic systems a private forensic science lab can buy, then!' he said again. 'Although I have to hand it to him, I could find nothing with you and him together. I have looked for some of the events that you said you have attended and it seems he is not happy to share you with the photographers of the world.'

Her spine went cold: say that to anyone else and they would not have reacted, but Lottie had heard that already this week.

Sensing her tension of the subject, he pulled his laptop out and said, 'Before we get too much wine inside us, can I just show you this.' He also produced a file. They looked at the information for a while. Steven had returned and vanished to the spare room. Lottie filled the glasses and found one of the other bottles and opened it in anticipation of refilling the glasses as required.

They had worked for about an hour when Todd said, 'Hey, guess what I also found?' He pulled a disk out and placed it in the machine. Clicking it to play, he smiled. 'Remember this?' he asked.

The DVD played and Lottie started laughing. It was when they had been at uni, one of the nights in the bar where they had played in the band. 'You have a few more pounds.' She laughed again, patting his stomach.

'Cheeky!' He stuck out his tongue. 'And of course you are just as beautiful.' He held her smile and she looked back at him. She leaned over his shoulder to get a closer look at them in their younger years. The next bit was Lottie playing the piano, with Todd sitting at her side playing a song together.

'You never could get that bit right.' She pointed at the screen at a specific point in the duo playing.

'Yes, I did, you had your arms in the way.' He was reaching over her, showing her, and their faces were inches apart. He could smell the sweet wine on her lips, the soft fragrance of her hair that he remembered. He could have kissed her there and then.

Neither of them had heard the front door open. Ed could hear the music and laughter coming from the kitchen where the door was slightly ajar. For a second, he looked in and observed the scene. His eyes narrowed, his nostrils flared, and the gut instinct was to crash through the door. He took a breath, with Dr Morgan's voice in his head: 'Control, Dean.' He said it to himself again. He knew that he could not give it another second, but he almost froze when he saw how close they were. She looked so at ease. Did she look like that when she laughed with him?

Lottie pushed back slightly, knowing that she was in Todd's space. The moment had passed between them, but it was undeniable that there had been something there once. Did they have unfinished business?

'Having fun?' Ed asked as he finally managed to control himself enough to open the door.

'Ed, you're early,' Lottie said, not in surprise but as a statement. Todd jumped up after she had moved towards Ed and they kissed quickly as a normal greeting. He kept his hand on her back, stating his male dominance over the other Alpha in the room. 'Ed, meet Todd Carter. Todd, Edward Dean, Ed.' She gestured with her hands as she said it. The men formally shook hands, both vying for the upper hand with the strength of the shake. They both nodded in acknowledgment.

'Started without me,' he said, looking at the empty bottle, taken aback that she had been drinking so much and still taking quite strong prescription painkillers.

'Sorry, we finished talking shop and we got carried away a bit,' she said, totally unaware that he had been observing them seconds before.

'I could see that! Your work looks far more fun than mine!' he said as an implication to the laughter they had been sharing as he arrived.

'We were just looking at this.' She spun round the laptop and Ed witnessed the two of them playing, just at the point when they kissed at the end of the number.

Awkward! Todd thought to himself. 'Can I get you a glass?' he said, trying to break the chill that had suddenly gone around the room, pointing to the bottle and getting up to grab a glass from the cupboard.

'Thank you,' Ed replied. He looked at Lottie. 'How have you been today?' He was trying to act normal.

'OK,' she said. He rubbed his finger over her forehead; she had taken the dressing off to leave the stitches in the air.

'Coming off tomorrow.' It was a statement more than a question from Ed as Todd went to refill her glass. 'So, should you have any more?' he finished.

'Hell, yes,' Todd replied for her. 'It's going to hurt like hell!' But he could see from the look on Ed's face that if he filled her glass, he was likely to get some stitches of his own. But he could not help but continue to goad him. 'Harley Street opens on a Saturday, then?'

'If you pay enough, yes,' came the curt reply.

Lottie jumped off her chair. 'If you boys don't play nicely then you can both get out!' She pulled the laptop lid down to stop the continuing music that no one was now listening to. 'This was supposed to be you two meeting each other as important parts of my life, not a point-scoring sheet to see who has the better hand, or the bigger balls. Get over yourselves.' She took the bottle off the table and filled her glass herself.

Both of the men looked at each other, wondering who would apologise first.

'Sorry,' Todd said to Ed, breaking the silence of wills.

'Sorry, Lottie.' Ed purposely apologised to her first, taking a sip of wine as if he needed to wet his mouth before he expressed the same regard to Todd. Lottie stared at him. 'Todd.' He nodded, still feeling the need to add his male dominance in some way by not adding 'Sorry'.

'Right, children, can we eat now?' she asked, pulling out the takeaway menu. 'And I hope that I am not going to have to clear up the mess in the morning after you have had a food fight!' She tried to lighten the mood, but she was goddamn pissed with them both. She took her phone from her pocket and punched in the number. 'Who wants what?'

It took time to get civil conversation going. Lottie did stop drinking after her glass was empty, not because she felt she should do as she was told, but she did feel quite giddy, and if it did kick off she wanted to be able to control the situation as much as she could. Well, or call Pete who was inevitably sitting outside, or somewhere close outside, at best.

If it was genuine interest or not, Ed asked about Todd's work at the Centre, and how it was funded. Slowly the ice had melted, although Lottie was sure that there would always be a tension between them; she supposed it was like that for men to meet ex-partners, and she had to think how she would feel if she met one of Ed's exes. In fact, the more she thought of that, the more she dreaded the day.

As it headed towards 9:30pm Todd said he needed to go to catch the tube home. As a peace-offering Lottie asked if Pete could take him. It looked as if she had asked for the remainder of Ed's fortune to be handed over at gunpoint, but he said yes.

She shut the door and walked back into the sitting room after Todd had left. She picked up the empty glasses and the plates and went to the kitchen and loaded the dishwasher.

'You're pissed with me,' Ed said, following her in.

'No shit, Sherlock,' she replied, not looking round at him.

'I tried,' he said and she spun round.

'Well, I would suggest you try harder next time. Todd and I have history, granted, but me and you.' She paused. 'I would like to think we have got a future, but I can't cope with that intensity Ed, I really can't.'

'Is this our first argument?' he asked with a little hope that she had still been thinking about the future.

'If you want it to be,' she quickly replied. She was half-tempted to bring up the subject Todd had noted about sharing her with the world. Let alone bringing up the comment about the necklace.

He was stunned with her answer. 'No, I don't want it to be, I don't ever want us to argue.' He really did mean that. 'I also don't want to see you so pissed off, but I have managed that again,' he added. He leaned against the worktop next to where she was still putting in the dishes one-handed. He leaned down and took her hand to stop her doing it. She looked as if she did not want him to stop her, but did not put up a fight in any case. He guessed he would just say it anyway while it was on his mind. He pulled her a little closer; again she did not resist, which he took as a good sign.

He put his hand under her chin, making her look at him. 'I meant what I said the other day, Lottie. I am falling in love with you and I can't deal with the emotion. I have never felt like this. I am a grown, professional businessman, with more responsibility than others. I have had to play hard ass or die for so long, I know nothing else, but you...' He ran his hand through her hair, aware not to pull the side that was still looking painful. 'You have spun me around on my heels and I can't stop.' He continued to work his hand along her neck, and down her spine. She licked her lower lip unconsciously and she felt him tense. 'I never thought this would be the outcome of our meeting. I hoped it would after the first night: you know that because I have told you before. But the control I find the hardest is with you.'

'You may be the most irresistible male specimen, and you really could charm the pants off a nun! Especially if you kiss me there.' He laughed at her metaphor after he had kissed the nape of her neck. 'But I also explained that you have me. This week has been an emotional roller coaster for us both. Life is not going to be simple and so the added issue of having to be on my guard all the time around men – well, damn it, other people full stop are tiring, exhausting.' She paused. 'And I don't think that I can do it.' She paused again.

Had he lost her with that statement? He had stopped kissing her: was she gearing up to say it was over? He ran his hand through his hair. She leaned over and flicked the kettle on, moving from his grip. It was not the fact that she revealed her bare flesh of her stomach in doing so that made him feel like his chest was being pushed through his throat; it was the anticipation of what she was going to do or say next.

It was not sexual desire that he craved from her now, it was the emotion he had expressed to her that he desperately wanted her to feel back. The long silence stabbed at him. She grabbed two mugs and put in the instant coffee.

'Lottie, tell me what you want me to do.' He was desperate for the conversation to continue. She wanted to laugh and say, 'Grab the milk!' But she would not be that cruel so she opened the fridge and got it herself. 'Lottie, stop the goddamn coffee shit, please, I'm dying here, talk to me!'

'And now you know how it feels,' she said, 'to know that life is so precious that you could lose it any minute, to know you feel something for someone else so strong, so deep, so uncontrollable that your life becomes inconsequential. Next time you get jealous think about it. Know that I have those feelings, too: nothing on this earth will stop me falling in love with you, because it has happened. I will do anything to try not to hurt you, but I will never give up the girl you are falling in love with, and by default that in itself will hurt you.' She stopped. 'Learn to share this world with me not continually defending me from the world.' It was her sweeping statement that jolted him back in the room.

'I don't want this to be over,' he said, not knowing if her statement was still open-ended.

'You're not listening, that is the last thing I want, but I don't know what you want me to be,' she said, walking back into his space.

'I want you to be my...' He thought about it: she was right, it came down to him stating his ownership every time. 'I want you to be with me,' he said, 'alongside me, an equal to share with, to always fill the part that you have become of me,' he said almost in a whisper as he understood his own words and what she was asking him.

'Was that a counselling breakthrough?' she asked. 'Are you getting my point?'

'If only you knew how much I get your point.' He knew he needed to kiss her, but he had to let her make that first move. As she went onto her tiptoes his heart finally took another beat as her lips were planted on his. He slowly pulled her to him and returned her kiss.

They sat on her sofa with their coffee and continued to talk. If it had been their first argument, no one had won. But they both had better respect for each other, so they agreed to leave it at that. But if he really had learned the restraint it would have to be proven and tested again, of that they were both sure.

As promised, Ed pulled back on insisting that Steven was her shadow. He had accepted that she would return to working for the centre and she had been going back to Kent alone one weekend out of two to catch up with life back there. They had both kept busy, but still been able to pull time together. Ed had more regular sessions with Dr Morgan, and it finally felt that it was working for him. They had been out as a couple and he had made the effort to let her socialise with Todd and his family. He had even been out with them for a meal and found that the more he knew Todd and the way he was with Lottie, the more he knew that he could trust him.

They had been seen in public and for the first time accepted that the papers were going to pick up on the fact that one of the capital's playboys had been seen with the same girl more than once. He had backed off on the gestures he showed by buying everything he thought Lottie needed, although when she had flowers she loved them.

It was late-August when Ed took a call from Alex that came through on his office phone.

'Well, stranger,' he began, 'I see you have a new woman on your arm and I have not met the lovely lady. Word on the street is that you're in lovvvvve!'

'And if it is, then they are right,' Ed retorted straight back at him. 'A strange concept to you, I'm sure.'

'Hell, yes, why commit when there are so many lovely ladies out there that you don't have to give them the world just promise them it, and then find another who does not know you did not mean it. What happened to the old Ed I know?' he asked.

'He may have grown up?' he said back.

'Or had too many counselling sessions by the sound of things. I may have to come back and show you the way again, old friend.' Alex had been in Europe for the past two months spending his parents' money and living it up as usual for the summer in some place or other.

'Ran out of places to cause havoc, then.' Ed referred to his last comment of coming home.

'No, just bored, and interested in your newfound love life.' He laughed.

'Nice picture from the charity awards: she does look lush. Nice necklace, too. Is she a true sub?'

'Fuck you.' The conversation turned within a second. 'Back off, you are overstepping the mark, she is no sub.'

'OK dude, understood. It must be love, love love,' he sang down the phone.

'Seriously, Alex, I'm not in this conversation. Now what did you want really?'

'Bit of bother,' he replied, knowing that he did need to keep his friend sweet as he needed some help.

'How many times do I have to bail you out?' Ed asked back.

'How many times did I bail you out over the years in that hell-hole they called a school?' Alex asked back.

'That's getting to be an old story now, this is the last time for whatever it is.' His friend continued the conversation to outline his predicament.

'Not drugs, no way, I'm not involved. You know my feelings on that, never have, never will.' Ed was mad now. The subject was still one he would never face: it was drugs that had allegedly killed Mitch that night as he drove his car off the road, and he wanted nothing to do with it. 'The fucking Russians, you are joking me,' he continued to say as Alex furthered his dealings and problems. 'You're on your own,' Ed replied to whatever he had been told. 'I said no, I'm not coming out there. I have not got that many people in my pocket: why can't you pay them off?' He continued to listen. He was pacing the floor as he walked round his office with the phone stuck to his ear. 'One phone call: if it does not work, then you're on your own. That's my final word.'

He put down the phone and called Pete. 'Shit, shit, shit,' he said out loud. He had only just got them back onside from the last dealings he had had with one of the top Russian families; that had cost him millions and they promised he would not be heard of again in their country. He would make the call as much as he did not want to, but the threat of them killing his friend was not an empty one. If they said they would, then give it 24 hours and they would. He had to think about this. That would fuck the rest of the plans up for the day, and meeting Lottie later and the weekend.

About six years before, he had an oil company that he had all but stolen in a card game of all things from a very drunk Russian guy who turned out to be the son of a very dodgy oil baron. He had sold it back to him for a high price, but then Ed was not to know that the reverse would run out within a year and that the family would never see the returns on what they had owned in the first place. He had paid them the money back, just to keep good international relations. They considered him good for his word and said that they would leave it at that.

Now he needed them to reason with a rival family whom Alex had slipped into the drug-buying world with, losing them over a million when he had lost the shipment to the police, he could see why they were pissed. He needed to raise the funds which would not be hard. But after speaking to one of their representatives on the phone, for some reason they wanted him to go over in person and hand over the cash.

The plane journey was long, and Ed really had no intention of hanging around in the country. He had pulled some strings and spent a lot of cash. This was the last thing he was doing for Alex, and he meant that. Worst of all, he had to lie to Lottie where he was going.

The drop had gone well and Alex was deposited back to Ed as promised and everyone was happy all round as they came back to the UK late on the Sunday morning. Then Alex dropped the bombshell.

'Well, mate, I will have your money back by the end of the week,' he said.

'If you had the money why did I have to pay?' Ed looked at him sitting in the back of his car on the way back to the city.

'Because they said that if you trusted me to come all the way over there then the deal had to be good, with no strings attached: you trust me, they trust you, all that bullshit.'

'There is a but?' Ed said; he could feel it coming.

'But the drugs had not been lost to the police, I just forgot what shipment they came in on and where they went, along with the other million pounds' worth they did not know I had.' He laughed. 'When I sell them, you get your money back, and the deal goes down in the U.S.' He looked at his watch. 'In about an hour's time! They were fools to trust that you trusted me!'

'You fucking wanker, so when they find out that you have ripped them off, they come looking for me, not you?' He leaned over and grabbed him by the throat. Pete looked behind him in the mirror: he had been listening to the conversation and was just checking in case he needed to stop the car.

'Chill, bro, the Yanks will bail us out, that's part of my deal with them. Nothing to do with you, Mr Dean.' Alex was grabbing at his captor's hand to release some of the pressure so he could breathe. 'They wanted a way into the Russian trade, so I gave it to them. My first business deal in ages should make some good profit.' He laughed.

'Oh God, what the fuck have you got me into?' He slumped back in his chair. 'Were you high when you thought this thing through!?' he shouted back.

'A bit,' Alex bit back. 'And shagging one of their wives!'

'When you get out of this car, we are through. If shit comes anywhere near my door I will kill you. Fuck the Russians doing it, that is a promise. I don't care what we have had in the past, count this as my last goodbye. We will not be speaking again, even think about coming into my life and it will hurt.' He tapped the window. 'Stop the car.'

'No, bro, you can't. We are not back yet,' Alex protested and Ed looked at him closer.

'You're high now?' Ed asked, prompting his friend to dip his hand in his pocket and pull out a large package. 'Want some?'

'This is just a fucking joke to you. If we had been stopped we would both have been done,' Ed retorted.

'Your corporate jet is never stopped. Customs don't bother Mr squeaky clean Mr Dean.' Alex lay further back in his seat as he exaggerated his name, unaware that the car had stopped now.

'My fucking corporate jet could have been stopped and that would have risked my business reputation, not just my personal one. You played me! Used my trust and played me for a fool.' How he had not hit him by now was showing some restraint, Pete thought, as he got out of the car ready to open the door and deposit the person he disliked most in the world on the side of the road.

'You've got lawyers and judges in the pay that can get you off.' Alex really was not in control of his senses. Whatever he had taken, whenever he had taken it, was having a good effect. He was truly off his head in both aspects of the term. 'Or you can sleep with them, or their daughters to keep them on good terms... Oops, forgot, almost married man now.' A red rag to a bull would have had a lesser effect. Ed placed his fist in his passenger's ribs, satisfied by the thud as he made contact. The next was to his face, instantly bursting his nose open. Like a whimpering child he went into a foetal position, but Ed laid into him again, and again.

Pete opened the door afraid that Ed truly would kill him in a public place, and instead of getting Alex out, he pulled Ed out in an attempt to cool him down.

'Not here,' he said, restraining him. 'Think of the consequences.' Pete almost pleaded with his employer as the muffled sounds of pain were mixed with: 'You bastard, you have broken my nose', 'I played you because you have gone soft', 'Never trust anyone, Edward, is that not what we used to say?' Pete put his head in the door. 'Shut the fuck up or I will finish you here.' Alex cowered again knowing that Pete would carry out a threat.

'Think, Edward, think, think,' Ed said out loud to himself. Just as he was pacing on the side of the road that was busy with other traffic, his phone rang. He looked at the screen and Lottie's picture and name came up. 'No, no, not now.' He gave the phone to Pete. 'Say something.'

As requested he took the phone and made an excuse that they had a flat tyre, as she had noted they were on a road and that Ed had gone into the garage. Satisfied she had taken the story, he hung up.

'Get in, take him back to his place. We are only half an hour away and just leave him,' Ed said.

'He is injured,' Pete said.

'Don't care. He won't die from his injuries: he has enough painkillers in him, he won't even notice. He's breathing, isn't he?' I will call his mother and say he got into a fight: she can look after him.' Ed pulled out the packet from Alex's pocket. He put his finger in the powder and rubbed some of it on his lips. Alex licked it off. 'Here, have some more and shut the fuck up!' Edward repeated the process.

Alex's parents lived in a respectable part of the city. His mother had taken the call, and as it was not the first time in their lives this had happened, she believed Ed and was waiting for him as they pulled up. She was beside herself, and though Ed felt sorry for her, had no compassion for the person he had called friend for many years as Pete rolled him out of the car and into the house.

'You picked him up from the airport like this?' Mrs Girski asked.

'Yes, he called me out of the blue, said he was in trouble so we went to get him.' He knew that Alex would not give her the real details, and quite frankly he did not give a shit if he did. They were over.

'Have you called the police?' she asked.

Ed pulled out the package from Alex's coat. 'I thought I had better not!'

She fell almost to the floor weeping: he knew how that would break her heart but could see it was the only way she did not get the police involved herself.

'Oh God, Edward, what has my poor boy done? Thank you.' She was fully crying now and Ed knew that he had to leave. The realisation of his lost friendship was hitting him; years of seeing Alex as a brother flashed past him and he wished he had just had a phone call to say he was dead. From experience of that night in New York, being told Mitch was dead, the feelings he was having now were the same.

This was bad on many levels and he knew it was not going to go away.

Pete took Ed back to the apartment. The first thing he needed to do was change and shower, but most of all have a drink.

'I will be back in about an hour,' Pete said as he was leaving, the car needing to be cleaned and he needed to get some other people up to speed with this in case it came back sooner than anyone had wanted.

Ed poured a large glass of whiskey and took it down. The hot liquor burned his throat as he poured another, and another, until the decanter was empty.

He stood in the shower and let the water cascade over him. Pete shouted out to him to let him know he was back. Ed still took his time getting out of the shower and put on some joggers.

Paddling in his bare feet, he found the whiskey bottle and filled the glass again.

'Fuck it, Pete, I was getting there with it all, you know.' He swigged the yellow liquid, now not a shock to his palate. 'Never fucking lost it in weeks. Even played nice in the boardroom to try to change, and for what? That little cunt to come and fuck it all up.'

Pete thought it best to let him get it out. After a few more rants he slowly put his hand in his pocket and put a disk on the counter.

'What's this?' Ed asked with a distinct slur in his voice. Pete walked to the office and fired up Ed's laptop. Ed followed and put in his password, putting in the disk ready. The scene was the back of the car just over two hours ago. Every word, every image was replayed out. The more he watched, the more he smiled. Pete remained silent.

'You fucking genius,' he said to Pete playing the recording again, and also burning it to his hard drive at the same time.

'Not to make light of the situation, but your little fetish which, may I say, has not been used in the past three months of videoing the goings-on in the back of the Bentley, may have paid off?' He never even had a smug look on his face, he just remained calm. 'I am not saying that they will not try to have a go at you, or your business, but this should show them that you are not their man after all?'

'I could fucking kiss you.' Ed smiled. 'You, my friend, have saved my life, potentially, literally for the second time.'

'I will ask around and keep my ear to the ground for any repercussions, but it should get them to back off. I'm not sure how they will deal with Mr Girski, though.' Pete took another disk out and made the third copy. 'I will get this to the safe deposit in the morning.'

'I meant every word, I don't care. I am through with him, make sure everyone knows that if he contacts, or tries to contact, I want him taken out.' Ed watched it one more time and could not believe how he had let himself be treated like this by someone whom he cared for.

Alex had spared him from some shit in the early days, but he had also caused a lot in the last few. Ed had put most of the details of his school years behind him, thanks to Dr Morgan, but that night as he tried to sleep they came back as nightmares. Dr Morgan had understood how the way some of the boys had treated him had affected him mentally. It had taken trust to detail some of the beatings, humiliations, that they had put him through. He had convinced Ed that such acts of violence, both physical and sexual, would have driven some people over the edge at the age of sixteen or seventeen, but Ed had used the positive side to build up his life to where he was today.

He woke up with sweat dripping from his skin. The sheets were off the bed, exposing his naked body, a reminder of how he must have tossed and turned in a bid to get away from the captors in his night terror. The nightmares had all but gone in the past few years, but the one still fresh in his mind for last night's sleep, of being held down and forced to do such acts of depravity, disgusted him. Sodomy, oral sex, the boys had stopped at nothing until Alex had come along. He had found it hard to accept that although they had affected him mentally, he still had certain sexual preferences that could have been seen as the same acts. Again, Dr Morgan had outlined one very plain difference: it was consenting adults doing the act, not a child who is being abused.

Standing in the shower, Lottie came into his mind. He recalled how she had been treated by the first prick she had known, that village boy, and understood how she must have felt. She had said she had had counselling, but it had not made her bad like him: it somehow had made her a better person. So, although they were again similar in one way, they were so very opposite in another. This, he thought again, completed them as a couple.

He owed her some time, but not until he owed Pete some form of reward. He faxed through his signature to the bank as he sat in his office. He had transferred a year's wages to Pete's account. He had asked him to take some time away and visit his family, but he had declined, saying for the next few weeks he needed to wait around to see if there was any comeback.

Monday was not a day to see Lottie but he wanted to, so he texted her to see if they could meet for lunch.

Miss Jenkins, I know this is out of your routine but are you free to have lunch or dinner today with me to make up for my last-minute plans ruining our weekend? Ex

It only took a few seconds for the reply. Although it was only 8:30am Lottie was up and about, just returning from a run.

Good morning handsome. I came to Kent when we changed things, so I am not in town just yet. Todd sent some work through, so I had not planned to come in until Wednesday. I could be with you for dinner later? Miss J x

Ed looked back at the text, fighting the urge to be angry that he did not even know she was so many miles away; he had been happy with the thought that she was in town. But he thought of her words to calm him down and sent his reply.

Can I come up to you then? Maybe we could have tomorrow together too if your work allows. Would Mr and Mrs Deakin like to have a bite of supper with us after? Mr E Dean CEO of missing you incorporated

He was being brave, sharing her with her friends.

Another company set up Mr Dean to add to your empire? She texted back.

He smiled at her reply and sent back **Yes and the main stakeholder has my assets at her disposal. Mr E Dean CEO Frustrated PLC.**

She started to giggle at the exchange of words: she knew that it would only be a few more messages and then he would call. He never ended a text session without finishing it with a personal conversation.

Well, I would hate that your assets are neglected and I look forward to their growth in particular! Miss Jx

His desire for her was mounting and he longed for her to be sitting next to him so he could smell her, feel her gentle touch and kisses. The more he thought of it, the more he became turned on.

Miss Jenkins, I believe you are flirting with me and that could turn out to be a dangerous business decision. E DEAN Chairman of Growth

She allowed another smile, just as her phone rang right on cue. She took his call and they continued to flirt and make the arrangements for later.

The one thing that he needed now was to tell the only other person this information. He had made an appointment with Dr Morgan that morning and, as usual, although he had to cancel other patients, he was able to see Ed. He had listened to all the details of the whole weekend, Ed satisfied knowing that doctor-patient confidentiality would keep the secret safe. He had been impressed with the restraint Ed had shown, and almost, though not totally, got why he had lost it. The old Ed would have put the guy in hospital if not worse. The session included Ed taking about their friendship he now considered lost, and of course this brought up old ground of the issues he suffered as a young adult in the later times of his school life.

'The nightmares will go, Ed, you know that,' the doctor had explained as he was informed of the bad night's sleep he had before he woke. 'Put them in the past and they will go, don't let your mind work with them. Taking yourself off for a day or so will help, but you have to tell her.'

Ed knew he was right. As it turned out, Lottie seemed to be a better counsellor than Dr Morgan at times when he had shared his problems with her, or maybe it was the fact that since Monaco their therapy sessions had involved wine, nakedness and fabulous lovemaking. Not a stark, clinical, white room and a single, black leather couch with a green plant in the corner that always seemed to need watering!

There were still things Ed had not shared about his childhood. 'The time is not right for it all, Edward,' Dr Morgan said, 'but there will be and right on, soon.'

As he jumped in his car he stopped and took a breath. He felt better, several of those sessions in the past had made him leave, go straight to some seedy backstreet club and drink until he could not stand. This session seemed to lighten his mood and he thought that a shopping trip was in order.

Parking in town was a nightmare in itself; as Pete was taking some time out he had driven himself and, although he was getting really frustrated, he was determined that it would not spoil his mood. He parked, not knowing if he would get a ticket; he jostled with the crowds and made his way through the grand front doors. The doorman tipped his hat to him and Ed smiled.

He made his way to ladieswear to seek out his goal. He was approached by several of the young female assistants as he walked through the maze of rooms asking if they could help him; he politely smiled and said, 'No thank you.' He turned as two of them giggled as he walked past: they must have been all of eighteen. It was not just the shop staff who stopped to look at him. Other women walking past did, too, almost tripping over to see this guy who was well tailored from head to toe. His musk aftershave filled the space and lingered as he walked past: this alone could turn your head. He walked with strong purpose, his defined shoulders showing through the shape of his Savile Row suit and, as always, a crisp, white shirt. No tie and the collar slightly open, just showing the relaxed look instead of full-on business professional.

He had spied his goal; the lady was straightening what looked to be already perfectly lined-up coat hangers with dresses attached. He walked up to her.

'Bella.' He shot out his hand to show the other staff this was still a formal greeting.

'Mr Dean, you are looking very well, how very pleased to see you,' she replied, taking his hand in a warm greeting.

'And you, Bella, I hope you are well, too,' he replied.

'No good comes of complaining,' she replied and he grinned. It was the sort of comment Lottie would make and he knew why she got on so well with this stranger to some, but friend to others. It was as if every woman had been drawn to his smile when he did it. Several admired the view that was lightening up this section of the store. 'How is our Miss Lottie? I can see from your smile all is well.'

'Very well,' he said. 'I need your help again: can you spare me an hour or so?' Ed looked around but he was not there really for clothes today.

'It's no trouble, the food hall is through here. I am not joined at the hip to ladieswear and it's good to get out once in a while,' Bella said as she walked in front of him to the rooms where the most spectacular array of food was on show. 'Hamper for tonight's dinner?' she asked, repeating what he had already said. 'Wine or bubbles?' she asked as she beckoned a young assistant to help them.

The food came together and then Ed asked to be shown to another section of the shop.

'I want something special,' he said as Bella walked through the glitter of the jewellery section. 'Something that she can wear every day.'

'Necklace?' Bella asked.

'No, she has one. Well, two, actually,' and it was not something to brand his ownership, remember? he thought to himself.

'Bracelet?' Bella asked again.

'Done that one, matches the necklace,' he said, glancing at the array of jewels for inspiration.

'Earrings.' She pointed to the most fantastic set of blue, shining stones surrounded by diamonds and the store attendant picked up her nose through the prospect of a sale no doubt, Ed thought.

'Done that, too, full set,' he said back, flashing his white teeth in the smile the young assistant got back as he walked off.

'Mr Dean, you are not leading me down the "I want to get a ring" route, are you? And we should have put in bubbles in the hamper, not red wine?' She turned to look at him and he stopped midstride to compute the comment she had made.

He thought about it: in his life the thought had never crossed his mind before, until now. His skin tingled and every hair on his body stood up as if a cold wind had blown over him. Was it a feeling of fright at the prospect, or a feeling of elation to the fact that he even contemplated such a day that he would ask that very question?

'Mr Dean?' Bella asked to bring him back from his wandering mind. 'Scary notion or future consideration? She is a wonderful young girl,' she finished.

'I have no argument with you on that, and when she is ready I will be back to visit you again, but it was not the item I thought of for today. But you have given me some hope to work towards,' he replied and continued to look around the displays.

'A watch, practical and beautiful, just like...' She never finished her sentence.

'Like Lottie,' he finished. Bella smiled. 'She has you gripped bad, Mr Dean, does she not?'

Could everyone see through him so much when it came to her. If he was weak around her did that make her vulnerable? He had no notion why his mind thought of that; maybe the weekend was not done and dusted. No matter what shit they threw at Ed or the business he could cope with, but what about her? He felt his colour drain. He put a hand on the counter and Bella asked, 'Mr Dean, are you OK?' He took a breath and said, 'Yes, fine. Excuse me, I need to make a call.' He pulled out his phone and called up her number.

'Hi, baby girl,' he started the conversation and Lottie greeted him. 'OK with you if I land a bit earlier than we arranged? I'm still in town but I thought maybe 3pm instead of 6pm?' He felt better once she had said yes. He had no Pete to send to check on her, and Steven was back at the office working with the other security staff today, so he had to go himself. She had asked him a question and he gritted his teeth to lie to her. 'Everything is fine, just.' He never said, I want you straight away. He wanted to say, I need to protect you, but he held back. 'Just cleared things sooner than I thought this end so, as the weather is nice, we could go for a walk or something.' She made a joke about the or something bit and he smiled to the handset in his hand.

He was satisfied she was OK and he continued to look at the watches. Bella took over from the young assistant, more to ensure Ed got a good item that was for the wearer, or the fact that the young girl looked like she would swoon into a puddle on the floor if she had any closer contact with him. The one they chose was understated compared to the others in the store. Plain, the only jewels dictated the quarter- and half-hour stations on the watch face. Solid gold in a loose-fitting bracelet. The clasp had a safety chain and Bella tried it on.

'I think you just need one link out, I can get this done in no time at all.' She beckoned over the young in-store jeweller. 'OK to wait, Mr Dean? Do you want to grab a snack or drink if you are rushing off after this? I can have it all brought to you in the bistro café.' Ed took her hand and gently shook it, saying so that other staff would hear, 'Bella, as ever, the best woman a man could ever wish for.' He took the hand and placed a kiss on the back of it. He looked at her and leaned in closer with a cheeky smile on his face. 'With the exception of you know who, no offence!'

She nodded as if the final bit of his statement satisfied her more than the first compliment. 'None taken,' she whispered back. She plumped out her chest as the other female assistants bitched at her, no doubt with comments about her intimacy with a client: she did not care. Even if Mr Dean was her only customer, she had one up on all of them, even if she had 40 years in age on most of them, too. They both noted the whispering assistants and she said, 'Jealousy is an evil feeling, do you not agree, Mr Dean?' He kissed her hand again as an agreement of the statement, but also just to make the point to the young girls who had now turned away.

He sat in the bistro clearing a few emails and talking to Zoe about the next few days and his plans. He had got some meetings that he should not be putting off again, but he would make the effort to get these in as soon as he could. He opted for a coffee with the prospect of a drive after a quick change at home. Mrs B was his next call to get some clothes out and his things ready. The sooner he could go, the quicker he could check she was OK.

Hamper in hand and the small box tucked in his pocket, he made his way back to the car. Not a parking ticket, just a young boy having his photo next to the car. As a rule, he never took the Ferrari out, but today he had felt like it, and it would help him get to Kent quicker now his plans had changed. He was just lucky Pete kept it full of fuel, as he was not sure how to fill it up! He opened the door and as it rose to the sky like a spaceship door the boy said, 'Nice car, Mister.' His dad put his finger to his mouth and uttered, 'Shush, come on, son!'

He must have only been about ten, eleven max, Ed thought. Totally out of character he said, 'Want to sit in her?'

'Oh yer! Cooool,' the young voice replied and instant enjoyment filled his innocent face. 'Sorry, sir, don't mind him.' The guy Ed guessed was his father by the next statement the youngster made, 'Oh Dad!' with a look of pure disappointment. 'Don't bother the gentleman, Simon, come on.' He put up his hand. 'Sorry,' he said in the direction of Ed.

'Really, it's no bother, she is a beauty, every boy needs his toys.' The boy was over like a shot and he jumped in the driver's seat that almost swallowed him whole, it was so big. He grabbed the steering wheel as if he was driving. 'Get a picture for Gramps, Dad! Go on, go on. He will be sad to have missed this, you know how he loves his cars!' Ed could not help but smile: such a small gesture had made this small person's day. The photo was done and the boy said, 'Bet she sounds like a dream.' Ed flashed the card at the console and pushed the auto button to start her up. With a thundering roar the £190,000 car kicked into life.

'Wicked, Dad, listen to her!' The boy was so excited that Ed felt he would burst. Oh, to be so young and full of life, so innocent to the world around. 'Oh Dad, if Mum, were here she would be stoked.' Ed noted the sudden sadness in the man's eyes as he mustered a smile back to the boy. He wondered why she was not there: divorce, maybe split up? But his father's smile was full of love and admiration, Ed could tell.

'That's enough now, son, say thank you to the kind gentleman,' and as requested the boy jumped out, rubbing his hand about an inch above the paintwork aware that, if he touched it, it would scratch. 'Gee Mister, thank you.' He walked off towards the back of the car to look at the exhaust where the noise was coming from. 'Thank you, you have made his day. I have not seen him smile like that for weeks now, thanks again,' the guy said to Ed. The boy ran back to his dad and hugged him around his waist. 'Wicked, eh, Dad?' He jumped up and down as he said it again. 'Come on, son, let's go find Gramps and show him the photo.' He bent down and kissed the boy's head and ruffled his hair as they walked off.

Ed sat in the car for a moment and watched as they reached the edge of the street. An older man met up with them. The boy started pointing at the car and grabbing the camera from his dad, obviously showing him the photo. He grabbed his wallet and pulled out one of his own charity business cards. As he slowly moved down the street towards him, the boy's excitement was refreshed and he pulled up by the side of the older man and said:

'Edward Dean, please take my card. Whenever you are free please give me a call and I can see if I can arrange for you to have a drive in something similar. Your grandson?' Ed questioned tentatively as the boy had called him Gramps: it was confirmed with a nod. 'He seems so excited it would be a shame not to,' he continued.

'I used to take him and his mother to the race days whenever we could afford it. She's no longer with us. I don't go as much as we should, but Simon is still fascinated by cars. I'm sorry he bothered you today.' He did reluctantly take the card and Ed felt the need to back up his request.

'Then seriously take me up on the offer for him.' He slowly pulled past the boy and his family and headed back to the apartment.

Along the way Ed's mind was awash with thoughts that had revealed themselves over the past few days. It made the journey shorter, that was for sure. What a mix of emotions that he had never felt before. But before what? he had asked himself. The only conclusion he came to was 'Lottie' – he said her name out loud.

He arrived on the drive and turned off the car. He knocked on the front door and waited; there was no reply. He knocked again, no reply. He stepped back off the step and looked in the ground-floor windows: no one around. She knew he was coming, so where was she?

He walked around the side of the house that allowed access to the garden and patio area. 'Lottie!' he shouted, starting to panic slightly; there was no reply. He increased his speed so that he could get a good look in the garden and the far side of the patio that was shaded, creating a suntrap. It was a nice, late-summer afternoon: as the house faced south at the back it was bathed in the rays and warmth.

He almost froze as he saw her there, lying on the sunbed. 'Lottie!' he called out again, moving in her direction. He could then see her foot moving and realised that she was listening to her iPod, eyes closed, baking in the sun. Thank God! His mind had gone straight to the sinister part of his world, thinking that something was wrong. Maybe he was not as far over that as he had been telling himself on the way there.

He just stood and looked at her: she looked so relaxed, surreal almost in shorts and a bikini top, oblivious to him. He did it again with the negative thoughts of 'I could have been anyone'!

'Lottie,' he called, trying to raise his voice, but at the same time trying not to make her jump.

She sensed someone there and opened her eyes.

'Ed, you startled me.' She quickly pulled the ear moulds and got up off the seat. 'I had almost dozed off,' she said. She embraced and kissed him passionately on the mouth. For a fleeting moment their tongues met and he grazed his teeth along her lower lip. 'It's so beautiful out here,' she said, hugging him.

'From where I am standing, I see no problems with the view.' He tracked a finger down along her shoulder and lightly ran his little finger down her sternum below her breast, and then grasped her by the lower back and kissed her again. His instant arousal exposed how much he had missed her, but he had to say it. 'I could have been anyone, though, creeping up on you!' He started to kiss along the side of her neck: he could still hear the faint flow of music from her iPod as it was now sitting on the chair, where it fell as she had got up.

'What, like the postman?' She laughed, not seeing his point completely. 'It's a woman so no issues there!'

He was not going to start this one off. He needed to grab a drink and go to the loo before he got into any deep conversations, and he was determined that he was telling it all. She went inside and slipped on a light top; out of the sun it was noticeably cooler. 'Make yourself at home!' she shouted back. 'I'll grab your stuff!' She took the keys from the worktop where he had put them before dashing to the loo, and she went out the front door.

'Wowzers!' She was expecting the Porsche not the gleaming red sports car she was faced with. She did not even know where the boot was if it had one, and judging by the bags on the passenger seat it did not. He came out behind her as she was looking into it. 'Nice!' she said out loud.

He grabbed her from behind and said, 'Better than that!' He rubbed his hand over her stomach so she was within his embrace and again planted a kiss on the nap of her neck. 'Beautiful,' he whispered. Smelling in her scent, mixed with suntan oil, her skin was hot due to the fact she had been sitting out for sometime and it made his lips tingle as he traced down her spine. He found himself pushing one hand down the front of her shorts and could feel the delicate lace of her pants beneath.

'The car or me?' she asked with increased breath, clearly turned on by his affection, and turned to face him, biting her lower lip.

'God, Miss Jenkins, you have to ask?' He took her full buttock in his hand and lifted, squeezing at the same time. Now she was facing him.

'Some men get this excited over cars, and things that go fast!' She was rubbing her hand over the top of his light cotton deck trousers, tempting the already hard dick below. 'Do you like to go fast, Mr Dean?'

'I will be going too fast if you don't move your hand away, Miss Jenkins.' He felt a bead of sweat trickle down his back as he kissed her full-on with urgency, hitting her teeth with his own, wanting to devour her.

He picked her up in a swoop, and he knew that he would not make it to the bedroom. Slamming the door behind him with his foot he lowered her on the cream mat that sat on the floor in the hallway. Urgently she ripped at his shirt, losing a button as she pulled them loose to reveal his torso. She kissed his chest, gently grazing his nipples, and he sucked the air past his teeth. 'That's how you want to play this?' he said, licking her ear. He pulled her top off and in one movement grabbed the bikini ties that undid in a second. He rubbed her chest with one hand, the other arm holding his weight above her. She had one leg out as his leg covered her, the other was bent at the knee, and she bucked her hips as an invitation to invite her sex to the show. 'What do you want, Miss Jenkins?' he asked, easing down her shorts. He had to take a look at the white lace, there was something clinical and virginal in his eyes with this colour. There was a time and place and a type of person for black underwear, Lottie. Here and now was not one of them. He placed a kiss on her mound as he pulled the pants down: shorts and pants and bikini gone, she was naked on the mat in her front hall. He leaned back to admire the slenderness of her body. He rubbed his hand down from her chest to her sex and with ease parted her lips with his middle finger. She was wet, so very wet and welcoming. 'Oh, baby girl so sweet.' He eased his finger into her and ensured that there was pressure on her sweet spot. She gasped and pushed her head back. He kissed her again, nudging his tongue into her, to taste her.

Her internal muscles contracted and she felt the shiver of desire running through her thighs down to her feet. She grabbed his hand, to increase the pressure on her and he responded. She was rubbing his dick with her knee and calf as best she could in this position. He needed to get the trousers off before he burst out of them. He undid his flies and she helped him remove them with her feet. He was not wearing anything under them and she commented, 'Commando, nice touch.' She dug in her nails to his strong shoulders and she could feel the muscles that covered his frame, defined and smooth. He worked his kisses back up her body, starting to cover her with his own naked form. Paying attention to each nipple he kissed and nibbled at the erect bud sending shock waves back to her inner sex, her first wave of climax was not far off. Her chest started to go pinker than it was from the sun and her skin burned underneath him.

The head of his dick nudged at her, as if it knew where it wanted to go. The slick of pre-cum mingled with her own wetness to give no restrictions regardless of his engorged size. She shifted her legs further apart so she could be entered and he thrust gently to ensure that she was receptive. The rhythm of his hips increased and she took both hands down to his arse to increase his actions. 'Impatient, baby girl,' he whispered. If truth was known he was really having a job holding himself back. 'Show me how much you want this,' he said, lifting her hips with his free hand so that he could be deeper in her with the thrusts that were coming faster. 'Show me, Lottie, let me know how much.' She gave out a scream. 'Please!' she panted as the first wave of heat thrust through her sex. He was pushing so hard into her that she could feel his bollocks hitting her. It increased his need to release and so he pulled back. 'No,' she said, 'don't stop.' He brushed the hair away from her face and said, 'I'm not stopping, baby girl, I want to see your face when you give me everything.' He kissed the small pink scar that sat along her forehead; it had healed but the sun had raised it up. 'Let me possess your very soul, you have mine.' His breathing was heavy and with the first contraction of her inner muscles around his cock he felt his lower stomach muscles knot and he looked at her face. She was releasing herself to him and he gripped her around her waist to ensure that he felt every last lustful blow of her. She screamed out, 'Oh God!' She was racked with shaking and he held her as still as he could. The vibration she was causing on his balls made him grunt and he was no longer able to control himself. 'Baby girl I love you,' he said and as if to confirm his words, he thrust harder into her. She was feeling the onset of another orgasm, or it was still the first one, she was not sure. He came hard into her, spilling his seed as deep as he could. 'I need you,' he said. He was still thrusting but the strength had eased and he released her slightly from his grip. He placed his head on her chest, still holding his weight with one hand, towering over her. She placed both hands on the side of his face and he looked up and opened his eyes. She gently kissed his face that was wet with sweat. 'I love you, too,' she said. His cock had lost some of its hardness but not all and it jerked inside her when she said the words. She had always said, 'You, too,' when he said he loved her, but this was the first time she had said it not as a reply, but as a statement.

He kissed her again: their bodies were still in contact like feral dogs. The desire was rising again within him and she knew that he would be able to do round two within a blink of her eyes. She pushed him off her and reluctantly he rested on his back. She smiled at him and sucked at his lower lip. He allowed her to straddle him and he lay back. She continued to kiss down his body and she licked the natural muscle lines that ran straight to his hips and to his groin. 'Lottie, Lottie, Lottie,' he said as she rubbed her nipples up his legs at the same time. She moved to his dick and took it in her mouth. She could taste herself which was mingled with his salty semen. She took him in her mouth and started to suck. He leaned up on his elbows to see her head going up and down on him. She took as much as she could in her mouth, and used her hand on the base of his dick to rub up and down with the rhythm. She licked at the top and rubbed her tongue around his head. The veins running the length of the shaft were full to bursting and tracked down them to the base and back up. He shot his head back and took small, shallow breaths. She looked up at him.

'Do you have a problem there, Mr Dean?' As she asked she sucked hard on the top of his dick, squeezing it to restrict the blood flow. She gently bit into the skin on his hips and he sat up. She pushed her hand on his chest to lay him back down, taking his full length in her mouth again. She continued to lick and suck and he had to lift her head: he was about to fill her mouth. 'Too fast, Mr Dean?' She bit his lip again as she kissed him. She had moved up his body although she was not able to hold her own weight on her wrist. He took the weight of her upper body but quickly rolled her onto her stomach. Holding her under the chest he knelt her up with her back to him, on her knees. Steadying her with his own weight, he entered her from behind; she bent forward with the pressure of his first thrust until she was on her knees and one arm, he counterbalanced her to ease the pressure from her wrist. He thrust and the position was so that he could get deeper than before inside her. With genuine gasps of pain, he was long hitting her cervix with each thrust. She tossed her hair back and it wiped across his chest. He leaned into her ear. 'Do you like it, Lottie?' he asked. 'Yes,' she spat out in the rhythm of his thrusts. 'Do you want it harder?' She did not reply and he grabbed her nipple and pulled. The shock of his action startled her at first until the pain merged with her pleasure and she said, 'Yes.' She groaned and he responded. She put her weak hand on the floor, taking most of the strain with her good side and he pushed back, holding her hips. Using his hands to push and pull her back onto him, he gritted his teeth. She shouted out as her flush of orgasm was so strong that she fell onto his elbows. He never stopped his ravaged thrusts, he was so close to losing it. Her pale arse was pounding into him and he wanted to hit it so hard and make her scream, feel the pleasure and the pain, but he resisted.

'Arrh Lottie! he grunted out as he exploded inside her for the second time. He grunted with each thrust and it shot her forwards. She was already limp in his arms spent from her orgasm that he had to hold her still but he continued to take her until he was done. He pulled her back up to him and turned her round. They were still on their knees and she was exhausted in his arms. He pulled her to a standing position. She had her eyes closed and he picked her up. He took her up to her room.

'I will run you a bath,' he said, kissing her. He had been the roughest he had ever been since they had met. God, he knew his thighs were hurting so hers would be, too: a bath would ease that. He filled the large tub in the main bathroom with sweet-smelling bubble bath and set out two towels. They both fitted in if he was sitting behind her: they had been in there before.

'Come on, baby girl, let's try to wake you up a bit.' He picked her up again and took her to the bathroom. He got in and she stepped in after him. Lying down she lay with her back on his chest and he started to sponge water over her chest to make sure she kept warm as her nipples were out of the water.

'Ummmmmm,' she said, 'this is nice.' He kissed her hair, and he continued to sponge her down. They sat for a while just enjoying the hot water. She had come back to the land of the living now and she was really relaxed.

'So, what was so important I had to wait an extra two days for this?' she asked. He had two options now. Lie and live with it or tell her the truth. He had battled with this in his mind on the way over earlier; his hesitation was noted. She spun herself round, making the water splash over the side of the bath. 'If there is a lie about to come out, think very carefully: it is to protect me, you or neither of us!'

He looked at her and he started to relay the story. 'It was business in a way, it was Alex.' He told her the truth about what he had got into. The drugs, his lost trust and how he had been used by reputation and his friendship. He explained the past dealings with the Russians, and the possible outcomes if this really pissed them off. She listened intently. He explained about the recording, and, although he said that nothing of the sort had taken place while she had been in the back of the car, she scowled. 'I had it installed because I do a lot of business deals in the car: it was a precaution and Pete did some quick thinking on the day,' he followed on. She put her head back on his chest. All of the time he was running water over her with the sponge, mainly to try to keep him relaxed more than her.

He said they had made copies of the tape, and hoped that it would blow over, although he doubted it: the part he missed out was the fact that this could have put her in danger. He sighed when he continued to explain that he had lost it with Alex and hit him. 'There is no excuse for the way I exploded with anger, I'm sorry.'

'Maybe it is not me you should be sorry with?' she asked. He stopped what he was doing and sat up slightly.

'I meant it, Lottie, I will not forgive him. It is a friendship lost, all the things...' He paused. 'All the things I went through when I was younger. I know I owe him, but he really betrayed me and I can't forgive that.' She kissed his wet chest.

'I'm sorry,' she replied. 'Thank you for being so honest with me.' It had changed the mood slightly so she kept quiet for a while then he said, 'I went back to Dr Morgan and talked it through. I think I can get there and this has certainly helped' he rubbed her wet hair back away from her face. She still did not understand his world, but she was glad that he was finally opening up to her.

'Hungry?' she said, sitting up slightly. 'I'm going a bit wrinkly!' She pointed to the skin on her hands that had become really soft from the water.

They sat on the sitting room floor in casual clothes, legs crossed, and went through the hamper. It was an indoor picnic because the weather outside had turned quite cold and windy. Ed explained his day and how he had been with Bella to get the food. Lottie asked how she was and they continued to make small talk.

'And he was so excited, I have never seen the joy on someone's face,' he said as he recalled the story of Simon, the small boy who had taken so much pleasure just sitting in the car that Ed really just took for granted.

She looked at him: finally he is learning to share something, she thought but did not say.

'Talking of helping children, I wondered if you could help me?' she said, swallowing a mouthful of cracker and caviar.

'You know if I can I will,' he replied, looking back at her and putting down his fork.

She explained how when they had been to the music recital she had heard about the young boy who played so beautifully, but was not able to get funding.

'Well,' she continued, 'don't laugh,' she said, 'I wanted to set up a scholarship, with some of the money from Mum's will and the income from the properties I have left.'

'Go on,' he said, listening and taking a sip of his wine.

'I rang the Royal Music School and they really did not seem to be so interested. I got the impression that they did not take me seriously, but they did give me the number of his school. So I talked to them. They seemed to be up for it, and they asked me to call them back once they had contacted his parents.' She, too, took a sip of wine. 'I wondered if using your name may be able to get the process going faster, as he will need to leave by the end of the month, but the Academy said that they could not set something up so fast. I've got the money, I am not asking you for that.' She thought that she would add that as she wanted this to be her venture. 'It's just if they hear from Mr Dean of Dean Charities they may realise that this is important to me. He really has a talent.'

He shuffled round so that he was sitting by the side of her instead of in front. 'Lottie, I would love nothing more than for you to have my name.' She stopped and listened to what he said. 'I mean use my name if it helps.' He thought he had saved that verbal error, although now he had also thought about this and Lottie having his name really was an option for their future, he hoped. He quickly saved the conversation 'Give me their number and I will ring them tomorrow. I also have a contact who deals with just this thing for scholars, mainly from overseas, but you can call her: I am sure she will help you.' He kissed her on the cheek: it seemed that the comment about having his name had gone over her head.

Lottie sat there, and missed the bit about contact for overseas. She was still running the words past in her mind: you can have my name! He really did only have a slip of the tongue there, I'm sure, but for him to say it, it must have at some point crossed his mind. 'Great,' she said.

They continued to talk about general things; the hamper had been put away and they were huddled up on the couch with the rest of their wine. She had put on a CD in the background and it was playing various songs for easy listening. Ed shuffled and said he just wanted to get up. He left a cool space where she felt the body heat leave and she shivered.

'Do you want another wine while I'm up?' he asked.

'Please, could you get my jumper from the other sitting room if you don't mind.' He pushed open the door and a black jumper was sitting on the piano stool. The lid was up as if she had been playing. He brushed the keys lightly, not enough to make them engage and make a sound, but enough to sense her sitting there, playing.

He returned and once the glasses were refreshed and she had put on the item he sat back down, with her wrapped around him. 'Feeling cold?' he asked.

'A bit, but better now,' she returned. 'So what are the plans for tomorrow?'

He explained that for the last day of her birthday they were going to go up to the farm: they had now made good progress in the month since this had passed, but he also had one more surprise that had been put on hold.

'Talking of not wanting any more gifts' – as that was what she had just said in reply to his last comment - 'I got you this.' He fumbled in his pocket and pulled out the box.

She opened it and the watch looked back at her. She smiled. 'Bella helped me choose it. I noticed that you don't have a watch, you always use your phone, so we thought it was the best one to suit you.'

'It's lovely, thank you.' She planted a kiss on his cheek. 'I don't need gifts all the time, though, but you are right, I don't have a watch: it got damaged last year and I never replaced it.'

'Well, there you have it, practical as well as beautiful.' He remembered the words that Bella had said and looking at her now, lying in his arms, it was so very true. He closed his eyes and allowed himself time to savour the moment. He never did this, never took time out to think about anything other than work. He had even left his phone upstairs, something that Lottie had said he was joined to at the hip. Maybe the ring could have been an option, and then he could have this all the time. This time thinking of it his skin never went cold, and the hairs on his arms remained still.

The disadvantage of the car was the number of times they had to stop and fill up going to Buckinghamshire! Lottie was now used to people looking and commenting on the type of car after their second stop. As they drove, Ed had his hand on her knee and often affectionately rubbed it. Although they had had a lie-in, she did find herself closing her eyes several times through the journey. He had joked a few times, 'What time is it?' and Lottie had looked at her watch and told him. It took until the second time of his asking that she got it, and why he was asking again!

They arrived on the site and it was totally a new place. Extended buildings, existing buildings that were being internally refitted, to the point of painting. It was on track for the opening in January next year. They stopped at a country pub just past another petrol station they had stopped at, and had some lunch. Instead of heading off home, Ed started to journey across country to the next destination.

'Where are we going?' she asked.

'I told you it is a surprise,' he replied with his cheeky smile.

As they pulled off a main road they went down a track. The car was not built for this sort of environment, and the scuffing sounds underneath made her wince at times, and Ed slowed down. They arrived at a set of large, electric gates with a sign, "Whitmore Stables and Stud Yard". Lottie looked at him, confused. Ed found a place to park and they walked over to the large, white mansion house where he had planned to meet the owner.

This green and pleasant land was for sure in this part of the world, Lottie thought. All she could see was fields and horses. A young woman came out of the property dressed in the tightest jodhpurs and riding jacket and boots.

She was well groomed, and made up to add glamour to her country look.

'Edward, so very pleased you could make it.' She held out her hand and she kissed him on the cheek. Lottie instantly guessed that they knew each other. 'You must be Miss Jenkins.' She held out her hand and Lottie gave it a shake, firmer than usual: was she guilty of trying to make her territory, something she had accused Ed of several times before, stating her dominance? 'Sarah Hargreaves, pleased to meet you.' Was she this friendly with all her male 'friends'?

Sarah linked in with Ed's arm and said, 'Come over to the stables: Joe and the others are ready and waiting.' Ed held out his hand to Lottie who instantly took it. It was not far to walk, but Lottie felt out of the conversation as they talked about Sarah's father. As it turned out he was one of Ed's lawyers, so that was the connection.

'Edward,' the handsome, young man said, holding out his hand.

'Joe,' Ed replied on their formal greeting. 'This is Leticia, Lottie.' A quick handshake and the young man looked her in the eye. He was dashing, blond-haired, blue-eyed and tanned, maybe from working outside all summer, Lottie thought. He was also dressed for riding, and Lottie felt the heat in her face as she couldn't help but notice the tightness of his riding pants. 'So sorry we were not able to meet before.' He turned to Ed. 'You have picked the most fantastic filly.' Lottie was shocked by what he had just said, thinking that he was referring to her.

'Not had to use the whip yet.' Joe made the statement and Lottie was sure that she was hearing things and looked across at Ed, who smiled as he thought she was not on the same line of conversation as everyone else.

Ed looked across and pointed. 'Look,' he whispered to Lottie. On the other side of the stable yard a bay filly was brought out from her box. The young stable hand was having a job to control her at first and Joe shouted across, 'Tighten that hold, Pip! Show her you are in control, not her!' He did as he was told and the horse flicked her tail as if in submission.

'Stunning choice, Edward,' Joe said again. If the noise inside Lottie's head could have been heard once the penny had dropped from the last few comments they would have all been deafened. She must have been as red as a tomato: how embarrassed to have thought they were taking about sex before. She instantly knew that she must have shown some form of concern to Ed as he whispered again, 'Happy birthday, Lottie, she is yours.' He kissed her cheek. 'Good to know she is well behaved and does not need a whip!' Lottie spun him a glance and he smiled again.

'Mine? I don't understand,' she replied as the fine-standing creature came to a halt in front of her. Joe stroked her nose and then rubbed his hand all the way along her back to her backside. He gave her a pat and she kicked out a back leg.

'Strong thighs: always a bonus, eh, Ed, in a filly?' He smirked at him and Ed resisted the urge to look back at Lottie.

They made conversation about her form in the last race and her breeding in general. It was a while before Ed turned to Lottie and said, 'You mentioned about a horse when we were racing. I know that she is not for you to ride, but I hope that we will get to have a few days out with her, watching her win. I thought - and she is yours after all, so correct me if I am wrong - that any winnings we could put to charity, or your scholarship you mentioned yesterday. I will pay her keep; it will not drain the charity coffers dry if I have made a poor choice, but from all accounts and her breeding she should soon be one of the best flat racers out there.'

She nodded as she could see his plan. 'She is called Lottie's pride,' he said. 'It was the name that drew me to her at first, but it is bonus that she seems to have a good race career in front of her.' She was actually stunned for words. That he had thought about this, and sometime ago now. The more she thought about the idea, the more she thought she liked it.

They had a tour of the yard. Lottie was a little more content when she found out that Joe and Sarah were married, although she had to say he looked a lot younger than her. She still sensed a connection between her and Ed, but she had to practise what she preached and not hold the past to what has happened in the here and now with friendships.

So, the day had gone well: they arrived back at the house and Lottie set about starting the dinner. Agnes and Dick were due over in just under an hour so she made a start in the kitchen. While she chopped vegetables, Ed seasoned the meat.

'So, your little smirks today at what Joe was saying, I take it from the look on your face you thought he was talking about you?' he said.

'No,' Lottie said in a matter-of-fact way.

'So, you don't agree that a firm pair of thighs is a bonus?' He smiled.

'Well, that would depend on which angle you look at them.' She smiled back as he spooned behind her.

'And you don't think that using a whip would make a difference?' He rubbed his hands up and down her stomach, reaching round her from behind. Suddenly he gave her a gentle tap on the arse with a plastic fish fork he had found in the drawer, and she jumped, giving a little yelp. He moved back and did it again. She spun round, trying to grab it from him; he snatched it back and placed another slap along her thigh, none of them hard but they left a tingly feeling.

'Edward!' she laughed, trying to get it off him.

'What?' He tapped her again. By this time they had skipped around the island and the breakfast bar in the kitchen. He landed another on her stomach, and as it grazed her nipple it instantly responded. She was amazed that the feeling had pulsed straight to her sex and it was a turn-on.

'Mr Dean, grow up please, I have the dinner to cook.' She fixed his eyes and bit her lip.

'Miss Jenkins, I was all set to admit defeat due to time constraints and then you bit your lip, I have told you...' – *thwack*, another on the backside landed - 'many times about that lip-biting thing!' Another tap of the plastic implement. 'That's for not listening!' he replied.

She was laughing. 'Ed, Please, we don't have time.' She caught him off guard and was able to hold his wrist from the next blow he had planned to place on her. Both slightly breathless, their bodies met and he kissed her forcefully on the lips. She responded by opening her mouth and teasing her tongue along his teeth. Slowly their hands came down to create an embrace and the kiss continued. He was aroused already: she could feel him straining against her, and she could not help but rub at him with her hips. As if she was feather-light, he lifted her onto the worktop and parted her legs. He stepped in between and, pulling her bottom back towards him, ensured that they were at a perfect height, although at present their clothes were the only barrier. She continued to rub. In a kissing frenzy he pulled her top over her head. She had a black bra on with just a hint of lace; it was low-cut and the playful running around had allowed the dark skin of her outer nipple to show along the lace line. He eased her out of the cup and sucked at the flesh, the nipple responded instantly. He licked it all round and she continued to run her hands through his hair. He put the kitchen tool by her side, but took care not to drop it off the countertop, and used the other hand to massage the other breast, rolling the nipple around in his fingers.

The feeling that was pulsing to her stomach and below was immense. Uncoupling her bra, he allowed her full chest to release and he continued to kiss her chest all over. He worked his way back to her neck and nipped her ear. 'So these strong thighs, what can they be good for, Miss Jenkins?' He squeezed her thighs, making sure his thumbs brushed the gusset lining of her jeans, which vibrated onto her flesh below. She drew in breath and raised her backside from the counter; as if timed well he pulled at her jeans and it left her matching black G-string on show. 'That leaves little to the imagination,' he said, implying the lack of coverage the light material gave as he started to kiss her between her legs. She pushed back on her elbows and some of the vegetables rolled off the end of the counter. He used his tongue to part the material to reveal her to him and he blew across her outer lips. She pushed back a bit more and some of the utensils fell with a clatter. He shot up with one sweep of his arm and removed the rest of the food, plates and cutlery to the floor with a loud smash and bang. He towered over her, pushing her back so that her upper body was fully supported on the worktop. He lifted her hips again so that he nudged her forwards slightly. 'Put your legs round me,' he whispered.

She did and he unzipped his trousers. His large erection glistened at the top and she could feel his heart beating fast; he was on his toes to make sure he had height over her and that he could thrust down. His thighs were flush with the units, so he pulled her forwards some more, making her use her thighs to keep her in level position. He used his hand to guide himself towards her opening, and then his fingers to tease her, rubbing himself around her opening. Arching his back, he lowered his head and kissed her flat stomach; she gave out a slight groan as her pleasure mounted. He thrust into her, but the angle was not right. In a flash he lifted both of her legs up and placed her calves on his shoulders; he pulled her hips again: that was a better angle. She bent and opened her legs so he could lean through, slightly resting his weight on his arms and hands on the worktop. She clasped his wrist to give her better support as he wildly pushed in and out of her.

'Should I whip you again now to learn your lesson?' He said he had kept the fish fork to hand, although the other items had gone from the worktop. 'Would you like that, Lottie?' She was not sure if she would or not, but she could still feel the sting on her thigh, and after all it was not that bad. Without a reply he tapped her on the top of the back of her thigh where her butt cheek started. She gasped. The sensation seemed to go straight to her sex.

With no complaints and no other words except moans and noises of enjoyment, he did it again. 'Seems Joe is right that the filly goes faster with a whip.' He did it again but this time he changed his target and he tapped her directly on the top of her sex. She shot her eyes open when the heat surge of pleasure focused on the spot that intensified her need to climax. 'Arh!' She grabbed and held his other wrist tight.

The submission of her allowing him to go this far was a turn-on for Ed, so much that he knew he had to stop before he pushed her limits.

'Miss Jenkins, you will be my ruination. I'm sorry I can't hold back for you any longer.' His dick thickened around her and she felt the first thrust of his climax. She wrapped her legs around his shoulders, allowing him to be more on top of her, and lifted her hands above her head. He knew that he could not restrain them there but he laced his fingers with hers, so she knew she could release them at any time. She dug in her nails as the climax came, bucking her hips with his rhythm. 'GOD, Lottie!' he hissed out through his teeth. 'Come with me, baby girl, please, I'm begging you.' As she did he filled her with each thrust, and as her inner muscles responded, she dragged out his orgasm, milking him, and he had to release her hands first to take his own weight before he collapsed. She squeezed her thighs with each pulse of her sex until her breathing slowed and she unarched her back.

He lifted his head: he was drenched with sweat. He ran a finger down her body from the necklace around her neck to her navel and then followed the track with his tongue. He pushed up, dropping his head back, and gave out a long breath. She sat herself up and placed her legs down either side of his, wrapping her arms around his neck. 'Mr Dean, I can see the need for strong thighs on a filly and I have to say that the application of the whip is an incentive to go faster, although I am unsure the rider would be able to hold on for too long if applied too often.' She gave him a seductive smile and then, knowing it would affect him, she bit her lip.

'I love you, Miss Lottie Jenkins!' he said, kissing her damp brow.

'Mr Dean, I love you, too.' She smiled and looked down at the floor. She made a point of looking at her watch: with the exception of her necklace it was still all she had on. 'No time to pick that lot up, takeaway meal for four it is, then, for supper!!'

They waited until Agnes and Dick arrived before ordering supper, as they did not know if Chinese or pizza was preferred. When Agnes referred to the fact that she thought Lottie would be cooking, she replied, 'We got carried away, so we are running a bit late!' Ed smiled at her when she said it and whispered in her ear and she giggled. Agnes looked at her and smiled. Well, he seemed to be looking after her well now, she thought.

Monday morning had arrived and it was back to normal. Saying goodbye at the door, Lottie arranged to meet up for their usual Wednesday lunch date; she would stay at home until then: she had some work to do, but it was a relatively easy week ahead for her work-wise.

Ed arrived in the office just before 11am: he was met by Pete.

'Anything to worry me?' he asked.

'Not yet, but you have a message on your landline from Alex.' Ed walked to the desk and pressed the play button to receive the call.

Chapter 13

Ed had called his lawyers, and against his better judgment met with them and explained the situation, handing over a copy of the tape. They had agreed to write to Alex and outline that they had evidence of what had happened, and if he tried to access, contact or visit Ed in any way the information would be passed to the police.

He had asked Pete to brief the staff and employ another guard for the office and the apartment: he knew either that Alex would try something, or worst case that the Russians would be on their way over. He had wondered if he should contact them to explain, but then knew he was sealing the fate of his friend for sure, and, although at this moment in time he hated him, he did not wish that to come sooner than it inevitably would. It would be a rough few weeks until this either exploded or died down.

Lottie had been at the centre all morning; she had travelled in to catch up with Todd, and by mid-afternoon made her way over to the flat. She pulled the car into the car park and went up the external stairs. She had leased the flat for a few months before making the decision to stay longer-term, and at the end of this week she needed to get back to the agent to say if she wanted to stay.

It had been working, she thought, sharing her time between London and Kent, she was going to talk it through with Ed tonight and extend her tenancy agreement for the next six months. She unlocked and went in and settled down to work on contacting the academy again. Ed's contact had been really helpful and it had been the breakthrough she needed to get them to accept the scholarship.

She was working away when the door went and she looked at the time on her watch. Ed was early so he made himself at home while she quickly changed and they went out for an evening meal.

On returning, they went up to the flat, and as they approached, the security light never came on.

'That's unusual,' she said. 'It usually comes on else you can't see to get your keys.' She fumbled in her bag and unlocked the door; well, she thought that she did, but it was not locked.

'Did you pull that to when we came out?' she asked Ed.

'You were last out,' he said. 'Hold on.' He pushed past her and went through the door first, hitting the light switch. They remained in darkness. 'Not a power cut. Lottie, go back down...' He was just about to say 'stairs' when the assailant hit him over the shoulder with something hard. It took him by surprise and he pushed back against the wall. As a reaction, Lottie grabbed out towards Ed to break his fall, but the person, all dressed in black, pushed her back to the top of the stairs. She hit her head on the side of the wall, but she was able to grab the person pushing past her. Her nails dug into the bare flesh on their wrists, but the push had unsteadied her and she let go, grasping to hold onto the handrail to stop her falling. Ed had scrambled to his feet and was following the person down the steps two at time. He knew that Pete would have gone by now, although he would not be too far away. He was too intent on trying to catch the culprit, instead of getting his phone out.

Lottie was dazed and grabbed her phone. She dialled Pete and, taking the steps as quickly as she could, she followed and made her way down the stairs.

Ed gave chase for almost two streets before the pain in his ribs slowed him down. Pete was driving back up the street and came to a halt in front of him. 'That way!' Ed shouted, pointing to the parkland in front of them. Pete took off with fresh legs. Lottie had caught up with Ed and said, 'You are injured.' He was holding his ribs.

'I'm fine, what about you? Let me look: your head, you are bleeding.' He wiped her hair away and could see the cut.

'It's fine, I am more worried about you,' she said. 'You took a blow to the ribs, let me look.' Pete came back out of breath but without anyone in tow, indicating that he had lost them.

'Fuck it, Pete, who was that?' Ed asked.

'I don't know but you need to get that looked at, Miss.' He pointed to her head.

'I'm fine, one thing I do need is some cling film,' she said.

'Sorry?' Pete asked.

'Cling film: whoever it was, I have a handful of skin under my fingertips, and we should get some DNA!' She held up her hands, not wanting to touch them and destroy anything she had been able to save. Ed laughed and grabbed at his ribs.

'We need to get him checked out,' Lottie said to Pete.

'I don't want the police involved,' Ed said. 'Let's get back to the flat and see if there is anything up there that would give us a clue who that was.' Pete grabbed his gun from his pocket as they walked up the stairs again. 'Lottie, stay in the car.'

'Does he really carry a gun?' Lottie asked: in her innocent world she could not believe that he had a gun, but then how did she think that he did close protection without one? 'I'm not stopping here,' she continued.

Ed argued with her, but she started to walk back into the flat. Pete had found the fuse board and turned on the lights, but the outside had been cut at the wall.

'Not sure what they could be looking for: did you see if they had anything in their hands?' he asked Ed.

'No,' he replied. 'Lottie, let me take a look at you.' She was in the kitchen with her work bag taking the tiny samples of flesh from under her fingers. 'What the hell is that going to prove?' Ed said, still wound up. She looked at him.

'Sorry,' he said, 'I'm just pissed at this.' He spread his hand around the room at the overturned belongings and damage that had been caused.

'I can get it tested, and ask Pete not to walk around too much. I was going to text Todd to come over to see if he could lift anything from the room, prints etc.'

'No,' Ed said. 'I will deal with it.'

'How?' she asked. 'My house: they were after me for some reason, it could be related to the case I am working on.'

'What?' he said. 'Why in hell's name would your work put you in danger like this?' he said, leaning against the worktop and still rubbing his ribs.

'Some of the cases I have worked on involve people going inside for a long time, they will do anything to not get caught,' she replied, still working away at her hands with tiny bags and swabs. 'They could want the laptop or the case files or anything.'

'Fuck it, Lottie, I thought that you would be safe doing your work. If I thought for one moment that this could happen I would never have allowed you to carry on!' he exclaimed, becoming agitated again.

'Really?' she replied. 'You would not permit me to carry on? Don't you think that I am the one to say what I do or don't do?' She was getting wound up now: maybe the adrenaline from the event, or the comments he just made. 'I am calling Todd because he needs to know if I have lost any data, he needs to inform the centre.'

'Maybe it was not you they were after,' Ed said. 'Maybe it was a way to get to me!'

'Well, either way, I would sooner Todd be involved.' She picked up her phone and dialled his number. 'It's not always just about you, you know, Ed!' she said, talking to Todd as he picked up the phone. She explained what had happened and he said that he would come as soon as he could.

Pete had looked around the flat and called Steven in. Her laptop jewellery and money were all still there. After a quick look round, she could not see anything missing. As they waited for Todd, Ed started the conversation about Lottie being safe again.

'Lottie, I never thought that you would be at risk doing what you do,' he started.

'I gathered that from your comment before,' she bit back.

'I guess it came out wrong, but you know that I only want to protect you,' he said, distracting her from what she was doing to hug her. She held back for a moment in protest of her independence, but then put her arms around his neck and received his kiss.

'I know but I survived long before you came on the scene,' she said, still a bit annoyed at him.

'But I won't have you at risk, Lottie. I'm not losing you for any cost,' he said back, holding her at arm's length to look her in the eye. 'What you said earlier about keeping the flat on, well, please don't raise the roof with this suggestion, but you can't stay here no matter why someone got in for whatever reason.' He took a breath, almost waiting for her to say something. He continued. 'Stay at mine, move in with me.' He noted the look on her face and was not sure what way this was going to go.

Was he asking too soon or had it been something he had thought about before? He was not sure but it did seem like the right thing to do. He quickly added, 'This may not be the time to think about it, so just for tonight, I will ask Pete to come back with you tomorrow to collect a few things, and you can think about it.' And then as a peace-offering: 'Or if that sounds too much, stay at the Kensington, I can arrange for it to be at your disposal whenever you want, I just don't want you here, as much as you love it – please, as a compromise?'

Lottie looked at him. He had a point for tonight, but was it a compromise or was it just another way to control her?

'I will think about it,' she said, 'But…' As she continued, Todd burst into the room.

'Bloody hell, Lotts, you OK?' he asked, slowing down as he noticed Ed wrapped around her waist. 'Ed,' he nodded, in a more hostile tone. She pulled away from Ed slightly. Ed nodded back in a reply.

'I'm fine, nothing taken by the looks, though.' She turned to Ed. 'Just go with us on this for an hour, please,' she said. He held his hands up in defeat and said, 'I'll be staying right here so let me know when you have done.'

'Let's look at your head.' Todd held her by the shoulders and looked at the dry cut. Ed would have boiled but he tried to show restraint, especially as he wanted her onside to make the decision to come and stay with him. The more he thought about her moving in, the more he wanted it.

'You'll live,' Todd said. 'Now show me what you've got.'

Ed watched as they worked, almost getting in the way as he was over their shoulders so much. He had to admit, as much as he still did not like her working with Todd, he was good, they were good together. They had found prints from the fuse board, the outside light, footprints on the carpet and the floor outside that could be something. Todd found the stool that had been planted in Ed's ribs so hard, and, although it looked like the person had worn gloves, they had not worn them all the time. It was someone who was not professional, that was for sure. They worked for about an hour, and then called it a night.

'I will get to work on these in the morning, will you come over?' Todd asked.

'Yes sure,' she replied.

'You staying tonight?' he asked without naming the location.

'With Ed, I will be OK. I will lock up here and see you later. Thanks for coming over, we may need to involve the Prof, depending on what we find, but we will know more in the morning, I guess.'

Ed and Pete waited for her and they finally headed back to his apartment.

He opened the door and Mrs B was waiting for them.

'Edward, this is terrible, are you both OK?' She never gave them time to answer. 'Tea in the pot is still hot and some food if anyone wants some?' She walked over to the kitchen as if to get them it anyway whether they said yes or no.

'Lottie,' he said, holding her wrist as she had started to follow Mrs B. 'My offer, it is a genuine one, I really would like you to consider moving in, more permanent, but I know you need to take some time so, this place is yours until you let me know otherwise.'

She smiled at him and kissed his cheek. 'It's been quite a night.' She looked at her watch: it was gone midnight. 'Let's sleep on it and work out where to go from there.'

She stood in the shower the next morning, the water just tingling the cut on her forehead. It was only a graze really: they had been lucky. She had been through the 'what ifs' in her head before falling asleep in Ed's arms: if she had been alone etc, but from the number of times they had both woken in the night, it was not a peaceful sleep for either of them. The bathroom door opened and she could see that Ed had come in through the steamed-up glass of the large shower. He placed himself in front of the mirror and started to shave. He was butt naked and she admired his body, his curves, his fantastic prick, that was not totally flaccid, and the red mark across his ribs.

'Like what you see?' he asked as if he could see her watching him.

'Umm, might!' she replied with a laugh in her voice.

'You might?' he retorted. 'Might? That does wonders for a man's ego,' he said, splashing his face with water to remove the rest of the shaving gel.

'I am sure, Mr Dean, your ego is absolutely fine. In fact I am sure that no

matter what is said it could not even be dented slightly by any comments.'
She smiled back as he appeared behind her. His body was cold as he pressed
up against her. The water jet was large and started to cascade down him, too.
He picked up the shower gel and rubbed some in his hands. Still standing
behind her, he placed his slippery hands on her shoulders and started to
rub. The bubbles ran over her shoulders and down her breasts. He put his
hands through her arms and started to rub the bubbles in, adding more to
his hands as he paid attention to her nipples. She placed her head onto his
shoulder as she started to enjoy the sensation the warm water was having
and the rubbing of his hands. He ran his hands down her waist and then
round, cupping her sex in his hand, allowing the water to build up. The
warm water splashed her and she parted her legs slightly. She could feel
the nudging of his swelling dick in the base of her spine and she could tell
he was becoming more than just turned on. She rubbed against him as he
started to kiss her neck. He rubbed his hand down her spine and reached
through her open legs, sliding one finger onto her outer folds of skin. His
hand was slippery from the extra wash he had put on, and without effort
he parted her and rubbed his middle finger into her. She gasped as the
sensation ran through her to the pit of her stomach. His other hand was
reaching round to her breast, pulling and squeezing her erect nipple. He
gently bit down on her shoulder and she felt the hot sensation of pain as his
teeth did more than graze the skin. The pain seemed to travel to her nipple
and then through her internally, focusing on her inner muscles, and her sex
throbbed. He was rubbing his finger in and out, using his thumb to circle
the sweet bit at the entrance to her clitoris.

He was fully erect and she could feel the gentle pulsing of him rubbing
up against her outer thigh. He placed another finger alongside the one
probing and reaching her inside to expand her slowly. She gave out a moan
as the pleasure started to grow to the start of her orgasm. He turned her
around, removing his hands to put more gel on them both. Kissing her on

the mouth, he pushed his tongue into her and she rounded her mouth in a gesture as if it were his dick in there. He ran his hands down her back again, soaping her arse cheeks, rubbing round and over them, slowly getting closer to the opening of her anus. He reached down and placed his hand between her legs again, and she parted them as before. He kissed her nipples, then bit down on them, again creating a shooting pain. Not so much a physical pain, more of a hot aroused pleasure to her sex. He put his fingers on her outer lips and she wiggled as if to get him to put them in the place they were before. He did, but his thumb gently moved back to brush against her private hole. They had never had anal sex, and she had never done it before. The soap allowed him to move gently as he fingered her, but his thumb just kept the pressure on her anus, gently rubbing around it. The sensation was not unpleasant; in fact, the throbbing of her sex was overriding any issue she had with where this thumb was. Each rub just nudged it in further until Lottie gave out a gasp: it seemed to intensify the feeling she was having. He never moved it, he just continued to circle the area that was becoming sensitive, but thrust his finger into her deeper.

Pulling her leg up, he pushed her against the wall; his throbbing cock replaced his fingers. He had no trouble easing into her: the soap and her own wetness along with the warm water that continued to flow made his access easy. Holding her by the inner thigh and butt, pinning her against the wall, he rammed into her. She held onto him, feeing that she would lose her balance; as the climax was coming, her legs felt weaker.

'Give me it all, Lottie, give me what you want, baby girl,' he whispered into her neck as he bit down onto her again. She was sure he would leave a mark, but as soon as the pain flashed over her stomach, the water turned her skin back to pink. He continued to reach around her arse, again probing her hole, this time with his fingers. His cock was bouncing in and out of her, his balls hitting her each time. He had to bend slightly to be able to reach behind her, but this gave him easy access to her full breasts that were pulsing, sore with the continued biting and teasing of each nipple. The more sensitive they became, the more she drove towards her end. He had worked his finger into the sensitive, soft skin of her anus, and she felt the intense burn as he pushed his finger in the most that he had. She gasped, not in pain or surprise but in the shock of how it increased the feeling in her sex, how it turned her on.

He knew that the penetration of his cock and the gentle massage of her inner arse would stimulate her G-spot from a whole new angle. He had not tried this before, although he had wanted to. It was the only part of her he had not had, but he knew he would have to take it easy at first. He gently eased again with his finger, knowing that she was overcome with the frenzied feel of climax very close. Her inner walls were so thin that when he pushed in for one last time, he could feel himself thrusting.

She could not stop even if she wanted to. She started to shake and grabbed his hips to pound into her more. The sensation of both her areas being stimulated was incredible, something she had never felt before. The thought of anal penetration had always put her off, but the sensation that she was having was so deep she could not stop.

'I can't wait for you, baby girl,' he said as his own release was about to fill her. 'Do you want me?' he asked, his breath laboured and gargled as the water went in his mouth. 'Tell me! Tell me you want me,' he said again.

She tried to speak out but found that all her effort was on the breathing. 'Yeess!' she managed. 'Oh God yes, Ed please, make me!' It was with this that he pushed his finger into her as much as he could. His cock responded at his own touch through her internal skin. She dug her hands into him, drawing blood on his side as her nails grazed the skin. The hot pain caused his dick to thrust as she climaxed over him and as he gushed inside her. He was trying to hold her, but found his release so powerful that he had to move his finger out of her to use his hand to steady them both pushing against the wall.

He grunted as his carnal pleasure was poured into her and she gasped at every last drop he gave. Both spent, they clung to each other for a few seconds as the water continued to flow over them.

He kissed her and she responded, gently working their mouths until they became one; they had to breathe and they pulled apart. His cock was softer, although she had to put her leg down before he withdrew.

'I have not hurt you?' he asked, placing kisses on her neck and applying more shower gel to his hands, allowing the water to wash them off.

'No,' Lottie said, almost embarrassed that he had touched her there, but more so that she had enjoyed it – in fact really enjoyed it. 'No, I'm good,' she said, kissing him back. 'Sorry.' She looked at the red marks on his side where her nails had been digging in.

'Matches the other side,' he joked and Lottie looked. His skin was red, turning almost blue and grey from where he had taken a blow the night before.

'Ed, that looks painful, why did you not say something?' she said, instantly looking at it closer.

'I am fine, now promise me that you are? We were a bit full on then,' he said, knowing that he had pushed her limits a long way, maybe too far.

'Well, I hope that is not the way that you are going to wake me up every morning!' she said, biting her lip.

'Miss Jenkins, you will have to expand a little to give me another clue,' he said, hoping she was about to make his day and accept his invitation: although his dick had not missed the lip-biting, he resisted commenting on it.

'Well, Mr Dean,' she started, 'it seems I have considered your offer and, it will take some getting used to but I accept your invitation to move in, although I will still be going home at weekends and sometimes in the week.'

'I can negotiate some terms and conditions, and that seems acceptable.' He took a breath. 'I cannot promise that there will never be some type of wake-up call, along similar lines. Although I do understand that I can't make you late every day for work, but you need to be aware that while you remain so incredibly beautiful in every way I am going to have to stress it will be hard not to.'

'I would like to set some boundaries, though,' she said, looking very serious because she meant what she was about to say. 'Even though I agree to live here, I'm going to need some space.'

'I will have as many wardrobes as you want put into your room, because you will be with me in mine,' he said, starting to wash his hair.

'Seriously, Ed, I don't mean physical space, I mean me time, people like Todd and Agnes visiting. You will have to share me, even though it is your home.'

'It's our home from now on, and if I have to share, I will try,' he said, washing the soap from his eyes. 'Try, Lottie. The apartment comes with some add-ons, though.'

'Now you tell me, after I have agreed. Are you adding to the original terms and conditions?' she said as she got out of the shower and he followed.

'It's Mrs B: you will have to get used to her being here. We may have to negotiate cooking if you want to do any, as she is very possessive over her kitchen.'

'I'm surrounded by obsessives,' she said, drying her legs on the warm, fluffy towel and rolling her eyes.

'Washing up, shopping, that sort of thing she is quite touchy about as well, not that I have ever overstepped the mark and muscled in at any point with chores, but you will have to get used to having a domestic about. She is not proud' – God, no, she has seen me enough times, he thought – 'but I can't have you wandering around when the guys are in.' He was referring to Pete and Simon.

'As if I would want to,' she said genuinely, but he was adamant and continued.

'And you may find it easier to let one of them drive you, just for ease of parking etc, I will ask Pete to employ someone else. You can have a say in who, but it is something that I want, especially in light of last night.' He had already asked Pete to do this days ago. She did not know that: in fact the guy was in training now.

'Really, that's a bit OTT for me,' she said, wrapping herself in the towel as she was now dry. 'I love my new car,' she said.

'Not stopping you loving it, just want to make sure that you don't get bogged down in traffic every day,' he lied. Just want to keep you in check, he really wanted to say.

'Not sure,' she said, walking out of the door into the bedroom to find some clothes.

'Miss Jenkins, its non-negotiable now, the deal is done,' he said, following her.

'I never shook on it!' she said. He was over to her faster than she had time to move out of the way. She felt her legs hit the side of the bed and he pushed her down. She gave out a little squeal and he put his weight down on her legs. He pulled off the towel to reveal her soft, freshly washed skin. 'Are you going for the pressure tactics to wear me down?' she said, biting her lip. He was already fully aroused and he climbed on top of her, forcing her legs out of the way to allow him room to enter her.

He was forceful as he sucked her bottom lip. 'I'm going to seal the deal, Miss Jenkins, if you want this...' As he said it his hard cock thrust into her. '...As much as I do, you will have to find some give and take, and my acceptance of sharing you, only occasionally, and to you accepting my way of life and having a driver.'

'You are driving a hard bargain, Mr Dean,' she said, gasping at the pleasure he had evoked in her again so soon from the shower. 'Although I am becoming quite warm to the idea.' She paused and he pulled at her hard nipple. 'Especially there.' She gasped again as he kissed and sucked it. 'I, I think I can try if you can.'

'Miss Jenkins, I can drive a harder bargain,' and to endorse this he pulled her hips up to adjust her position so he could get all of his length into her. 'And I truly look forward to negotiations, in the office, or the shower, or the sitting room, wherever you choose to make the executive decisions.' His breathing was hard and he was about to release into her again she gasped out. 'I will try, too, as long as you know that.'

He tried to resist the release but she had won him over with her words. He felt her inner muscles tighten around him and he knew that she was climaxing, her breathing was quick and she grabbed the sheets at her sides. 'I will do anything for you Lottie, my baby girl, you know that?'

'Yes!' she whispered as if the energy to talk had left her. He slowed himself down and truly wanted to reach her soul. The heat washed over his face that was again wet, this time from his sweat. He poured what he had left into her and she clung to him as he juddered and spasmed as his orgasm sealed the deal.

'I love you,' he whispered without moving, savouring the moment, feeling her inner warmth on his shaft as he started to be flaccid again.

'I love you,' she said back, kissing the flushed cheeks as they hovered above her.

She had gone with Ed to the office and then Pete dropped Lottie off at the centre just after 10am. Todd was already in working on the evidence they had gathered the night before. He had informed the Professor who, as soon as she arrived, went to meet her.

'Is there any other reason to think that this could not be work-related, Lottie?' he asked. 'Of course we want to find out what happened, but I wish that you would bring the police in.'

She had explained that she wanted Todd to look into it first. After a long conversation with Ed he had offered the centre a large sum of money to get their help, and to buy their silence, more to the point. This satisfied the

Professor that they worked on it for the day. 'But no longer without telling the police,' he had asked.

They managed to get good samples of DNA and fingerprints, but if the person had not been put on the police database, then they had no leads. Todd sent the samples to Interpol, hoping that spreading the search wider could bring something up, but they would not get any news back for a few days from the other agencies. They had placed it into their database, but again it did take time for these things to be looked into.

Lottie relayed all of this back to Ed on the phone during one of his phone calls that morning.

'He calls you a lot,' Todd commented when she came off the phone. 'Don't you find that a bit overpowering?'

'Not really, I have not really thought about it,' she said back. It was a lie of course; she had thought about it, but it was just the way he was. She had also had a missed call from Agnes so at lunchtime she called her back.

'Lottie, do you really know the guy enough to move in?' she had exclaimed when Lottie revealed their plans for her to give up the flat. She had not gone into the details of the break-in. Maybe if she had, her friend would have welcomed the news a little more readily. 'Don't you think that you should wait a bit longer?' she said. 'What about your house here?' she asked Lottie explained that she would not be giving up her home, but it did not make Agnes any less wary. 'I'm not sure I approve, although my approval is the last thing you need if you have made up your mind,' she said, knowing her all too well.

'Come down to see me, have a look at the place, maybe then you will put your mind at ease,' Lottie asked.

'I'm guessing that it is a palace with staff running around fulfilling your every need!' The hint of sarcasm was almost not far from the truth, although Agnes did not know this.

'The offer is there, and I would love you to come. I will back on Saturday anyway so maybe we could catch up then?' The conversation continued and Agnes said that she would not be able to make it this week, but she would come over at some point and see them, if not to satisfy her own curiosity then to catch up on some of Lottie's accounts, something else she expressed concern with, that she was spending money and giving it away left, right and centre. After half an hour, and the fact that Lottie's phone was low on battery, they said goodbye.

They went back to work, not picking up on her break-in as promised to the professor, but on the case that they had already concluded. They just needed to complete the paperwork for Todd to take it to court. As always, Lottie was not going to court, she would just stay in the background: as long as justice was done that suited her fine.

She was not due back in to work now until Monday next week, so bade Todd goodbye. He went to his desk and noticed that an email had flashed up. It was from the Metropolitan Police: they had a match for the DNA, not from a live person but someone who had died a few years ago. Traces had been found on his body, or at the scene. So it looked like whoever had broken in was noted in another case marked 'Case closed.' This was accidental death. He was not sure that this would come to anything so he went through to the Professor and outlined the facts.

'I would leave it, Todd. Case closed, nothing else to go on really, a few years old, not going to be much use, looks like it has been dug into quite a few times without resolve. I would leave it at that.' Todd did as he was told. No need going over old ground, the Professor had said. Properly true, he had thought as he bade him goodnight.

The weather had taken an autumnal turn. As planned, Lottie was going back to Kent for the weekend. Ed had managed to clear his afternoon meetings, and said he would drive back with her if she could wait until lunchtime. She had phoned Todd to ask if there was any news, but he had held back on the information that he had found something.

She was bored of sitting around the apartment so went down to the gym and took the opportunity to work out with Ed's trainer. She showered and dressed and was looking out of the windows at the rain when Mrs B came in.

'Morning, dear,' she said.

'Morning, Mrs B.' Lottie hesitated, not sure if she wanted to be called that or if it was a pet name that Ed had given her. 'You are OK with me calling you Mrs B, are you?' she asked, still aware that she was new around here.

'You are welcome. If you want to call me Mrs Bracklestikic you are still welcome, but you can see why I got nicknamed Mrs B!' Lottie tried to say her name under her breath but she was right, it was a mouthful. The women made small talk mainly about the weather and what they liked to eat. Mrs B said, 'Edward has never had a young lady to stay for very long, so please excuse me if you feel I take over too much here. I know that it is now your home., Edward and I have talked, but my old habits die hard and I have a habit of taking over. My late husband said I fussed over him too much, and I am afraid I do the same to Edward and his boys.' Mrs B was referring to Pete and the security team that often hung around the apartment. 'I will help out in any way you need me to, just don't forget to ask, dear,' she said, walking out of the kitchen with a cloth and cleaning products in her hand.

'I feel a bit bad leaving the housework to you,' Lottie said, following her through.

'That's what I'm here for, you and Mr Dean just have fun.' She disappeared into the en suite and started humming as she worked.

Deep down Lottie would not miss another day of ironing in her life, as it was the one chore she hated, but still she was not too proud to do cleaning and cooking; in fact, the latter could be enjoyable. She thought about her last attempt to make a meal and she smiled, thinking of Ed. She sat on the sofa and turned on the TV, trying to work out all the remote controls for the gadgets he had. At first, she had turned on the lights and closed the blinds instead of turning the channel over. Once she mastered the control she just sat watching daytime programmes of no real interest until he returned and they could set off for the country.

It rained all the way to Kent, and never stopped after they arrived. Lottie put on the heating as the house seemed cold to sit in, although they chose to go to the village pub for their evening meal, so did not stay in there too long. Ed had been there before, but still seemed to be the topic of conversation for the locals. Agnes was not able to join them, but they were able to make conversation with the others enjoying an evening drink. They sat by the small open fire: it helped to dry their coats out as they had walked the distance, like many others in the room.

They were in conversation with a couple sitting next to them. Lottie only knew their faces from seeing them in their gardens, or walking around the village. She had only smiled and said hello before this. They were slightly older than her; they were married and had a small boy. Anita and Paul: she was now a stay-at-home mother and Paul still worked in the city in insurance.

'Mr Dean,' Paul replied when they were formally introduced, as if he knew of him. The men shook hands and the ladies formally introduced themselves, too. Pleasant, small talk about how long they had been in the village and a short story of their lives were exchanged. Ed offered another round of drinks as they were getting low and the couple accepted.

'He's far less imposing in person than from what you read,' Paul said to Lottie as soon as he was at the bar. 'He just about owns a part of most things, doesn't he?' he continued to say. 'I have dealt with some of his companies before and he is ruthless.'

'Well, as you can see, in the flesh he is quite harmless,' Lottie put in as Anita tapped her husband's leg as if to say don't be so personal. Ed returned with a bottle of wine and four glasses and started to pour. Lottie noted that Paul continued to be fixated on Ed's every word once the conversation continued, and wondered that when he returned to work on Monday he would be the topic of conversation. They talked about local things, but not once did the conversation turn to business of any sort; as soon as it did, Ed managed to change the subject. It was something that Lottie noticed a lot: he never did discuss it when they were out. Always kept the conversations to work time, private time, although she had pushed him on occasion to say what was on his mind at the end of a day to just help him destress.

They had looked at several new arrivals coming in the main front doors, wet and bedraggled from the rain, and on this occasion as the door opened they all four looked up, but Lottie put her head down instantly. As with other new arrivals into the dry surrounds of the building, the two men shook their coats and took them off as they made a beeline for the bar area. Once they had a drink, they walked over to some spare seats, where one of the two men made eye contact with Lottie and nodded, as if to acknowledge her. She quickly smiled and looked away, hoping that Ed had not noticed. She carried on talking in the group they had formed.

The evening went by and Ed and Lottie were left, parting from the other couple with the agreement that they should meet up again at some point, a genuine offer from both parties. Lottie stood to go to the toilet: they, too, had decided to leave for the evening. On the way the young guy who had made eye contact with her earlier spoke as she walked past them.

'Nice to see you, Lottie, it's been a while.' He should have been aware that she was with someone; he had seen them all at the table together, but he acted as if she was on her own. 'Looking hot: that city air must be agreeing with you.'

'It's good to get back from time to time,' Lottie said, not really stopping to talk as she was heading to the ladies. She also did not want to make polite conversation. She continued to her destination. On re-entering the room, the guy had stood up from his chair and spoke to her again, this time standing in her path, making her stop.

'Don't be so quick to get past, we should catch up.' It was clear from his voice that he had drunk a fair amount, if not in the pub, before they had come out. 'I am sure Dad would love to catch up with you, too, at some point.' He continued to hold her up. Lottie was now aware that Ed had seen her obstructed return and knew that, within a second, he would be across to her. She sidestepped and put herself between him and the guy.

'I hope that your dad is well,' she replied, meaning the sentiment but still not wanting to make conversation.

'Everything OK?' Ed asked, walking towards her.

'You are?' the guy asked.

'Just leaving,' Lottie interjected, pushing her way towards Ed. 'Everything is fine.' She mouthed the words. 'Please, Ed,' to him. He stood his ground. 'You must be the reason we miss the lovely Lottie,' he piped up.

Ed replied, already rising his shoulders, the body language one that Lottie knew all too well. 'And you are?'

'An old friend, go back years.' He smiled. 'Don't we? She's a bit too high-flying for us all now, though,' he added. Lottie held Ed's arm, knowing that this was going to turn ugly and he could easily swing a punch before anyone could take action, and it was the last place that she wanted it to.

'Give my regards to your dad.' Lottie pushed Ed to turn around. 'Please don't make a scene, he is drunk, please don't, not in here, everyone is looking.' She looked him in the face and could see that the green mist was rising in his eyes. 'Please,' she pleaded one more time. He picked her coat up and helped her on with it. 'Coat, babe,' he said as he did so. With almost relief on her face she slid her arms into the jacket that was being held out. One or two people started talking again, but most still had their eye on the guy standing at the bar. He grabbed his own coat and put it on, then he held the door open for her. As she walked out Ed turned to the guy at the bar and took a good look at him. He would remember his face.

'Thank you,' she said as they started walking back. He squeezed her hand but did not say anything. He was painting a picture of the guy in his memory; he almost knew what she was about to say. 'I'm sure that you have guessed who he was?' She was not sure if she should say it so close to the pub, still within bolting distance for Ed to turn around and vent his anger on the guy she had talked to him about on her birthday.

'I guessed,' he finally said, not wanting to say anything else as it was only the fact that she was standing by his side that he had not punched the twat's lights out. If it had been a meeting in town he would have done, but she was right: not there, in front of so many witnesses. Not in the place where he hoped to spend more free time in the future. There were other ways to show people that he was not be messed with. The subject was closed, for now.

The rain stopped on Sunday, allowing them to go for a run. Nothing had been said during the evening, and Lottie hoped that was the end of it. After showering and having lunch, Lottie reminded Ed that she had her bike test on Tuesday.

'Oh, I had not forgot,' he said, smiling at her. 'I spoke to Joe: he said you should be OK, Miss Clever Clogs passing the written exam with 100%!' She had taken that the week before, insisting that she went on her own. He had given in to the lessons, as long as she used who he recommended, and finally got his way to pay for them, but this was his compromise: he had to let her do it on her own. To his better judgment he had, although Steven had been asked to drive her to some lessons, and also to follow them at a safe distance. She had been so engrossed in her lessons that she had not seen him or recognised the car at all. 'Nervous?' he asked.

'A bit,' she replied as she sat on his knee in the living room where they had gone after their meal. 'I guess I will just have to go with the flow. If I can remember everything Joe had taught me I should be OK, oh and as long as it stops raining. I hate the rain.'

'Fair-weather biker,' he laughed. 'Being able to handle the changing conditions is important, because you can set out in good weather and it can turn at any time,' he said, rubbing her legs gently. 'And you have to be sure that you don't get distracted by anything.'

'But my leathers get wet, and they stick to me,' she said.

'What a wonderful image, you and your leathers, tight and clinging to your soft skin.' He rubbed down the inside of her leg with one hand, purposefully brushing the top of her sex. 'How a man could be driven to distraction thinking about it.' He spun her around so she was facing him and straddling him in the chair. She giggled at him as he cupped her backside in both hands. 'Just thinking how the leather moulds better when it is wet, and your skin is hot and sticky. But you should not be distracted.' He placed a kiss on the outside of her jumper, on the spot where her nipple was showing through. It was not cold, but he was guessing that she was enjoying her current position. 'Keep your hands on the handlebars' - he put her hands on his shoulders - 'and pay attention to everything you can feel.' He ran his hands down her sides. She closed her eyes. 'Get to the place in your mind where you are sitting on the bike. Feel the power between your legs when you start it up.' She had her eyes closed as he talked her through the procedures. 'When you feel the bike engage, ease the clutch out to move off, adjusting your position to be at one with the seat.' She wiggled and could feel the growing expanse in his trousers. She smiled. 'Concentrate. Don't get distracted,' he said, knowing that she could feel his mounting desire. 'You are riding along the road, change gear,' and she moved her hands and feet in response as if doing so.

He rubbed his hand down her chest. 'Feel the wind increase along your body as you change gear again.' This continued through his imaginary ride along the road. 'You are waiting for the traffic lights to change.' He put his hands under her top and felt her hard nipples through the lace of her bra. She gasped. 'Pay attention, they changed!' He pulled hard on one, making her open her eyes. 'Road, not me! Eyes on the road.' She closed her eyes again. He continued to give her instructions, as if she was turning in and out of streets, asking her to speed up and slow down. If he did not feel the right movement of her body, he nipped her with his teeth on the area he was kissing, or flicked the outside of her jeans where the zip was. This had a direct effect on her, and she felt the inner muscles of her sex clench. She was trying hard to concentrate but she felt the wetness of her sex between her legs and she shifted. 'Is it getting warm in those leathers?' he asked.

'Yes,' she whispered back.

'Do you want to take them off?' he asked. 'Yes,' she replied. He shot his hand up the back of her bra and undid the clasp. He then cupped her with both hands and squeezed. 'Well, you can't,' he said. 'It is designed to protect you, keep your mind on the road!' He continued to ask her to imagine she was going in between lanes of traffic, swaying with the bike. He slightly parted his own legs, allowing a gap to form between her own; he slid his hand between, using the heel of his hand to apply pressure on her outer sex. 'Feel the vibration of the engine,' he said, rubbing her as hard as he could at this angle. She took off her hand to wipe the sweat that had appeared on her forehead. He lifted his other hand and slapped the side of her arse cheek: *crack!* She jumped and squealed with the surprise. 'Keep your hands on the controls. Come on, Lottie: you would have fallen off then!' He lifted her top to expose her nipples to him and he sucked hard. 'Open her up now, the road is clear, how fast can you go?' She replied through increased breathing. He continued to rub her and suck the soft skin that was now becoming sore with the continued attention; she moved her hips to counter the swaying from side to side that he was doing as if she was on the road. She purposely pushed down harder on his hand to get more friction to the spot that she wanted him. *Crack!* the other hand slapped her arse again. 'Concentrate, too much movement and you will be out of control!' He was not too sure about her, but he was sure that this had to end soon or he would crash and burn!

'Slow down to a stop,' he said and she responded as if going through the gears to lower the engine. 'Turn off the bike and dismount.' She stood to her feet and swung her leg over his to the side and stepped away, taking her hands from his shoulders. *Crack*: another slap on her arse. 'You dropped the bike, what about the stand?'

'You're joking!' she said, aware of the game he was playing, but so aroused that she wanted to play along. She bent down slowly in front of him, purposely pushing her backside into his eyeline; she bent her knees and slightly parted her legs as if picking something up, she then made the gesture with her foot to imitate that she was pushing out a stand to secure the bike where it was parked.

She rubbed her jeans with her hands as if wiping the leather trousers, running her hand along her butt cheeks and down the seam of her fly zip to her crotch. She took her hair out of the band it was in and flicked it, rubbing her hand through it as if taking off her helmet. He watched as she performed for him, and he rubbed himself to try to arrange his erection better in his trousers, but he was feeling uncomfortable with the engorged, pulsing shaft that was pressed hard against the fabric and his pelvic bone.

'Arriving home at least,' she said, 'safe and sound. I had just better check I am all there.' She ran her hands down her chest and through the fabric of her jumper and felt her breast, not supported by her bra that he had undone earlier. 'Umm, they feel OK.' She rubbed her naked stomach and pushed her hands down the front of her jeans. She made sure he saw that she pushed her finger between her legs and closed her eyes as she felt that her pants were wet with her own excited juices.

'Come here and ride this baby girl,' he said, making her open her eyes. He had undone his trousers and the thick, purple shaft was glistening as the head had the slick trickle of pre-cum on it. She slid off her jeans and remounted him in the same position she had been in. She lifted up her arms so that he could pull off her top. She held onto his shoulders and with one hand pulled her delicate lace pants to the side. He guided her onto him and she used her knees at the side of sofa to control the depth, with just his head inside she pushed her chest into his face. He licked at her nipples as she pulled away. She held him at arm's length 'You have to start slowly before demanding full power.' She was again referring to the bike when you turn in on. 'You have to ensure that the engine is warm before opening the throttle to ensure that something does not blow,' she said in his ear.

Fucking hell, Lottie, something will blow in a moment if you don't get on with it, he thought! 'So, just easing the throttle gently.' She pushed her hips and he went in deeper, down and up, deeper, down and up. 'Until you can feel the tune of the engine.' She took one hand off his shoulder and rubbed it down her chest, over a nipple, down her stomach and then between her legs. With her palm facing downwards she rubbed the top of his pubic bone, allowing her hand to circle his cock; with just the head inside her, she squeezed his shaft.

He pushed his head forwards and sucked her nipple. He used both hands to pull her towards him. She moved her hand and pushed down; he pushed her hips down at the same time and from being just inside her to fully thrusting in one movement Lottie felt him hit the very inside of her and she gasped. He used her hips to thrust her up and down. She felt her head fall back and closed her eyes. The hot clenching of her internal muscles reacted with every brush of her sweet spot. She felt him breathing hard on her chest.

'Ride me, Lottie, let yourself go as if you are on the bike with the wind in your hair, free to feel everything.' He speeded up and she could feel the urgency in his fingers as they dug into her side. The pain from this was like a lightning bolt to her orgasm that was building so fast she could not speak.

'Tell me, Lottie, how does it feel? Let me have everything, let me possess your feelings and tell me!' he gasped.

'Auhh!' she could not get the words out, she was wildly flinging her head back and forwards, and as the slicing, hot spasm flushed over her, sending her chest red, she screamed out, 'Yes!'

'Can I have you?' he asked. 'Can I take you?'

'Oh God, please!' she begged. He thrust in her and she knew that she was going to come again. His cock throbbed inside her and he sucked hard on her nipple. It was painful, but it released the second uncontrolled wave of spasm through her. He pushed her so deep when his first release of ejaculate forced into her, she gasped again. With a rhythm in tune with his heart he pulsed and pumped himself into her, sweat dripping down his forehead, and breath short and in gasps. She put her head on his shoulder and whispered in his ear, 'Did I pass my test, Mr Dean?' She was starting to regain her own breathing now.

'I see that you have studied hard and learned how to control the beast and I insist that under no circumstances do you ride with anyone, only with me, Miss Jenkins,' he replied, kissing her neck. 'And I can only ask that you enjoy each trip. I can say that the more you ride, the more pleasure you feel and experience you gain.'

'Well, Mr Dean, maybe we should see if you have enough petrol left in your tank to go again?' She pushed herself back off his legs and bent down to take his flaccid dick in her mouth. At first, she could taste his salt and her sweetness. As she gently sucked he began to harden and she sucked in air past his teeth, making a noise. As she licked the top of his cock, a small drop of cum came out and she licked it like a lollipop she looked at him and grinned with a mouth full.

'Lottie, you are incredible,' he said, pushing his head back into the sofa and closing his eyes.

Chapter 14

She had been really nervous, but wondered why when the examiner said, 'Congratulations, Miss Jenkins, welcome to the world of bike riding, now the fun can begin.' She gave out a little cry as he handed her the document that she needed to send off to the DVLA to upgrade her licence.

Joe smiled at her when she arrived back at the test centre. 'Bet you can't wait to get a bike, then?' he asked, knowing full well that Mr Dean had given him enough warning that she was not to pass unless they were totally sure she would be safe. He had not dared to tell the examiner this, or the fact that Ed had paid him to fail her if need be. She had passed on her own merits and he could see she was genuinely excited. On cue her phone rang, and it was Ed: she chose not to take the call, and without fail Joe's phone then sprang into life.

'Tell him I am not back yet, or something: I want to go to the office and surprise him,' she said.

'Do you think he will believe me?' Joe asked, fully aware of how persuasive the mighty Mr Dean could be.

'Say that the other people before me were late and they are about an hour behind.' She was still smiling from ear to ear. Joe did as instructed and when he put down the phone he said, 'I am sure he knew I was lying.'

Lottie said her goodbyes and kissed him as a way to thank him for the lessons and helping her through this. She hailed a cab and made her way to Ed's office. When she arrived outside, Pete was there with the car.

'Miss,' he said, bobbing his head and going in his pocket for his phone. Well aware of what he was about to do, Lottie said, 'Let me surprise him.' He put his phone away and continued to stay by the car as if it was going to walk off on its own.

She pressed the button to the office floor and bounced out to see Zoe sitting at her desk.

'He is busy, Lottie, at the moment,' Zoe said. 'Let me call through.'

'I wanted to surprise him. That would sort of spoil it,' Lottie replied, looking like a puppy to try to win her over and stop her doing her job.

'I am sure that he will not be long. Do you want a coffee while you wait?' She stood up, not waiting for the reply and moving towards the coffee machine.

'That would be nice.' Lottie walked over to her. 'Any one important in there?' she asked, just making conversation she was not really being that nosey. Zoe sort of faltered in her reply as if she really had to think about the answer. Lottie looked at her, this time with a 'well tell me, it must be a woman' look on her face.

'Not sure I should say,' Zoe finally said, handing her a coffee.

'I was not being nosy, it does not matter really,' Lottie replied, still happy from her achievement earlier. Ed's voice came through on the intercom, as Zoe was away from her desk she had put it on speakerphone so she did not miss anything.

'Zoe, get me Parsons, I need a barrister. Ask Pete to come around the detectives are just about to leave.' He sounded pissed off. 'Has Joe called yet?'

'No, Mr Dean, he has not.' She looked at Lottie who was shaking her head. She pressed a button and Pete picked up. 'He's done,' was all she said. The door to his office opened and two tanned men in suits walked out. One of them spoke to Zoe in a very strong accent.

'Madam, thank you for your hospitality, we will be back at some point, of that I am sure.' They pressed the button and went into the lift when it arrived. Lottie was able to catch the door to the office before it closed. Ed had walked into his bathroom and obviously did not see her.

'Fuck it, Pete, what did you do out there to him?' She could hear water and so presumed that he was washing his hands. 'They found him dead, said he had been dead for weeks. They have traced him back to the fucking hotel and are interviewing everyone who stayed there at the time, apparently looking at me because of what happened by the pool with Lottie and the fucking dead prick.' He had continued to talk while he was drying his hands. 'Are you listening?' he was still in the other room, but he then heard the door close again. It was Pete this time walking in and he saw Lottie standing still in the middle of the floor. He said, 'Mr Dean?' Pete almost said as a warning of her presence, not a question as to what he had been saying before he walked in.

Ed walked out and looked straight at her. 'How long have you been standing there?' he asked.

'Long enough to hear something I maybe should have not,' she said. He walked over to her and she turned away. Ed tipped his head to Pete and without a word he went out of the room. 'Lottie, how did you do?' He was referring to the test.

'Changing the subject will not stop me from drawing my own conclusions as to the conversation you just thought you were having with Pete, so maybe you should explain.' She looked out of the window at the busy world below.

'You first, it's more important,' he said.

She looked at him and raised her eyebrows. 'Really, needing a barrister after a visit from the French police, quoting that someone is dead and asking your hired muscles what he did to them: let me guess, my dear acquaintance Monsieur Orange?' She took a breath as her skin crawled as she thought about the birthday visit to Monaco. 'You are not referring to the fact that Pete had lunch with him, are you?' There was a hint of sarcasm in her voice.

'Lottie,' he said, standing in front of her making her look at him. 'It was nothing,' he said.

'Nothing? Right, let's take a think here. They never travel out of the country if they can help it, unless they have good reason. You would not ask for your barrister unless you thought you needed him. I have not worked with the police and dead people for the past two years, and I was not born yesterday.' She looked at him with her arms folded.

He was trying not to smile as he knew that she would totally take that the wrong way, but he could not help himself. She was so right, and so sure and so beautiful when she was right, and she knew her stuff, that he could not deny it and he loved her for it all. To lie to her was wrong in every way, but not quite as wrong as wanting to pick her up and take her there on the desk. He knew that she was being serious and all he wanted to do was ravish her. He put the thoughts to the back of his mind and held up his hands.

'OK, I'm not going to belittle you by lying, I just don't see the point in you bothering with this. I will have it sorted by the end of the day,' he said, walking back to his desk to sit in the chair.

'Really, then humour me,' she said, still standing by the window. 'Tell me that Pete did not go to see him and that you know nothing of what they were talking about,' she continued.

'It seems that they found a body, just outside Monaco, it turned out to be Monsieur Orange.' He started to relay the story. 'They have been investigating for a week or so and during this time they gathered information from our visit to the hotel, and...' He stopped, then continued. 'What happened according to their witnesses, they were given my name as to the disturbance.' He stopped again. She never spoke. 'So, they called and asked if they could come over and interview me.' He stopped again and she walked round and sat at the other side of the desk. 'They just wanted to ask some questions, all of which I answered.' He leaned over to focus on her. 'Pete did visit him, yes, just to warn him off. I never asked for any more than that, and he did not do anything more than that.' He sounded sure of the fact.

'And I am expected to believe that?' she put in.

'Yes, because I just said I was not going to lie to you.' He had his business face on and she looked at him as if to say continue then. There was a silence. 'They suspect he was drugged in some way.'

'But they suspect foul play?' she asked. 'Not an overdose.'

'It seems so, Inspector Clouseau!' he replied. 'They know that I never left your side, the doctors have confirmed that; they just wanted to know if I could shed any more light on any facts about the guy. I had never set eyes on him, it was you getting up close and personal.' Although he had meant his comments in jest, she took it the wrong way.

'So maybe it was me, then!' she snarled, this being the first time since they had met she had ever retorted at him.

'Lottie, don't get pissed with me,' he said back to her, 'I am being honest here. They want to come back to speak to Pete. I said that they would have to do that after I had spoken to him and with legal representation, as a precaution, something I would do for all my staff.'

'Sorry,' she quickly apologised but just wanted more information, 'I want to speak to them.'

'No,' he firmly said, 'absolutely not!' He stood up and paced to the window. 'What does that achieve?'

'I do this all day, remember? Maybe I could help them,' she replied.

'It's not even a UK case, once they have the facts it's nothing to do with me, you, us.' He finished. 'Their problem, and no!' He turned to look at her. 'No way, I won't let you.'

'You won't let me?' she asked, standing up to face him where he stood.

'It's not for you to "let me" do anything.' She exaggerated the 'let me' part. 'What don't you want me to find out?'

'Damn it, Lottie, I said no! I am not lying here, I have been truthful and you won't let it go, just leave it to run its course.' He was now quite stern-faced. Something he never wanted to be with her. 'I won't let you go around investigating something that could put you in danger. You need to be here where I can keep an eye on you. I don't want you to do this sort of stuff at all, but it seems to keep you happy. I hate it, let alone for something that has nothing to do with...' He was not able to finish.

'You don't want me to continue to work, you hate my job choice?' she asked. 'What makes you think it is for you to decide what I do for a career?'

'Lottie, I don't want to have this conversation now,' he said, trying to lighten his tone.

'Well, tough, I do,' she said. 'Do you want to control me that much that you expect me to give this up?' It was a statement as much as a question.

'I will look after you, you live with me now, and you don't need to work.' He paused. 'The work you do is only minor stuff. The professor said you stay away from the dangerous, complicated stuff, keeping a low profile.' He rolled it off his tongue as if he was in a business meeting, but Lottie's mind had already clicked.

'You have spoken to the Professor about my workload?' She faced him again. 'What else have you said to him?'

'Nothing, I just wanted to keep you safe,' he said. 'How the hell did we get onto this conversation anyway?'

'I don't know, but I wish we had not.' She pushed away from him as he tried to put an arm on her waist. 'What else have you talked about?'

'Nothing,' he said, trying again.

'Get off,' she said, walking towards the door.

'Lottie, where are you going?' he asked, following her.

'Leave me alone, I need to think.' She was quite confused. Ten minutes ago, she was on top of the world; now she was not sure about anything anymore. He grabbed her arm. 'Get off me, Edward,' she said with tears in her eyes. 'I mean it.' She had her hand on the door handle. He dropped his arm. 'We can finish this some other time. Right now, I need you out of my space.'

'Lottie!' She had gone through the door: both Pete and Zoe looked at her. She pushed the call button to the lift. Ed looked at Pete who never spoke. 'No,' Lottie said, 'don't even think about it, Pete!'

She tapped the wall as the lift seemed to take forever to get to the bottom floor. She knew that he would get one of the security team to follow her, so she sat on the bench outside and rang Todd.

Ed stood in the corridor looking through the darkened glass at her sitting on the bench. While she was there he was happy she was safe. He resisted the burning urge to go to her and pick her up in his arms and tell her he was sorry, but was he really sorry for not wanting her to be in harm's way? He did want her safe: he never wanted her to be in danger from anything. He would provide her with everything she could ever want and more.

'What was that all about?' Pete asked.

'I tried to be truthful and fucked up!' he replied. 'Never seen her like that, she really is fired up. I will give her a minute and then go out.'

'Is that wise? Do you want me to follow her, find out who she spoke to?' Pete asked.

'No,' he replied, 'I need you to speak to Parsons about the other shit. Get your story straight so that the police go home and then she will forget about it,' he hoped. 'Where is Steven?'

'Took the car to the wash, and then back to the apartment to get the Bentley cleaned for tonight. I will get him back.' He picked up his phone.

She sat there seething. He wanted to control her that much that he wanted her to stop work? Was this why he wanted her to be involved in his charities, and so eager for her to set up scholarships, to turn her into the little lady? It was over ten minutes that she sat there; she had calmed down, but still needed to get away to clear her mind. Todd's text came through and she looked at her phone. He was sitting in the entrance to the car park; she could see him. She quickly jumped up and ran to the car.

Ed noticed her move and tried to get out the door, but the security door jammed and held him back.

'Fucking thing!' He kicked the door, hoping it would let him out, but he should know that his security systems were so good it was not going to work. 'Get this fucking thing open!' he bellowed at the guard behind the desk. He already had his phone out, ringing Pete. The car left the car park and she was away before he could even ask for him to get down, let alone to get the car to follow her. He called her and it went straight through to voicemail. He dialled again and again, getting the same tone each time. 'Fuck it!' he shouted.

She did not want to go home – well, the apartment, was that home? She just wanted to be free to think about everything.

'Where to?' Todd asked. She looked up at the signpost. They were heading south out of the city.

'Brighton,' she said, looking at one of the destinations on the sign that they were about to pass.

'What?' Todd laughed.

'I don't know, just somewhere I can put some of this together in my head,' she replied. 'Can I have your phone?'

'You have lost the plot, Lottie. Can you fill me in a bit?' he asked, following her instruction to go to Brighton.

She looked for the Professor's number and dialled.

'Hi, Todd,' he replied.

'Sorry, Professor, it's Lottie,' she replied.

'Oh Lottie, sorry, it's Todd's number!' he exclaimed, surprised at her voice.

'I want you to be honest with me, Professor, I will not be mad,' she started. 'Has Mr Dean asked you to keep me away from any cases that could have turned out to be, be, difficult?' she finished and allowed him to speak. Todd looked at her.

'N-N-Nooo.' He was a poor liar as he stuttered. He was too square, too academic to lie.

'Really?' she asked. 'What about when you asked us to only work on my 'break in' for a few hours, no more than a morning? Was that because you did not want me to find out what happened, or to keep me from some sort of truth?' she finished.

'Mr Dean has...' He paused. 'How can I put this? Contributed well to the centre since you started working for us. Lottie, I don't want to say this, as I value you and your work, you know that.' She was boiling in her skin. 'You have really done some great work but...' He stopped.

'He pressured you to keep me safe!' She said the last word as she thought Mr Dean would put it.

'No, well, yes, but I never stopped you working on anything. Todd...'

She pushed in. 'Todd, what?' She looked at him and the mention of his name made him go red.

'Todd was happy just to go along with whatever I gave you two: he did not know anything about it. I never mentioned anything about...' He paused. 'Oh Lottie, I am digging myself a hole here. Whatever has made you call and ask me I am sorry. I totally value you and your work. I, too, did not want you to get harmed and nothing we have really done has made me have to pull you off any work, it was just... 'Yes,' she said. 'Mr Dean asked me to keep you safe: it has not really turned out that I have had to.'

She continued to talk to the professor and then returned to look at Todd.

'I guess you got most of that. Well, today has been an eye-opener,' she said. 'You will be no marriage guidance counsellor to know that Ed and I have had a row, our first really, but...' she continued to tell him the story.

'Wow, you go from passing your bike test, to overhearing the French bill investigate a murder of someone who hit on you on your birthday, all in one morning. I could not write a book, Lottie.' He laughed.

'I suppose when you put it like that it does sound so far-fetched.' She laughed, too. She looked at the clock, it was almost 3pm. 'Maybe I joked about Brighton.' She looked at the road and they were already well on the way. 'But a night out will make him stew. Did you bring the laptop?'

'Real row, cool. Your phone will be on overload, Mr Control will blow a fuse not knowing where you are,' Todd said, pointing to the computer in the back.

'I'm sure he will have the phone tapped or something, someone will be following us so don't get too excited, but sadly that's the point!' she joked as she turned the phone off, knowing that the thing could not be tracked if it was off.

The receiver on the computer that they were looking at had picked her phone up from when she had left until that point.

'I've got her,' Pete said. Ed was already standing there with his jacket on. 'A23.'

'Where's she going?' he asked.

'Should you follow her?' Pete asked.

'Fuck yes,' Ed replied. 'Why the hell not?'

'Maybe she just needs to calm down.' He knew that he would not want to hear that, but it had to be said.

'With him?' Ed had already asked who she had left with, and from the CCTV Pete was quick to find out that it was Todd's car.

'Lost it.' Pete hardly dare say it. Ed smashed the computer screen with his phone. 'Fucking piece of shit!' he shouted, putting his hands on his head. 'Now what?'

They reached Brighton and they had looked around for a hotel. Most were full, so as they hit the side streets they found a B&B on the way to Worthing that had a vacancy sign. They checked in with the cheery guy, who was clearly part of the bright, bustling gay community in the city. His partner had showed them to their room. Lottie went in the shower, without a change of clothes or anything; she just wanted time to calm down. She washed her face and ran her hands down her neck; she touched the choker and was now regretting running away and really wanted to ring Ed to say sorry. The longer she left it, the harder it would be. She really wanted him there, but then her gut churned. They had not had a row in the six months they had been together. They had had a few cross words, but then made up with usually the most sensational sex, and a talking session to iron out the issues. She really was afraid that she loved him, but there had always been those niggles that he smothered her, and today it seemed to click. She thought she could cope with it, but obviously not.

Todd had fired up the laptop and was looking for some of the information they had talked about on the way there. She came through to the basic little room, with a bed and a table, and the en suite she had just used.

'I'll sleep in the chair.' Todd pointed to the old, pink-coloured single sofa seat.

'Don't trust yourself to top and tail?' She laughed, still drying her hair with a towel.

'Maybe a few months ago, when we first got back in touch I would have said no, but I can see the way you feel about him and as much as I love you, I know it is as the friend I always knew you would be,' he said, looking up from his work. 'He is a lucky man, even if he is a fool for suffocating you.'

'You are sweet.' She kissed his head. 'Thank you for dropping things and just turning up for me. I am not sure what came over me, but I panicked. There have been a few things that have happened that just seemed to join together, and I feel that I have lost myself, in a whirlwind, I suppose.' She continued. 'I need to let him know I'm OK: I would want him to do the same.'

'You have got it bad, girl, but you are right: I would want to know. Here.' He passed her the laptop. 'Log onto the centre and email him from your account. It's not traceable!' he added. So she did:

Ed

Sorry, I am not sure what went wrong today, but you need to know I am OK. Please let me just have a day or so to get my head in the right space. We have done so much, moved so fast. I have become lost. But please know I love you. I know that you can't help but need to know where I am. I had to contact you because I need to have you here with me, too, but first I need to be sure that I really know who I am, and so I need to be here.

You can hate me for acting so strange, leaving like that, I will understand. I will email you again soon, and if you still want me around we can talk.

Know I miss you,

Love Lottie.

She pressed the send button, knowing that it would come through on his phone. She wanted to wait for a reply but she had done what she needed to, and let him know she was OK. She logged off and passed the computer back to Todd.

The ping on the phone that had not left his hand since he changed the SIM card to a new handset made him look up. He had stood at his office window since they had lost the connection. Pete had tried everything to guess where they were heading, but the A23 could have taken them anywhere. He had tried to talk to Ed but got no response. One good thing was he had not hit anyone, or headed for the whiskey that he knew Ed kept in the office cabinet, although there was time. One thing he knew his employer could not cope with was personal stress, emotional pain, and drink usually was the answer, which led to trouble.

Ed looked at the email.

'Is she OK?' Pete asked as he seemed to stare at it motionless.

'Yes.' He started to move his fingers over the small keys to pen a reply. He moved over to his desk: he felt, for the first time since he was young, that he could do nothing.

'Edward, are you OK?' Pete genuinely asked as a friend, not his employee.

As Ed pressed the keys, a small tear dropped on his fingers. He never looked back up, he simply replied, 'No.'

Lottie had fallen asleep as they both lay on the bed looking at documents and anything they could get from the French police at this time of night. Todd wrapped her in the quilt and sat still tapping away well into the night. He heard the noise of the other guests coming back in, and several others walking past the ground-floor room. He had managed to get an email conversation with the forensic team in Monaco, but lost them around midnight. So he, too, decided that it was time to give in. One last search and then he could leave the genius of the network to look for anything overnight. He placed the computer on the table and shut the lid. He found a sheet from the small wardrobe and wrapped it around himself. He was going to be cold, but never mind, one night never killed anyone.

'Morning you,' Todd said as Lottie woke up. He had been right that he would be cold, and he really was exhausted from catnapping all night.

'Morning,' she said.

'Sleep OK?' he asked.

'More than you by the looks of things!' she said, sitting up. She was still dressed.

'Are you saying I don't look at my most handsome at this hour of the morning?' His words prompted her to look at her watch. The watch Ed had brought for her, and she started to cry.

'Hey, hey, I am really not that bad-looking, am I?' He moved over to her and took her in his arms.

'What am I doing with my life?' she asked. 'It was going so well and I had to mess it up. Most people would think I had everything, in fact I am sure they would say perfect. I love him so why do I feel like this?'

'You just need to get your answers. I know you, Lottie, you hate to be in the dark. It has to be black and white for you: everything has an answer and you have to find it to be happy.'

'I thought I was happy,' she sobbed.

'And we will find you some answers to make you happy again,' Todd reassured her.

'What if he thinks I am a head case and does not want to see me again?' She tried to wipe her face. 'Agnes was right, I put all my eggs into one basket in a hurry and now I have smashed them.' He smiled at her metaphor.

'He won't hate you,' Todd said softly. 'Look at everything he has done for you.' That made her worse and the tears started again.

'That's my point. I have started a business, charity things that will all need me to be with him, even if not with him as a couple, with him from time to time. I am not sure I can do that.' She stopped herself. Just the thought of seeing him with someone else, months down the line, would kill her.

'Has it come to that? Really, Lottie. Everyone has an argument. God alone knows two strong people should have a difference of opinions, that's what makes us different.'

'We never argued all the time we were together.' She sniffed.

'Yes, but we were not to be,' he said. 'We had had different views.'

'Professionally, yes. Most to be proved right one way or another,' she reminded him.

'I say it again: we are different people. This hurts right now because you care so much.' He looked her in the face. 'Look at your emails, just to check, and then we can go get some breakfast and think about what you want to do from here.'

'What if I log on and he has dumped me, or he went to some club last night and got steaming drunk and pulled a beautiful girl and has forgotten about me?'

'You are being stupid now, get a grip. He will not have dumped you: if he has, I will go to his big, posh penthouse and knock the fucking life back into him. And to be honest, he could not pull the most beautiful girl ever as she is sitting here, looking a bit rough, granted, and acting and saying the most stupid of things, for sure, but he will not have, Lottie, trust me.' He looked at her and almost shook her shoulders. 'Email, shower, breakfast, then I will keep looking for something to give us some clues to this mess.'

'OK,' she smiled. 'I need the loo first,' she said, getting out of bed. She looked in the mirror: well, he was right she did look a bit rough, and yes, she did need to get a grip. In fact, she could hear Agnes's voice again saying just the same thing. She wanted to ring her friend; she wondered if Ed would have called her, and would that have made her panic, but if he had not she would have to go over the story one more time and get the 'I told you so' or the 'don't be a fool' lectures, so she left her phone off.

Todd jumped in the shower, complaining that the complimentary toiletries would make him smell like a woman, while Lottie logged on.

19:45

Baby girl, thank God you are OK, please come back, don't leave me, I don't know what to say. I guess I fucked up big time, said just the wrong things, always doing the wrong things. This feeling I have for you is so new I don't know how to deal with it. Please reply and let me know where you are, I will be with you as soon as I can.

I love You,

Ed x

19:52

Baby girl why are you not replying? I am out of my mind thinking that you will leave me, please.

19:55

This night will kill me without your reply, but I guess you don't want to.

19:59

I'm doing it again, stalking you, bombarding you, I just need to know I have not lost you.

20:02

I love you!

The single email one-liners went on until just after midnight, all along the same lines. She replied:

Sorry I logged off after sending it. We will be back later, as soon as I know, I will let you know when.

Love Lx

She logged off again, as she knew there would be a barrage of emails; as much as she wanted there to be, she wanted a conversation face to face. She had made up her mind how this would pan out, and email was not the way to do it.

They sat in a café eating breakfast - well, Todd was, Lottie just pushed the food around the plate. They had taken the laptop with them and once Todd had finished he started to go through what he had found. He logged onto his page and looked at his email replies.

'I've got something,' he said.

'What let me look.' She quickly came to life.

'Hang on, let me read it.' She was sitting on his knee almost wanting to read it with him. He shifted over in his chair.

'What? I don't see the connection,' she said.

'Wait.' He pulled up another document.

'I don't get it. The break-in at mine, what has...'

He stopped her. 'Look.' He pointed to the screen. 'DNA pattern.' He pointed again.

She looked and had to look again. The results of the post-mortem on Mr Orange had showed he struggled, so no wonder they suspected foul play. In doing the detailed examination of his body, or what seemed to be left of his body, they had found some evidence on his clothes of someone else's DNA.

Todd tapped the screen and it changed to the DNA profile of the person who had been in the flat. She looked again.

'Can you bind on this laptop?' She wanted the patterns overlapped, not sure if outside the lab he could do that.

'Yep!' He pressed a few more of the keys and the two images wrapped around each other. They matched perfectly.

'Means only one thing,' Todd said.

'They match!' Lottie exclaimed, almost letting all the other diners know the information, too.

'They do, but whose?' Todd asked, looking around at some of the faces that were still staring over on their direction. He gave them a little smile and they soon turned away.

'I need to be back in the lab for sure, but I found something else on this, a cold case that the professor said was nothing, but...' He tapped a few more keys. 'No, I can't get access remotely, we need to be there, but there is something else. I never told you as he said to leave it, but I think we need to see all the evidence to get a picture.'

She had not really been listening; she was going over in her head who could have been in the same places at the same time. Pete. He had been with them, but he had to be called back that night to the flat because he had driven off, or had he? Could he have been in there somehow? Surely if they searched the military server system they could find his DNA. Steven, he was nowhere near the flat, not even on duty: again they could check the military records. Ed... Now you are being stupid, she thought. He was by your side all the time: it was someone else who ran past them.

'Can you get the MOD data on here?' she asked.

'No, need to be at the Centre,' Todd said. 'Why?' he asked. She explained her theory. 'We need to get back there, don't we?' she said back to him.

'You need to get back to Ed first,' he said, 'and I need to have a proper shower and get changed.'

'That's going to take too long,' she said, a wild look of a thrill in her eyes that she was on to something.

'The facts are not going to go away. If we take a few hours out, Lottie,' he said, 'the Prof can have a look for us.'

'No, I want to do this,' she said. 'I don't want him to know too much until we have some facts to go to the French authorities with.'

They paid their bill and returned to the car. They chatted all the way back in the car; she was still undecided about going back to the apartment, but had no option as all her things were there. They had a clear plan of action, and it needed to start with her seeing Ed, so she turned the phone back on to make the call.

He looked down at the display and her number came flashing up. It was not more than one ring when he hit the answer button.

'Lottie, where are you?' he asked. He was still dressed in the same clothes as yesterday: the growth of stubble on his chin showed he had not washed or taken his normal morning shower. In fact, he had been up all night pacing around waiting for any call or correspondence at all. He did sleep, but only in the chair in the sitting room. Both Mrs B and Pete were now giving him a wide berth as they had both been heavily scolded over the course of the evening. He had even placed a call into Dr Douglas around 1pm, who through sleepy comments had calmed him down a little. He had hit the bottle of whiskey in the study around 3pm: this mainly was the reason he had fallen asleep, but as nights went, it was one he did not want to remember. Pete had been grateful that he had stayed in, so if any good was coming from the situation at least he had not been in any trouble that his team needed to deal with yet.

'We are on our way back,' she started to explain. 'I will come back to the apartment and explain everything: will you still be there?'

'Where do you think I would be, baby girl? I need to see you are OK,' he asked, not in an angry voice but one of relief that she had chosen to go back to him and not as he feared to her home in Kent. Not that it would have mattered: he would have driven over there as soon as he knew she was heading back. 'Where have you been?' he asked.

'We stayed in a B&B,' she said. 'Just outside Brighton. Don't ask why there, I am not sure. I am not sure I can explain the last 24 hours, to be honest, but I will try, if you will listen.'

'I will listen, of course I will, as long as you come home to me,' he said. 'We do talking well, remember!'

Maybe not well enough as it has led us here! she thought. She could hear that he was calm by the end of the conversation, although she had said enough for now. She did not want to mention the rest of her plans to him until she was face to face.

'The traffic is doing well so I would say that about two hours and we will be there,' she said, looking at Todd for confirmation of the time, and he was nodding.

As he put down the phone, he stopped feeling sick and jumped up. He needed to get washed and ready for her. He went into the kitchen where Pete was watching the TV.

'Mrs B, get the kettle on, and we need some lunch.' He went to the fridge to see what was in.

'Don't you think that she will want to freshen up first?' Mrs B said, coming back into the room.

'She can do what the hell she likes as long as she walks back in the door in one piece,' he said back to her, drinking out of the bottle of orange. She snatched the bottle off him.

'Edward manners, please!' she said. He kissed her on the cheek. 'Sorry!' he said.

'Will you really?' Pete asked.

'Will I really what?' Ed asked back.

'Will you really let her do what she wants?' he asked, lengthening out the question that he first asked. 'Without biting my head off, can you say that you will?'

'I am going to try. I know I can't face the fact that for all the money I have, all the things I can do, everything I can have on demand, she is the only one thing that if I lost, I could not breathe.' He had both hands on the worktop. 'Never thought I would hear myself say that. Even I am shocked, so I am sure that you are, but I can't help this feeling, Pete. I hate myself for being so out of control about her. If I have to give everything up within an hour I will be as poor as a beggar, but I will not give her up for nothing, and if it means I have to change, then I do. The last few weeks I thought I had changed, but last night showed me that I still have it in me to be dominant, overpowering and possessive.'

'Then take the necklace back off her.' Pete came out with it without prompting.

'Sorry, not with you,' Ed asked.

'The necklace, admit to yourself that it was a way to claim her as yours, to show the world you have taken her.' He focused on his face. 'I know you better than most: admit the fact that you thought this was going to be a bit of fun, but it has turned out to be much more. Not a usual submissive girl who was happy to be claimed but innocent of your true intentions.'

'What the fuck has this got to do with anything?' Ed asked, getting angry again.

'You know where I am with this. Own it, put a brand and label on it, and it's mine, hands off! The usual Dean way. If she has rattled you so much allow her to be herself.'

'If I want counselling from you, I will ask,' he said. Pete held up his hands and continued to sip at his tea.

Ed stood under the water in the shower and reflected on his words. It had been the norm, chase a girl, in some cases only for an hour, get what you want, if they hang around make a statement to everyone she is yours, or get rid of them. Usually buying the expensive necklace was a way to do both. They were labelled as his, and when he did not want them anymore, they were usually happy to come out of it with some expensive piece of jewellery as payment. 'Shit,' he said to himself. 'Why does that prick have to be right, every time?'

He was thrilled by her chase to start off with, within seconds of seeing her, and then somewhere along the line, and he was not totally sure where, he had fallen for her. In fact, to think of it he knew where. It was when she had sat playing the piano, in the Tap and Tune. He had fallen for her by then.

'I don't want you anywhere near the Centre today, Lottie, hear me?' Todd said as he was about to pull up outside the apartment block. 'I am not going in and I don't want you to. This can all wait until tomorrow. And I will see you there at 8am. If I have to I will get security to block your clearance and then you will have to wait for another day before the Professor can get you put back on the system. Understand?' he said.

'Yes, yes, I'm on the page and I get it, but then you will stick to what we have agreed?' she said, getting her bag in her hand ready to get out. He nodded and said, 'Good luck.'

She was aware that he would have eyes everywhere and, as predicted, he was waiting for her at the top of the lift. Clean shave, smelling fresh and looking as gorgeous as the first day she had seen him. No words were spoken and she dropped her bag and nestled into the comfort of his arms. Both had their eyes closed and they held onto each other; the silence was only broken by the sound of their breathing. He gently kissed her hair, rubbing it tenderly as she clung to him. She broke the bond first and spoke.

'I'm sorry, Ed, I am not sure what happened but I just...' She took a breath. 'Wobbled.'

He smiled. 'Shusssh!' he said. 'You're here now.'

'I'm almost embarrassed at how I reacted.' She looked down at the floor and he picked her head up to look at him.

Mrs B had left the kettle on. 'Do you want some lunch?' he said.

'You're not going to avoid the subject, are you, skim over it like it never happened?' She was worried that he would and within a few days she would feel the same way again.

'No, quite the opposite, I am not rushing you to do anything, or say anything.' He placed one hand on her cheek. 'I want to get this right and I can see that I said things that upset you, and maybe I should have thought more before I said them.'

She put her hand on top of his and replied, 'Maybe you needed to say them, but I did not want to hear what you said?'

'You see, you do it: within seconds, you see the best side to everyone and make it look bright and cheerily.' He kissed her tenderly on the lips. Oh, she felt good. He had points last night where he could have said his heart stopped because he thought he would not get to taste her again, or feel the warmth of her through his lips.

He opened the apartment door: there was a light playing of music in the background as she walked into the sitting room. She could smell the coffee and had to say it smelled good. He lifted up the pot on the warmer.

'Want one?' he asked.

She screwed up her nose and went to the fridge. She smiled to herself as she noticed the bottle of champagne in there. They should have drunk it last night, as she had asked for it to be ready and chilling in the anticipation of passing her test, a fact that she had put well at the back of her mind. She closed the door and held up the bottle.

'Bath?' she asked with a smile and bite of her lower lip, the deliberate lip thing to tempt him in. 'We always do so well at chatting in the bath.' She finished grabbing two of the crystal flutes from the open glass cabinet. 'And after all I did pass my test, but I am sure that you know that already!'

'Miss Jenkins, I am not sure how you ever expect me to turn down the invitation you have just given. As a business deal I have to say I am sold. Be very careful now what you ask for as I am afraid that I am liable to offer anything at any price.' He started to undo his top, and he kicked off his shoes, following her to the large tub situated in his en suite.

She placed the bottle in the ice bucket she had picked up on the way past, and placed down the glasses. As the steam from the water started to fill the room she poured a large glug of sandalwood bath foam into the water. The spicy, sweet smell soon filled the room. She kicked off her shoes and took off her light jacket. Ed had stayed outside momentarily, then walked in behind her, without his top, just his loose-fitting, baggy joggers. Barefooted he paddled over to the bottle and pulled at the cork. Still they remained silent, the look in each other's eyes as they visually followed the movements of each other seemed to speak volumes. When the pressurised cork popped he poured two glasses and handed one to her. She smiled at him and raised her glass; he did the same: still no words. He took her glass and set it down beside the bath that was now becoming quite full. She continued to undo her blouse: he watched as it slipped to the floor. She pushed down her jeans, leaving her underwear that she had on the day before showing. She turned her back to him and undid her bra and took down her pants, kicking them out of the way. He walked up to her and placed a small kiss in the middle of her neck. He swept her hair to the side and nuzzled at her neck. Her nipples were erect, although it was not cold in the room. He placed both hands on her shoulders and tracked down her arms, kissing and licking her ear, neck and shoulders.

He moved in closer to her and reached one hand over her shoulder, cupping her breast as he did so. She gasped and took in a longer breath. She laid her head back onto his shoulder, closed her eyes and whispered:

'I'm so sorry.' She paused momentarily. 'I really can't explain what happened yesterday but...' He changed attention from her breast to her abdomen, rubbing from one hip to the other. She felt her inner thigh muscle tighten as he continued to press himself against her bare backside, and he laced his other hand across her stomach, confirming that he was aroused, as his erection strained in his loose pants.

'Shush, baby girl,' he whispered, continuing the onslaught of kisses to her neck and shoulders. He moved to the side, pushing her hair over to the other shoulder, releasing new places for him to kiss and pay attention to. His grip on her waist never lightened. He kept her as close as he could. He could feel her breathing, feel her heart beat.

He turned off the tap and picked her up, walking back into the bedroom. He laid her back onto the bed. To start with, there was no urgency in their touching, but it soon became apparent that they had missed each other. He straddled her, using his upper body to hold his weight. He slipped a finger inside her, feeling her soft, wet juice warming the area he most wanted to be in. He nudged her with the head of his enlarged dick and she shifted her hips in reply that she wanted him. He bent his head down and bit on her nipple. She gave a yelp as the pain crushed through her, peaking at her sex. He repeated the motion at the same time as he pushed himself into her. His first thrust went all of the way, and it took a moment for her to adjust to his size. She pushed her head back in the bed as he thrust again, using all of his weight to trap her. She felt his breath on her face, he was breathing fast. He usually went slowly, enjoying the moment, but it was the first time Lottie had ever felt he was just there for the sex, not the pleasure. He pushed up on his hands and increased his speed. Although it was not making love, his actions were turning her on and so she pushed back at him with the same rhythm. He gave a grunt, a primal grunt showing that he was close to completion.

'Fuck me, Lottie. Come on, give me what I want,' he said, grabbing one of her hands by her side and pinning her to the bed. She felt his weight on her hand and could not move it. She placed the other under his backside and pulled at him to make sure that the base of his cock hit the sweet spot of her sex, and she shivered with the increased intensity of her orgasm. He was wild, the roughest he had been, but she was with him in the moment.

'Oh God yes, fuck me like you have never before, Lottie!' he spat out. 'Faster!' he said. She felt her muscles explode and as she did he grabbed a handful of hair and pulled her head back. He bit down on her neck and it took her breath away. 'Yes! Take it from me!' He said each word with a thrust of his hips as his seed forced into her in thick gusts.

He was starting to pull her hair again, but this time it was not gentle. 'GUR,' he said, 'did you like that? Did you miss that? Lottie. Tell me you did.' He kissed the area on her neck that he had just bitten down on. 'Um baby girl, are you glad to be back?'

'Yes,' she said, slightly shocked by his rushed nature, but as she looked up at him, he had his eyes closed. He was still inside her, the hardness starting to subside. He lowered down on his elbows and whispered in her ear. 'I do love you, Lottie, you are mine forever, don't forget that.' He kissed the line of her necklace from shoulder to shoulder, careful not to crush her under his weight. He pulled slightly to the side of her and pulled up the sheets. It was still only lunchtime but she felt tired.

'Sleep a while,' he said. He laid her on his chest and she welcomed the feeling that her eyes needed to close.

It had only been half an hour but he had watched her for all of it, the slowing of her breathing as she drifted into a light sleep. The rise and fall of her chest: he watched the sheet lift and fall where her nipple pushed it up; he resisted the urge to blow it to see if it would react, as he did want her to sleep. He knew that he had been rough with her, but he was so pleased to get her back in his arms, to mark her again as his. He placed his hand over her necklace and ran his hand over it. He had bought it at first to give to her as a submissive, but when she had been given it for her birthday, he knew that she was not going to fit the usual role: in her eyes it was a gift, like any other.

His phone had been vibrating away and he tried to pick it up without disturbing her. She opened her eyes.

'Sorry,' he said, kissing her head and settling back down.

'Did I nod off?' she asked.

'Yes.' He kissed her head again. 'Sorry, the phone does not want me to have a moment's rest today,' he said.

'Well, get it, I will go and have that bath.' She sat up. 'Do you want your glass back?' She poured the flat champagne down the sink and used the bottle in the ice bucket to fill it up again. She took a sip of her own and placed his on the bedside table. He was in conversation with someone, his upper body revealing his tight chest and biceps. She kissed his chest and smiled.

'One moment,' he said to the caller as he grabbed her hand and placed a kiss on her lips, making her stop in her tracks. She smiled at him and continued to walk into the bathroom.

Lottie placed her hands on the side of the bath and slowly eased into the water, allowing it to work around her body. The water was a shock to her sore inner thighs; she noted that he had been quite rough with her, nothing that worried her, but as she lay there she thought that she had not taken her pill for the last two days and they would need to be more careful for a couple of days at least.

Ed paddled into the bathroom and sat by the side of the bath. He had put some joggers on, and a light top, although Lottie could still see the lines of his pecks through it. 'I just need to get some emails out and make a call. Keep the water warm, I will be back in half an hour.'

'I will look like a shrivelled prune by then!' She laughed.

'OK but come in and get me if I am any longer.' He filled up his glass and put the rest of the bottle into Lottie's. He kissed her head and caught some of the water and flicked it in her face. She was quick to react and she splashed a large handful of water that hit his back.

'Miss Jenkins, really?' he smirked at her and she splashed again. 'Declaring war is a dangerous thing to do, Miss Jenkins, and if I did not need to catch the Chinese Embassy before they leave I would get right back in that bath and spank you to within an inch of your life!'

'Promises, promises,' she said, biting her lip.

'Oh, they are promises, believe me.' He smiled back at her, shaking his top to remove some of the water as he walked out. He felt the stir in his loins at the thought of spanking her, and wondered what her reaction would be if he really did. Just the thought of it made him hard, and he had to give his phone call a moment to compose himself.

Lottie had finished her drink and the water had gone quite cold now. She washed her hair and rinsed herself down under the shower to get warm and remove the sandalwood bubbles she had put in the bath earlier. She dried herself and put on the dressing gown/nightgown set from her top drawer. It was cream silk, with a black trim. Not really warm, but would cover up as she walked back to the kitchen. She did not go past the study; she could hear Ed's voice and knew that he was still on the phone. Although he had said that she should disturb him, she did not want to. It was still a working day, after all.

She picked up her phone: no calls and no text messages. Sad, really, that the only person who really ever called or texted her was sitting in the next room! She poured some of the coffee from the pot into two cups and walked through to the office with one for Ed. She could hear him so just put her head round and gestured the cup, so as not to disturb him. She was aware what a mess she got into the last time she had listened to his conversation the day before and did not want a repeat episode.

He raised his eyebrows and nodded to her to come in. She danced along as she walked over to him and he smiled, patting his knee, asking silently for her to sit down. She did as he asked and he wrapped a hand around her.

'Mr York, I have to go for now, but if the figures do not add up call me back, I am pleased that you are happy with the original offer, but I can assure you I am not going to pull out at this rate of return. I am disappointed that your father will not come to the UK to make the deal, but that can be worked around, I am sure.' He said goodbye in Chinese and then put down his phone.

'Impressive,' Lottie said, 'bilingual.' She giggled.

'Don't be too impressed. It does not go further than hello and goodbye for some countries, but Chinese is one that I have learned to get along with. I do a lot of business out there. In fact, it looks like within the next month I will need to go: do you want to come with me?' he said, referring to the double entendre of his last statement.

'Mr Dean, always so rude, I knew that you meant to the country!' she replied.

'Not to Heaven and back, then,' he butted in and kissed her neck.

'One-track mind!' She laughed. Was now the time to say that she did not want to do anything but go to the centre and get her teeth into the investigation. They had not really discussed what he had said about her not working, and it had gone so well: was now the time to rock the boat?

'Do you want to go out for supper?' he said. 'Somewhere nice, Ivy or The Shard?' he asked.

'Will we get in at short notice?' she asked and her phone beeped as if the battery was going flat.

'Do you have to ask?' he said back.

'Sorry, Mr I get whatever I want!' she said back, standing up to get the phone charger. He slapped her backside.

'Don't you forget it,' he said, following her to the sitting room. She pulled her phone from her bag and looked around for the charger.

'Damn, the charger is at the Centre, I will get it tomorrow,' she said.

'Are you going into work?' he asked. Well, now must be the time to bring this up, she thought. She sat on the sofa.

'Yes, I had intended to.' She wanted to say 'if that is OK', but did not want to give him the option. It was her choice and he needed to accept it. 'We've got a lead that I want to follow.' He was quiet: she wondered if she should keep talking and explain that the case looked like it was linked with the break-in, but then thought better of it.

'I stand by what I said yesterday: I really don't like the thought that you do something that puts you in danger. I want to be able to keep you safe, but I need to realise that you do what you do, and maybe after some time you will change your mind, and find that working at something else works better for you.' He stopped. 'I hate the very fact that you may need to be away from me, but I have to get over it.' He sat next to her. 'I want you to be honest with me, Lottie, and tell me everything. If it even looks like there will be any trouble, or you need me, you ask. And I want you to keep one of the guys with you.' He pulled her hand out to him. 'This is my best compromise and no negotiations.'

'I guess that a compromise is something I should consider, as I know how much you are against this, and I will.' He noticed that she played with the necklace around her neck: she often did that when she was thinking about something. 'You will be the first to know if I need any help.'

'Pete has a new guy who is ready to come to work for me, I will get him to introduce you tomorrow, even if you accept a driver, and someone around when I am not, it will make me feel better,' he said, looking at her and trying to smile.

'What has happened to Steven?' Lottie worried that he was no longer around.

'He is still working with us; he has had some time off because of a family thing, plus the fact that the last time I left you two alone it went wrong!' He paused. 'I did mention sometime ago for you to have your own CPO, so Pete is sure that Phil will work out OK.'

She wanted to say that this was far over the top. Being followed like a child was something she could not get used to, even with Pete sometimes, but she had to give it a go for him, as he was making so much of the effort. Their conversation was interrupted again by Ed's phone and he looked at it.

'Table booked for 7pm.' He sipped at his coffee that was old and cold by now. He pulled a face and Lottie noticed.

'Want another?' she asked.

'No, I really need a few more hours of work, I missed so much yesterday: catching up would be good.' He still had a hold of her hand. 'Could I ask a favour?' She nodded and he explained to her what he wanted. He wandered off and fetched a letter and continued to explain.

'I have made a few notes, but I wanted you to have a look and tell me what you think. I will fetch your laptop: you can connect in here, but promise me that you will not sneak a look at any of your work while I am gone!'

'OK, message understood.' She opened the letter. The address on the front was to Ed at work. The handwriting was the best effort, but you could tell it was from a child. She opened the neatly folded document and started to read.

Mr Dean

My father asked me to write to you thanking you for the small replica of your cool car. I have put it in my bedroom. It was really cool to get in her and hear her make such a cool noise.

Your offer to Gramps and me would be really cool, too, but I need to ask if my mate Paul could come along as he has a birthday soon and his family don't have much time to have a party for him, it would be like a birthday present from me.

I hope that you don't think I am too cheeky in asking,

Many thanks

Simon Cooper

Lottie smiled at the letter. Ed had told her about the young boy, who had been so made up with getting in his car. She was not aware that he had been in touch with him and sent along a car. Ed had also arranged for a visit to a racetrack one weekend and said that he would call to arrange a time and date, but he had asked Lottie to do it as he thought it would be great for them all to go.

The Ferrari track at Goodwood had replied to Ed, giving him a corporate day for any Saturday in September: the first was only one week away so they needed to make the arrangements soon. She picked up the phone and called. Mr Cooper had been really nice on the phone; Lottie had explained who she was and asked if any dates would fit in with them. It had been arranged for the last week in September, four weeks' time: she thought that this would give her time to work, just in case she wanted to go to Monaco, and Ed had spoken about China.

She slipped in a quick email to Agnes, too, but did not log onto the Centre, she was content that she was going back in the morning. She was just looking at the internet when the reply from her friend came back.

Lottie

I would love to come down to see you for the weekend. Can I bring Sarah, some time away from the kids will do her good, we can have a right old girly shop and a pamper. Not sure if we can all stay, but let me know if not, I will book a hotel or something.

Let me know how you get on and more arrangements, I'm just popping to the shop for some tea for Dick, I'll mail you later.

Ax

Lottie put the laptop on the sofa and wandered to the office door. Ed had his head in a document and she spied on him. He had his laptop open in front of him, documents in one hand and was writing something with the other hand to the right of his desk. So, this is how a multimillionaire works all day: man can multitask after all! She smiled as she thought it to herself. He never noticed her there - well, maybe not! she thought as he dropped his pen. She giggled and he looked up.

'Sorry, I did not want to distract you,' she said opening the door.

'You are a most welcome distraction,' he said, smiling and putting down the papers.

'All arranged for young Simon, maybe I can give Zoe a run for her money as your new PA?' She walked over to the window and looked out.

'It can be arranged: when do you start?' If only she knew how serious he was with that statement. 'Although I have to say you will need to turn up for work in something a little less seductive.' He had moved behind her with stealth, and ran his hand up her short silk gown. 'I would never get any work done, and I do not welcome sharing this view with any visitors!'

He pulled her close and kissed her; she welcomed his closeness, and was highly aware that he was becoming aroused by their kissing.

'You are easily distracted, Mr Dean, are you not?' she asked, pulling away slightly. 'Do all your female business acquaintances have the same effect?'

'You are kidding me, Lottie!' he said, not playing the game of using their formal titles. 'Don't ever think that! I would have 'Taken don't try it' tattooed on my forehead if it made you feel better. You really have to understand that I am true to my word: we are together and I have never been shared, and will never share.' His face was all serious and Lottie regretted saying it now. 'I have to be around women, work with them, even accept that they flirt with me to get business, or something, but none of them affect me like you do, and the something will never be strong enough for me to even consider losing what we have.'

'Sorry, I was only playing.' She let him go as he was walking back to his desk, seeing how sincere he was with her.

'Sorry, too, for snapping,' he said. She draped herself over his shoulders and kissed his ear. 'Maybe the tattoo should say: 'Hot property of Lottie Jenkins'? She had to take the jest too far, and his silence was noted, so she changed the subject.

She explained about Agnes coming over: he was not best pleased as he would have to give her up for the weekend, but he could get some gym time in, and she would be staying at the apartment? It could have been worse, she could have said she was going back to Kent which meant he would not be invited.

'Ring the Kensington: the suite is still booked out in my name, and it will be free. Pete will need some time off but it will be good for Phil to get used to driving you around, maybe we could all meet up for dinner.' It would be a way of him being with her and keeping tabs at least.

'How about making it a real social and meeting with Todd and his sister? Maybe we could go to the Tap & Tune to see Scotty, too. We have not been there for a while.'

He hated the very thought of it, but could see the joy in her face, so agreed. She kissed him. 'I will take my newfound skills at PAing and book it all.' She skipped off and he shook his head as she left the room.

How does she do it? he thought to himself as he could hear her on the phone making some arrangements. She winds me up, with her comments, but has me wrapped around her finger. I am supposed to be the dominant one, but I give in to her every whim! He shook his head again, and then laughed to himself.

It was past 6:30 when Pete called to say he was waiting for them outside. Lottie had a summer dress on, but needed a coat as it had turned cold. They had generally chatted in the car and she thought to herself how different it had all looked 24 hours ago.

The Ivy was packed as normal. Front of house greeted them both. 'Mr Dean your table is ready.' As they walked in, Lottie took off her coat. Various heads turned and Ed spoke to one couple as they walked past the table. The waiter was walking ahead of them; Ed has his hand in Lottie's lower back following behind as she made her way to the seats. Several eyes looked at them: maybe as they knew Ed, maybe as they were just an attractive young couple.

But one person had watched them from a distance, and made sure he was not seen, as they sat and ordered a drink and looked through the menu. He left as quickly as he had arrived.

Chapter 15

'So, it does relate to the case, then?' Todd stood back from the monitor looking at the results from DNA tests they had run through the computer.

Lottie had arrived on the Thursday with her new driver after being introduced as arranged, and they had a full day working on the leads they had found a few days before. Todd made no comment, although he was dying to, but he could tell she was not impressed with her newfound shadow who hung around in the car park, or car, or walking around the site, or chatting to the centre security guards. Thankfully he was not allowed in the labs, so she could work undisturbed. Through the first day he never mentioned how it had gone making up; it seemed everything was OK. Lottie had been the first to bring up the compromise as they chatted while they worked. The days were flying by and the professor had asked them to come in to see him after lunch on the Friday. They both sat at his desk, waiting for him to come back in.

Both were surprised with his request.

'I know you both are taken up at the moment, but last week I was asked by a colleague if I had anyone who would like to work with Professor Channing on his new research project. I was meaning to ask you both last week. It slipped my mind. Well, he emailed this morning asking if we were still interested as he has another couple from Italy who have shown an interest. He knows we have been working with the new technology and wanted someone who has an interest in buying one of the programmes to work with him. The Italians are not interested in buying, but we are.' He paused. 'Lottie, I know that this may be a no from you.' He wanted to say, 'Mr Dean will not agree to it,' but held it back and added, 'As I am sure that you don't want to put on hold what you are looking into right now, but Professor Channing cannot come over here. It means a trip to the US, so I wondered if, Todd, you would like to go for a few days?'

'Really!?' Todd exclaimed. Professor Channing was the leading expert on pathology and forensic science. Todd had seen him at several conferences and was engrossed that the guy could be top in both fields and so well published for his new techniques and research with various books and papers that he had written. 'I would love to, Prof, what an opportunity!' he said. 'When can I go?'

'Maybe book a flight for next Thursday, he said he was free after then.' Todd looked at Lottie.

'I don't suppose that there is the slightest chance of you dropping this for a few days to join me?'

She had to admit, the timing could not have been any worse. The opportunity to work with Professor Channing was a once-in-a-lifetime offer. She was going over in her head how she was going to explain that she wanted to go to Monaco to help the French police, but the thought that asking Ed this as well would just blow all negotiations out of the water.

'I never asked you, Lottie, as I, too, thought that you would want to pursue the case you are working on, but I have every assurance that there is space for the two of you,' the Professor finished. 'The ball is in your court, my dear, but I am happy, Todd, to reply saying you will be out to see him soon.'

'Can I think about it?' Lottie asked.

'Of course, maybe let me know as soon as possible so we can make the arrangements, flights, accommodation, that sort of thing. New York is a busy place, exciting, though.' The Professor got up. 'I'll leave you two to have a chat and work something out.'

'Lottie, you can't give this a miss. Surely old Bossy Pants must see that this is a career move. To have a chance of working with Professor Channing on your CV, I can't miss it for the world. Would you mind if I go, and pick up the case in a week or so. After all, we seem to have come to a standstill even with the first basic enquiries.'

Todd was right. The MOD system had not shown up any DNA match. The UK and Interpol had no DNA matches: short of going to Monaco to look at the scene and the body they could not find any more. The scene had since been worked on by the builders who found the body, and Monsieur Orange was on ice and would not be buried for weeks so could wait their inspection if required. The French police were eager to get some help, but could wait as it did not seem to take priority now that Ed had made a statement.

'Please don't call him Old Bossy Pants when we are out tomorrow night, or I will have no chance of persuading him.' She laughed.

'But you would ask?' Todd seemed tentative at the question.

'Yes, why not?' she enquired, getting up to leave the room.

'Well, you know with everything that happened this week, about him hating your work, letting you out of his sight for more than an hour, etcetera!'

'Don't make it sound so bad,' she said as they walked down the corridor.

'Well, from the outside looking in, that's what it looks like,' Todd replied, stating the facts in true Todd style.

'I will ask him on Sunday. I don't want to take the fight on until after we have been out, so keep it shut at dinner,' she instructed.

'What a way to carry on: does he really have you that much to heel. I am surprised it is a gold necklace and not a leather dog collar, or do you change into that at night?'

'That's bloody rude, Todd, what are you insinuating?' She came to a stop and faced him.

'Joke, Lotts, just a joke. It's just ironic that he gave you the necklace like some sort of...'

'Token of affection, birthday gift?' she cut in before he could finish his sentence. 'I have a bracelet and earrings and a watch. Are they all marks of ownership, too?'

He never answered but thought maybe, or just generosity from a rich boyfriend? He knew which answer he favoured the most out of his conclusions.

The rest of the working day was quiet. She mulled over in her head what Todd had said. She was no prude: she knew about dominant people and how they placed a collar on their submissive as a sexual branding, but he had never been like that to her. Never showed her that's what it was.

It was after 7pm when Ed came back from the office, he had called several times and they had chatted, his usual way to check up on her. Lottie had showered and sat in a soft, white jogging suit. Mrs B had made dinner, so with a glass of wine she turned on the TV and sat and chilled out.

After a quick shower Ed joined Lottie and they ate at the breakfast bar, passing comments about their day and the next days to come. Lottie was excited to be meeting with her friends, but never once mentioned the possibility of a trip, albeit to New York or Monaco.

Once they had gone to bed, they made love. Different to the last time, Lottie thought, when he had seemed aggressive; this time he was tender and caring, like he usually was. She had woken to still find him there, sleeping. She looked across at the clock and could see that she had woken before the alarm. Mrs B no doubt was in the kitchen as the smell of breakfast wafted past her nose. She hugged him tight and it was enough to make him open his eyes.

'Morning you,' she said, kissing his nose lightly.

'Good morning to you, too, what time is it?' Ed replied, stealing a kiss from her lips before she could answer.

'Time to get up, I am afraid,' she said back, knowing that he had awoken as usual with a full, glorious erection, 'So you need to put that on hold.' She looked down at the covers and it confirmed he was aroused.

'Oh Lottie, how can you leave me like this?' she said with a sad face.

'Easily.' She jumped up and he ran after her into the bathroom. After a short embrace and kiss, they started their morning routine, and had breakfast that was timed to perfection, waiting for them as they arrived in the kitchen.

Phil dropped her off at the Kensington, and she made her way upstairs. She knocked on the door and waited for Agnes to open it. They hugged and she went inside.

'Really, Lottie, this is marvellous!' Agnes exclaimed, looking around the room. Lottie greeted her old friend Lynne, Agnes's daughter, and they chatted. 'And the driver was simply delicious! Do you have him all the time?'

They giggled and chatted and caught up while sitting drinking coffee. Lottie's phone beeped and she looked down at the message.

'We need to go into town, those shops will not wait for us!' she exclaimed. She had planned a day shopping, with a visit to Bella for a new outfit. A few drinks in the bar at The Ritz and then back to get changed for the evening meal. They had arranged to meet everyone for 7:30pm.

'Lottie, Phil is outside, get a shift on!' Ed called through to her; she was still getting changed. They had been back later than expected due to the number of shops that had visited.

She emerged in a new pair of black, fitted trousers, and a high-collar top that was cut away at the back. Due to the design of the dress she had taken off her necklace and chose not to wear any jewellery. As she had taken it off, Todd's words came back to her and she was going to be interested in Ed's reaction to this. As she walked out she was about to find out how he felt.

'Like it?' She gave him a twirl.

'Bella, I'm guessing?' He came closer to her and ran his hand down her back. He noticed the missing necklace, and his stomach turned for a moment. He unconsciously ran his finger around her neck where the gold band should have sat.

'No necklace?' he asked. 'I guess it does not go with the outfit?' he wanted to sound relaxed about it, but it was a blow to him all the same.

'Not really. Is that a problem? I can wear it underneath, but no one would see it.' She put her hand on his 'I'm going to be with you, so no need to show the world in other ways that I'm yours: they will be able to see it by the smile on my face!'

'Is that how you see it, a statement of ownership?' he enquired. Looking directly at her, had she known all along his true, original intention?

'No just a beautiful gift, gratefully received and proudly worn, just like the watch, and the other gifts you have undeservedly bestowed on me over the past few months.' She pulled towards him and smiled.

'You deserve them and more, Lottie, for understanding me even when I don't know myself so well.' He kissed her. 'Please let me go or we will not make it out on time, and the necklace will not be the only thing you don't have on!'

'Mr Dean, really, is that all you think about?' She playfully slapped his shoulder and felt the power in his upper body as he grabbed back at her hand, holding her still.

'Not **all** I think about, but with regard to you, there is so much more I think about, too. The thoughts I have right now are just a fantastic, pleasurable by-product.' He smiled at her and kissed her hard on the mouth as he whispered, 'And don't you forget, you're mine, statement of ownership or not.'

She thought about his comment in the car on the way to the Tap and Tune. There was an underlying something, but he had seemed to dismiss it with ease, and so maybe she should not make a great thing about it. She had to confess to herself that she did feel slightly naked without it: for one reason or another she had hardly been without one or the other necklace on since her birthday, months ago.

They did not say anything during the drive and Ed wondered what was going through her mind. He was sure he could live with the fact that she had taken the necklace off, couldn't he? Pete had said take it off, Dr Morgan had said try without it if it was such a big deal to him. So, he would see how tonight would go. As if she was reading his mind, Lottie wandered her hand over to his and held it, giving it a squeeze and smile as they arrived.

As they stepped out of the car, Lottie pulled him back and whispered in his ear.

'Just wanted to get your mind back on that train of thought you mentioned in the apartment.' She stopped and bit down on her lip as she looked into his eyes, and in a low voice said, 'I also don't have any underwear on; maybe that's all you can think about for a few hours?!'

The statement was so out of character for her, he almost choked on the next breath that he took. Without allowing him to reply she thanked Pete for holding the door and walked in ahead of him into the crowded bar.

'Alright, Mr Dean?' Pete asked, noticing the look on his face, and the shallow coughing sound he was making.

'Yes, fine,' he gasped, 'I'll ring you in a bit as arranged.'

They were the last to arrive and the large party of friends soon fell into conversation. Ed stuck to her side while they stood at the bar drinking. As they were shown to the table, Lottie took the seat opposite him and smiled. He had offered the seat next to him, but she wanted to sit where she could see more of what was going on.

They ordered food and quite unannounced she took off her shoe and rubbed it up the inside of his leg. The conversation he was having with Lynne, who was sitting to his left, stopped, as if he had been shot. He looked across at Lottie who was talking to Agnes, but had a smile on her face; she bit her lip and looked out of the corner of her eye and caught his gaze. She pulled away her foot. She worked out that if she shuffled the chair in a bit more she would be able to make it higher up his leg; he had put his napkin over his lap when the first course arrived, and just as he was taking his last spoon of soup she did it again, this time starting at his knee and pushing her foot upwards.

How lucky she was not to share his soup that he resisted spitting it out in the surprise again. Without a word she bit her lip and his nostrils flared as he looked at her.

'Edward, are you OK?' Agnes looked across to him, noticing that he had gone slightly red.

'Soup's quite peppery!' he lied back as an attempt at a reply. This sparked a conversation over the table between them about food they liked and disliked, and Lottie smiled under her breath at the effort he was making.

Scotty was having a busman's holiday; he was not working, but had joined the party, and could not help dipping into work when the bar got busy. It was halfway through the meal that the resident pianist sat at the piano and started to play upbeat tunes. Lottie's attention was instantly drawn to him.

'Trade seems to be going well,' Sarah said to her younger brother.

'Yes, the addition of the playing seems to have helped, although Lottie, I have to say, I wish you had taken up my offer months ago. He does not have quite the same eye appeal, good to listen to, not so good to look at!' he joked, but several of the party's eyes seemed to fall on Ed, as if waiting for a reply to the comment on Lottie's looks. She looked up at Ed, too, and smiled, trying to see through his eyes into his thoughts. He remained quiet, just sipped at his drink. She put her foot up on his chair about to reach his thigh, and he caught it and squeezed. Instantly their eyes locked and it could have been that no one else was in the room. The split second seemed to last for an hour. The heat burned from her face down to her toes and she felt an instant stir in her own thighs. He squeezed again as if to bring her to the present and let her go. She returned her foot to the floor.

'Should I thank you for that backhanded compliment?' she asked Scotty.

'Maybe we should see you play, Miss Jenkins, and then we can make up our own mind,' Ed cut in. He held her eyes as if they were invisibly connected in some way. 'After all, it is one pleasure you have so far denied me!' he said in a low voice.

Sarah spoke to Todd in a low voice. 'Now there is some deep sexual tension. Whew, I can feel that from here, he just oozes man!'

'Sarah, you're married!' Todd said, amazed at his elder sister, and not quite sure he wanted to see one of his exes have some sort of verbal foreplay over the table.

'And your point is?' She laughed and he shook his head, trying to get the thoughts out of his mind.

During the sweet course Agnes said to Ed.

'Edward, have you really not heard Lottie play?' Although Lottie was eating, she never flinched. Her foot had been resting on his thigh for the past five minutes, admiring her handiwork that he was almost fully aroused. He had pulled into the table and neatly pulled the cloth over his legs, allowing her to move her toes on the seam of his trousers between his legs for a while now. He put down his spoon and pushed his plate to the side, leaving his half-eaten chocolate dessert. He placed both elbows on the table. He rested his chin on his hands and smiled.

'I had the fortune to overhear her playing once, sometime ago, but no, I have not had the direct pleasure.' He looked under his eyes at her, and she felt her heart skip a beat. In an effort to relax to everyone else around the table, he pushed himself back slightly in his chair. For Lottie she felt his groin push hard against her foot, as if an invitation to increase the one pleasure she was giving him now.

'How strange that you have not played for him, Lottie. Well, Edward, you have not lived,' Agnes said, the mixture of wine and champagne clearly warming her cheeks and greasing the volume of her voice. 'Lottie, give us a tune,' she said, looking at her friend. 'Her fingers are so nimble they caress the notes as if they are in love, it's so effortless to her, you know,' Agnes said.

'There is something to be said for such a talent to have dextrous digits!' Ed retorted. Maybe no one else got the pun, but Lottie coloured as if she was about to explode, instantly moving her foot from its recent mooring.

He leaned forward again, putting his elbows back on the table, and in a deep, seductive voice said, 'Would you play, for me, Miss Jenkins?'

'See,' Sarah again whispered in her brother's ear. 'Look at him: does he just not captivate her? He has a hold on her that is incredible, like an invisible hand drawing her in, holding her still.'

'You read too many of those fantasy books!' Todd retorted, but he had to admit it. He had noticed the lack of necklace when she arrived, and was almost sorry now that he had mentioned it to Lottie the day before, but he had to say, there was a power between them that he could not explain. Did he have a pang of jealousy, or did he have to admit that Lottie was right? This guy was truly besotted with her. God only alone knew how that felt: he had felt it, too, and the more they were together, the more she was having her hold.

She protested slightly, asking that they finish the meal first, but had promised to play something before they left. She excused herself from the table and headed towards the toilet. She was about to leave the small cubicle, unlocking the door when the power that forced it from the other side took her unawares and almost knocked her back on the toilet seat. It happened so fast that she only caught a glimpse of him forcing down onto her lips before she recognised who it was. The smell of him confirmed that this powerful man was Ed. The hot pounding of his lips and the taste of his tongue as he thrust it into her mouth, confirmed his hunger for her. She gasped. He had made his way into the toilet and like a praying mantis had waited outside for her to unlock the door.

'Ed not here, someone...' She did not get out the words before the next assault on her mouth started. He pushed her up against the door and was fumbling at her breasts. 'Oh!' she gasped out again, trying to be quiet.

'Not here?' he asked. 'You tease me all night and then say not here. Miss Jenkins, never start a business deal that you can't carry through!' Her protests were not serious. She did want him and, although he was commanding over her, she was not being unwontedly forced. He slid his hand between her legs, where he found her, slick wet opening and glided his fingers in.

'Oh yes, Miss Jenkins tell me that you want me to stop, and I will,' he whispered in her ear. There was no reply.

He undid his flies to release his throbbing dick, already releasing the life juice, making the bulbous head shine. Her trousers fell to the floor and he lifted one of her legs to gain the urgent access that he wanted. The urgency of their kissing, biting his neck, and licking her ears added to the urgency of the release that was building up in her inner muscles. If anyone was going to walk in there was no going back now. The only way that this was ending was in them both being satisfied with the hot passion and urgency of coming. He thrust himself into her and she stifled her cry out on his shoulder. His large frame moved her up and down, with her only supporting foot leaving the floor with each thrust. 'Lottie, possess me, take it, please baby girl, I need your connection to never end with me.' He panted out his words. 'Show me, show me that you want me.' He felt her inner muscles clash at the start of her climax: it was like a flame to a firework for his own explosion which came fast and hard, pushing her back on the wall in a powerful thud. He pumped into her, breathing out with each powerful lift.

Both spent, momentarily they held each other up, trying to contain their breathing.

'Miss Jenkins, there is going to be a day that you kill me.' He held his head back and gave a large breath out. 'I swear any more of that and you will be close.'

She ran her hand through his hair: it was damp from his sweat. 'Can you think of better ways to go, Mr Dean?' she asked.

'Not right now, although we may have room for improvement the more we try!' He kissed her nose and closed his eyes, his mouth remaining in contact with her hot skin. 'I love you,' he whispered, his breathing back to some sort of normal now.

'I love you,' she said back. The door to the toilet opened and Agnes walked in. Lottie put her finger to his mouth as if to silence him.

'Lottie, you OK?' Agnes came in and opened the cubicle next to them.

'Yes, fine, I just got a bit hot and needed the loo.' She quietly opened the door to allow him to slip out. Agnes had started talking to her totally unaware that he was in there, due to the fact he left with the same ease as he had got in. Lottie adjusted her clothes and flushed the loo as if she had been again. She opened the door and looked in the mirror. Her hair was a mess, her face was as red as a tomato. Oh GOD, she thought, they will all know what we have been doing. She splashed some water on her face and reapplied the small amount of lipstick she had been wearing. Dabbing her face with a towel that she drenched in water, Agnes walked out.

'Oh, Lottie, you do look flushed, are you OK?' She started washing her hands.

'Just a bit hot, I will be fine.'

They both walked out together. Ed was not sitting at the desk. She could see he was outside on his phone. At that point her phone beeped as a text came through. She took it out of the small bag she had left on the table and looked at the text.

Miss Jenkins,

I just need some air. I will be back in a moment.

Yours forever

Mr Edward Dean totally fulfilled CEO of Dean Holdings

He was also desperate to put 'and Tap and Tune owner' at the bottom, as he was fed up of the conversations they had all had over dinner trying to guess who the owner of the bar was, but held off as he did not want to have to explain.

Mr Dean
Your shirt needs tucking in!!
Yours
Miss Jenkins (doing the PA thing again looking out for you!)

She smiled at him through the window as she saw him look down at the shirt tail that was sticking out of his trousers. He hurried to tuck it in as he continued the conversation on the phone.

He returned to the table.

'Everything OK?' she asked.

'Yes, I was just calling Pete to give a cover that we were not together.' He smiled.

'How about that tune, then, Lottie?' Scotty asked. 'Jed asked if you need any sheet music.'

'Really, there must be enough music in that head of yours to do a full session at Last Night at the Proms,' Todd butted in.

'I'm only doing a few, you two, no matter what you say.' She looked at Ed. 'Any requests?'

'Mozart, in G major,' he said without even having to think. He had listened to it enough since the first time she had played it.

'Very precise, Mr Dean, I had no idea you were such an aficionado.' Lottie smiled: she had heard him playing classical music before in the apartment. She wiggled her fingers in a gesture to warm them up. She walked to the piano, and ran her fingers over the keys as if to introduce herself to them. She stroked the seat and sat down. She folded the sheet music up that was on the stand and placed it on the top of the piano; she hated looking at the music if she was not following it.

She closed her eyes and took a breath. She could feel the effects of the few glasses of wine she had drunk over the course of her meal, but she soon focused and started to touch the keys. She started to play and for a moment the hub of the noise in the bar seemed to go quiet as they heard the music start to play again. Lottie soon blanked them out as if she was the only one in the room and the joyful tune filled the air.

Ed sat fixed on her every move, every pulse of the fingers, every breath that she took.

'Good, isn't she?' Agnes said, leaning in close to him.

Lottie continued to play a few favourite soundtracks from her all-time favourite film *Pride and Prejudice*, the 2005 version. Light and airy tunes came from the white piano, and its young proficient player: 'Georgiana', 'Liz on Top of the world' and 'Your Hands Are Cold', and her final favourite, 'Dawn' – all perfect piano pieces showing her dexterity and ability to create light and dark shades and moods with the music. She knew that she was a romantic at heart and loved the music as soon as she had seen the film. She had searched high and low for the score when it had first come out, and at every opportunity practised until her few favourites were note-perfect.

She could have been alone in the room, she became so lost. She came to the end of the final piece and stopped with her eyes closed. Jed clapped as loud as he could. He had sat at the end of the bar to start off with having a drink, but had wandered over closer to admire her playing. During the last piece, he had sat on the step at her feet as if in awe of her.

'I can't say how fantastic that was, Lottie. You are a marvel, my playing holds nothing in comparison to that.' He sat on the seat next to her, even though there was not enough room. 'Was that the music to a soundtrack?

I am sure that I know some of the pieces.' He did not give her chance to answer. 'Can we play together?' He riffled through the sheet music she had folded up. 'How about ragtime?'

Ed walked over to her and placed his hands on her shoulders. He gently kissed her head and whispered in her ear, 'I am spellbound, Miss Jenkins.' He handed her a glass of champagne that he had asked for at the end of a meal. 'I want to invest in a piano for the apartment: you must play more often.'

She took the glass from him and said to Jed, 'Just one piece, I am neglecting my friends.' She looked up at Ed and smiled; he winked back to her.

He chose a piece that she vaguely recognised so had a quick look through it. She moved over on the chair, aware of his closeness, and he started to play. She picked up the pace with her hands and at times they had to cross over. As she brushed hands with him, she could feel that were hot and sweaty, and she had a sudden feeling of being uncomfortable. No one else in the room was watching them, apart from Edward. He must have picked up on her body language so he went over to her again and rubbed his hand on her shoulder while she played. Just knowing he was there made her more at ease.

They did not stay very much longer. Agnes and Lynne had been dropped off at the hotel, and after saying goodbye they made their way back to the apartment. They had not arranged to see them the next day: they were heading off home after breakfast.

'What do you have planned for tomorrow?' Ed asked as they drew up to the apartment. She replied and they continued to chat.

'Well, how about a ride out to the farm? The weather should be OK if we go once the morning dew dries.' She accepted the offer as they walked back through the door. Both exhausted, they fall asleep embraced in each other's arms.

She was clad in her leathers. They had become far more comfortable now that she had worn them in. Gloves and helmet in hand, they walked down to the basement car park, where only Ed's vehicles and the company cars all sat.

'She is only on loan, but if you like it we can look at getting one for you.' He pointed to the red, shining bike parked next to his. 'I need to make sure the seat height is OK for you.'

She looked at him in surprise. 'Mine?' she asked.

'If you like it, as I said I did not buy it without you trying it.' He smiled at her 'I know you are going to say that I should not have, but I need to make sure you don't get something that is going to increase the chances of you being hurt, or some slimy salesman giving you something that is totally useless, just because it sounds good!'

'Oh, so you get to ride the beast, Papa bear, and I get the baby bear version?' She was smiling. She knew that it would happen: he would want to control what type of bike she had, so it was not worth the fight. She sensed that the conversation she was planning to have with him today would prove enough of a challenge later. She needed to give the Professor and answer tomorrow, so it was today or tonight, whichever way she looked at it.

'Start small and sensible and then we will see!' She walked to it and gently felt the fuel tank. Just because the engine was smaller, it looked the same physical size.

'The plate, however, is yours.' He pointed to the large yellow number plate at the back: MissJ 1.

She swung her leg over the machine and tried it out for size. He gave her a quick overview of the controls; she let him humour her. She could have worked it out but enjoyed his masterful instruction. His face was close to hers and she looked at him straight in the eye. She could feel his breath he was so close. 'Ready?' he asked. She nodded. 'Best zip up tight.' He pulled the zip that was at her chest level up to her neck. As he did he noticed the gold choker sitting in the hollow of her neck. She must have put it on after her shower as she had not worn it the night before, even after they had got into bed. He touched it lightly with his middle finger. He then drew a line directly from it up under her chin and he pulled her face up to present her lips to him. He kissed her on the mouth, just pushing his tongue to her enough so she had to respond to him. She did, with her eyes closed. He pulled back and smiled at her.

'You first or me?' he asked.

'You had better show the way, and if I stall her you will not be able to laugh!' She grabbed her hair and scrunched it up in a bobble so that it fitted under her helmet.

They started the journey and Lottie impressed herself that she was only nervous for the first few miles. She could tell he was easing back all the time to ensure she was with him. On a few occasions when they had to stop at traffic lights, she pulled up beside him, but resisted the urge to glance across. By the time they had reached the open road she was more relaxed. As a normal Sunday the traffic was light, but it did not seem to matter as Ed dodged and weaved through anything, and she followed.

Halfway up the motorway, he indicated and they pulled off at a service station. There were other bikes alongside, with several people dressed as they were, full leather kits, drinking coffee and talking outside. He had parked up and got his helmet off before she did. Pulling up a bit further back she, too, stopped and dismounted. She pulled her helmet off and allowed her long, blonde hair to fall free.

'Where have you been all my life, beautiful?' a guy shouted out from a small group that were standing around. Another wolf-whistled as she walked past. 'Wrap those thighs wound my weapon, love!' another shouted.

'I'll wrap my fist round your face, you wanker!' Ed barked out as he reached them, clearly pissed off with the comments. Lottie was bright red, not just from the comments but not knowing what to say or do. The two guys locked imaginary horns and had a face-off of silent wills. One of the group stood in between them.

'Sorry, mate, no offence!' he said to Ed, clearly trying to defuse the situation.

Lottie pulled off her glove and just held out her hand, not turning to the group or making any comments; she just picked up his hand as she walked past and put it around her shoulder. It was her own way to mark his ownership, she thought, but a necessary reassurance that she was his.

'I'm a big girl!' she said to him as they walked off. 'Coffee!'

'I can't let them talk to you like that,' he said, still seething inside. 'If they are like that when I'm here, what are they going to be like when I'm not?'

'They will still be wankers!' she said. 'But that's life.' He stopped her in midstride and laughed.

'Lottie Jenkins, I do declare I have never heard you swear before!'

'It must be the biker chick in me, and the type of girl it brings out!' She smiled and bit her lip.

He kissed her and the wolf whistles started again, but this time the cheers were: 'Get a room!' and 'Please, man!' and 'Lucky bastard!' all of which he could cope with.

They were both pleased they had spent the day together, although there were no workers onsite they were amazed at how the project had moved along. They dropped into the hospital as well, and were made as welcome as ever. As the night would be drawing in sooner for the last few days of August, they headed back after having a late lunch at a small pub. Lottie could feel the change in the temperature of the wind: it felt colder as they headed towards 5pm.

Entering the apartment and placing her helmet on the table she shivered.

'Take a shower to warm you up, I will get the kettle on,' he said. 'You did really well for the first long journey out, it can be quite enduring.' He kissed her forehead. 'I still have to say I prefer it with your arms around me holding on from behind, and you would not get so cold!'

'Well, forget the kettle and come and join me in the shower, then.' She smiled with a seductive smirk.

'If this is still the biker chick talking, then bring it on, I am not objecting to that!' he replied. As she turned around he slapped her backside as she walked towards the bathroom.

There was no sexy way to peel off the leather outer skin, but both of them managed it, leaving them on a heap on the floor.

Lottie turned on the shower and the instant water was hot on her skin. Ed stepped in and hugged her from behind. The jet of the water was so large that they both became covered with the water. As it ran over their bodies, they kissed and caressed each other's necks and upper bodies. Lottie looked down at the obvious arousal that he had and she placed her hand firmly round the bulging shaft; he took an intake of breath. She started to rub her hand up and down the shaft from tip to his ball sack. He pushed his head back against the wall to enjoy the feeling she gave him. She bent to her knees and replaced her hand with her mouth. She needed to make sure that the water was running away from her face so that she could still breathe, as he filled her mouth, leaving no choice but to breathe through her noise. She started to rub her lips up and down his shaft, paying attention to the tip at the end, where she could taste a hit of salt for small amounts of pre-ejaculate. She rubbed her hand around his balls, finishing around his inner thighs. She rubbed her hand along the lower part of his stomach, feeling the definition of his lower abs, and the predominant muscle group of his hip flexors. She continued to suck at his length, using fast, harder strokes, allowing her tongue to brush from side to side as she sucked. He started to thrust: she could feel him hit the back of her throat and she had to get the timing right to prevent his length from making her gag. He placed his hand on her head to steady her movement to bring them together. The increased amount of seeping cum indicated that he was close to release. His breathing was heavy and he had increased his grip to her shoulders. He was making gentle noises of a man about to release his juices. He whimpered, 'Oh God, Lottie, I can't hold back if you do that!' several times.

He wanted to come inside her, to feel her around him and to make her feel the pleasure that he had coursing through his lower body, but the selfish male in him allowed her to continue. He was trying to hold back, to keep himself on the edge of the pleasure as long as he could, but it was to no avail. If he did not withdraw he would be spent. She squeezed his balls and he thought he was about to burst with the searing pleasure.

'Stand up' he gasped, 'I need to be in you.' Lottie did as she was asked; he turned her around and bent her over. She placed her hands on the wall in front of her to steady herself. He parted her thighs and ran his fingers between her legs. The water had not reached the parts where her own juice had moistened her hole. Two fingers went in with ease and he rubbed her, continuing to brush himself against her outer thigh. The other hand was used to find her nipple, hanging down with hot water dripping from it. With a flick and a rub, the soft, warm flesh responded by becoming hard and also by waking the internal muscles in her inner sex. She gasped out. Her hair was wet and clinging to her face and shoulders. He moved some of it out of the way and bent to kiss her back. He nipped at the skin and licked around her ear. He rubbed the outer lips of her sex and the sweet spot at the top, she shivered as the nerve endings were stimulated hard.

With a water slap, he raised his hand and it came down hard on her arse cheek. The shock at first made her cry out, but the second slap confirmed that the jolt was more of the reason and the scream was a release of pure pleasure. He parted her sex from behind and moved in to fill her with his exaggerated organ, which was becoming purple with overfilled pressure.

'OHH,' she cried out as he thrust hard and deep into her. She shifted her hands to get a better grip on the wall. He slapped her again, this time leaving a red mark where his hand had been.

'I have wanted to do this all day, those incredibly tight leather pants around this perfectly formed arse!' He spanked it again just to remind her whose arse he was talking about. 'Tell me, Lottie, did you like those guys shouting out at you, did you like the fact they ogled you and wanted you, like I have you now?' She got a slap on her arse for not answering him. 'I did not hear you.'

'Yes,' she said between gasping for air and not taking in any of the water that was still rushing down her face. The trickle of it over her nipples and down her stomach was adding to the climax that was pending with the tingling of the skin on her backside. He pushed hard. 'I can't hold it, Lottie.' He pushed again. 'Do you want it?' He grabbed the wet hair and pulled her head up so she could speak. 'Tell me that you want me.'

'Yes,' she said, 'oh God yes, please, quick, yes.' She spasmed and the orgasm almost took her off her feet; he had to hold her as she uncontrollably shook in his arms. He steadied her and himself and placed his head in the centre of her back. In one movement he guided himself to the final place: as he shot into her, he grunted loudly. He was aware she was still unsteady on her feet, the internal contractions of her sex indicating that her orgasm was just as powerful as his, but he needed to control so that he did not push her over. He thrust again; he pulled his inner core muscles trying to slow the ejaculation but he could not. He thrust again harder, and again and again, lingering deep inside her as long as he could before he gave the final thrust and he knew he was spent.

They lounged on the sofa, in shorts and tee shirts watching the TV. Ed wanted to watch some news; Lottie did not really care as she was relaxing in his arms. They had a glass of wine, and a small selection of cheese that they were grazing on. Every now and then he kissed her head, and she rubbed his knee or thigh.

'Happy?' he asked.

'Ah ha,' she replied, nodding her head.

'Comfy?' he added.

'Yep,' she said through a sleepy voice. She was almost on the edge of starting the conversation that she had avoided all day when his phone rang. He looked at the screen and said, 'Oh, baby girl, I need to get this.' He shifted her slightly. 'Ni hao,' he said in Chinese for hello. 'Wǎn ān, good evening, Mr Yok. One moment!' he directed at the caller. Then turned to Lottie. 'Sorry baby, don't move I will be back.' He squeezed from behind her and she shifted to let him move away, he continued to speak in Chinese to the person on the end of the phone. Lottie could hear him; she was never sure if the raised voices and hurried words were just the way the Chinese spoke or if he was angry with someone! She turned the TV over to find some American mindless series, and she found *CSI*, how fitting, she thought, in mind of where she wanted to go and what she wanted to ask when he got back in the room. It always amazed her how factually incorrect such programmes were, so much so that she only watched for a few minutes and then turned over again.

He had been on the phone in his office for over twenty minutes when he came back in; he did not look pleased. He plonked himself back down and shoved a large lump of cheese in his mouth and picked up his glass.

'OK?' she asked. He swallowed the contents and washed it down with the cool Pinot Grigio.

'Yes, but no!' he said as a contradiction. She looked at him to explain if he wanted to, and he continued, 'Just brokered a deal for almost 7 million after taxes.' His face showed no emotion or elation to the fact.

'Most people, I guess, for a Sunday night would be happy with that?' Lottie was sure that she as hell would be.

'I'm sure they would, but not to be flippant, it is a lot as it goes direct to the charity base: it is not strictly my money.' He shoved more cheese in his mouth and refilled their glasses. Lottie put her hand over hers as she did not want any more; she had helped herself while he had been on the phone. 'While it is great for the charity, it has one major drawback.' He tried not to speak with his mouth full, but the cheese was taking some going down, so he had another mouthful of wine.

'They want it delivered in blood?' she asked, trying to make light of it.

'It may as well be: I need to go over and sign the documents in person, on Tuesday,' he finished.

'You have time to arrange it, don't you?' She wondered about his point really, and it was sounding better for her side of her plans if he did have to go somewhere.

'You said that you would not come and I don't want to leave you here.' There it was, he had said it. 'I know that I said I was happy for you to carry on with this case, but I don't feel happy you working on something that may be dangerous if I am not here.'

'Well.' She started what was now looking like it could have been a calculated plan of some sort. 'I needed to speak to you all day about this.' She stopped and took a sip of her own wine. It seemed to work for him to get the conversation going: maybe it would work for her. 'What if I said we have put the case on hold for a week?'

'And you come with me?' he asked, his face alight at the thought.

'Not quite, and I go to New York!' She quickly drained the glass, avoiding his eye contact. He sat back in the large, cream sofa and turned fully to look at her.

'Where did that come from?' he asked. 'When were you going to drop that little bombshell, Lottie?' She could see his was pissed now for sure.

'I have been trying to say something all day but I did not want to spoil the mood.'

'And not dropping that on me until I was relaxed and enjoying time with you would not spoil the mood more?' he said back to her as a question he almost knew the answer to. 'Care to explain?'

She did as he asked and he listened without butting in. In fact, he said nothing at all even when she had finished speaking.

'Todd knew this last night?' He had not raised his voice at all.

She looked under her eyebrows at him like a frightened child who had done something wrong. 'We were asked on Friday.' He got up and looked out at the night sky, which was black, but washed with colour at floor level from the orange haze of the city light pollution.

'Say something, shout if you have to, although I hope that you don't,' she said. He turned around. His fists were clenched. He hated this, the idea was wrong: he never wanted her out of his sight. But he fumed inside knowing that she had needed to work up to this, to get the courage to ask him at all.

'Do I frighten you, Lottie, do I bully you?' he asked out of the blue.

'No,' she said back, 'on both counts.'

'Then why did you have to say you needed to build up the courage to ask me? What do you think I would do? At worst, shout and scream, swear and object profusely. And I have to admit I want to do all of that, but even if I did I would have got over it. I did last time, didn't I?'

She got up and paddled over to him. 'I realise how you are making such fantastic progress with... me... well, everything. I really see the change, the guys today, the gestures yesterday.' She was going to say 'the disappointment in your eyes when I did not have the necklace on', but then would have to say 'and the joy when I put it back on today', so she left that bit out. 'But this is a big ask from me, even though I will take it on any of your terms. It is also a big ask of me to go and leave you: maybe I was reluctant to be away from you for so long, too.' That was a genuine plea: she had given it the thought that it was not all a one-sided loss.

He opened out his arms and invited her into the warmth of his chest:

willingly she went. He kissed her hair that was still damp and smelled sweet from the shampoo and earlier shower.

'I love you more than the breath I need to take, baby girl, and with each living moment that gets worse.' He held her tight and she could feel his heart beat and the breath he was talking about. 'But when you went and I was not able to do anything, I was out of control not knowing you were coming back. I need to accept that I cannot always control you, should not always control you because you need to be you. If I can help you do what you want then I can put my take on it and in some way have influence, not control.' It was the hardest thing he had said for years. He had never even had that breakthrough with Dr Morgan, but with Lottie it just came easily.

He looked down at her as she had not said a word. She could not: she had tears streaming down her face. It was the finest thing anyone had ever said: genuine affection and care, consideration and, she supposed, love. He wiped her tears away. 'What are these for?' he asked. She took his face in her hands and reached on her tiptoes and kissed him. Deep and full on the mouth, she sucked in his breath, wanting to feel him so close. They stood entwined for what seemed hours, kissing, holding and loving each other.

Was this the breakthrough for the rest of their lives? God she hoped so. They had stayed up for several hours the night before arranging things and talking things through of how the next seven days would work out for them both. Pete had been at the apartment since 6:30 that morning making arrangements and calls in response to the emails he was sent the night before. Lottie guessed that Zoe would have an early morning start, too; she was also bombarded with instructions and requests for things to be arranged.

Lottie had even managed to drive herself to the Centre, to give Pete and the team time to do other things. It felt strange being behind the wheel again; she was set on taking the bike after the successful ride, but the rain clouds had gathered when she was in the shower, and Ed changed her mind for that! Riding in the wet was a far more dangerous habit, one she had not experienced due to taking all her lessons and her test in the summer.

She used her ID to let her in and Todd was already waiting in the office. He had seen her arrive and pull up in the parking spot.

'Oh no' were his first words. 'You told him and you walked out again?'

'Good morning to you, too.' She put her bag on her desk and looked back over to him. 'I told him and you don't need to book an airline ticket, or a hotel. You are going on a private charter and you are staying in an 11 million-dollar skyline penthouse apartment in central New York, so kiss my sorry ass, you pessimist!' She was smiling from ear to ear. He picked her up and swung her around.

'Wowzers, that is fantastic, let's go tell the Prof. I guess there is some sorting out to do this end, too.' He put her down and headed straight out the door.

Ed had to leave for the airport a few hours before Lottie, so they had arranged to meet back at the apartment for 4pm. Mr York had arranged for Ed to travel out and stay until Thursday. Although it would be a killer of a journey, and he was going to gain some air miles, he was then arranging to meet Lottie in New York for the Saturday. They could then have some time away, like a mini-break, and come back to the UK once they had rested up.

Todd could catch the chartered flight back anytime from Friday onwards, although Ed had said he was welcome to go back with them if he could spare the time away. Apparently, the penthouse was big enough so that he could do his own thing, and they would not be disturbed. Lottie liked that idea as it showed that Ed was accepting her friend and former lover into their lives. Todd had liked the idea as he had never been to New York, and with not having to pay for travel and accommodation he would be able to spend some money on having some fun of his own, whatever that had been, Lottie thought!

She had to get a move on as she wanted to go to the city to collect something she had put on hold online the night before. The tube had been packed but the freedom of not having Pete or Phil with her had allowed her to achieve her task in only a few hours.

Bags packed, she was looking around the apartment for the last-minute things. Ed was an old hat at travelling light. He bought most things when he needed them when he got to wherever he was going. Lottie was still trying to find toiletries when she heard him walk in. She took one last look around and thought, oh well, not taken them for nearly a week, I will start again when I come back. She was referring to her contraceptive pills.

'All set?' he asked, kissing her on the cheek.

'I think so. When does Pete pick you up?' She had made a fresh coffee pot and was pouring her own. 'Time for one of these?' She held up the pot to offer him a cup. He walked over to her.

'Sooner have one of these.' He kissed her and squeezed her tight. He was reluctant to let her go. She pushed him back slightly and looked up at him.

'Hold that thought just there, don't move.' She ran to the bedroom and fetched the item she had been so keen to go into town for earlier.

'Lottie?' He looked puzzled at her when she came back to the kitchen. He had a mug of the hot brown liquid in his hands. 'What you up to?' he asked. She handed him a small, wrapped box. 'What's this?' he asked.

'Open it and find out.' She looked more excited than he did. 'I know you hate surprises, but I saw this when I was with Agnes, and thought of you. Maybe...' She paused as he opened the box. 'You can look at it and think of me!' She finished the sentence.

He looked down at the small gold band inside the jewellers' box. He lifted it and held it out. She took the small signet ring and placed it on the little finger of his right hand. He did not wear any jewellery at all, and the small, dark pink stone was swamped by the size of his large, powerful hands.

'It's the same stone as mine.' She affectionately touched her necklace. 'I'm glad it fits.' She was desperate for him to say something. 'You don't like it' was the only conclusion she could draw from his complete silence.

He swallowed hard; it took a moment for the words to come out of his lips, although he had opened his mouth moments before to speak.

'I love it, but I don't need physical gifts to think of you, at all, you're here.' He looked down at it again and put his other hand on his heart. 'Here,' he said again.

'And neither do I.' Again she touched her neck and stroked the gold band. 'But I wanted you to know how much you, and this trip, and the prospect of, who knows, the whole future mean to me, too.'

He pulled her close and hugged her. He looked at the shining gift and kissed her hair. Through gritted teeth, for fear that he would cry, he said, 'I love you, Lottie Jenkins. Baby girl, take care, won't you?'

They were still embracing when his phone beeped, and then beeped again. Pete was reminding them it was time for him to go. Their final farewell did see Lottie cry. Ed left and passed Phil standing at the door.

'You take fucking good care of her, you hear me. I want every call answered, every email replied to, and every request from Pete, or me, followed out, get it?' He had to show aggression in his voice as he was still close to a newfound emotion of crying if not.

'Mr Dean.' Phil nodded. He had been made more than aware from the hours of grilling and instructions from Pete up until less than ten minutes ago that his balls were totally on the line for the next seven days. Something he was being paid more than he had ever earned in the last three years of the armed forces, even though he had been an officer in the secret service, and in one of the highest paid positions he could have achieved in his fifteen-year military career. He knew that this was important to his boss, and knowing Lottie, he could see why.

Chapter 16

Planning was the key. They had been in New York for three days and everything had so far had been plain sailing, and one of the best times of her life.

The flight was good: they ate, slept and chatted, and Lottie took calls from Ed! They were taken to the penthouse by Corry, one of his top men stateside, as Ed had explained in his call as they drove, moments after landing and clearing Customs! They had settled into the most fantastic place she had ever seen. Ed owned it and had lived in it when he was there before they met. Dorothy was, as promised, the perfect housekeeper, although Mrs B had outlined some of her flaws, Lottie could only conclude that it was a hint of jealousy for the attractive, middle-aged, tanned American, who reminded her of Mrs Dean, Ed's mother in some ways. She said this to Ed and he laughed as she spoke to him on the phone that night when he called.

The theme of communication between them was the same throughout the days, and Todd made a joke of it every time her phone rang, beeped or flashed.

'Before you ask, no, it's not annoying at all!' Lottie said, looking at him on the Thursday night while they were out eating a meal and a text came through.

Miss Jenkins

Business done, few hours' sleep and then I'm on my way, baby girl
Mr Edward Dean
Chairman of a now very wealthy Dean Charities LTD (but missing a
hug desperately!)

She quickly typed back:
Mr Dean
Get more than a few hours' sleep, as I have more than a hug waiting!
Miss L Jenkins (hugs are not a PA's task unless I change careers I hope!)

Their days had been filled with a whirlwind of new technology and learning. They had met and been introduced to lots of leading scientists, doctors and professors in the States. Todd was in his element, and on more than one occasion had said he would love to stay longer and work over there if they offered it to him.

They were driven everywhere by either Phil or Corry, and throughout the day one of them was around if anything at all was needed. Lottie was more relaxed about Phil being in the penthouse than Todd, but she made every effort to make him feel part of the team, not an employee.

'Miss Jenkins, I am happy to eat alone. I can't...' He had corrected himself. 'I don't want to interrupt you and Mr Carter at any point.' She knew that he would have been told this, but she still insisted that he joined them at night when they chatted or watched TV, as part of his downtime. Corry was a bit more stand-offish with her, but she guessed that was the years he had worked for Ed, and with Pete, and she guessed he had seen more issues and knew the score better. She would make sure that Ed did not chastise Phil for any of this if it did get back to him when he arrived.

She lay in bed on the Thursday night and touched her necklace, smiling to herself on how well it was all going, although she was missing him more than she had thought. They had spent nights away when she stayed in Kent, but not since moving into the apartment; maybe she had taken this for granted. She rubbed the gold braid around her neck and thought of his face when he had put the ring on. In a way, maybe that was her way of branding him, if the conversation about the necklace had been true. Some physical way to claim ownership that was understood between the two people who were involved?

The thought of Ed and her stomach churned; the light, silk sheet rubbed against her nipple and it became erect. She closed her eyes and imagined his face, his hands on her, making her nipple erect. She felt her inner sex tighten at the thought of him touching her. Now she knew that she missed him, she turned her head to the side, trying to focus on the soft humming of the traffic way below, and the dull scream of the police and emergency vehicles that spread through the surrounding streets, but the aroused feeling would not go away.

She pushed her hand under the sheet and rubbed the light silk nightdress she was wearing over her pubic bone. Her nipples reacted as if a cold chill had spread over her, but she was warm: the brush of her finger onto her outer sex lips had confirmed that as she could feel her arousal soak the top of her leg.

She closed her eyes again and imagined Ed's hands on her there. His masterful fingers, massaging her and gently easing into her. She pushed one finger into the entrance of her, opening her legs slightly and relaxing her shoulders back. She took a deep breath out as the pressure on her sweet spot was rubbed by her palm. She extended her forefinger to join the one already circling the outer areas of her clitoris, and probed them into her now receptive area. She brought her other hand up under the silk and located the hard nipple: she gave it a squeeze.

It had been a long time since she had needed to pleasure herself; the longing for Ed, the smell of his skin, came back to her as she continued to stir her arousal. She pushed her fingers in deeper, exploring the area she knew he would have filled by now with the size of his manhood. She eased another finger in as best she could to try to replicate the pressure that he caused as he entered her with his engorged dick. She gasped and licked her lips as she remembered how he tasted the last time they had showered together. How he had taken her and driven her to the surging orgasm by the pleasurable pain when he slapped her bare ass. She increased the speed of her rubbing, feeling the sweet spot swell and spasm as the nerve endings were exposed to the friction her hand was creating. She pushed as hard as she could, leaning to one side to get a better position to reach her internal G-spot. Oh! She gasped as she touched it with her nail; the sharp touch added a pleasure, and with the soft scratch she did it again. 'Oh Edward!' she softly moaned out as her chest became warm and her breathing increased. The flush of her cheeks and the sudden uncontrolled surge confirmed that she had reached the point of explosion. She arched her back trying to get the full stimulation that would take this to the end. She could feel her own inner muscle contract and squeeze her fingers as the orgasm pulsed through her. She imagined that this was the trigger for his own surge of power that often allowed him to ejaculate into her simultaneously as the conclusion to his own pleasure, with her mouth open and his name drifting over her lips; she used her other hand to touch the necklace around her throat and she said his name one more time: I love you! In the aftermath of her self-gratification she fell into a deep, relaxed sleep.

Friday came and went with the speed that the city worked at. Nothing in the city stopped or seemed to close. The bustle in the streets always seemed the same, regardless of the time. They had been able to take in some of the sites, but most of their waking hours were consumed with meetings, lectures, meals and networking. Lottie had got used to being called 'Dr Jenkins' again, a title she never used. She had worked hard to gain the qualifications that allowed her the status, but somehow felt it too formal.

They had been invited to a charity event that the US DuPont Centre was holding. Like back in the UK, they relied heavily on donations to keep their work going. In true New York style the event was far more over the top than those she had attended at home. She had not packed anything to wear, so had to go shopping. Dorothy had offered to go with her; Corry drove them to the location. As Lottie hated shopping, unless she had Bella with her of late, she did not want to walk from street to street. 'Get something and go' was the motto. The little boutique was on the corner of 58th Street, and as the car dropped them off they got out and walked to the window. The women in the shop looked at them both as they walked in and instantly they were approached.

'Good day, madam, how can we help?' the assistant asked. Lottie thought she looked like an over-preened peacock and would have been better off with less make-up to let her beauty through.

'Miss Jenkins is attending a high society ball and needs a suitable dress,' Dorothy explained, without allowing Lottie to speak.

'Well, let me see. Colour, size, any design or names you are interested in?' came the reply.

'No, all black,' Lottie said, hearing the words of Bella in her head. 'I'm guessing long?'

'Well, Miss. This season is long, or very short, and if I can say, those legs should be on show.' She wandered off. I have a list of other purchasers who are attending your charity ball.' (This was something that they did back in Harrods, too. It had impressed Lottie at the time because it meant that you would not turn up in something the same as anyone else who had been to the same high-end shops.)

'Short seems to be the way forwards, there have not been any pale blue items.' The girl spotted Lottie's necklace as she took off her jacket and sat on the small sofa arranged in the middle of the floor. 'I have something that will go with that.' She touched her neck as if to indicate to Lottie's neckline where the gold and shining choker was still on display.

It would not cover a postage stamp, Lottie thought as it was brought out and shown to her, but it was the most fantastic deep purple, that shone pinker in the lights. It was low-cut to the front and back, made of a stretched material that would hug every curve. Lottie was not sure. She tried it on. The inner silk lining made it feel incredible to wear, although she was sure that her modesty was on show more than she would like. The low neck meant that she would not be able to wear a bra; luckily it had bones to give some support, but it did show the necklace off, and the sporting curves of her shoulders and athletic figure she had. She rubbed over her stomach to flatten it. She had not worked out for a few weeks and promised herself that she had to get back in routine as she was starting to forget the gym, and eat and drink too much. She was sure that Ed's trainer could whip her back into shape. There he was in her thoughts again! They had exchanged texts earlier, but she now guessed he was mid-air and catching up on the sleep he had said he needed to get.

'Bit short?' Lottie said to Dorothy.

'Mr Dean would love it, I'm sure,' she replied.

'Think so?' Lottie was sure he would, but maybe if he was not there to show her off in it. 'Legs are very pasty,' she said.

'You need some hoes.' The assistant rushed off.

'Tights,' Dorothy said as Lottie looked confused. Once the sheer light tan 'tights' were on, the shoes and matching bag, Lottie was almost convinced.

'Is it a yes?' the assistant asked. Lottie bit her lip, took one last look and nodded. Dorothy reached into her bag and pulled out a card.

'Pay on here please.' She handed the assistant the plastic. 'And another pair of hoes. Spare,' She said to Lottie. 'I usually put a finger through them!' she said. 'You never know!'

'I'm good to pay,' Lottie said as the assistant walked off. She did not want to say anything in front of her.

'I've had my orders, dear,' Dorothy said. 'Mr Dean has been quite clear with us all about your time here.'

'The guy may be a multimillionaire, but he will be broke soon if he does not stop indulging me!' Lottie was quite serious in her statement.

'Miss Jenkins, I doubt that. He has the reputation in this city for being a hard-ass businessman, sorely missed in the past two years, but he makes money that makes money without trying - it's his way. If he chooses to spoil you, let him,' Dorothy said, and then to herself noted, 'You're just another way for him to invest in his future.'

The gift-wrapped dress was in the bag. As it was warm Lottie left her jacket off and put it in the bag also. It was nice to feel the sun on her skin as they made their way out of the shop. Lottie had looked up the street and Corry had parked some way down due to traffic. She looked in the shop windows as they walked along. Lottie did not see the young lad walking behind them; he had his hoodie up over his head. He knocked into Dorothy, and with a flick of his hand had her bag off her shoulder. The reaction was instant for her to cry out and Lottie looked over. The assailant was off faster than a bullet from a gun. The reaction for Lottie to give chase came from somewhere, she was not sure, but she ran after him. Her sprint speed impressed her and she was able to catch him by the arm. He turned and she caught a glimpse of his face.

'Let him go!' Dorothy shouted, exclaiming that it was not worth it. Corry had seen the scene and was out of the car coming in the opposite direction. Lottie had managed to get a better grip and she had tackled him to the floor. Without noticing, he had pulled a knife from his pocket and the blade shone in her face as he flicked it around. She hit her shoulder on the floor as she let go of him. Luckily for her, Corry was quick and had the guy by the arm, the knife on the floor and boy in a face plant on the floor immobile. Lottie stood up and grabbed the bag back from him. Dorothy had caught them up.

'Miss, how stupid of you. Are you hurt?' She looked her up and down.

'No,' Lottie said, rubbing her shoulder.

'Whose blood is that, then?' Corry asked, phone in one hand, prisoner in the other. Several people walked by, some taking notice, others not looking as if it was an everyday occurrence. Lottie looked at herself again. There was a small cut on her arm. She looked at it closer, not sure if it was a scratch from the floor or a clean cut from the knife. She wiped the blood off, just to see if it was only a slight flesh wound.

'It's nothing,' she said, although she now noticed her hand shaking. The young boy was swearing and cursing his jailer, even when the police arrived. The ladies had gone back to the safety of the car while Corry dealt with them.

'You should have let him go. My purse is in my pocket: he would have only got a few pens, and hankie and lipstick and some perfume. You need to learn about living in this city, Miss: that cut could have been a lot worse.' Dorothy looked at her and Lottie knew that she was right.

'I just acted on impulse,' Lottie said, holding the said hankie to her arm that Dorothy had got from the retrieved bag.

'Need a medic?' Corry asked as he came back to the car.

'No, it's stopped, it just needs a clean.' They made their way back and Lottie sat in silence. Her phone was ringing and she knew who this would be. One of the others would have made the call, sent the text and regardless of whether he was 30,000 feet in the air, he would have found out, and no doubt been pissed off! She took a breath and pulled out the phone. How right she was. She pressed the accept call button and waited for the onslaught of words.

To her surprise it was Pete.

'Mr Dean is asleep, Miss Jenkins. Corry called me and I wanted to ask if you are OK before I wake him.' Lottie took a sigh of relief.

'Really, I am OK, nothing you can do, Corry has it all in hand. It was my fault, I reacted, sorry!' as if she should apologise really, but she did not want Ed pissed off, even if it was just for the sake of Pete having to put up with him in a confined space for the next few hours. 'Really I'm OK, and I have learned my lesson now.'

'Sounds like I should be employing you on my team!' Pete made light of the conversation. 'Really, though, you should have just let Corry handle the thug. I will let him know when we land, so keep your phone on, you have a few hours yet. Oh, and Miss Jenkins...'

'Yes,' Lottie said.

'He is planning on joining you about 10:30pm at the function. We have made good time and he wants to come straight there. If you go back to the apartment or move on to another venue, please make sure Phil lets us know.'

'I will,' she replied. 'Thanks, Pete.'

'Jesus, Lottie, who do you think you are? Wonder Woman? Todd exclaimed as the story was relayed to him.

'OK, I have the message loud and clear: no more lectures, thanks.' She was making a drink as they talked.

'I'm sure there will be another one when the call comes through!' Todd added with a smile. She stuck out her tongue at him. Both Phil and Corry looked at each other, knowing that this was true, and that they were sure they would also be in the firing line.

'Give me a look, have you cleaned it? Does it need a stitch?' Todd said, moving towards her with his hand out.

'Don't fuss!' Lottie said back, but his persistent look made her lift up her arm and he cleaned and dressed it again, needing some skin closures to make sure the cut stayed closed. 'It should have a stitch or two,' he commented.

'What type of a doctor are you? No, it does not!' she said and the subject was closed.

'You scrub up well,' she said to Todd as they sat in the back of the car.

'I like to make the effort for you,' he said, fidgeting with the collar. He had commented on how beautiful she looked as they had left the penthouse, although he had noted to himself that she was still fit and looked hot in the dress.

As they got out of the car Corry opened the door for Lottie.

'Miss, please keep this in your bag. We can't come in but if you need us at all we will be parked up and within access within seconds if you press it.' The small black button was passed over and she looked at it. 'Can you just try it so Phil and I can check.' She did as she was asked and he put his hand to his earpiece. 'Roger copy,' he replied, presumably talking to Phil on the other end of the radio system. 'Thanks, just a precaution,' he added.

'Very James Bond!' Todd remarked as they walked in, Lottie linked her arm in his as they were surrounded by the glitz and glamour of the event. 'You may need to use it when the call comes through: only a few hours to wait, I'm guessing.'

She slapped his arm and laughed. 'You'll need it in a moment if you don't shut up!' She smiled at him and hurried along the red carpet. She thought it was more like the Oscars than a normal charity event, although she was pleased to see that most of the other female guests were in short skirts, one thing she had got right at least.

His chartered plane was a luxury one. The bedroom he had occupied for the last ten hours was like a high-end hotel, and he had not known that he was flying for the whole time. He never slept, but the trip and amount of travel, along with some jetlag, had caught up with him. He looked at his phone, and as they were due to land in under 30 minutes he could not make any calls; he would do that later. She would be sitting down to eat by this time, anyway he thought, looking at his ring shining on his hand.

Every day, and several times a day, he had been drawn to it, various thoughts running through his head. He had even wondered back to the day with Bella, looking at different types of rings, gifts for the wearer for a different meaning. He recalled a conversation he had with Alex once.

Engagement means entrapment; wedding means she's off-limits (but you can sleep with me if my husband does not catch us!) and eternity means I own you now! He tried not to think of his old friend, but could not help it. No matter what had come between them of late, he had had some good times with him.

He dressed and took one last look in the mirror. He changed his watch, looking at the LCD console just to confirm the time difference. His sleep had left him refreshed; he opened the cabin door and saw Pete sitting reading, and the hostess sitting neatly with her legs crossed in the chair at the back of the cabin.

'How we doing?' he asked. Pete put down the book and hostess jumped up from her position.

'Drink, Mr Dean?' she asked, already with coffee pot in hand. He nodded. It had been an easy flight for her: it was only really the crew and Pete she had been serving, as Ed had worked or slept most of the way.

'Good. We have about fifteen minutes to land.' He took a deep breath. Ed knew his employee by now and instantly looked at his face: something was wrong.

'What is it?!' It was a demand, not a question. Pete sucked in another breath and did not cut to the chase; he laid the facts out to him, knowing there was no pretty way that this would turn out.

'For fuck's sake, Pete, why did you not wake me up this was hours ago?' He picked up his phone. The hostess said in a brave tone, Pete thought, 'Sorry, sir, we are landing: you can't make a call.'

The fire in Ed's eyes was just about to spurt out of his mouth, saying she could not tell him what to do when Pete felt he needed to save her the pain and the wrath of his tongue.

'It has all been dealt with, her injury...' he never finished.

'Oh, it gets fucking better – she is injured?' Ed was pacing around despite the seat belt sign being on and the movement of the plane as it came back through the cloud layer approaching the landing strip. 'Anything else you have missed out?' He still had his phone in his hand and he was impatiently tapping it while it was turned off. He walked to the drinks cabin and poured himself a whiskey and emptied the glass in one mouthful. He left his coffee on the side, and poured another of the amber liquid.

'Every fucking time I'm not there. You need to sort your fucking team out.' He pointed his finger towards the head of security for his whole organisation. Pete remained quiet: anything he said would not make the temper cool. He was just best left alone when he was like this, although he had taken it better than he had anticipated. To his surprise he had now sat down and only had the two drinks. Progress in some way, he thought.

Ed had taken a few deep breaths; his voice had returned to normal when he asked, 'How long when we land will it take to get there?'

'Under an hour if the roads are good, once we clear passport control,' Pete returned as if not a cross word had been spoken. The plane bounced as the wheels on the undercarriage hit the ground, and Ed pressed the button on his phone to turn it on. The doors had not even opened when he punched in the speed-dial for Lottie's phone.

She was talking to another of the professors from the centre when she felt her bag vibrating. They had eaten and were taking drinks in the lounge area. It was a bit old-fashioned as the men seemed to have stayed at their tables, whereas the women had retired to the lounge for coffee. 'Very 19th-century,' Dr Corbett had commented at the start of her conversation. As soon as she felt the bag vibrate she excused herself. Not wanting to let him ring off, she hit the receive button but did not put the phone to her ear for a few seconds until she was out in the corridor. They had done this before when they called: it was a way for the other to know that they needed a bit more privacy to talk.

'Sorry,' she finally said, 'I just needed to get outside.' She would have been fully aware that he knew now about the incident so continued without hesitation. 'And before you say anything, I am fine, it was my fault, I never thought, and about the outcome I tried to act the hero and I should not have done.'

'Do you want to breathe now?' he asked in a perfectly normal voice. 'You are right to think that I am a bit pissed off, but I am trying to get over it! So how are you anyway?'

'You sure?' she said, not answering his question.

'Trying to get over it if people let me,' he said back with a smile on his face. 'How is your night?' he asked again.

He was relieved just to hear her voice. He was not over it, but putting a brave face. It was over and done with: past history is not important and can't be changed. She had once said that to him during one of their bath time counselling sessions. It just seemed that when he was not there, when he thought he had control of her, or thought others in his employ had control, it still went wrong.

They continued to talk while he went through Customs and he explained that they would be about an hour away. Lottie was sure that she would still be at the venue. Todd was making the most of the night, both in talking to anyone and everyone, and also partaking in a few drinks – well, more than a few.

After she put down the phone she wandered round the room to find him. She smiled and stopped to make conversation with only a few people, but she could see him over the other side of the room so she headed over.

'Is the amazing Mr Ed on his way?' Todd asked with a slight alcoholic slur to his voice. She looked under her eyebrows at him and he held his hands up as an apology. 'Here, meet Professor Smyth.' He pointed to a middle-aged guy who currently had his back to them. 'I told him that you know Mr Ed,' he whispered with his hand over his face. 'Not the horse! The billionaire. Did you know that he is a billionaire, Lottie?' he sarcastically said and she scowled at him again. 'And he said he wanted to meet you.'

'Todd, you've had a fair drink, have you not?' she said, holding his arm as they approached the guy he was referring to.

'May have.' He smiled a childlike grin. 'Last night to enjoy the corporate hospitality.'

'Yes, and tomorrow morning to face the hangover!' she said back at him. He raised his hand and said, 'Good point!' He grabbed a glass of water from the next waiter who went past, and then waited for the conversation to die down so that they could interrupt them.

'Hum!' Todd coughed as an interruption and the party looked round. 'Professor Smyth, I said that I would introduce you to my colleague, Dr Lottie Jenkins, from the DuPont Centre UK.'

He turned to face her and extended his hand. Lottie took it and shook it; he held it for slightly longer than she would have liked and he rubbed his finger over the top of her hand before he let it go.

'Arh, Miss Jenkins, Todd here told me so much about you. However, he omitted to state what a stunning beauty you are.' She knew that he was looking directly at her chest when he was talking to her. He was in his early fifties, she guessed. No wedding ring, not all of his own hair, and she guessed he had dyed it. His over-polished teeth shone with his smile, and she could see that in his time he must have been a handsome man. The round stomach and developing crow's-feet showed his years, and to be sure he was an intelligent, professional man, but there was just something about him that she felt she did not like. It was maybe the lecherous looks he was giving her.

'Nice dress, I have to say.' She thought it was a weird thing for a man to compliment but she smiled back at him.

'Good to meet you,' she said. She had to show some manners, although she purposely did not say 'Nice to meet you', as it really was not!

'So, Todd, our Miss Jenkins knows Mr Edward Dean, does she?' Lottie disliked the guy more and more. They made conversation which she really only listened to. She tried to ignore the innuendos and comments about her and her long legs. Todd had turned to talk to the lady next to them and the professor leaned in to Lottie and whispered, 'He has you tamed, I see, just like Ed to put such a hefty price tag around your neck. I guess not for sharing?' Lottie blanked the comment and replied:

'I am sure that Mr Dean will enjoy your company when he arrives, so for now please excuse me.' She turned and walked away from him, looking for somewhere to go. She thought about a quick trip to the loo. She looked at her watch: she was sure that he would arrive soon and then maybe they could get out of there. It was quite clear that Smyth new Ed, from sometime in the past, she guessed. To be honest she was not really bothered how, she just knew that the last few hours had been the worst of him being away. Being a superhero, even if an airhead one, she could cope with; being lusted over by a sad old man she could not.

She looked in the mirror and adjusted her dress. She applied some more lipstick and walked back into the room. She resisted the urge to text him: she was sure that she would know when he arrived.

Several other people had heard that she knew Edward; as it turned out that he attended many charity dinners. This annual one had been one until he had moved away. Lottie overheard a conversation which made her smile.

'Well, I heard that he is dating some French supermodel, totally off the market.' She soon stopped smiling when the next woman commented. 'I am sure whoever it is he will lose interest, he always seems to after a week or so.'

'Well, as none of us would ever get a look in, I don't know why you are speculating,' another one said.

'He looks more than lush, but I have heard that he is far too overpowering: these dominating men always are!'

Todd put his arm through hers as he walked up to her.

'Earwigging, are you?' he asked, still with water in his hand.

'What have you said about Ed and me, about our relationship?' she enquired.

'I said that you knew him,' he stuttered. 'Did business with him.' He tried again. 'Never said you were together, though.'

'Reason why not?' she asked.

'None really apart from...' He stopped and she lifted her eyebrows. 'Well, I might have said we were together at some point and, well, never really corrected anyone!'

'Todd, you pain in the arse, really, and they believed you?' She shook her head.

'Why is that so hard to believe, it was true once,' he said back. 'Am I so easily forgotten?'

'No,' Lottie said, 'but we really made all this clear: it was in the past, fun, great and I am grateful for your friendship still, but Ed and I – well, let me just say. You and I are friends, no hope of anything else.' She was not mad at him, just a bit annoyed that he was under some sort of illusion that anything could change between them. She felt like she was going back over six months when they first had this conversation.

'Don't be mad at me, Lotts, you just look so great and I really enjoy being around you and...' She stopped him.

'You need to sleep it off!' she said. 'I'll get you a cab back.' She went to the front desk and asked for them to order a cab. He got in and this was the last she saw of him for the night.

She was talking again to Dr Corbett. She was married with two children; her husband was somewhere in the room, but they had both moved around, talking to friends and colleagues.

Lottie thought that was so nice that they could do that, and she could tell by the affectionate way that she spoke of her husband that she clearly loved him. She felt an arm around her waist and gasped with the surprise. She turned around to see the most welcome face smiling at her. She should have known by the hush that seemed to have come over the room that he was here, but the reaction the room gave as he kissed her tenderly on the lips made a buzz of chatter and noise.

'Hello, baby girl,' he whispered.

'Hi,' she said, not taking her eyes off him. 'How are you?'

'Better for seeing you.' He pulled up her arm to look at the cut that had not been dressed. He shook his head.

'Sorry, Dr Corbett, this is Edward Dean. Sorry, Ed, Dr Corbett and I were just chatting.' He held out his hand and shook it.

'Mr Dean, there has been some chatter in the room that you were attending. I was not aware that you came as a guest with Dr Jenkins, though, there will be many hearts breaking as we speak.' She smiled.

He had not taken his eyes off Lottie. 'Let them break Dr Corbett, Miss.' He corrected himself: he had never called her doctor before. 'Dr Jenkins and I have been together for some time now, although I have to say the past few days we have been apart, so if you will excuse me, I would ask if we could have a moment to catch up?'

'Of course.' She said goodbye and Lottie thanked her for her time and was hopeful that they would meet again.

'I hope that was not rude but I want to see you for myself. Can I first say I have missed you, and second, how bloody short is that skirt!?'

'You don't like it?' Lottie asked, looking down at her legs and shoes: there was not much else covering anything.

'I love it, but I am not sure I approve of something so short when you have all these men around you to admire my handiwork.'

'Oh, your handiwork, is it?' she asked, biting her lip.

'The legs, incredible. The short skirt leaving nothing to the imagination, stunning. The lip-biting thing, insatiable, and I have been away for almost a week. Miss Jenkins, Dr Jenkins, whoever, get your ass in that car and let me take you home!' He smiled at her and she understood that he was not angry at all.

As they started to leave the room, Ed was approached by the CEO of DuPont US and he stopped to chat. He held out his hand for Lottie to hold as he walked back slightly.

'I was unaware that you and Dr Jenkins were acquainted, Mr Dean. It is good to see you once more stateside.'

'Travis, it is good to see you, too.' The men shook hands and Lottie smiled; she had not formally met the CEO, but she was aware of him over the past few days. It was a brief conversation, but in that time Dr Smyth had managed to make his way over to them.

'The famous Mr Dean!' he said once the conversation with the CEO was over. Ed nodded. 'Smyth!' The greeting was far from friendly.

'Well, you have done well this time, brains and beauty, no wonder your mark is an expensive one.' The guy was drunker now than he had been before when he spoke to Lottie. Ed scowled and still held Lottie's hand. They started to walk away, although the grip was tighter and she could feel the rage building up in him. She quickly hit the button in her bag. This was not how she wanted the night to end, nor was it how she wanted to be remembered in New York.

Ed walked up to the man and faced him nose on. 'Need to lose all the funding for the Centre, do you?' he threatened. 'Or just your front teeth for tonight?'

'No need to be like that, Edward. She has made it clear she is not for sharing, although when you have done with her, I would pay for a taste!'

Pete was like a ninja catching the hand that was about to hit the guy square in the jaw. Lottie had not even seen them turn up. Ed turned around and Corry had put himself between the two of them. Only a few people saw the commotion that was as quickly dissolved as it had started. Lottie let his hand go and walked towards the door. Something this guy had on Ed certainly railed him. The biker guys the weekend before had been rude but he never offered them out: there must be something else.

They sat in the back of the car, with the privacy blind down. Lottie huddled in her coat; it had turned cold and, after all, she had not got many clothes on! Ed pulled the middle screen up and slid over to her.

'Sorry, that was not much of a "I've missed you all week" reunion was it!?'

She knew that he did not have to explain himself: he could offer the information at any time. She was tired; as a gesture of peace she put her head on his shoulder and he cupped her hand in his.

'I guess you sense we had a history. Well, I used to go out with a girl, only for a couple of weeks, who – how should I say? – was happy to be with several people at one time. Smyth was the other man and as soon as I found out I finished it. I was one of the charity backers that helped Travis start his company, and when I found out about Smyth, I pulled the funding. Smyth was not flavour of the month and not sure how he kept his job, but he did. I did not know that she was a relation of Travis's, so it all got a bit messy and…' She put her hand to his lips to stop him.

'Enough, other people and the past: you me here now!' she said, smiling at him. He leaned in to kiss her and then sat back in the seat.

'Todd bailed, then, did he?' he asked, changing the subject as if the conversation had not happened.

'Yes, we had a bit of a word, he had drunk a bit and…' He stopped her this time and repeated her line.

'Other people past, here and now.'

She nodded. 'Something like that.'

Once they had reached the penthouse, Lottie was happy that Todd had arrived back and was snoring his way towards the headache she no doubt knew he would have the next day. She undressed and got into bed. She pulled the sheets around her and found that sleep came quickly.

Ed walked in the room and looked at her. She looked beat; he dimmed the light and stripped, climbing in beside her; she did not stir. He placed her in his arms and he watched her sleep. He was not feeling tired so he put his iPod on as low as he could and listened to music. Pete had found the soundtrack that Lottie had played the scores to at the weekend and he played them over, reliving the scene in his head. He had also asked the DVD to be sent over so that they could watch it: after all, she had said it was one of her favour chick flicks, and he had never seen it, too girly!

Her phone had buzzed and several messages had come through. It was in the purse where she left it the night before. Dorothy noted it as she arrived at the house, and after the third call in as many minutes thought that it was something urgent. She would not go into the bag but thought that she needed to say something. No one else in the house seemed to be awake. She started a coffee knowing that soon Pete or Corry would be around, and she made herself as busy as she could while remaining quiet. The phone rang again, so she dared to go into her bag and pick it up. She stood outside Ed's door. If he had been alone she would have gone in, but she was not going to listen or invade their privacy. She put the phone back and tried to ignore the repeated beep of another message.

The front door opened and Ed came in.

'Edward,' she said, 'I had no idea you were awake.' He had been for a run; he could not sleep. Either too much on the plane, or his body clock was catching up with him.

'Morning, Dorothy, no one else up?' he asked, taking off his tee shirt as it was sweaty. She glanced at his perfect body and commented, 'Still keeping in shape, then?'

'Trying, been missing it over the past few days, though.' He grabbed a bottle of water from the fridge.

'She's nice.' Dorothy commented. 'Are we seeing a serious Mr Dean?' She had always told him how it was: over the years of knowing him his lifestyle had, at times, made her frown and given him comments that he had not welcomed. She had on more than one occasion been reminded that he was young and would do as he pleased. But she noted in his voice from the phone calls, and just the way he was now, that there was a change.

'Dorothy, you may be looking at a changed man, yes.' He took more water. 'I find myself in a place that I have never been before and I have to say that I like it. I'm not saying it's not hard.' He jumped up on the counter and watched her while she started breakfast. 'But I may be finding my karma after all.'

'And is she lying in your bedroom, this karma?'

'I believe that she is,' he replied, draining the water and throwing the bottle at the bin: its lid was up and he made a direct hit as the plastic rattled in the container. He punched the air as a celebration of his skills.

The housekeeper smiled, he would never have been so relaxed, she thought. 'Well, I am pleased to see you, and I hope that we see you both soon over this side of the pond.'

'I'm glad that you missed me.' He jumped down and kissed her on the cheek, and she pulled away a little. 'Stop it, you will make me blush.'

'Thank you for looking after her the past few days, I hope we come back soon. I was worried that she would find the house a bit...'

'Playboy,' she interjected.

'Yes, so thank you for the flowers and the touches you made to make it feel more homely.' He looked round as he heard a ringing phone. 'That you?' he asked.

'No, it's Lottie's, it's been going off a lot since I arrived, about four times.'

He wandered to the bag and picked out the phone. He would never have answered but he saw the missed calls from Agnes and thought it may be urgent.

'Agnes?' he said as he hit the accept button.

'No, it's Lynne.' She sounded distressed. 'Is that Edward?' she asked and he replied. 'Is Lottie with you?'

'She's asleep, yes, why?' He moved to the window and kept his voice low. So many thoughts went through his head, but the main one was that she was OK because she was with him, selfish, but it would steady the blow that he was about to give her.

He listened to her and finished the call by saying, 'I will, yes, don't worry.' He put the phone in his pocket and walked back to the kitchen.

'Get Pete up here please ASAP, we will need to get back to the UK fast, and I may need you in a few minutes after I go in to see Lottie.' He explained why and took a deep breath and walked towards the bedroom.

She had woken and seen he was not there. The iPod was left on the bedside cabinet and she had put it on and lain back. She guessed he had listened to music before he went to sleep; she had woken in the night, felt his arms and soft breathing, and fell back to sleep. Surprised he had got up and not woken her, she was relaxing in bed hoping he would come in and rejoin her.

He put his head around the door and saw she was sitting with her upper body out of bed. He smiled at her as he could see she was listening to his music: she had her eyes closed but her feet were tapping and her fingers slowly moving as she played the air piano! He ran his hands up the sheets as a way to attract her attention and she opened her eyes immediately.

'Morning you, fancy leaving without saying goodbye!' He was now sitting half-stripped on the side of the bed. Still sweaty from his run, he pulled her in his arms and kissed her. 'That's better,' she said, suddenly noticing his face. 'What's wrong?' she asked. He pulled the phone from his pocket and said, 'It has been ringing, sorry I saw who the caller was and answered.' She looked at the missed calls and text messages. They had been coming through for the last two hours. Her hands were shaking and she was trying to get the messages up to read. He held her hand and stopped her.

'Lottie, it's Dick.' He stopped and she looked at him. 'He has...' He faltered. 'He has had a heart attack, and, oh God I can't say this, they lost him last night.'

It was as if a hot rod had been rammed through his heart as he saw her weep uncontrollably. He held her tight, rocking her, trying to give her some comfort, but it did not seem to come.

'Shush, baby girl, I'm here!' He stroked her hair and kissed her head. 'Shush,' he continued to say. He knew that Dick was the father she had not had for all those years. He had seen the way that she was the second daughter he had when they spent time together. He knew this was hurting and he couldn't do anything to help her. She tried to talk to him through her sobs, but he could not make out what she was saying.

'Oh God, Agnes, he's gone... He can't have, what about... is she, who called, when...' She sobbed out all at once, repeating it.

'I know, shush.' He continued to hold her and Dorothy put her head in the door. Ed looked up and shook his head: she closed the door to again to leave them alone.

Lottie finally pushed herself back and wiped her face. Her eyes were red, her nose was running, her face hurt from the sobbing. She sniffed back and wiped her nose on her wrist. Ed jumped up and grabbed some tissues from the bathroom and gave them to her, returning to his place and sitting next to her as close as he could.

'I need to be home!' she said, her voice wobbling and small, like a child's.

'I know, I will see to it. I've asked for Pete. It's going to be a few hours, but we will get a plane as soon as it is possible.'

'I don't understand, he was OK when we left. I only spoke to them on Tuesday when I got here.' The sobs started again and he held her once more. He heard the door go and Dorothy's voice: she must have been talking to Pete about what had happened. He would not let her go until she was OK, but the quicker he did things, the faster they could get back.

Todd was now up, after hearing the commotion, and he put his head around the door. Ed looked up. Under any other circumstance he would have ripped into him for being so personal, but this was not about him. Lottie looked up at him and wiped her face again. 'Sorry,' she said to them both, 'I must look awful.' She used the damp tissue again to blow her nose.

'Baby girl, it's OK.' He smiled at her and kissed her face.

'What can I do?' Todd asked. He was brave enough to put his head in the door, but did not want to go in, although someone biting his head off at this moment would at least stop the throbbing hangover. Lottie turned over and put her face in the pillows. Ed put his hand on her back.

'Stay with her. I need to get things sorted.' Against every bone in his body, he needed to leave. He had hoped that Dorothy would sit with her, but then Todd knew her, and he hoped would be able to make her feel better in some way.

'Baby girl, I will not be far.' He kissed the back of her head; she never moved apart from the jerking of her body from the silent sobs that still came out. He got up and grabbed a top from the wardrobe. Todd edged his way in and sat on the bed.

'Look after her, fetch me if she needs anything,' Ed said, looking directly at him. 'Anything,' he said again, giving her one last kiss.

'Hey, now, Lotts, come on,' Todd said and she spun round and hugged him. How Ed moved his legs when he saw her reaction with Todd he did not know. She clung in Todd's arms like they fitted her like a glove. His fists were tight and his stomach knotted. 'Fuck it!' he said as he walked out the door. Pete met him instantly and passed him the phone.

Within half an hour it was all sorted: they had twenty minutes before they needed to go. The plane was already waiting and they had an hour's drive to the airport. Ed had tried to get a helicopter but could not get permission to land on the helipad. Dorothy would pack up the cases, Pete would need to get his stuff so had gone, and they needed to find out what Todd wanted to do. They were not going back originally until tomorrow, and Ed was not sure if there was anything left for him to do at the Centre. He went back into the bedroom. Lottie was lying on Todd's side: she was motionless, no tears; she looked exhausted. She never looked up as he walked in. Todd moved over and stood up. Ed replaced him and she looked at him and smiled.

'20 minutes, baby girl, I need you to be ready so we can go.' He kissed her.

'OK,' she whimpered. 'I need to have a shower.' Todd walked out the door and pulled it to.

Ed wiped her face again. 'Thank you,' she said, pushing up trying to make the effort to move.

'For what?' he asked.

'Being here, arranging to...' He kissed her lips to stop her talking.

'That's what I'm here for,' he said. 'I hate to rush you, but we need to get going. Can you manage it? Dorothy is coming in to pack and get you some clothes out. I just need to see what Todd is going to do.'

She pushed the sheets back and moved to the edge of the bed. He picked her up and took her into the bathroom and stood her up in the shower. She wobbled slightly then got her balance. 'I will be OK,' she said, as she turned on the hot water. He got wet kissing her and then he left her, leaving the door open in case she shouted him back.

Grabbing some bits, he used the other bathroom to shower and get ready. Dorothy worked like lightning to get the bags packed, and left out some clothes for Lottie to put on.

They were all ready for her when she emerged from the room, hair still damp and pulled back in a ponytail.

'Good to go?' Ed asked as he put his arm around her waist. Lottie nodded.

'Todd, are you not coming back?' she asked, confused as he was still dressed in his joggers and tee shirt.

'No. I want to tie things up here. I was going to hang on for a few days, and I guess work will wait so I may as well stay here.' Ed kindly paid for the ticket. 'I can use it up to seven days' time.' She went over to him and hugged him. She lingered in his arms for a moment, and Ed felt his stomach churn again as Todd brushed her hair and kissed her forehead.

'Ring me, keep in touch, won't you?' she said in a voice dulled by his chest as her face was tight against it.

'Lotts, of course,' he replied. 'Keep smiling, kid,' he said to her, trying to lighten the mood and he did manage to break a smile from her. He nervously looked at Ed, knowing the stare he was getting was one to back off, but it was Lottie clinging onto him as he tried to release her grip.

She finally let go and Ed moved towards her, Todd almost glad that he had been able to break the release before Ed broke a part of his own body.

'Thank you, Dorothy, I am sorry we are going so soon.' She hugged her and could see that she had tears in her eyes.

'Jeez, you'll be back and we can catch up again soon. Go home to your family, they need you,' she said, hugging her back.

She smiled at them all one more time and they left, Pete was in the car and Ed opened the door for her. He shot in the other side and they were away heading to the airport.

Chapter 17

Lottie went straight back to Kent when they arrived. Ed stayed the first night, but to his annoyance had to get back to London. Phil stayed to be there if she needed him, but she spent most of the days and nights with Agnes and her family. Ed called constantly and texted. He kept in touch with Phil until he could return the following Thursday to be with her for the funeral.

He arrived and let himself in. Lottie was in the kitchen and Phil met him by the door.

'How is she?' he asked, putting down his bags and coat.

'OK, looking withdrawn, hardly eating, but she says she's OK.' He went outside to give them time together.

'Hey, you,' she said as she saw him walk in.

She was dressed in black; he instantly noticed she had lost weight and she was looking pale and drawn.

'Baby girl.' He kissed her and she felt so fragile he thought he would break her. 'How are you?' he asked.

'OK,' she replied, still taking his hug. 'Need to get today over with and then get back to normal.'

'No one's rushing you,' he said, worried that she was not going to take the time she needed to get over this. He knew from their conversations that she had taken this badly, it had been a shock. He guessed in reality it was still fresh from her own mother passing and it had brought back the thoughts of how her own father had died.

It was a sombre day, and as they returned in the evening Lottie went back in the house and sat on the sofa and took off her shoes. She had no more tears to cry. She looked up at her mum and dad's photo and walked over to the fireplace, smiling at it as Ed walked back in. He had made a drink and had some biscuits. He handed her the coffee and she put it straight down.

'You need to drink and eat, you have had nothing all day,' he said, worried that she was running herself down.

'I'm not hungry,' she said. 'I feel sick and it just will not stay down.'

'Please? I don't want you to be ill.' He picked the drink back up and gave it to her. She took it, but it did not reach her lips.

'I'm just exhausted, I'm going to bed, you can stay down here if it is too early to go up.' She smiled at him and walked toward the stairs.

He felt useless to help her. He wanted to pick her up and take all the hurt away from her, but there was nothing he could do. Every time he tried to console her she had been cold to him. He had spoken to Dr Morgan, who explained it was normal grieving to let it run its course; she would come back to him when she was ready to. Being there mentally for her, if not physically, was natural and he needed to show her he had patience. 'That's what love is all about, Edward,' he said when they met the day before. 'It is not just the sex that shows you deeply care.'

He followed her upstairs and they climbed into bed. She hugged him and linked her hand in his and closed her eyes.

'I love you,' she said out of the blue. He could feel her rolling his ring around with her finger and he smiled to himself. She's in there somewhere, just give her some time, he thought, remembering what his mother had said to him when he called her because he did not know what to do. They were alright: it was just another emotion that he had never felt and needed to deal with. He thought back to how he had been when his father died: he had no emotion, no feelings, or at least he had not showed them if he had. When Mitch passed, he became a monster, drinking, going off the rails, and then being consumed by finding out what happened. Immersing himself in work and being ruthless with others' livelihoods. That was how he dealt with grief, and this was her way.

The house was dark, but he was woken by a noise. He shot his hand out to feel for her and she was gone; the sheets were cold. He called out her name with no reply. He grabbed his tee shirt and hurried to put it on. As he opened the bedroom door wide he could hear the delicate sound of music. He made his way to the top of the stairs and sat on the top step. She was playing the piano: he never recognised the tune, but it was slow and sad. He put his head in his hands and ran his fingers through his hair. Should he go to her, should he leave her? He did not know what to do. He let her play for a while. Twice he went to stand, but thought better of it. She carried on playing and he could hear the soft whimper of her crying. He had to go to her, he could not bear it. He paddled down the stairs in his bare feet, feeling the cold floor as he hit the bottom.

She was so taken with her task that she did not hear him. He watched as her body swayed and her hands moved effortlessly over the keys. He wanted her so badly. He drew in a breath and gently said her name: 'Lottie.' She turned to him, but continued to play.

He walked behind her and placed a kiss in the middle of her back. She had a thin nightdress on, revealing her naked shoulders and arms. She was freezing; she must have been there for a while. He draped his hands around her to try to pass over his body heat; she put her head back, and her fingers never missed a key. The tune continued and he ran his hands over her arms and back up slowly. Kissing her neck, and the flesh he could reach around her collarbone. He knelt behind her, running his hands down to her waist. She never stopped him, but she stopped her hands playing and put them on his. He kissed around her necklace, reaching over her to kiss the hollow of her neck. She turned around to face him, spinning her legs around to straddle his body. Her nightdress uncovered her lower body and exposed her to him. He kissed her cheeks and she moved her face so that their lips met.

She needed to feel his intimacy, his soft, delicate touch. She wanted to feel his breath on her skin and the smell of him next to her. She pushed her tongue into his mouth and he responded to her, licking her lips and biting gently on hers. She ran her hands down his hard chest, feeling the ripple and shape of each muscle, which contracted at her touch. He moved his head down her chest and kissed her through the soft material that covered her nipples that were erect, from the arousal or the fact that she felt like an ice block, he was not sure. She sighed as he took the other breast in his hand and gently rubbed. They felt tender, but she enjoyed the heat of his hand.

He ran his hands down her ribs: she had lost so much weight, he thought again, each one defined and easy to touch.

He pulled her closer and moved the assault back to her nipples. Her breasts felt hard, firmer than normal; she was so cold and he did not dare to take off her only layer of clothing.

He pushed his hand under her and used his powerful legs to lift them both, him from the floor, her from the red stool. She laid her head on his shoulder; without words he took her back upstairs and placed her in the sheets.

She spread herself out on the bed, lifting her arms above her head. The light from the moon outside cast shadows, but allowed him to see her taut breasts, and he followed the shape of them with his hands.

'Lottie, tell me to stop if you don't want this,' he whispered in her ear, aware that was fully erect and turned on so much that he was going to find it hard to stop if she said no.

'I want you so much,' she said as she reached for his head to kiss her again. Her words were like sweet joy to him. He kissed her shoulders and she bit him gently on his exposed neck.

She felt his swollen dick on her thigh react and pulse to the nuzzling, and she did it again. She ran her hands through his hair, releasing the smell of his showered body. She took a deep breath in. She guided her hand down his back and around his thigh until she touched him; stroking him, she could feel the heat in his arousal. She trapped his cock between her thigh and her hand, and she rubbed him. He reacted by pulling down her top to expose her nipples and he kissed one, licking all round the raised skin and gently biting with his teeth.

They felt more sensitive than normal and the shock wave was directed to her sex: she clenched her inner muscles. There was no urgency in their touching, although it had been well over a week since they had enjoyed each other this way. She used her hands to wiggle her nightgown off over her head, and he helped her. She again raised her hands above her head holding onto the headboard and he worked his tongue down between her breasts to her navel. She gave a gasp when he brushed his lips over the top of her pubic bone, and around her bikini line. She bucked her hips and he licked the top of her opening.

He could feel her wetness, the sweet musk of her, and he licked his lips to taste her after he had put his tongue inside her, parting her lips with his chin. He sucked at her and she responded, arching her back and whimpering, as her increased breath left her mouth. He sat between her legs and slowly kissed every inch of her back up to her neck. The gold glimmered in the light: the pink, purple stone shone bright.

He rubbed himself along her pelvis, leaving a trail of his pre-cum on her. Using his hips, he guided himself into her, gently probing the entrance allowing the lubricating juices to ease his large dick into her. It had been a while so he needed to ensure she could take him.

As he pushed down she dug her nails into the sheets above her head and he placed both of his hands by her shoulders so he could take his weight and bear down on her more.

'I love you,' she said again in a whisper as he kissed her cheeks. He felt the words in the heat of her breath on the soft part of his ear.

'I love you, Lottie,' he responded and she moved her hands to clasp his face, forcing him to kiss her. It was soft at first but then she increased her urgency as she ran her hands through his hair and onto his shoulders. She dug in her nails and pulled herself closer to him, urging to increase the rubbing of his abdomen on her pelvis. She moved her hands down to his backside and pushed him into her, making him totally fill her. She gasped out as his balls hit her arse cheeks; she widened her legs as much as she could and tilted her hips to feel him all the way inside her. His pace increased and he started to breathe quickly. The tension building in them both turned their lovemaking into a frenzy of lust and passion, pulling and grasping, thrusting and biting.

Hers came so hard that she shot her eyes open and grabbed the sheets at her side. 'Oh!' she panted out. 'Oh God! she exclaimed as her inner sex spasmed so hard she felt the pain in her stomach.

'Oh, baby girl.' He wanted her to keep coming, to feel the pleasure as their bodies were one, entwined in her wetness he felt her contracting around him. He felt the second wave of pressure on his cock as she came again, instantly bucking her hips and crying out his name.

That was the final act, the release that sent his world in a frenzy; he thrust into her and spilled himself out. He almost had a head rush as the blood left to fill his swollen prick as it throbbed.

'ARHHH!' he grunted out. 'Oh baby!' He tried to slow down in fear of hurting her, but he was overcome with his own needs to be this close, to feel this need that she was still responding to each thrust trying to get him deeper and deeper into her. He never thought that this level of pleasure was possible with basic sex: it was truly feeling as one, making love, which was the all-consuming feeling. And if he had asked, she would have told him that she felt it, too.

It took them both time to come down from the high and regain their breath. He withdrew and lay on his side. He pulled over the sheets and gently kissed her shoulder.

'Thank you,' she said. He leaned up on one elbow and kissed her earlobe.

'What for?' he asked, still slightly fuzzy-headed.

'Getting me through this,' she replied, rubbing her hand along his other arm. He held up his hand and she entwined her fingers with his. She brought them down and kissed the back of his hand. 'I'm sorry if I have been...'

'Never apologise for being you, Lottie, never.' He kissed her hand back. He did not think that it was possible to love her more, but he did. He felt a warm, wet patch on his arm that was close to her face and he looked down. In the light he could see the single tear falling. He pulled her onto his chest and hugged her.

'Sleep, my love: let me hold you and you sleep.' She did.

'Well, Mr Dean, here you are sitting in my surgery telling me that you are going to propose to the woman you love, and you ask me if you are mad?' Dr Morgan smiled at him. 'I would say I need to meet this woman and offer her a job. Nine months ago, you never had one feeling bone in your body, now all 206 of them are like a teenager who has just found his dick: they are all out on show. Where has this playboy, 'I will never have feeling for anyone', hard-ass businessman gone to?'

'So, it's not too soon?' Ed asked, playing with the ring on his finger.

'I am a physiatrist not a marriage guidance counsellor. You came to me because you could not express yourself in any other way apart from in the bedroom through rough, unadulterated sex. You want my advice on marriage?'

'Don't mock me, I am asking as a friend,' Ed retorted.

'I see the change in you, if this is what you want then who am I to stop you? What's your concern - she does love you back?'

'Yes,' he nodded.

'That she will take you for everything you have got?' Ed replied with a NO. 'That she will leave you?' He did not need to reply. 'That's it, the rejection: would she leave you?'

'That's out of my control.' Ed shifted in his chair: the mere thought of it made him uncomfortable.

'Right, so we do still have a bit of that control freak lurking in the background, then!' The doctor leaned on his desk. 'How many business deals have you made when you take a punt, a gamble? Not knowing how they will turn out.'

'Not many.' Ed sat up, priding himself that he always thought them through and did not go for non-starters.

'But you have taken some?' he asked. Ed nodded. 'So what makes them different?'

'I have a gut feeling. It felt right,' he answered the question.

'And so, my friend, does this feel right, gut feeling?'

Ed left the surgery having answered his own question. It felt so right, so very right.

It had been two weeks now after Dick's funeral; Lottie had come back to London with him, after they stayed the weekend in Kent, but had not returned to work. Todd had stayed in New York for longer that the first week. Ed had agreed that he could use the penthouse. It just sits there anyway, he said someone may as well use it. She said that she could not face any more death until he was back and she felt happy to be there again. They had spent time together every day; she had even got her scholarship placement up and running and Ed was now on his way to meet her at the

College for Music after his appointment with Dr Morgan. He had told her that he still wanted to go to see him, even if it was only once a month; after today's session he could see that going to once every two months the way he felt now.

He found himself whistling as he walked down the street to the car. Mid-September and, although the wind was colder, today the sun was shining finally: some of the years of cloudy skies seemed to be parting for him.

They were made welcome at the College, being shown round by the Principal and some of the pupils. They were shown what their money offered talented youngsters, and Lottie would be able to pay for at least two per year, for the full terms, which what she had pledged.

She smiled and laughed, and she even had a go on one of the new Steinway pianos sitting in the corner of the studio. Ed watched her as she seemed really happy for the first time in weeks. He wanted to fill his promise to get a piano for the apartment: there was room for one like she was playing and he asked about where to go to get one. They spent the whole afternoon together and then went to eat out; as they had not booked anywhere they called into one of her favourite cocktail bars in town. They ordered, but when the food came she chased most of it round the plate.

'Still not hungry?' Ed asked as he noticed had not really eaten much of the lobster she ordered.

'Not really,' she said as she sipped at the water in her glass. 'I'm fine, though.' She gave him a smile and they continued to chat into the early evening. Pete picked them up and they spent the rest of the night in the apartment looking through some of the hospital plans and arrangements for the next charity event. Lottie reminded Ed that they had the day booked with young Simon the next weekend, and it was also the first time her horse was running in a big event. She hoped it would win as it would boost the coffers for her scholars, and he noticed how she really was getting involved with working at home and making plans to fill her days, other than at the centre. He quietly hoped that she would lean towards this. Maybe one of the reasons he thought that if Todd was in New York she would not want to work on the case they had started and be safe for sure.

She sat on the sofa looking through her emails and her own accounts.

'We should get you space in the study,' he said. 'You'll get neck ache working on the sofa.' He walked over to her and kissed her head. She smiled up at him. 'I'll put it away in a minute,' she said.

He looked over her shoulder at the screen: she was looking at some sunny beach.

'Where's that?' he asked, sitting next to her.

'The Maldives.' She clicked on one of the cabins that were situated in the sea.

'Thinking of getting away?' he asked. Maybe a holiday is what she wanted.

'Just fancied some sunshine, really. Agnes said it was one place that they wanted to go, but never made it. I wondered if I could treat her.'

'What, the two of you go?' he replied, a surge of panic in his throat which he managed to hold in.

'Maybe, and Lynne and her family, just to get away from it. What do you think?' She turned the laptop round to him so he could see the resort pictures.

What did he think? No was the first reaction, he did not want another few weeks of her away.

'Do you think you could get away from everything for a few weeks, too? Without Pete and the crew and the phone, internet and the rest of the world?' Her question surprised him as he expected it to be a girl request and he would have to think of how he would survive her being away. He would never have the heart to say he did not want her to go, but her request was a welcome one.

'Um, not sure, maybe with a bit of planning, I did not think you would want me around,' he replied with a hint at his honesty.

'Why, I wanted it to be a big family holiday, maybe even your mum? Would she go for it? I am sure Agnes and her would get on well.'

The notion started him thinking: could this be a plan? 'When were you thinking of going?'

'Start of November maybe, after we have had the charity ball, but before the Christmas rush comes upon us.'

He was really pleased she wanted to include him in this: she had said 'big family thing' and he almost grinned inside himself knowing that was how she was seeing them, a family. The old Edward would have kicked himself into touch at the very thought; instead his brain was in overdrive thinking that maybe this could be the opportunity. She jumped up. 'Want a drink?' she held up the decanter of whiskey.

'Trying to get me drunk to take advantage and persuade me?' He laughed.

'Do you need me, too?' she asked, pouring the drink and taking it back over to him.

'You want to go, don't you?' He took the glass from her and she nodded. 'Big family holiday, could we put up with everyone for so long?'

She walked into the kitchen, saying, 'They have individual apartments, although I am not sure about one in the middle of the sea for me, with my history of seafaring!' She referred to the boat trip that went so wrong. He carried on looking through the resort and some wedding photos came up. He smiled to himself.

He took the photos off the screen when she sat back down next to him.

'What do you think? Can I ask around, see if anyone is interested?' She took a sip of the milk she had fetched, but it seemed to have funny taste so she put it back down.

'You don't have to, I will get Zoe to do all the arrangements.' He held her hand. 'If you want to go we will.'

'Oh, don't want my PA skills, then?' She looked disappointed. 'Just thought it would give me something to do.'

He had to agree she could arrange it, but he would not be able to do what he was thinking of. 'Maybe you can work on it together. Come into work with me tomorrow and talk to her.'

'I will.' She kissed him on the cheek. 'I want to phone Agnes and see if she wants to do it.' She jumped up off the sofa and grabbed her phone.

He lay awake listening to her sleep. So many things going through his head. If he could pull this off, it would be a triumph. He had promised himself that he would not lie to her, but to achieve this he would need to be cunning and put some little white lies out and about, and hope her friends and family did let it slip. He was going to marry her out there. Without her knowing, he was going to arrange it all.

The first part of the plan was to propose. That would be easy. He was going to go and get the ring tomorrow. He could get out when she was at the office, some meeting or other, and then pop the question. Where, how? he thought. His palms started to sweat and he found himself thinking. Maybe not, Dean, not a good idea. Then he shook his head: yes, it is a great idea. Oh God, could he do it?

They got up and showered and dressed to go to the office together. Lottie took her pills from her bag and took one. She should have waited until her period, but with all the goings-on she just thought that she would take the rest of this pack then get back into the rhythm. She had done it before when she went away and did not want to be on, so she should be OK, wouldn't she? Maybe that was why she felt drained and sick skipping her last period and taking them randomly. She washed it down with some water and cleaned her teeth.

Ed was dressed in a dark grey suit, white shirt and pink tie when she walked back into the room.

'Meeting someone important?' she asked as she walked behind him and ran her hand over his powerful shoulders.

'Yep, then I thought maybe we could do The Shard for a late lunch?'

'Sounds nice.' She reached for her jeans and a sweat top.

'Do you want to put a dress in to change for dinner?' he asked. He did not want to tell her what to wear, but jeans really were a no-no in the well-known restaurant. She did as he said. 'This one?' She held up a long-sleeved black dress with see-through lace over the top. He stood next to her. 'If you're happy, that one.' He kissed her head. 'Breakfast?' he asked.

She put the carry bag on the side and sat at the breakfast bar. Mrs B had made pancakes and coffee. Lottie made a cup of tea: she really had gone off coffee.

'Sorry, Miss. If I knew you wanted tea I would have done that,' Mrs B said as she passed her a plate with pancakes and syrup.

'Just lost the taste for coffee,' and she took one bite of the sweet food and pushed it to one side.

'And your food by the looks of it.' Ed walked back in as Mrs B made her last comment and took his plate of food, sipping his coffee as he stood.

'Do you want to try some toast?' Mrs B offered.

'Do we have any peanut butter?' Lottie asked.

'Somewhere. Edward has it when he's been running.' She pulled the jar out of the back of the cupboard. 'I'll get some more, there's not much left.' She started to spread the mixture on the toast that had popped quickly.

Ed was already on the phone, eating his pancake whilst he walked around dropping crumbs on the floor.

'Edward!' Mrs B shouted at him for making a mess, even though he was in a conversation. Lottie laughed as she devoured the toast, putting some more in the toaster. She spread the rest of the peanut butter but it did not cover all the toast so she finished it off with jam.

'Got your appetite back?' he asked, kissing her hair as he walked back to the breakfast bar. He was really pleased she was eating something at last. She nodded and smiled at him, wiping her mouth. 'Even if it looks gross, jam and peanut butter: an acquired combination I am sure!' he said. Mrs B raised her eyebrows.

'Mission complete,' he said to Pete. 'Are you happy with the rest of today?' he asked as they pulled away from De Beers jewellers. He had to tell him all his plans because he was instrumental in getting them to work and everything booked with Zoe. He trusted both of them in their own way not to let anything slip. Pete had said he was happy for them, but had also asked if Ed was sure this was the way to take it forwards, so quickly. His question really was fruitless as he knew best that if Ed wanted something to happen, it did.

Lottie was changed when he got back to the office. She chatted all the time in the car about how they had been able to get a seventeen-day stay in two weeks' time. Enough rooms and the most fantastic apartment for the two of them, and beach huts for the others. She was a bit confused as to seventeen days, but it was something to do with getting some free days. Really it was because they had to be in the country long enough to get the licence; Zoe omitted that bit of information to her.

She turned to him in the car on the way to their dinner date with a very serious face. 'Ed,' she started.

'Miss Jenkins?' he replied. 'I feel a compromise on my part coming here!' He smiled as he knew that face. One he had missed for several days.

'I want to pay for Agnes and her family, I don't want this all to be down to you. Zoe was really not happy for me to pay, but I'm not going if it is all on you. It is not my intention to fund everything through you.' She paused.

'I made Zoe transfer money into your account, so that you could not do anything about saying no. I just wanted to get that out there so you know.'

'Well, Miss Jenkins, it seems to be done and I can't change the deal anyway.' He squeezed her hand. 'But if it is mine, it is yours, you know that, don't you?'

She smiled back at him and they continued the journey.

He seemed odd all through the first part of the meal. She ate small amounts of the food; it was nice, and they had an expensive bottle of wine. The seat was the best in the house; the view across the city was, as always, on a sunny day breathtaking and they made conversation without any issues.

He had arranged for roses to be on the table and they smelled sweet as she put her nose to them. Lottie noticed that he had not taken off his jacket and wondered if he was not hot. He, as always, looked fantastic, and many of the other women in the room looked over at her. They ordered coffee, and he asked for tea for her, remembering what she had said at breakfast. She smiled at the attention to detail he gave her.

'Happy,' he asked as he caught her smile.

'Very,' she replied as he leaned over and held her hand over the table. She automatically played with his signet ring, something she had done since the day she had given it to him, but more of late.

'Do you want anything else?' he asked as the waiter came to the table with the drinks. He had again noticed her lack of appetite, and he still maintained she was losing weight.

'I'm good,' she said sipping her drink with the hand that she had spare. She put her glass down and he took her other hand.

'Lottie...' Here we go, he thought, never done this before so I don't know how it will go. His hands were shaking and she picked up on this.

'What's wrong, Ed?' She looked concerned at him. 'You're sweating, are you ill?'

'Maybe?' he started. 'I have to say that I have not been feeling myself for the past seven months.' He rubbed her hands. 'Lottie, you have changed my life so much, I am the luckiest man on earth right now, and I have you to thank for that.' He let her hands go and quickly got up from the table. He stood behind her and placed both hands on her shoulders. He took the champagne out of the cooler that the waiter had brought over and placed it by the side of her. He bent down by her side and she turned to look at him.

He had the box in his hand and he was not sure if he should kneel, or get her to stand up, so he knelt by her side.

'I love you, Miss Jenkins, will you marry me?' He held out the box and stopped breathing. She had to speak before he could take another breath.

The couple at the next table had looked across: they must have heard what he had said. It was as if a hush went over the room.

'Edward,' she said, 'I don't...' She paused and looked at the box that was closed. He opened it and the largest diamond and platinum ring she had ever seen sat proud in the red velvet box. She looked up at him and bit her lip, genuinely not sure of what to say. They had never even discussed this; she did not think that they were anywhere near this. Agnes had joked about it. Lottie had never given it any thought.

'Lottie, say something, I am dying here! I can't breathe,' he said, pleading with her. He really could not find the breath.

She put her hand to her face: she was not sure to laugh or to cry.

'Yes, yes of course.' The words seemed to come from her without a second thought. She stood up and he pulled her into her arms. The couple on the next table smiled, and the rest of the room could have left for all he cared. She had said yes. They kissed and several other people guessed what had just happened and the atmosphere became light-hearted.

'Oh God, really?' he said.

'Did you want me to say no, Mr Dean?' she said, biting her lip again.

'I want to kiss that lip,' and he did. This public display of affection would no doubt make its way around the gossip columns, but he seemed not to care. 'Thank you, baby girl, I love you so much.' He took the ring out of the box and slid it down her finger. 'Perfect.' he grabbed the champagne and popped the bottle. He poured two glasses and they clinked together. He sat back down but did not let her hands go.

'Surprise me, then, why don't you?' she said to him.

The smile on his face was hard to miss. He ran his hand through his hair. 'I thought you were going to say no!' he said, taking off his jacket and relaxing now.

'How long have you been planning this?' she asked, looking at the rock on her hand.

'Since I first saw you!' he said.

'Cheesy or what, Mr Dean? Do better than that.' She smiled at him. Her stomach was fluttering and she was glad that he had sat her down again as she felt her legs go weak when he had said it.

'I have been falling in love with you since we met. I am going to be honest, I never thought about marriage until, well, I knew I could not live without you. I want you to have everything I can give you: my name seems the next thing as you already have my heart.'

'And your body?' she asked, flashing her eyebrows.

'Without question all yours,' he said, smiling at her lurid comment 'Whenever, however, you want it!'

They finished their meal and went home on a high. The next morning Mrs B was pottering in the kitchen when Lottie walked in.

'Congratulations, Miss,' she said to her.

'Thank you,' Lottie replied, looking down at the ring that sparkled on her hand.

'Do we have a date soon?' Mrs B never looked up from her task as she asked.

'We did not set a date. I'm sure we will wait a while, I'm in no rush.'

Lottie made a tea and poured a fresh coffee in another mug which she took back to Ed who was getting dressed.

'Oh,' Mrs B replied as if she still had something to say to finish off the comment.

Lottie watched him as he dressed. She lay on the bed and stretched out, after leaving the drinks on the side. She was smiling as he walked back in, brushing his hand through his hair.

'You OK?' he asked, picking up the cufflinks he was about to put on. Lottie gestured for him to come closer so she could help.

'Yes. Mrs B just asked about a date: what do you think, maybe next spring? Our local church in the village is so nice then, and...' She stopped and looked at him. 'I know this sounds silly, but Mum and Dad would be there.' She referred to this as they were buried together in the churchyard in the village in Kent. He looked at her.

'Is that what you want?' He fiddled with the first link that was already in his shirt. Shit, he thought to himself, never planned for that!

'Yes, but it's not just for me to decide, it's a joint thing you know.' She kissed his hand as she completed the task on the other wrist. 'Done,' she said, turning around to get her tea. She took a mouthful and he was fiddling with the other cuff to get it straight.

'Maybe we could talk about it later, set something up with a wedding planner?' He was panicking now, not sure what to say.

'Have you gone off the idea already?' she asked, sensing his hesitation.

'No, God, no, I just had not thought much past asking you really. I was so nervous about it, I never got past the part for more details.' He was now struggling with his tie and the lie he was starting to spin.

'Mr Dean not having a plan, now there is a first!' Lottie sat up on her knees and helped him with his tie. She pulled him close and stole a kiss. She lingered on his lips and licked the bottom one. He put his arms around her and responded to her.

'If you don't stop, all the effort to dress me will have been worthless!' he whispered as he slipped his hand under the tee shirt she wore to feel her breast and erect nipples. 'And I need to be in the office within the hour.' She rubbed her hand along his thigh and felt his groin, hard and bulging against the grey pinstripe suit trousers he had on.

'Maybe you can keep this thought until later, then?' She rubbed his erection one more time, and it responded with a spasm.

'My first appointment will be more than shocked when I meet them if it stays on my mind too long!' He laughed, picking up her face to give her a final kiss. He purposely held her hands so that she could not touch him again: getting to the car at this rate was going to be hard enough!

'See you later, baby girl, be careful.' He left her sitting on the bed drinking her tea. She had planned to go shopping for some clothes for her holiday.

'Any requests for small bikinis, thongs maybe, or white tee shirts that will be see-through after swimming in the sea!?' she shouted after him as he went out of the bedroom door.

He burst back in the room, took the tea out of her hand and pushed her back onto the bed. Bearing down all his weight onto her, she gave a yelp of surprise as he pulled off his tie.

'Miss Jenkins, you are now in the greatest of trouble!' He pinned one of her hands down and started to kiss her neck. Lottie scrambled for his belt as he kissed her. She unbuttoned his shirt but never pulled it off, as it was attached at the cuffs. His tight torso flexed as she took the weight towering above her.

Quite undignified with his trousers by his knees, shoes and socks still on, he pushed her legs apart and guided himself towards her opening. He struggled to get her tee shirt over her head between the urgent kissing and licking of her neck, ears, face. She bucked her hips to him and he pushed his hard head into her, just enough so she could feel his size.

'Is this what you have been asking for?' He pushed a bit more and she gasped as he stretched the soft skin of her sex. 'Miss Jenkins is this what you want?' he asked again.

'Yes!' she said, holding his backside to get him to push further.

'Not had enough last night?' he asked, grinding his hips into her pubic bone. 'You are greedy, are you not?' He pushed further sucking the nipple that was looking lonely to his left. He sucked the other just to ensure he did not leave it out. He grabbed her hips and withdrew from her, turning her round onto her belly in one easy movement. He moved himself further up the bed and knelt behind her. He pulled her backside to meet him and he plunged his fingers between her legs. She flung her head back as he dipped the digits in and out.

'So very wet,' he said, pulling out his fingers 'And so sweet to taste.' He gently took the wetness in his mouth and then leaned over her to whisper in her ear. 'You are holding me up, my client will not be happy that I am making them wait!' He slapped her backside as hard as he could and she shot forwards, not expecting the blow. 'You know I hate to keep people waiting, now you have made me look bad!' He slapped her again, seeing the instant colour of her skin where his hand had landed.

The pain shot to her core, but was radiating through her sex, making her clench her inner muscles. He pushed himself towards her opening and smacked her hard again on the other cheek, perfectly timed with the first full thrust of hard prick into her. 'Ah!' It was painful and she gripped at the sheets to steady herself. He pushed again and she could feel his balls hit her as his full length went into her. He held her by one shoulder and slapped her again on the outer thigh. 'You are being punished for making me late, Miss Jenkins, as a reminder that I don't like to be late!' His thrusts were fast and she tried to join his rhythm. He slapped her again; again she gasped but the power of the pain brought her orgasm faster than she realised and she pushed her head back into him. He moved his hand and it was now over her throat. He applied a small amount of pressure, more to hold himself in place than to stop her breathing. She tried to swallow, but he was restraining her. He slapped her again and her orgasm came, she bucked and arched her back, panting for breath.

'Miss Jenkins, you really do need to learn to wait.' He pulled her back up as she had slumped for exhaustion onto her chest. 'Although I am finding it hard to demonstrate the same control.' He pulled at her nipple that was rubbing on the sheets as he moved in and out of her. She could feel herself building up again, as her soft skin was sensitive between her legs. 'You will have to wait!' he said, pulling out of her. He gently slapped her arse and she fully fell to the bed.

'Mr Dean, really, if you are going to be late at least conclude this deal before you move out?' she rolled over and smiled at him, biting her lip. 'Or should I show my business strategy and finish myself?' She moved her hand down to her swollen lips that were wet, not just from her cum, but also from the ejaculate that had leaked from him, showing just how close he was to full release.

'Not a chance.' He grabbed her hand away from the area. 'It's mine, remember?' He leaned over her again, pulling her backside up to him. 'I'm not even sharing you with you.' He forced into her again and pounded her. The urgency made him sweat and breathe heavily. He gritted his teeth and used her hips to speed up the rhythm. He tilted her hips and she could feel his brushing her G-spot. She gasped and whimpered as she could feel another release coming. Before she could he thrust his first primal spasm into her, then again. 'Oh Jesus, Lottie!' he exclaimed in a euphoric state. 'Fuck!' he said, giving in to the last thrusts of his own orgasm.

He ran his hand from her face to belly button, still leaning above her. 'Where did that come from?' he asked.

'Not sure, but do you want me to ring them to say you are going to be late?' She wiped the sweat from his brow. 'You're going to need another shower!' She smiled and he rolled off her.

'I'm going to need another set of lungs and more stamina, too!' He started to undo the cufflinks and regain his normal breathing. 'If you keep that sort of pace up, you will be burying me before spring, let alone marrying me!' She jumped up and straddled him. 'Don't you say that.' Her face was really serious. 'Don't you even say it in jest, that's not funny.' Using his abs to pull him up while she sat on his legs, he held her in his arms. He could see that it was not quite the right thing to have said. Timing was poor and wording inappropriate given the past few weeks.

'Sorry, I did not think it was purely a metaphor!' He kissed her. 'If a rather insensitive one!' They hugged for a moment until he was happy that she was OK.

His visitor waited in his office for well over an hour before he arrived that morning. The greeting was formal and Ed could tell he was displeased at having to wait.

He played the recording through his desktop and the well-dressed man with a strong Russian accent nodded at various points.

'Well, Mr Dean, it seems that you have good reason to distrust Mr Girski, as we were mislead that this was any of your doing. You must be pleased that your man here' – he nodded over to where Pete was quietly standing by the door – 'was quick to think to make a recording of your conversation. It is conclusive that you had no part to play in this. I have to say my boss will be pleased as he was quite unimpressed at the thought you had double-crossed us. So there, happy all round.' He stood up and shook Ed's hand. 'It is good news, I hear, congratulations on your engagement. She is a very fine young woman for sure, very pleasing to the eye.'

'You've followed her?' He suddenly got the drift of the conversation.

'As a precaution you understand, Mr Dean. My boss was eager to ensure that you knew we were not happy with the conduct and getting to know young Leticia may have been a bargaining tool!' The man held no expression on his face. He did not need to. Ed knew what he was implying without doubt.

'You tell your fucking boss that this is over. If she has any reason to feel threatened, or I know about anything like this from this second onwards, he had better watch out.' He had his fists clenched and was standing up from his chair. The man-mountain that was also in the room as protection to the Russian visitor moved slightly towards his employer. The Russian held up his hand as if he was OK with Ed's fury.

'It's OK, Steven, Mr Dean would be understandably upset to lose such a jewel, but he knows we are OK now, so no harm done.'

'Was it you bastards that broke into her flat a few weeks ago, trying to frighten her?' He slammed his hands on the table and the protection officer again moved forwards.

'No, Mr Dean, it was not, you have my word on that. Although I guess by the speed that she moved in with you after that you were worried?'

'Don't fuck with me, arsehole! Is our business done here?' he asked, pacing by the window.

'For now, Mr Dean, yes. I will happily say that our relationship is back on track, with no issues with you, your businesses, or your family. If we can assist in any way please do contact us: relations across the water can be so beneficial sometimes.' He stood and held out his hand. Ed did not want to shake it, but knew that he had to, to seal the deal: it was the Russian way.

'Mr Dean, we may meet again: if we do, I look forward to it.'

'Don't hold your breath!' Ed said as he sat back down and Pete opened the door for them to leave.

'Did you have any idea she was being followed?' Ed asked as he walked back to his desk and sat down.

'None. Neither Steven nor Phil noted anything unusual: they would have said,' Pete replied.

'Where is she now?' Ed asked, picking up his phone.

'Shopping. Phil is sitting in car waiting for her,' Pete informed him.

'So, she is not in eyeshot?' Ed asked, punching the number for Lottie.

'No,' Pete replied.

'Maybe she fucking well should be!' He put the phone to his ear. Pete picked up his phone also.

Bella had been pleased to see Lottie and had marvelled at her ring. She grinned from ear to ear and was more than happy to help Lottie pick out some new clothes for her holiday. They had only been sitting discussing the sort of thing that she wanted when her phone rang.

'Missing you already?' Bella asked as she said could she just take the call.

'Lottie, everything OK?' Ed asked.

'Yes, fine, why?' she replied. Should she be worried?

'Just ringing to reply to your question earlier.' It was a lie, but an excuse to call her all the same. 'Nothing too revealing: I don't want to be distracted for the entire time we are away!' She laughed, totally unaware that this was a guise for calling her.

'Shame,' she said, 'but I will think of you when we visit the lingerie!' She coloured as Bella was in earshot.

They made conversation, and Lottie noticed Phil appear and speak to Bella.

'Is everything OK? Phil has appeared,' she asked. She said that she did not need him with her all the time while she was in the shop: it did feel too intimidating.

'He must have fancied a change of scene,' Ed added.

'Well, rest assured he won't be getting a preview of anything I buy.' She sounded at ease.

'I hope not from the underwear section!' Ed added, genuinely meaning the comment.

Bella and Lottie were in the changing room.

'He must get incredibly bored just sitting there,' Bella asked, helping her on with a light summer dress.

'I guess. I have to say I find it all a bit too much, but it saves me carrying the bags and having to drive through the traffic!' She smiled.

'I guess he is quite handsome, too, so not too bad a deal after all!' Bella remarked.

'Well...' She looked at the ring. 'I can't say that I have noticed!' She had noticed that he was an attractive man when they first met. He had strong facial features and a body that had worked hard to get so defined.

'I'm sure that Mr Dean is all you need to be looking at.' Bella laughed. 'I'm sure I would not be distracted if he were mine. Do we also need to be looking at a dress for an engagement party?' Bella changed the subject.

'Do you know, I had not even thought of it, we never talked about it,' Lottie replied with the idea now in her head.

'I'm sure that you had other things on your mind last night!' Bella raised her eyebrows. The two of them laughed.

'Maybe we could plan something for after the holiday,' Lottie said as they sat eating their evening meal. They were talking about the idea of an engagement party. It had played over in her mind since Bella mentioned it earlier in the day.

'Maybe,' Ed said, not really wanting to give it too much detail as he had other things to plan. He had already thought that after the holiday they would have a party for other reasons; this could be one way that he could do something, and not have to lie to her about his plans. 'Maybe, yes, that sounds like a good idea,' he finished. 'How's the rest of your day been?' He tried to change the subject, and it worked.

She made general conversation on what she had purchased then asked, 'Why did Phil come up to me? I was happy he was in the car?'

Now did he lie to her again, or did he tell her the truth? 'I did not want to alarm you...' He started to explain the events of this morning's Russian visitor, and what he had said.

'I don't know what to say,' Lottie started. 'I never knew anyone was following me. I'm glad you told me the truth, I am sure that you struggled to tell me in case...' She stopped. She wanted to say make her panic, and she had to admit it was disconcerting to know these people had such power. 'It just makes it easier to know why you want them close to me all the time.'

'Miss Jenkins the optimist strikes again!' he said, smiling at her. 'You see good in us all and for that I am most grateful, but please be careful, Lottie, these guys don't mix business and pleasure. I totally believe that if I had not been able to help them today, there would have been repercussions at some point: it's how they operate.'

Time moved on for them and it was the Saturday morning before they were due to fly away. They had attended several social events where they had been a topic of conversation. Several glossy magazines were eager to get their photo together and then print stories that the most eligible bachelor in the city had been taken by a nobody. Some stories were kind, others had some choice comments. A bit like the reception she got from meeting various guests at the social gathering they attended.

Ed had already been in touch with his solicitors to get the stories stopped, and he was on the phone again as he had flicked through the local paper to see another small story.

'I want it stopped! We are going away and I don't want to see anything, nothing at all, whatever clauses they have to sign, get it arranged,' had been the conversation Lottie heard as she walked back into the room. She felt sick again. Maybe nerves for flying away, but she could not face the fry-up waiting for her on the stove top.

'Toast again, Miss?' Mrs B asked, noticing the jam also out on the top.

'I just wanted something light really,' Lottie said, not even sure she wanted that. She sipped at her tea.

He finished on the phone and walked back over to the worktop to get his coffee.

'I don't mind, you know,' Lottie said, and both Ed and Mrs B looked at her. 'Whatever they write, it will be old news tomorrow.'

'I mind,' Ed said. 'Our lives are ours: if we choose to live on the moon no one should judge us. They are evil, Lottie, you can't see the good in the vultures who thrive to make or create gossip.' She could see he was angry; she pulled the paper towards her and read the section. She did not manage to get to the last line before he pulled it away.

Has he been trapped and will we soon here the pitter-patter of tiny Dean feet? Watch this space!

'Well, we know the truth,' he said, putting the paper in the bin. 'That's all that matters.'

'Yes, that's all that matters,' Mrs B said, looking at Lottie with a smile. She had seen the paper well before the two of them and had read the item with the heading **Billionaire off the market**. 'Being truthful to each other, and with each other,' was her parting comment on the subject.

'Anyway, it's a nice day, do you want to go to the track on the bikes?' Ed stood behind Lottie and gave her a hug as if to reinforce that he wanted to keep her safe. She was not sure she did, she was feeling tired. It was not a long drive, but it could have been to get home again after a long day.

'Don't you want to take the car? Isn't that kind of the whole point?' she asked. 'Simon will be disappointed.'

'He won't, my car has nothing on the ones he will get to see at the track, trust me.' He sounded like a child himself.

'So, remind me, this day is for which big kid? You or him?' She smiled as he kissed her hair.

'In no way is this for me!' he said, sipping his drink again. 'Well, only to see the excitement and joy of others of course.' She tilted her head to the side and looked under her eyes at him.

'Really?' she asked.

'Honest!' He put up his hands and had a grin like a Cheshire cat.

Ed had driven: they did not have Pete or any of the team with them as they were on some time off. He had guessed that when the two of them were together not much could go wrong?! Simon and his family had turned up early and were waiting for them, along with his friend and his family, so far, the day was going really well. Simon's friend Paul had a baby brother who slept most of the time in his pushchair. Lottie looked at him and chatted to his mother. When they ate their lunch, he had woken up and was so well behaved. Everyone seemed to make a fuss of him, even Edward, which came as a surprise to her.

'The little feller seems to like the cars, too,' Simon's gramps had said, noting the smiles and the way he kicked his fat legs when a car went past them on the track.

'Yes,' Ed said, smiling.

'Want to see them closer?' Gramps pulled him out of his chair and lifted him up. The baby giggled and blew a bubble in his face. 'Gosh, what does your mother feed you? You're heavy.' He bounced him around. 'Could you? Your arms are younger than mine.'

Ed held out his hands as if to take a radioactive bomb from someone, knowing it had about three seconds to go off. Lottie smiled at him and offered, 'Here, let me, you boys go play with your toys!' To Ed's relief Gramps offered him over to her instead.

Ed looked over at Lottie who seemed at ease with the youngster. He laughed and giggled as she talked to him in a baby voice.

'Suits her,' Gramps said as he noticed him looking over.

Ed had to agree it did suit her, she looked at ease. Maybe the interaction with Simon's family had put her at ease.

'Maybe you will be next?' Gramps asked. Ed smiled politely back but he knew it was something he wanted to wait a long time for. A child would mean he had to share her, something he had said he would never do.

Chapter 18

It was warm: the feeling of the hot air as you walked off the plane met them all as they landed on the small island. It had been a long day, flying to the mainland and then hopping to the small Rangali Island where they were staying. It should have been a boat trip, but they had added the extra flight because of Lottie. Rangali Island has 50 water villas of ever-increasing degrees of luxury. The elegant villas set on stilts over the ocean offer sweeping views of turquoise surrounds. The rooms that the rest of them were booked into all had ocean-view baths, private sun decks, espresso machines and a jacuzzi in the bathroom with inbuilt satellite TV. Ed and Lottie were staying in one of the two Sunset Water Villas which stood on terra firma in a secluded part of the lagoon with a private butler, glass-floored living room, two sitting rooms, a super double master suite with large, open bath and a free-standing, walk-in shower. It had a separate pool in the ocean and one on the deck. Sun decks all around leading from each room, with several sun loungers and the use of a personal jet boat.

Everyone was in really high spirits. Lottie looked around her. Agnes was smiling and looked happy, Lynne was trying to control the boys who had finally been able to run around after being confined during the journey. Ed's mother was smiling and had made every effort to enjoy the trip, although she had to admit she hated flying so she, too, was pleased to get her feet on the ground.

'With you not liking boats, and me not being in the air, it's a wonder you have been able to pull this off,' she said to Lottie as they waited for their bags and the directions to their rooms. 'Although you look beat, Lottie, do you feel OK?'

'Oh, it's been such a long day. I could do with a shower to refresh me, that's all.' She was fanning herself to try to keep cool. Maybe the idea of a bit of sun would have been better for Europe, not the extremes they were having here in the Indian Ocean at the moment, as it peaked at 40 °C+ every day.

They arranged to meet up in two hours' time for something to eat, as it had been a day of travel so they arranged to make it a short meal so they could get some rest, or explore if they wanted. Lottie dropped her bag on the floor and walked around the large apartment. It was almost as big as the London place, but on the ground, although she wobbled a bit when she saw the ocean under the floor.

'You get used to it, Miss,' a booming voice said. 'It is quite safe to stand on.' He held out his hand. 'My name is Gerald I am your butler. If it is not me then my colleague Alf will be serving you any time of the night or day.' Ed wandered over to see who Lottie was talking to. Gerald introduced himself again.

'Can we get you anything?' Gerald asked.

'Cold drinks please, bottle of Cristal on ice and once the bags are away, that will be great, thanks,' Ed said, flopping in the large sofa and holding his arms out for Lottie.

'I need to put the stuff away,' she said.

'What do they get paid for?' Ed said, pointing his finger to the attentive man; he beckoned her over. The air conditioning had kicked in and it was feeling cooler in the room. 'Come here, woman, at once and kiss me.'

She jumped on his knee and did as he asked. 'Do you like it?' he asked.

'The kiss or the resort?' Lottie asked.

'Funny! Miss Jenkins,' Ed gave a reply.

'Well, Mr Dean, good choice of resort by me, although I would like a second opinion on the kiss.' She giggled as he tickled her and kissed her hard on the lips. He continued to tickle her and she got up and ran to the bedroom.

'Stop it, Ed, I want a shower.' He continued to tickle her.

'Oh, I can help with that bit,' he said, pulling at her top and taking his own off as well, leading her into the room she had requested.

The shower was all that was in the room, which had glass on two sides, the others were the internal walls of the villa.

'How cool is that? Two-way glass: we can see out,' Ed said, 'but no one can see in. I like that idea!' He started to kiss her neck and undid her bra. He could feel her skin was hot. 'Wow, Lottie, you are on fire. You have not even been in the sun for any length of time yet, you feeling OK?' he asked, putting his hand on her forehead.

'Yes, just warm from the trip, I will be OK after a cooling shower,' she said.

'You make sure that you keep a hat on all holiday, I don't want you to get ill,' he said.

'Yes, Mother!' She smiled at him. 'Maybe you could pay more attention to my neck here.' She pointed. 'You may be able to kiss it better?' She bit her lip, knowing it would be an instant draw for him.

'Incorrigible Miss Jenkins.' He kissed and sucked at her neck.

With no shower walls to support her, he laid her on the floor, with the warm water flowing over his back. His large frame stopped her getting wet, but the floor was hard. He jumped up and put a towel down; although it got wet, it just took the harshness of the floor tiles. He started to kiss her from her head to her toes. As he moved she gasped as the water finally reached her. It was cool and refreshing. He placed his head between her legs and led his tongue to the spot that was still warm. He put his hands under her backside and lifted her up to his face. His nose pressed down on her sweet stop, while his tongue licked and pushed on her labia, sending pulsing nerve waves down her spine. She slowly gasped as she could feel the start of her orgasm, and he dug his tongue into her deeper. Using both hands to feel for her breasts, he pulled at the hard nipples. She noted that they were tender and very responsive to his touch, as if they were attached to her inner core. She started to push towards his mouth in urgent waves to feel him deeper. He pulled back and said. 'What's wrong, Miss Jenkins, in a hurry?'

'Yes,' she gasped out.

'I am not sure you should have all the fun on day one: we have a lot more time here to enjoy, you know.' He put her down and started to rub her with his hand, resisting the urge to put his fingers in where his tongue had just been. He pulled himself up and kissed her: she could taste herself on him.

'Tell me what you want, Miss Jenkins,' he whispered in her ear, biting the lip after he had spoken.

'You,' Lottie said. 'This.' She wrapped her hands around his fully erect shaft and rubbed from tip to head, squeezing as she did and making it turn dark purple with the constricted blood. Ed sucked in air through his teeth and he pulled her hand away. 'Oh, Lottie give me a chance to make it last!' he pleaded with her as he pushed his way between her legs. The floor was hard on his knees, so he pulled at the towel. He entered her, lifting her legs up with her ankles on his shoulders, the water running down him onto her, or missing her and hitting his back as he thrust in and out of her.

The angle of her legs was such that every time he pushed her G-spot was hit by his large head, and she gasped. He landed forwards, taking the weight on his hands; she was supple enough to be able to keep her legs where they were and she was bent double underneath him. He felt her sex tighten and constrict around him: he knew she would come soon, her chest was red and her breathing fast, restricted due to her lack of movement she had from this position. He held her hips to get better traction from her as they were both wet. It was almost an instant command to make her release: as she did she screamed out, as if in pain.

'Baby girl, you OK?' he asked, stopping moving.

'Don't stop, don't stop!' she yelled, indicating the scream was of pain, but in a manner that she enjoyed. He began to thrust again, sorry that he had spoilt her moment, but she soon picked his pace back up. She wanted to finish what he had started, so she pushed him backwards. 'Lie down, I want to suck you,' she said and he showed no hesitation.

She knelt above him and took him in her mouth. He filled her and she tried to move up and down his whole length without getting any water in her mouth. Her hair wrapped around him like long ivy around the base of a tree. As she moved up and down the gentle glide of her hair tickled his ball sack and added to the feeling that he was pulsating in her mouth and he would soon lose himself to her. He bucked his hips up out of rhythm and he hit the back of her throat. She gagged but tried to carry on: it brought tears to her eyes which mixed with the water already falling. She steadied herself as she knew this was it: he came with force and she swallowed as hard as she could. The strong salt tasted of him, some had leaked onto her lips and she licked it as she released him from her grip. He looked up at her wiping him from her mouth with her tongue and his dick thrust again, jetting the last drops out onto her thigh.

'That is fucking sexy, watching you lick myself off your face, almost as bad as the biting the lip thing you have going on.' He pulled up to kiss her: he could taste his own salt and he licked her lips to mix the taste with her. 'I will remember this whenever you lick your lips again.' He kissed her softly. 'Although I have a feeling I will remember every second of this holiday. Lottie, I love you so much, thank you for saying you wanted me to come with you.'

'Thank you for coming with me, in more ways than one!' she joked. 'I love you, too!' She planted a kiss on his lips, it was a bit strange but they just lay on the floor in each other's arms for a moment, with the overhead jet of water falling down on them like a cascading waterfall, in their own private room.

The evening meal had been quick: everyone was exhausted, and they said their goodnights and went to their own accommodation.

Lottie lay in bed. She heard Ed chatting to one of the butlers, but she was not sure who. She relaxed and found sleep soon took her before he came to bed.

As the sun rose, Ed looked out to sea. She slept in his arms; she had not woken when he got into bed, just as she had not woken as he now crept out. He was grateful for the hour he had to finalise arrangements. She paddled into the open room, feeling the cool floor on her bare feet. Ed was reading a book, sitting with coffee and a finished grapefruit.

'Morning, Miss, tea is on the way, what can I get you to eat?' Alf asked, and she turned to see the array of food he had on offer. 'Mr Dean had a full English, can I do you the same? It will take me ten minutes only.'

'Oh no, fruit would be fine,' she said as he put her tea down in front of her. She picked it up and walked out to Ed who was just in shorts lying in the sun, his hair rough and damp, as if he had been swimming. She kissed him as he looked up at her.

'Don't you get eating full English every day, or you will be charged extra baggage on the way home!' She sat on the edge of his sunbed and poked at his stomach that was rock-solid.

'You will keep me trim, I'm sure!' He smiled and licked his lips as if remembering their first night's shower. 'Either that or I will need to swim to that far island every morning before you get up.'

'Did you really go that far?' she asked.

'Yep!' He rubbed her leg. 'You need some cream on if you are going to sit here.'

'Miss,' Alf said as he presented with a tray of fruit.

'I will sit inside, thank you, out of the sun.' She tapped his nose. 'Just to keep you happy!' He put down his book and wandered in to her, pinching one of her strawberries. Once he had finished it, she pulled the stalk of another and passed it over. He let her feed him, and she kissed him as he put it in his mouth.

The holiday continued in the same sort of vein: Lottie slept in, he swam, they ate, met the others, walked, lay around in the sun, ate, walked more etc. The only time they were out of eyeshot was when Ed took out the boat, with the others on-board. Lottie and Ed's mother stayed firmly on the sand, but they could hear the squeals of Lynne's boys as they crashed through the waves and could see the boat dashing side to side in the clear, tranquil sea. It was the Saturday a week in and the same sort of day occurred: Ed was up and swimming before she got out of bed. They ate breakfast and went to the spot on the beach to get the boat out.

After half an hour of crashing around they came closer to the beach and moored the boat. They could see Ed swimming with the boys, or jumping in off the boat with them. His mum looked over her sunglasses to Lottie. 'I have never seen him so happy, and I have you to thank for that.'

Lottie looked up at them and smiled. 'I wonder who the bigger kid is?' she said, seeing he was having just as much fun as the boys.

'I was hesitant at first about the timing of the holiday, but I am glad we are away, today of all days. Ed often goes astray on the anniversary of his brother's death. It hit him hard, but today he seems to be happy.'

'I'm sorry, I never thought. I mean, Ed had mentioned Mitch, but never gone into details. I knew it was around this time of year, but I would not have booked for now if I thought it should be a private time.'

'We never forget him, no matter where we are, and he would be overjoyed to see you two like this. He really wanted to settle down, that's why it hit us so hard that he seemed to go off the rails the day of the...' She stopped, not even bringing herself to say the words.

'I'm sorry,' Lottie said as a natural reaction.

'Look at him. I'm not dwelling on the past, not today, or this holiday. It was just Ed tried to get to the bottom of it all, but just got nowhere. Has he ever asked you to… No, I'm sorry, I should not presume he would…' She stopped talking, but Lottie guessed what she was getting at. 'Sorry, it is just with your line of work, I wondered if he ever talked about it.'

'No, as I said, we have skipped over it mostly, I have never pushed. I know how hard it is to lose someone and, well, I guess that he respects the findings that were given at the time: hard to do, I suppose.' It had to be faced sometimes that accidents happened. That sometimes the truth was hard to face, another reason why they never talked about it.

His mother just looked and smiled and continued to read her book. When the boat came in, Lottie got up and waded into the sea. Ed dived into the water from the jetty and swam over to her. He waded into the water, holding her up. 'I'm exhausted, these kids have so much energy!' She gave him a kiss and she could taste the ocean on his lips.

'I love you, Mr Dean.' She hugged him tight. If he wanted to talk about it, he could, but she would not push the subject. He smiled at her. Only for one more day, Miss Jenkins! he wanted to say, meaning that after that he would have to say 'Mrs Dean'. 'I love you, too, baby girl.' He dunked her in the water and she playfully splashed him as she spluttered to the surface. 'Edward!' She scolded him as she came up for air. 'What?' He splashed her again and she dived and grabbed him by his feet, trying to knock him over. She came off worse of course, with another dunking for her efforts once she had surfaced.

He paced the floor just gone 1am. He could not sleep. If he had to ask if everything was set one more time, Agnes had said Lottie would know that something was wrong. He had checked the rings at least twice since she had come to bed. What if she does not want to go through with it? What am I going to do if it all goes wrong? he thought to himself. He hated that he could not control her reactions, or even predict them. 'She will be fine once it sinks in,' Agnes had said. He had asked her the same question the day before, and the day before that!

Lottie stirred in the bed and could feel he was not there. She looked around in the moonlight to see if she could see him. She blinked to try to see outside, and made out the top of his head over the chair on the decking. He had a glass of whiskey in his hand and as she reached down to kiss his head: she could smell the sweet liquor.

'Sorry, did I wake you?' He tapped his knee for her to sit on him.

'No.' She smiled in return. 'Your mum told me about, you know...' She stopped short of saying Mitch's anniversary.

He pulled back. 'What do you mean?' He panicked. 'How dare she?'

'Well, it affects her, too,' she said. 'Don't be hard on her. I did not want to say anything yesterday just in case.'

'In case what? I flew off at her? She had no right to tell you.' He swigged his drink down.

'She misses him, too,' Lottie said and Ed looked confused. 'The date of...' Again she stopped. Somehow it was hard to say, even for her, as if she had known him. 'His death,' she finished.

Ed dropped to the same page with a thud, so loud he was sure that she heard it. 'Sorry,' he said, almost glad it was just the anniversary date. He had not forgotten. He had tried to react differently this year, maybe that and the other reason was why he could not sleep.

'I guess that is why you are out here alone?' Lottie asked.

'Maybe,' he said, 'I tried to overcome it...' He started. 'I did not want to dwell, others here have lost so much it seems selfish just to focus on my loss...' She rubbed his face with her hand and he kissed her fingers as they passed his mouth.

'It is because we have all lost that we would respect your behaviour, your grieving and your loss. No one expects any of us to forget, I never wanted to say anything as I think you need to be happy with your feelings before I probe into them. If you had wanted to talk to me, I know that you would, you said you would not have secrets and lie to me, and I believe you don't anymore: that's how much we have grown together.'

He hated himself because she was right: he had promised and, although the biggest secret would be out in just a few hours, once more Lottie could see the good side to everything. He hoped she kept those thoughts after breakfast in the morning.

'If you need to sit here and have a drink alone, then please do.' She took his glass to fill it again.

'Stay with me then,' he said, 'let me tell you about him.' She grabbed a bottle of water and a light sheet from the bed. It was not cold but she thought of anything eating her alive while they sat outside. She shared the seat with him and settled down to hear some of the stories of their childhood. Almost an hour passed and he finally said: 'We need to sleep.' He kissed her cheek.

'We don't have to be up in the morning for anything special.' He picked her up and carried her inside. Oh yes, we do, he said to himself.

'I know, but there will be other times to remember him.' He put her down on the bed and they picked up the same position they had adopted on the lounger outside. This time the air conditioning was cool, keeping the bugs away, and he pulled the sheets over them to give them some warmth.

She woke as normal: he had gone. She looked out to the sea but could not see him swimming. After finishing in the bathroom, she wandered out to the lounge. Gerald was making breakfast and she willingly drank the tea that was placed ready for her. Ed was not eating, or sitting around the pool.

'Where is Mr Dean?' she asked.

'There was something at the reception he needed to collect: he has walked over.' Gerald never stopped making the food that he then gave to Lottie. She heard the door to the apartment close and she looked eager to welcome Ed, but it was Agnes.

'Morning,' she said very cheerily. She was asked if she wanted anything by the butler, and was served her request. 'Not much sleep last night?' she asked, looking at how pale Lottie looked.

'We did talk for some time,' Lottie said, putting some of the toast in her mouth.

'That's what you youngsters call it these days!' Agnes replied with a smile.

'Shocking! No, we really did talk.' She put her hand over her mouth as the toast was not going down well.

'Are you sure you're OK?' her friend asked again just as Ed walked back in the door.

'Morning,' he said, walking round to kiss Lottie who smiled at him, but needed to be excused. She walked quickly to the bathroom.

'Is she OK?' Ed asked Agnes.

'She said so; she still does not know anything, I take it?' Ed shook his head. 'Good, so I will stay here, have you got it?' He nodded again. 'Are you sure that you want me to tell her?' He nodded for the last time, grabbed a small bag that had been placed by the door, and went out.

It was about twenty minutes when Lottie returned. She looked more drained than she did before.

'Now I am worried,' her friend said, putting her hand to her head and feeling if she was too hot.

'Too much sun, I think, or last night's seafood taking hold!' Lottie took some water from the small fridge.

'You need ginger, Miss, good for upset stomachs out here.' He set to and made a small cocktail of ginger and lime. Lottie sipped it and she screwed her nose up at the taste. 'It does not taste too good, but will work a wonder,' Gerald told her in a bid to get her to drink the rest.

'Has Ed gone again?' she asked, reluctant to drain the rest of the mixture.

'Lottie.' Agnes took a deep breath. 'I want to show you something.' She stood her up and hoped that the item had been left as arranged. She held out her hand and led her to the bedroom. Gerald had been in and tidied round, and there was a large bag and items scattered on the silk sheets. 'Now,' her friend began, 'take a deep breath,' she directed to Lottie who was looking confused, her own hands shaking.

'Edward has left you this.' She held up the bag and started to open it. Inside a long, cream, silk halter neck dress revealed itself. Crystal details around the bust and along the hemline made it shine in the sun. 'He wants you to put it on and meet him on the beach at 10:30: we have just over half an hour.'

'I don't understand, Aggie, what's he playing at?' She took the dress and admired how soft and light it was.

'He has arranged for us all to be there, and well, you're getting married!' She looked at her to get the first signs of a reaction.

'Get away, you are joking with me, right?!' Lottie replied, putting down the dress. 'Say you are joking with me!'

'He arranged it all, knowing we would all be here. In fact, he has even asked a few people to come out here just for today: they arrived in the night. He has arranged the whole thing since you mentioned wanting to come away.' She could see that Lottie had tears in her eyes, but could not tell if this was a good or a bad sign. 'Can you say something?' Agnes asked. Lottie sat on the bed. She was not sure if she would be sick again or faint.

'I don't understand. He never said a word, in fact we arranged an engagement party for when we got home, and he knew this all along. I'm angry he did not share it with me. In fact, I am fuming as he knew I wanted to get married in Kent, where Mum and Dad are at the village church.' She wiped her face because she was crying now. 'How could he do it without asking? He is so controlling,' she asked her friend who was sitting by her side hugging her now.

'He wanted to surprise you. We all have kept it from you, Lottie. It's not lying, just a small secret with a happy ending. The party you are talking about is going ahead, and I'm sorry but he was going to tell you this.' She paused. 'You will be getting blessed at the church. He knew how important that was to you so when we get back you can go to the church and be with...' She stopped because Dick was also buried in the churchyard. 'He's not controlling, it's a really romantic gesture.' She got up and went to Ed's wardrobe and pulled out another bag. It had a pretty floral dress that she held up to herself, 'Am I putting this on or not?' she asked her friend directly.

'So, you all knew, and it's the only reason you're all here?' Lottie was cross and it showed in her voice. 'You have all lied to me every day we have been here?' She stood up and walked out onto the decking.

'It's not the only reason we are here. You asked us all and each one of us had said yes, before he explained the plans.' Agnes had joined her outside. 'I knew that you would be shocked, but I guessed that you would want to do it, once the idea had set in.'

'Well, maybe I don't!' She walked back inside and closed the bathroom door. Agnes heard the lock snap in the clasp. Oops, she thought, not in his plans! 'Lottie, open the door!' She did not reply.

Lottie heard the front door close and came out of the bathroom. She walked out of the apartment and sat on the beach looking out to sea. Gerald came to her.

'May I?' He asked if he could sit with her and she said yes.

'It must be a shock, I'm sorry that we all had to keep it from you. We were all asked to make it a surprise for you, but I see you are upset.'

'It's not your fault; to be honest I should have expected it. Mr Dean seems to get his own way with everything, and I'm sorry for reacting a bit like a child but…' She stopped. 'I guess Agnes has gone to fetch him? So that he can persuade me. I do want to marry him, it was the point of saying yes.' She looked at her hand where the large rock gleamed in the sun.

'It's a lot to deal with in the space of an hour?' Gerald added. 'I am, was, married since we were eighteen years old. I came to work here when I was 21 and I did not see my wife for six months of every year. I worked as much as I could and sent the money home to make a better life and one day a family. Two years ago, I went home and she… had gone. No one let me know. She had been ill and passed without me knowing. But I am not sorry, I was happy to have known her and called her my wife for the short time we had. I would not change it. We were as one, and I guess that Mr Dean wants you, that he also needs to be at one with you. It is most special for a man to call his lover his wife.'

Lottie looked at the man: she could only guess he was as young if not younger than her. She had a great sadness in her heart for his loss. 'I'm sorry, my worries are nothing compared to yours.'

'You have to take every moment, Miss, you never know when it will change: if it is right, then today you two become as one, and only you know it is right.' His gentle smile warmed her. 'I will carry on working and one day I may be lucky again to feel such joy, maybe go to another country and find a life. If it is meant to be it will happen for sure.'

Lottie asked him to go and meet up with Ed: she knew Agnes or both of them would be on the way back. She started to get ready.

'Sorry, Ed, she just lost it and locked herself away in the bathroom,' Agnes explained to him, breathing heavily as she had rushed down to the beach where everything was set up. 'I'll go back if you want me to, but maybe you can talk to her.'

'Shit, yes, it had crossed my mind this would happen, but I hoped it would not. Shit!' He looked at everyone else who had gathered. 'Don't make a fuss, just keep everyone entertained. If I'm not back, please come and get me within half an hour. I hope it does not get to that.' He pulled off his jacket and started to make his way back to the accommodation. He was met along the path by Gerald who explained their conversation.

'Good man, you are a life-saver. I owe you,' Ed said, shaking his hand. 'Oh God, thank you!' He rushed back to Agnes and gave her the thumbs-up.

'Touch and go, then?' the voice asked him and he turned around. Todd had been invited over, and when he knew the ticket was paid for, said he would be able to make it. Pete and Mrs B had also been flown in, and were sitting together on one of the white chairs that had been put out.

'Never a doubt!' Ed lied, wanting everyone to know it was all going to plan.

He adjusted his jacket it was hot. The thin, cotton, beige trousers and cream tee shirt were really smart casual. The red flower, picked from the tree outside their room, gave it a glimpse of colour. He had hand-picked them himself before the sun had come up. Lottie had a large bunch of them to hold, to go with her dress, and a single one that Gerald had placed on a hair clasp. He kicked the sand with his bare feet. He could feel the sweat running down his back: was it hot, or was it nerves? His mother came up to him and kissed his cheek.

'Well, I hope that you are not rushing this for any other reason than you love her?'

'What other reasons would there be? I do, truly,' he replied, kissing his mother back on the cheek.

'Then all is well, my beautiful boy.' She squeezed his hand and he showed her to her seat. He sat next to her, momentarily rubbing his hands nervously.

Agnes walked into her room and looked at the vision in cream. 'Wobble over?' she asked.

'Yes, although I can't say I'm not still a bit annoyed, but this dress is divine.' She smoothed it over her hips, noticing that it showed all her curves.

She brushed over her stomach, pulling it in.

'Don't even think you have put on weight, you look stunning.' Agnes complimented her, picking up the hairpiece and putting it in. She had her hair down, with the flower tucked behind her ear. 'Bella sent you this.' Lottie opened the box and took out a pale blue garter. The card read:

'My very best wishes, Miss Jenkins. I hope I chose the dress well. Here is a little something for Mr Dean!'

Lottie smiled at the thought of how excited she must have been when he placed the order or went in to see her.

'Now I will give you away today on the understanding...' She paused. 'You do come back to see me, often.'

Lottie hugged her friend. 'Of course, my name changes, but I am still the same person, and you are one of the most dear, dear friends to me.' She felt as if she was going to cry again. 'I guess we need to go?' she asked. Agnes nodded: they were late but it did not matter.

The chairs were set out to create a small isle, and a hoop of flowers set the altar place where they would marry. To the right was nothing but aquamarine sea; above, not a cloud marred the blue sky. Lottie stood looking at the few friends that had gathered and some other guests who had hung around to watch what was going on.

'Ready?' Agnes held her arm. 'Yes,' she replied. She saw Pete and Mrs B, and Todd, and she smiled at them. Her eyes were then drawn to his back: he stood facing away to start off with, and then his mother touched his arm and whispered to him, and he turned around.

She was every bit as stunning as he had imagined and more. The dress was perfect, her hair gently blew in the wind and her smile burned into him. She bit her lip as he smiled back at him. God, if I never remember anything else let it be this day, and I will get that lip under control if it is the last thing

I do! he thought to himself.

Finally standing by his side he took the arm that Agnes was holding and kissed her cheek, gently whispering, 'You are stunning, Miss Jenkins, amazing. Am I forgiven?' It would be the last time he would call her by that name.

'A little, Mr Dean.' She held his eyes and he kissed her again, not caring if the rest of the crowd looked on, or vanished into the vast expanse: it felt like they were alone.

It was done. As they kissed as Mr and Mrs Edward Dean, small petals of flowers were thrown and they laughed and hugged the gathering of friends and family who had witnessed the day. Lottie was amazed to see Mrs B and Pete, and also Todd. They had chatted via Skype but she really wanted to catch up with him: he seemed to be having a great time in America.

Ed never left her side, as if the ring on his finger was bound somehow to her waist. They had photos, passed amongst their friends chatting, and took time to admire the view in the sun. Then they had a formal sit-down meal. Lottie had never seen so much food. The whole island seemed to have come out to celebrate with them as the sun set and they continued to celebrate into the night. It was after 1am when Ed carried her all the way to the apartment, her head on his shoulder: she was totally spent, exhausted with the day. He stood her by the bed, brushing all of the flowers and cushions out of the way. He had told her so many times throughout the day how stunning she was; he had kissed her and held her, but there was time for one more opportunity to say it.

'Mrs Dean, I love you.' He kissed her while she stood with her eyes closed, saying it felt good. 'Come here, baby girl, let's get you into bed.' He unzipped the dress as it fell to the floor she stepped out of it. He noticed the blue garter. 'Maybe something for breakfast,' he said, referring to the fact that she was just so tired he wanted her to sleep. He bent down and took off her lace underwear, kissing her hips and stomach as he came back up. He noticed her small stomach just pushing out and hoped that she would continue to put back on the weight that she had lost when Dick had died. He kissed her stomach again, holding her backside to steady her.

He needed to stop or she would not get any sleep. He took off his own clothes and they got into bed. He listened for her breathing as she fell asleep. He had finally got her: he tracked the line of her necklace, and she had not taken it off all holiday. He looked at her hand and held it with his own, comparing the rings that were identical and inscribed inside with 'Neverending love'. The world was good for him, for now.

With a few days left of the holiday, which was now part of their honeymoon, Lottie and the group enjoyed each other's company and the sun, but it was all too soon to return to the reality of everyday life.

Chapter 19

They had been home for two days and Ed had been asked to go Paris for a meeting. He wanted Lottie to go, but since returning, she needed to sort some of the issues out with the plans for the charity hospital; she may even need to visit the site. As it was midweek she was sure that she should cope overnight, if he had to stay away.

'I can get Phil to drive me: we will not even be apart for 24 hours, and it will be over sooner than you know. Maybe if you made it Thursday we could meet back up and have the weekend in Kent, just to see how the house is and check everything is OK there for next week. I need to make a decision on the house soon: if we don't seem to spend much time there, someone needs to look after it,' she said as they ate breakfast – well, Ed ate and she drank her tea.

'Do I suspect that there is a cunning plan coming in here, Mrs Dean?' He tried to use her married name as much as he could: it still had a certain ring to it.

'Well, you know you said you owe Gerald a favour for his persuasive chat?' She continued to ask if he could come over and be employed to look after Lottie's family home when they were not there, like a housekeeper. Lottie had really bonded with him after the wedding day, and, although some may see it as taking a job away from someone over here, he showed the potential to be a great asset to them.

'I need Pete to do some digging: it's not that easy to get someone a visa,' Ed explained and looked at her. She gave him the puppy-eyed look and he finished. 'But I will look into it if it makes you feel better.'

'I don't want to sell the place, but I can't help but worry about it being broken into or becoming neglected,' she replied. 'After all, it is somewhere nice to get away to, our second home.'

He smiled at her, the fact that she had said 'our second home'.

'Well, technically it is my fourth!' he smirked and she stuck out her tongue at him. He then corrected himself. 'Our fourth.'

She went back into the bedroom and started to get dressed. She pulled her trousers up and pulled the button that she was struggling to do up. Ed smiled at her. 'So you blamed me for eating too much on holiday. Don't say that now you are married you are going to let yourself go, Mrs Dean!' He grabbed her by the waist and kissed her neck. He was more than happy that since they had been home she looked healthy, with a tan and not looking so pale. It had done her some good.

'Maybe I don't get the right type of exercise?' she smirked back. Within a shot he pinned her to the wall and kissed her on the mouth.

'Really? Well, last night I seemed to think you were busy working off the calories.' She struggled against his powerful frame.

'I'm already late,' she said, referring to her appointment with the Music School Scholars. 'Edward, please.' She laughed as he tickled her. 'Edward!' She raised her voice again, with as stern a tone as she could. He huffed at her and let her go.

'Just this once, then, I will let you go,' he said. 'I'll ask Pete to wait for you, he can drop you off first and then come back when you are ready if you like.' He walked out of the room, and she quickly sat on the bed. Her own words sprang back to her and she looked at herself in the mirror.

Oh God, she thought, I can't be late.

Ed opened the door for her at the steps of the college. They said their goodbyes and kissed. As the car drove off she tried to focus on why she was there, but her train of thought had gone.

She had taken her pill, apart from the birthday incident, and the week after Brighton. She had taken two months' worth, well with a few missed, but put the packs back to back without stopping: that was all it would be, a couple of days and she would be on. She just had a swollen stomach, and the pain in her boobs, just tender from this, surely.

She walked in the college and met her intended member of staff. The meeting took up until lunch, when she knew Pete would be expecting her call. She Googled the closest chemist's to where she was and set out for a short walk. She nervously looked around her to see if anyone was looking and then purchased the test. Quickly putting it in her bag, she went back to the college steps and called Pete to collect her to go home.

'Mr Dean has asked me to take you to the office, if that is OK. He wondered if you would like to look through a proposal,' Pete said as he helped her into the car.

'Oh, er yes, I suppose so.' She had really wanted to get home to do the test, but it would have to wait.

Ed had made plans while they were away to change his office around to allow her to have a permanent space. Although she had every intention of going back to work at the DuPont Centre, she did spend time working on the charities, her own properties inherited from her mother, and now the scholarships, so it would help.

It was an identical-size room, made up from splitting his office in half. It was divided by glass panels, which could be pulled back just to make one room if required, but would give privacy if required.

'I just thought it would get you out of the apartment office.' And I can see you, and know where you are, he thought to himself. 'It can be me and you against the business world now, no one else.'

'Thank you, that's really sweet for you to do this.' She walked over to his desk. He had placed a photo of them getting married on the beach and she picked it up. He walked over to her and put his hands around her waist and squeezed her, kissing her neck.

'Are you looking forward to next Saturday?' he asked.

'Yes.' She leaned back against him. She was not thinking of the blessing and the party that had been arranged for the following week in the village church, or the large marquee that was going in her garden and the guest list that seemed to be growing. She was wondering if she was pregnant and, if she was, how the hell was she going to tell him?

They stayed in the office for a few hours and did not go straight back to the apartment, as Ed decided to go for a meal out.

'Anywhere, I don't mind,' she replied when he asked her. So he directed Pete and she was surprised that they turned up at the Tap and Tune. She smiled when they arrived, and her spirits were lifted when she hugged Scotty who was on shift.

'Hi Lotts, congratulations!' he said. 'Here, Shelley, get some champagne out over here, my treat!' He shook Ed's hand and passed on his congratulations to him, too. They sat down at a seat in the bar. The room was busy with commuters having a drink before going home, or couples having their evening meal. Scotty poured two glasses, and after being offered one by Ed, he poured his own.

'The happy couple,' he said, raising his glass to theirs. Some of the other bar goers looked over, and made conversation on the celebration; others continued to talk amongst themselves. 'Don't tell the boss we are drinking the profits!' He laughed and Lottie smiled at him. 'I'm supposed to get to meet him tonight, so keep your eyes peeled for the mystery shopper!' he said with sarcasm in his voice. Ed smiled to himself.

'I hope you are coming next week,' she asked, referring to the blessing 'And Sarah and Bob?'

'Sure thing: we are all coming over together and then staying in a guest house in the village.' He told her which one.

'Well, I will make sure Annie knows, and you're not to pay, that's one of mine,' she said and they chatted for a while on the coincidence of that. Scotty was needed and they were left alone.

'Well, Mrs Dean, I can see I the need to teach you some business techniques: if you are going to give free stays out in your accommodation how are you ever going to make a profit?'

'Maybe I don't want to make a profit as long as Annie gets paid and the accommodation is kept in good order.' She sipped her drink quite mindful now that if she was pregnant she could have done all sorts of damage to the baby. She had drunk on holiday and taken her pills: would that have an effect? Ed was talking to her, but she was lost in her world of the unknown and she started to feel quite faint. She went pale. Ed stopped talking to her and asked, 'Lottie, are you OK?' He held her hand. 'You seem miles away.'

'Sorry.' She gathered herself: she could be worried about nothing. 'I'm hungry, and the bubbles have gone to my head. Shall we order?'

When the food arrived she ate a small amount, but her stomach was still churning. She was not prepared for the next bombshell Ed was about to drop.

'Lottie, I have to tell you my confession: it has played on my mind for a long time now,' he started and she looked at him with some concern. Had he guessed?

'I own the bar!' He just thought that the straightforward answer was the best way. 'I bought it months ago because...' He paused as this was the bit that was going to hurt. 'I saw you playing the piano and overheard it was for sale. You took my breath away and I had an instant reaction. I kept it from you, well, for God knows what reason, events just sort of took us over and…' He stopped talking. Her face had not changed expression. She was not running off, that was a good start, but he was unsure how she had taken it. 'Any thoughts, want to throw something at me, hopefully not the knife,' he said, looking at the implement in her hand, but trying to make light of the facts. 'Earth to Lottie, did you just get that revelation?'

'Yes,' she said slowly. It was clicking into place. The night, the day after with flowers. The comment on the card.

'So, you have kept it from me all this time that you brought me a drink in the hotel, and then…' She stopped herself short. 'Oh, I get it now, you had me followed here?' There was no anger in her tone.

'Not quite followed, but I knew you were here the next night.' He was amazed she was staying so calm.

'And the flowers the next day?'

'Guilty Your Honour, and sadly even Scotty got the rough business end as I threatened to sack him if you did not play at the bar. It was the only way at the time I thought I could see you again.' He watched as she rubbed her forehead, closing her eyes momentarily, thinking.

'Is sorry enough? I needed to come clean, Lottie. I respect you too much to go back on my word to keep things from you. This was one that I knew I had held onto for too long, but I just did not know how to tell you or how you would react.' He was getting worried as she was not reacting.

She heard his words, in fact they played back over in her head. 'Did not know how to tell you or how you would react.' That was the problem with secrets: somehow they come out. She had to tell him.

'I'm…' Her mouth closed. Don't be stupid, Lottie, you don't know yet, she told herself. She carried on 'I'm…' She stopped again.

'What? Angry, pissed off with me? You have every right to be.' He held her hand over the table.

She took a deep breath. 'I'm glad you told me, eventually!'

Ed's breath seemed deeper than hers. 'I wanted to tell you last time we were here and everyone was guessing and throwing accusations around, some of which I guess I deserve for not being honest, even with the staff.' He filled up his glass. Lottie put her hand over hers: she did not want any more. He put his hand in his pocket and pulled out an envelope.

'Here are the deeds and the contracts. They have all been changed to your name, Mrs Dean. You are now the owner, it's my wedding gift to you, and confirmation that I will not hold anything back again from you.' He smiled. 'I love you so much, nothing will change that: remember it is just me and you, we need no one else.'

She looked at the documents, still not really taking in what he was saying.

'I am happy to explain to Scotty.' Ed looked up to beckon him over.

'No, no,' Lottie said focusing back to the here and now. 'Thank you for being honest.' She started to relay the events that came from that night and her receiving the flowers. Ed was really shocked that he caused her the pain of thinking she had a stalker and that she was put off working there for that very reason. 'If it is controlled through your letting company, do we have to tell him?' she asked.

'No, but...' He was about to say it was a lie.

'It's not the truth, granted, it is just not all the facts,' Lottie said. 'As long as we know, is that all that matters?' She smiled at him. 'And as a gift, it is a very nice one, now that I know it was how we began.'

'Mrs Dean, the ever-forgiving person strikes again.' He leaned over the table and kissed her.

They arrived back at the apartment and Ed took some calls so that he was ready to leave early in the morning. He was due to land in Paris for 10am, so that he could be back to meet up in Kent for an evening meal at least. Lottie was going with Phil to Derbyshire, but it was only for a short meeting: she would be back before him, she hoped.

Lottie kept looking at her bag but could not bring herself to get it and do the test. She went in the bathroom and closed the door; it was only seconds before he knocked and asked if he could come in. She turned on the shower and made the excuse she was having a shower, but this was not enough of a deterrent to keep him out.

'Need a hand?' he said with a mischievous smile. He started to help her unbutton her blouse and he gently kissed and caressed her neck. She placed her head on his shoulder and allowed him to feel her. She was receptive to his touch: even with her head on other things, he could bring her out to realise her need and her own arousal. He quickly stripped and they got into the warm flow of the water. Using her scented gel, he rubbed the sponge over her, massaging the muscles in her back and neck that seemed so tight. As he ran his hands over her nipples, she tensed as they were tender. 'Sorry,' he said, easing his grip on them.

His hand slipped between her legs and she almost wanted to stop him, but a carnal desire was forcing other thoughts from her head. With one hand he reached for her soft, inner sex and massaged; she gave a pleasing groan and he stood in front of her, kissing all the way back up.

His swollen erection pushed against her stomach and she reached down to him, feeling the length and the power he had as he twitched in response. He dropped the sponge and continued to rub bath oils into her shoulders. She rubbed him from root to tip, gently working the water along his ball sack and the upper part of his legs.

He flexed his core muscles as she touched a tender part of his dick, and sucked in air, letting out a moan of pleasure. She was transfixed on his muscles in his shoulders as he continued to plunge his fingers into her, creating their own warm, wet area.

'You're so warm,' he said. 'I want you so badly, Mrs Dean.' He pulled up and kissed her nipples, lingering around the soft, dark tissue. She had been able to sunbathe topless a few times, but he had insisted she kept her top on where anyone would see her, so the pale, white mounds were prominent as her skin became darker-looking with the addition of the water. He turned her round and she faced the wall. He looked at the line of soap trailing down her spine and to the cleft of her backside. He tracked it with his fingers from her necklace to her hole. She gasped as he gently rubbed it as he reached under her to find her sex again. She leaned against the wall as he started to ease himself into her, using his hand to guide his way. Once the tip of his engorged dick was resting just inside her, he stepped forwards, putting his hand round to feel her chest.

They felt firm and warm in his hands and he rubbed the nipple between his thumb and finger. Slowly he pushed and he could feel her tightness enlarge to accommodate him. She lifted slightly onto her tiptoes, and he felt her internal angle alter. He could not wait for her: his thrust pushed her forwards and he had to hold her to stop her hitting her head on the wall.

'Arh!' she cried out. 'Ed!' she gasped. He came within the moment, watching her backside hit against him as he pushed her up and down his length.

'Sorry, baby girl, I could not wait.' He put his head on her back and slowly withdrew. 'It's because I will miss you.'

He never noticed the small amount of blood that flowed quickly into the water. Lottie still had her eyes closed.

'Stay there, baby, I'm going now,' he said fully dressed, showered and ready to go. She had moved when she felt him get up; she had been lying on her stomach and she felt like she had PMT or stomach cramps. Maybe she would not have to do this after all. She dozed and found sleep again for a short time. The door closed and he said goodbye to Mrs B, who must have been in already.

She sat up. Come on get this over with, she said to herself as she slid from the sheets and went to the sitting room. She hurried to her bag and took it back with her. The eagle-eyed Mrs B shouted through that she would put the kettle on, and Lottie replied with a 'Thanks!'

She sat on the loo and opened the pack. Having never done one of these before, she quickly skimmed the instructions. She followed them to the letter, holding the thin, white stick until she was happy the task was competed. She carried on sitting there with her eyes closed as she counted to one hundred. As if a monster was sitting next to her, she did dare not open her eyes. When she did, she felt the world stop.

Was it disappointment or joy she felt as her stomach turned? The hairs on her arms stood up and she felt like she had stopped breathing.

She double-checked the instructions to make sure that she was reading it right. The blue line was for positive and the indicator will say how many weeks. No blue line not a positive result.

She looked again at the indicator stick. There was the blue line and 11–13 weeks showed next to it. So, she was pregnant.

She sat, looking at it, thinking that if it faded it would be wrong. But it did not. No need to ask how this could have happened: she had gone over it in her head before. Timing was the missed pills the day before and after she went with Todd, after their first lovers' tiff. Turned out her little wobble would have a long-lasting effect after all.

So, if it was right, why did she have such stomach pains? Were her breasts supposed to be so tender? It was only under three months, if that. She knew nothing about how much she would be affected by the fact that she had continued to take the pill, quite recklessly, now she thought. What about all the drinking: could that affect the baby? The feeling sick and being off food made sense now. She stood up and looked at herself sideways in the mirror. Was she really developing that quickly? Was that possible to see or was that her imagination? What about sex? Would that affect the baby? 'The baby,' she said out loud as if to make it seem real.

There was a gentle knock at the door. 'Mrs Dean, your tea is getting cold.'

Lottie wiped her face and looked at herself in the mirror. God, she even looked different, she was sure. 'Yes, I'll be there in a moment, just washing up.' She turned the tap on to make out that she was, but she kept both hands on the side of the bowl and looked at her own image.

Oh God, how do I tell him? When do I say something? Now, on the phone, tomorrow, never? Maybe I can find a... She paused. The thought of getting rid of her, their baby. But it was there in her mind. We are not ready, I am not ready, she continued in her head. How am I going to be able to go to the doctor's without him finding out? Could I face doing it alone?

Another knock on the door. 'Lottie, love, are you OK?' Mrs B had only ever called her that once before. She always remained quite stern and professional towards her, maybe thinking at first that she would not be around in Ed's life for too long, so best not to build any relationship, but since the wedding she had seemed less hard-faced towards her.

'Sorry, finding it hard to get started this morning!' Lottie called back. She splashed her face again and used the towel to dry it. She wiped her face again, but still the same face and voices in her head asked her the same questions.

She walked into the bedroom and went straight to the wardrobe, so as not to make eye contact.

'Phil wanted to know what time you want to go to Kent?' She was making the bed as she talked to her. 'And Mr Dean phoned and said you did not pick up, so he called me. I said you were in the shower. He said he would call later, after he gets off the flight.'

'Thanks, Mrs B.' God, even thinking about what to wear was hard work. She pulled out a loose top and jeans, looking at them and wondering if they would fit. They would have to, she thought. Without noticing, Mrs B had busied herself in the usual way, clearing and tidying. Lottie never saw her go to the en suite. She walked back out and Lottie turned around to her. As if telepathy existed she knew she had seen the test, or the box. In her rush she had not put it in her bag to go in the bin.

'Oh, my dear.' Mrs B held out her arms. 'You know, I knew, suspected a few weeks ago something was not right.' Lottie went to her as if a child needed their mother to comfort them and keep the world at bay, even for just a few moments. 'Does Edward know?'

Lottie shook her head. 'No,' and confirmed it through the sobs with 'No, he does not.'

The two women sat on the bed and Mrs B handed Lottie a tissue. 'This is all my fault. We were going so well and I…' She could not get the words out.

'Shush,' Mrs B said. 'Have you just found out?'

'Yes, I messed up on my pills, and seemed to blank out any other signs. I can't tell him, not yet, I don't know what to say. Mrs B, please, I beg you, don't say anything to him. Please you must promise. I want this clear in my head first before…' She stopped.

'Before?' Mrs B asked.

'Everyone will think this was on purpose, but I promise you it was not. I want to do so much more, I want to be so much more before. Don't get me wrong, I am not saying I don't want his children. I'm his wife, if he wants…' She stopped again. 'We have never even talked about it.' She sobbed again. 'It looks like we were rushing to get married, like the paper said. He's going to hate me.'

'One thing Mr Dean will never do is hate you.' She comforted her again. 'He may shout, swear and get a little drunk. He has his own little ways, but he will never hate you: he is in love with you too much, that's so easy to see.' She passed her another tissue. The door went and Phil shouted out that he was there.

Mrs B wandered to him, and Lottie heard her say, 'Make a drink, Phil, Mrs Dean will be ready soon.' She went back in.

'Mrs Dean.' She paused. 'Lottie, make your phone calls, I will pack for you. Go to Kent, see Agnes, talk it through with her, but tell Edward, he needs to know.' And she finished: 'Sooner rather than later.'

This was what she did. Sitting in the car, she talked to Ed, but put on a brave face not saying a word. Once she was with Agnes, she would be able to see a doctor. She would be able to make up an excuse not to be taken there by

Phil, or say they were doing something. She put on her headphones for the car journey and blanked out as much as she could. She used her phone to Google as much information as she could with regard to the damage and possible issues there could be from her taking the pill and drinking in the early stages. She also looked at the implications of abortion. The thought kept popping up in her head: even if it was an unthinkable solution, it was a solution.

Agnes was in the house when they arrived. Phil had phoned Pete who relayed that it had become foggy and the take-off was delayed, asking if he could hang around until they arrived, which looked like it was going to be the early hours of the morning.

While he was talking, Lottie was in the sitting room doing the same. Getting the same information, but with no doubt from someone who was far more pissed off. She tried to cheer him up: she said that her phone would be with her all night and she would call before she went to bed. Phil was still on the phone when Ed hung up, so she went to the car, swung open the boot and grabbed her bags. A shooting pain hit her from her pelvis bone to her spine, and she bent and clutched herself. As soon as she stood up the pain went and, taking a breath, she continued to carry the bags inside.

At every opportunity she tried to talk to Agnes, but it never seemed right. She asked Phil to take a few hours off, she would stay in, just to give him a rest, or to sleep if he wanted. She would wake him when Agnes wanted to go home. The three phone calls from Ed still confirmed he was going to be late, but by any means he would be back before she woke up. 'I will get the bloody train if I have to,' he said to confirm he wanted to be with her. Part of her wanted him to stay away: if she could not tell Agnes, how the hell was she going to tell him?

They ate a meal and went through all the wedding photos; she even got away with crying, Agnes joining her, putting it down to joy, but deep down it was just the opposite. She was doing the very thing she asked people not to: lie.

Phil checked that the doors were locked and had a quick walk around outside before he took Agnes home. She was only five minutes down the road so he was happy that, as he heard the front door lock behind him, Lottie would be OK. She wandered back to the kitchen after putting her phone down in the sitting room, telling Ed she was on her way to bed. He had finally been given a flight time and would be in the air within the hour.

She bent down to fill the dishwasher with the few plates from their meal. The same pain in her stomach pulled again, more violently this time; it made her buckle at the knees and she gasped in agony. The ripping pain came again as she tried to stand, knowing that before this had taken away the pain, but it did not work. Something was not right.

She tapped her pockets for her phone: it was in the other room. As she moved her legs to try to get it, they buckled again with the surge of pain, and she had to grip the worktop, trying not to fall. Although she knew she was alone she shouted out for Phil. The pain spasmed and a cold surge went through her as she used one hand to clutch her side and the other to stand. She gave in to holding herself up and slipped to the floor. Another rack of pain gripped her: she had never felt pain like this before.

She tried to hold her breath. 'Oh God. NO!' she shouted. 'Please not like this, I'm sorry, but not like this.'

As she went into a foetal position on the floor she looked at the top of her leg: it felt warm and damp, as if she had wet herself, but through the colour of the blue material, it was more than obvious it was blood.

It was the shock or the pain that made her black out.

Phil used his key to get in, and as he could see the kitchen light on, he walked back through. He called out, 'Mrs Dean?' but he did not need a reply when he saw her lying on the floor, out cold, with a small patch of blood on the floor.

'Oh shit.' He grabbed his phone and dialled the emergency services. His basic Army training seemed to kick in and he found himself checking her breathing while he talked: it was so slow, it was as if she was in a peaceful sleep; she was as white as the kitchen floor, and it was more than apparent that she was not asleep. Her pulse was so weak that he had to concentrate to find it. Due to them being miles away from the nearest A&E he had asked if he should drive her, he would be quicker. They assured him to stay there. They would be out quickly: as it was late, the roads would be OK. He stayed on the line listening to the operator ask him more questions.

'I don't know,' he replied. 'Yes blood, no head injury, yes blood from there.' He explained the staining on her jeans and the growing stains seeping onto the floor. 'I don't know, Christ I don't know, just hurry up,' he said. He rushed up the stairs and fetched a blanket to try to keep her warm as she was going so cold.

'Mrs Dean.' He gently tapped her shoulder. 'Mrs Dean, it's Phil, can you hear me?' He paused and then said, 'No she is not replying,' to the person on the end of the phone. 'Where will they take her so I can contact her husband?'

Being on his mobile phone meant he was not making any other calls. So he got up quickly and went into the sitting room and picked up Lottie's phone. It was locked, but that was not an issue: the first thing Pete had told him was the password, so he put in. He filtered out 'Hubby' and then passed it to Pete's caller ID. He texted as fast as he could.

Mrs Dean has been taken to Tunbridge Wells meet us there. Urgent. I will call when I get off phone to the Emergency Service currently awaiting ambulance.

Pete never saw the point of turning off his phone when flying, although he did have it on silent. They were over the Channel, and only had a short time left of what had been a long day. He read his message, and momentarily paused to assess the situation. Without any words to Ed, he got up and asked if he could speak to the pilot. He wanted to know if there was anywhere to land closer than Heathrow; as it was a charter flight it may be possible, although his car was there. They could get a taxi so that really was not the issue. It was just as far from Gatwick, but the pilot tried to change course: it would be hard as they were already on descent.

On hearing the news that it was not possible, Pete made the decision again not to say anything until they landed. It felt like this was déjà vu. He had already had to rush Ed to her hospital bed: maybe he needed to say that he would become her protection officer and let Ed have someone else, as these days he caused less trouble. It would give him less of a headache.

Almost as the scene played out he knew how it would go. He called Phil the second they landed. He had ignored the hospital signs to turn off the phone, but did go towards the entrance doors to make the effort not to flaunt the rules.

'Details,' was all Pete said as Phil relayed the message from the doctor. 'OK.' Pete put down the phone.

Ed had shared the flight with his barrister, and they were chatting as they got their bags. 'Mr Dean, please can I have a moment?' Ed walked over to him.

'Please tell me this is good news, I am beat and I need to go home.' But he could tell that the look on Pete's face was about to say it all again.

'No, please, why does this always happen?' Ed froze on the spot.

'It is some sort of haemorrhage, and she is in surgery. It is not an accident.'

'That makes it better. I don't care if I never do business in any other country, she is with me next time, even if I have to drag her by her hair,' he spat at his phone as he called Phil for more details.

He could not give him any as she was still in surgery. With not being her next of kin they would not say any more to Phil until Mr Dean arrived.

'I would have been there with her if the bloody flight was on time,' he cursed, trying to call the hospital, but no one was picking up. The fact that it was almost 2am may have contributed to that, and also his abusive language which, when he did get through, meant the operator put the phone down, which did not help his mood.

47 miles is a long way: Pete repeatedly had to slam on the brakes and endure the abuse from his boss and the drivers of other cars that appeared to be going too slow for Edward. At 110 mph, most people are going slower! he reassured himself.

Pete had spoken to Phil and pre-warned him that he had better make sure that there was someone there to show him where to go and be prepared to talk to him as soon as they got there. His mood was boiling in the back of the car to the point that Pete had put the privacy screen up. As a last-ditch attempt to get any answers, he rang Mrs B.

'Oh, Peter that is just horrid news, you need me to do anything?' she asked, putting on the light in her room and pulling her dressing gown on that was always by her bed just in case.

'Did she seem ill when she left? Did she seem in any way different? They have said haemorrhage of some kind but that she is in surgery,' he asked.

'Oh my goodness, poor Edward must be beside himself.' She stopped. 'Oh goodness,' she said again.

'What?' Pete barked.

'You need to prepare him for this.' She paused, knowing it was the right thing to do. 'She was pregnant.'

'And he knew?' he asked. When the negative reply came back he simply said, 'FUCK!' Knowing that the housekeeper could not tolerate that sort of language, he quickly said, 'Sorry, Mrs B, but how do I tell him that?'

He leapt from the car as Pete pulled up by the main doors. Phil was waiting for him with a doctor, dressed in a white coat.

'Mr Dean, this is the junior doctor who has been with Mrs Dean.' Ed quickly shook his hand. Pete had not been able to pre-warn him; he had not found the words in the time.

'Junior doctor? Where is the main guy? Where is Lottie?' Ed asked in frustration. Phil mouthed 'Sorry' to the doctor as if he had prepared him for how he would be greeted. They walked and talked.

'Mr Dean, your wife has been in surgery, and we have been able to make her stable: there was significant blood loss,' the young man started.

'What the hell happened?' The question was both to Phil and the doctor.

'She haemorrhaged, Mr Dean.'

'I know that but why? What sort?'

'She has miscarried.'

Ed's feet froze to the spot. The doctor had verbally punched him in the face as he was hit by the information.

'We have not been able to speak with your wife, but from the levels of contraceptive in her blood, we are guessing that she may not have known she was expecting. We estimate around eleven weeks. I take it this is the case for you also?'

Ed simply nodded. The doctor started them walking again, and they headed to the suite where Lottie had been transferred to for recovery.

'I don't understand. How could she be? I would have known,' Ed asked.

'It is common in the first few months not to be aware. Some women's bodies do not change, others feel different from the start, changed eating habits, sickness, increased sleep, and tender breasts, that sort of thing. Other women, especially if they are still taking the pill, do not realise.'

'So why did this happen?' Ed asked.

'Mr Dean, we are never sure, it can happen for many reasons. Stress, flying, intercourse, abdominal straining, over-exercise, weakening of the womb, family history, the increased hormones from the contraceptives, the body's natural reaction... I could go on.' The young man knew his stuff.

Ed thought of everything he was saying. It could have been all of them, but why had he not noticed? The young man stood by a door. They could see a nurse in the room and Lottie lying in the bed asleep. 'She needs as much rest as she can, but please go in.' He opened the door and Ed just stood in the doorway. He turned around and walked backwards to the wall opposite.

'I need a moment.' He looked at the doctor and Phil, who both nodded and smiled.

She must have known, when I left yesterday, before the wedding, she had to have known? He was getting angry with himself. I should have noticed, he continued to say to himself. He punched the wall and put his head in his hands.

Pete had arrived and said to Phil, 'Go get some coffees.' He grabbed change from his pocket. Phil handed over Lottie's jewellery. He had been given it when she went to surgery for safe keeping. He gave it to Pete. He walked over to Ed; although Phil had told him he had requested to be alone, he continued to walk to him.

'Mr Dean?' he tentatively said, seeing his mark on the wall. 'Edward, go in and see her.'

'I can't, I don't know what to say, I can't get my head around it. I should have been with her. She should have been with me.' He had loosened his tie ages ago; he now took it off and put it in his pocket.

'It would have happened wherever she was. If it had happened during a flight we may not have been able to have got her here.' Pete tried to give him some reason.

'Did you know?' Ed asked, looking at him.

'Not until...' He stopped and took a breath. 'Mrs B, I phoned her. She said that Lottie found out today before she left.' It did not help him: he was still angry.

'She suspected and did not say anything, waited until I had gone. Would she have ever said anything?' He rubbed his hands through his hair again. Pete passed him the gold choker, her wedding band and engagement ring.

'Right now, she needs you. We can ask all the questions you need when she is better.' Pete took the coffee that was handed to him as Phil had returned. He passed it to Ed. 'Get that hand looked at please.' As Ed ran his fingers over her wedding ring, Pete saw the blood on his knuckles; the wall came off better on that occasion, he thought.

The nurse who was tending to Lottie came out and looked at the three men. 'Mr Dean?' She opened the question, looking at them all, but staring at Ed, admiring how he looked.

'Yes.' He looked up. She noted his deep blue eyes and strong jawline, and blushed slightly at the thoughts she was having at such a time. 'Your wife is almost awake.'

He wanted to go in there and pull her into his arms, kiss her, hold her, feel her, but he could not move with anger and frustration. Once more he was not able to help, not able to do anything. He gave the coffee back to Pete, fearing he would drop it.

'Both of you go, I will call, maybe you could get us some things?' he asked, looking at Pete who nodded and patted him on the shoulder as a sign of comfort more than understanding what he was asking.

Ed looked at the expensive handful of shining gems he had and took a breath. He looked at her through the glass in the door one more time and he could see that she was moving her arms slightly. There was an assault of questions he had and they needed to be answered, but first he had to hold her. He opened the door and went in. She turned her head to see him, still quite drowsy from the anaesthetic, and the painkilling drugs she was on.

He kissed her forehead and wiped the hair from her face, and smiled, reaching out for her hand.

'Baby girl, we must stop meeting like this.' It was a stupid statement, but he did not know what to say. He kissed her again, this time on the lips.

'I'm so sorry, Ed, I never knew.' She began to talk and licked her lips that were dry.

'It does not matter now, you need to rest.' He reached for the small bottle of water on the side and she took a sip. It did matter now as he wanted to know some answers to the questions in his head.

'I never... I only found out in the morning. It is my fault I forgot to take my pills, when I ran out on you weeks ago. I'm sorry, I never knew until today, I swear.' She had tears in her eyes, and he kissed her cheeks again.

'It's OK let's talk about it when you feel better,' he said.

'But I can see you're so angry with me.' She looked at her bare hands, noticing the jewellery missing.

'I'm not angry with you, I am just a bit confused as to the situation, and once more I was not around to help, stop it happening, save you the pain.' He put his hand out and showed her the jewellery as if to reassure her where it was. She held out her hand and finger in a gesture to put them back on, and he did. She leaned forward and he put the necklace back around her neck and she touched it, making sure it was sitting right. She smiled.

'Maybe if I had known sooner, it would have been different,' she said.

'Only maybe. Does that mean you had doubts about telling me?' he asked, sitting on the bed.

'Doubts about how I felt about it. It only hit me when we came back. I just took the test to ease my mind, I was so convinced it could have not happened, I did not want it to happen, maybe that was it.' He looked at her, more confused.

'Everything has come together for us, this addition was too soon. We have not had us time, sharing you so soon had not crossed my mind.' She continued. 'I was in denial, but looking back at how I felt, I should have known. Mrs B had picked it up!' He should have been the one saying this, as it was one of the things he was feeling, and he had to admit, looking back, maybe he should have picked it up, too.

'I am trying to feel sad for losing your...' She stopped herself saying it, but she knew she had to get it out. '...Our baby, but a part of me feels it happened for a reason and it is not our time for this. Part of me is guilty as I could have caused the miscarriage, not knowing, taking the pill, carrying on as normal, and that makes me feel ashamed. I had so little time to think about it, but even the thought of not keeping it crossed my mind.' She looked at him, concerned. 'Ed, you're not saying much, talk to me.'

'Lottie. I don't know what to say. Did you think I would ever want you to consider not having it, whether this is the right time or not? I am the first person to say that I am not sharing you, but to think I would not want whatever you give me, this gift of a life that we have made... You're right, it is too soon, but I would never have wanted this option. I would have willing learned to share you.' He rolled his ring around on his finger. 'I am just so sad that you had to keep it from me. The second you doubted, suspected, knew, I should have been there. You had the option to do something the night before, and I can cancel any meeting; business is not that important compared to you. Then maybe this would not have happened and I would not have found out like this.'

'I did not have time to compute it in my head what I wanted to do. I could not even tell Agnes because I knew you had to know first. No matter how long I had left it, I would have never lied to you,' she said.

'You would just have held the truth from me for a while?' he asked. 'I guess this is another dose of my own medicine, but I have to say this one hurts like hell.'

And it did hurt. Was it the emotion of the loss, what could have been, or the not being in control again? As the night went on towards dawn, Lottie slept. He sat in the chair at the side of her bed and he had to admit to himself that maybe it was the possible loss that pulled at his chest. The idea, had he known, would not have been all that impossible to live with surely? He needed a session with Dr Morgan and a shave - he looked a mess.

Pete had turned up as requested with some clothes and bits so that Ed could have a wash. He was pushing for her to be released to go home. Pete had called round to Agnes's quite early: Ed thought it was best coming from someone face to face. She called him as soon as she could and he gave her more details. He felt sad at her surprise; Lottie had not even told her and had the opportunity that night and then disappointment as she had said sorry for their loss. He told her he would try to get her home so that she did not have to come in.

'We cleaned the house up, too,' Pete said, detailing the mess that had been left in the kitchen. 'Phil has gone to get Mrs B to give the place the once-over.'

Ed walked back looking refreshed. The surgeon was in with her, and the young doctor who must have still been on shift was waiting outside the door.

'Sorry for my behaviour last night,' Ed said to him as they stood waiting to be let into the room.

'Mr Dean, we all take news like this differently. I have not personally experienced it, but in my short professional time I have seen it affect many couples in different ways, regardless of the circumstances. My only advice is that you heal with time, Mrs Dean physically and both of you mentally, but do, both of you, talk about it.' He smiled at him and Ed smiled back.

'Will she be OK, you know, could we, does this mean there will always be problems?'

'The surgeon will go through all of that with you, after he has just checked her over. We don't see why there should be any issues at all: it was just a sad occurrence. However, we would advise that she stops taking her contraceptive in clear time of any chance of being pregnant, just to be sure.'

'So you think that is what caused it, Lottie not knowing and carrying on as normal?' Ed asked. Was this going to give him closure? A black and white answer: was that what he was looking for?

'Sure no, but it would never have helped the foetus's chances, but then neither would all the other factors we mentioned last night. Women are amazing creatures. Their bodies will tolerate so much and they were designed for it. I go to church, Mr Dean, and I am a true believer that things happen for a reason, whether you say because of God, or just because they do. I am sure in your world there are clear-cut deals, answers, but where the human body is concerned, we have research and technology but we will never be 100% able to predict such things.'

The door opened and Ed was asked to come in. The young doctor smiled and said, 'After you.'

Lottie was able to go home.

Chapter 20

The next few days were spent at the house in Kent. At times it was like walking on eggshells, wondering if each one should bring up the subject or not. Lottie had spent most of her time in bed resting, and Ed had made the small sitting room his office base. He held her while she slept, and kissed her if she cried. He spoke to Dr Morgan on the phone several times. Although the surgeon had talked about them being intimate again, it did not feel right and he wanted to talk it through with someone who knew him. He felt he was in a better place but he was not sure about Lottie.

Agnes and Mrs B had been around at the start, but now they left them to it, so they could have some time on their own. The nights were longer and the weather now colder. They had planned their blessing in two days' time, but he still felt that they should call it off. Ed was on the phone, having left Lottie asleep once more.

'I just don't think it is a good idea, Mum,' he said, explaining that he wanted to cancel the event until another time. He had called his mother and, although she had planned to visit for the blessing, she wanted to come over sooner. Without warning she broke into a conversation about how, when she had first met his father, she had fallen pregnant. She, too, had lost the baby before she was twelve weeks. This was something she never shared with him or many people. He had been their first-born.

She explained that getting back to normal was the thing to do. 'You never forget, Edward, but it must make you stronger,' she explained. 'Your father and I were nowhere close to a perfect couple like you two. I never thought it would affect him; if it did, he never showed or told me. That's what made it hard.'

Her words played over to him as he sat at the desk watching the rain fall in the garden. Lottie wandered in dressed in her baggy pyjamas, hair not brushed. He looked over to her: she still looked beautiful, irresistible in fact. Colour had returned to her cheeks and she had a faint smile on her lips, without trying.

'Hey, you,' he said. She pottered over to him and sat on his lap. 'Careful,' he said, breaking her fall, not that she would hurt him, but herself.

'I won't break.' She pulled up off him, feeling the rejection. He looked back at her, and he patted his legs as an invite, saying he was sorry as she sat back down. 'I miss you,' she said, putting her arms around his neck, kissing him. 'I just want a hug.' She pulled him closer.

The problem was he wanted her that much that he wanted more than a hug, and her physical contact had, and he hoped always would, brought out the same male urges he felt when he had first seen her. He could feel himself getting hard just thinking about trying not to get hard!

She wiggled. She, too, could feel how she made him react, so did it more.

'Mrs Dean, you're not helping, at, all,' he said, steadying her so she had to stop.

'But I miss you!' she said with her sad eyes, running her fingernail down his chest bone to his waist. He grabbed her hand and she bit her lip. 'Good God, woman, stop it!' He laughed. She had shown this desire after Dick had died and he knew it was a coping mechanism for her. This was very different. Mentally she may need the same, but physically they both knew she needed time to heal.

'You heard what the surgeon said, Lottie: a few weeks.' He still held her hand and she playfully shrugged and looked away, putting her head on his shoulder, looking at the rain, too.

'I hope it stops for Saturday. I know that we would not get such perfect weather as the wedding, but a break in the clouds for the marquee would be nice. When are they coming to put it up?' she asked.

'It should have been this afternoon, but I'm not sure,' he said.

'Not sure if they are coming, or not sure you want to have a blessing with me?' she asked, looking back at him.

'Of course I want the blessing, no question, but are you ready for this? I want to postpone if not,' he said.

'No, no, no, you don't. I want to do this: please don't postpone,' she pleaded with him. 'I don't want people asking questions, upsetting you.' He turned her to look at him.

'What people, what questions? It will be a difficult subject for a long time, you know. Those who know are our closest friends, none of whom would allow it to become gossip.' She put her hand on his face. 'If we ask them, they will understand it's private. It would take more explaining, lies as to why we put it off, and cause more gossip anyway. Look at me, I'm fine.' She ran her hand along his shoulders and down his stomach one more time. He tensed his muscles at her touch.

She was able to lie on his hand, that would have come over to stop her doing it, but she rubbed his groin before he could stop her. She undid the top button of his loose-fitting shirt and placed a kiss and licked his chest, sliding herself from his knee to kneel in front of him. She pulled at his button and fly.

'Let me show you how "fine" I feel.' She kissed the outside of the fabric and fumbled with the zip to allow him to become loose.

'Lottie?' he tried to protest. 'Stop.'

'Really, Mr Dean?' she said, taking his already semi-hard cock in her mouth and sucking. She linked the fingers of both their hands and held them on the arms of the chair. She worked her mouth up and down along the growing member. He put his head back with a thud on the headrest and closed his eyes. She licked around the top of him, tasting the salt and his sweet shower gel overtones. She then plunged him back in her mouth taking him as far as she could to the root of his pelvic bone. He grew thicker with each soft stroke. She took one hand and helped with the rubbing motion, wrapping her thumb and forefinger around him and squeezing. He gasped. 'Mrs Dean, you are wicked.' She carried on rubbing, and she looked him in the eye as she licked the top of him like a child has an ice cream. She smiled and bit her lip.

'Arrhhh,' he said, knowing that he wanted to draw her up to kiss her, straddle him and sit on the very organ she was sucking. Restrain, Dean, he said to himself as she licked her way around his balls and he reacted instantly to the touch.

His breathing increased as she speeded up and slowed down using her hand, her mouth and her tongue. She rubbed her breasts up on his thighs and he could feel them harden through the soft material. He dug his hands into the chair and then used one hand to hold her hair back so he could see her face. He guided her head to the rhythm that he wanted: he was close to climax. Lottie licked at the liquid leaking from his tip and tightened her grip at the base of his shaft. The reduced blood flow made him pulse harder and as she let go she sucked him with hollowed lips to protect him from her teeth. He let out a gasp as he thrust for the first time, releasing the salty fluid into her mouth; she swallowed knowing that the next thrust would fill her equally. He had both hands on her shoulders, coaxing her to his rhythm, as he spilled freely into her mouth, gasping between each pulse. She waited until the last jerk was over before she looked up at him and smiled. She licked her lips and wiped them with her finger. She kissed his body all the way back up until she was sitting back on his legs, aware that she did not sit on his sensitive semi-hard, totally spilled state. She kissed him and he responded, tasting himself on her mouth.

'See, Mr Dean, fine, would you not agree?' She smirked and kissed his nose.

'Mrs Dean, I submit, you're more than fine! Deal concluded. I will ring the company to chase their sorry asses.' He dragged the words out, still trying to ease his laboured breathing.

It was all systems go for the next day and the first part of Saturday. The guest list invited several of the charity acquaintances and partners, Lottie's Scholars and some of the staff from the college. Simon and his family, including Gramps, who looked so different in suit and tie to when they had been racing. Belle and her husband, who arrived at the house early so she could help Lottie get dressed. Zoe and her husband played important parts, helping people find their places in the church.

The house was a buzz, with catering and florists all being charged around by Mrs B. It was almost 2pm and Lottie and Ed were the last to leave. Although she loved it and knew she would wear her wedding dress again, maybe for a charity function she wanted something warmer – well, Ed wanted her in something warmer – and Bella had pulled out the cards again.

The cream underdress was low-cut right down to her lower back, almost reaching her rose tattoo. It cut straight across her shoulders, baring her neck enough for her to have the diamond choker on display. It had no sleeves but covering down to her hands was the overdress. Again, full length, this time gold-embroidered hand-sewn lace that covered the bare back and hugged her figure. It had a kick from the knee out to allow her to walk, and a slight train that followed her as she walked. Her hair was up supported by a gold and diamond slide, that matched the bracelet and the earrings from the matching birthday set. A short, fur, matching gold muff covered her shoulders, following the top line of the dress. She looked in the mirror and flattened her stomach. She took a deep breath as she opened the door.

Ed stood waiting at the top of the stairs. As he always had a suit and tie on; he wanted something different so had opted for a morning suit with tails. The black, striped trousers and the matching tailcoat, set onto the cream shirt, finished with a gold cravat and gold hankie, just showing in the pocket. She smiled at him and twirled, showing the low heels under the dress. She shimmied up the skirt to her thigh and showed the little garter from her wedding day.

'Remember this, Mr Dean?' she asked, her beam wide as she had remembered the effect it had on him the day after their wedding.

'Do I ever, Mrs Dean?' He pulled up her skirt higher with his hand and ran his hand up her inside thigh, dropping the material and stopping his hand at her waist. He kissed her bare neck from one side to the other and whispered in her ear. 'You are the most stunning woman in every way. I thought that day you could never look more irresistible, and I could never love you more, but I was wrong.' He kissed her again, realising that he was supporting a full erection just from her touch. He put his head in her back and breathed the scent of her perfume in while he composed himself.

'Problem, Mr Dean? May I help?' she asked, knowing full well what the issue was. Through the trousers the bulge was unmissable.

'Hold that thought just a few more days!' he said to her, putting out his hand to help her down the stairs. As they left she picked up the small posy of cream roses, gathered in a gold ribbon, and they got in the waiting car.

The clouds had broken and the rain had stopped to allow the late-afternoon sunshine through. There was a no photo clause in the church, the only ones being taken by the hired professional, who was being paid not to sell them on anywhere. One reporter had made his way to the church, sitting outside, and Pete had despatched him without any issues, but really it was not a big thing. The house was, however, off-limits to anyone who had not been invited. Some of the local villages had popped over to offer their congratulations and needed Lottie or Ed to OK before the beefhead on the gate would let them pass.

The house and grounds were alive with music, chatter and laughter into the night. The first dance had seen Lottie and Ed take to the small dance floor. He held her in his arms as if she was a feather. His grip was tighter when she started to whisper in his ear, teasing him to the point of distraction. He had to hold her away from his body before the whole room saw something totally embarrassing. She laughed and smiled and he knew that she was back with him. He just had to get to the same place. He was not far away, but he still could not dismiss the feeling that they had lost a baby. Was that the real truth here, was he was ready to be given the chance to be a father?

The piano that had been hired in was cream and had been dressed in gold, carrying on the whole colour theme. Towards the end of the night Lottie and her young scholar wowed the crowd with a duet; despite requests for more, she only did the one score. With the exception of going to the toilet several times and hugging various guests, it was the only time she had left the physical contact of her husband since he held out his hand at the top of the stairs several hours ago.

With no neighbours to complain they were still outside well after midnight. If it was cold she did not feel it, although her feet were sore and she had sneaked in the odd yawn.

'One more hour, Mrs Dean, and then bed,' Ed said in her ear. He did not want her to be overtired.

'If that is the offer, please ask Pete to clear everyone out and I will see you up there in five!' She bit her lip in a seductive manner.

'Mrs Dean, you are going to regret this flirting and taunting. After your appointment on Tuesday you had better be prepared for a full-blown Dean Enterprises CEO assault. That is a statement, not just a promise.'

'I will clear my diary!' She giggled as if they were teenagers and in front of everyone still present he kissed her, lifting her off her feet.

And so... The story continues...

Following on from the last book 'Let the story begin' we pick up with the whirlwind romance of Lottie Dean and her new husband Edward as they start their married life.

As with the first 10 months of their relationship, they continue to battle with emotional situations and their own demons from the past which have not yet been laid to rest. They suffer the stress and consequences of being strong-willed professionals and business people in a modern world. People can change the things they want, their desires and needs, their hopes and their futures.

Money can buy anything. They have more than most people could dream of; some may say they have it all.

But do they have all the answers from their past to complete the story and have a perfect life. If they can, will it come at an unaffordable cost?

'The Story Continues ...'
